Eerie

C.M. McCoy

OMNIFIC PUBLISHING

LOS ANGELES

Omnific Publishing
2355 Westwood Blvd, #506
Los Angeles, CA 90064 www.omnificpublishing.com

First Omnific eBook edition, December 2015
First Omnific trade paperback edition, December 2015

Library of Congress Cataloguing-in-Publication Data C.M. McCoy.
Eerie / C.M. McCoy – 1st ed.
ISBN: 978-1-623422-32-5
1. College — Fiction. 2. Romance — Fiction.
3. Pittsburgh — Fiction. 4. Paranormal — Fiction. I. Title

10 9 8 7 6 5 4 3 2 1

Cover Design by Micha Stone and Amy Brokaw
Cover Art by Robin Lynne Schwind

Printed in the United States of America

For my husband, my hero.

Prologue

There he was again.

Hailey snapped her head around, hoping to catch more than a glimpse of the glowing creature, which once again zipped past the very edge of her vision.

It was real, she knew it was.

Frozen in place, she scanned the horizon, hoping to find *where* it was so she'd have more than a millisecond to determine exactly *what* it was.

Finally it halted with its back to her, on a hill next to her favorite tree—a giant sycamore, which usually stood in her neighbor's yard. But now it stretched high into the swirling purple skies of her dream.

The figure standing next to the sycamore looked like an angel, lean and pale, and as bright as the moon.

Curious, Hailey crept closer, not meaning to disturb him. But as she drew near, he whirled around.

Hailey stopped, mesmerized by his violet eyes.

"Hi," she breathed with a gentle smile.

He gave her a quizzical look.

"I'm Hailey."

"I know," he answered softly. Hailey let him study her for quite a while before she glanced over his shoulder.

"This is my favorite place." She nodded to the tree-lined river valley stretched out behind him.

"I know," he said again.

"Well, what don't you know?"

The creature merely gazed at her.

She lifted her shoulders. "Do you have a name?"

He looked away.

"What's wrong?"

"We've met before, but you never remember me." He drew a slow breath. "And I'm afraid this is the last time I'll see you."

"Why?" As the word passed her lips, a cascade of memories tumbled forth, whispers overlapping whispers until a single thought emerged. "You're an Envoy."

"You're remembering."

"And the other Envoys—they're coming, aren't they?" She glanced at the trees in the valley, their shadows taking on a menacing shape. "Make them go away. Why can't you make them go away?"

"Because you must die." He tilted his head, as if this were obvious.

Hailey's heart constricted. She staggered back.

"Don't run from me, Hailey," he warned, lifting his hand.

Hailey braced for a beating, but he merely caressed her cheek. Calmed by his touch, Hailey looked up and found herself staring into the most beautiful swirling eyes. But he had just said something…something important, she thought…

When he stroked her cheek again, she was certain this strange creature—this Envoy—was watching over her. She knew he wanted her to live—to grow up, to grow old.

But he jerked his hand away, and Hailey opened her eyes to a dark bedroom.

As she woke, the wisdom and maturity of her eternal soul faded. The memory of her Envoy dream dissolved

Chapter One

A Good Man

"All that is necessary for the triumph of evil is that good men do nothing."

— Edmund Burke

Professor Simeon Woodfork shuffled into the observatory shivering wildly and waving his papers, as expected.

Asher knew he was coming—he'd sensed his approach. Still, standing behind his telescope, Asher made no movement to acknowledge the professor at all. His smoldering purple eyes never shifted, never broke their gaze into the clear winter night.

"It must be exciting," Asher said without a hint of interest, "if you've made your way here in stocking feet." He finally turned to the man.

Woodfork stood coatless and covered in frost next to the door. He glanced down and seemed shocked to find he'd also forgotten his boots. Looking up, he attempted an announcement.

"Th-th-th-they'rrrrr…" he began, still shivering as he held his papers high.

"Forget her, Simeon," Asher boomed, his voice echoing inside the dome. "Forget them both. You cannot protect them. They'll be dead before your semester starts."

Asher already knew why the professor had come. He was well aware the girls had applied for scholarships at the school and that Woodfork had just discovered their essays. He'd seen it inside the man's mind.

Woodfork stared at Asher in astonishment for some time. He opened his mouth, closed it again, and turning to leave said quietly over his shoulder, "This is evil, you know." He waited a few seconds for a response that wouldn't come. With a heavy sigh he shook his head and walked out.

As soon as Woodfork left, Asher blinked and quite unexpectedly found a tear had escaped his eye and was traveling down his perfect cheek. He plucked the drop from his face and stared at it in awe. Rubbing it between his thumb and forefinger, he realized…

Sadness.

That must be what he was feeling.

Another tear trickled from his violet eye and dropped to the observatory floor, reflecting the starry night above. Asher watched it, his brow furrowed in concentration. Of course he knew what a tear was, but he'd never actually produced one. He'd come close once—on the night he first saw her magnificent soul. Naturally, she was deep asleep, and her soul, like all human souls did, had wandered into the Aether in what humans call a dream.

Asher was there. He was always there, in the Aether. Half in and half out. That was his curse. Three thousand years he'd endured it—shackled to the Earth, trapped among the humans, condemned to exist in both worlds—longing, always longing to be wholly in his home in the Aether.

It was there that he'd noticed her standing lonely and lovely, looking very curiously at him, which itself was a rare occurrence, as humans usually didn't see Envoys in the Aether, but that wasn't as rare as what she'd done next. Instead of avoiding his penetrating gaze, which most humans cannot tolerate, she met it. And smiled.

It was rapture.

And he hated her for it.

Soon after she smiled, she turned and ran from him. And though he hadn't meant to frighten her, he knew why she fled—he was a monster after all...an ender of life, and he shouldn't blame her for fleeing.

But it was devastating.

Since that night, he couldn't stay away from her. Like a Siren, she drew him in, and she'd challenged him like no other dared, her delicate voice ringing with scorn and defiance and forgiveness all at once. It was maddening—and addicting.

His eye released another tear.

Asher found this "sadness" utterly unpleasant and realized he would not take the advice he'd just given Woodfork. He would not simply forget the girl with the beautiful soul—the girl who'd found him in the Aether. The one—the only one—he ever wondered about, ever cared about, ever—resented. In his three thousand years stuck on this Earth, of the millions of souls he'd seen come and go, it was hers he longed to know, longed to reveal himself to. Always hers.

And as deplorable as it was for an Envoy to express such a sentiment, Asher could think of nothing other than his sudden, intense desire to see her in her waking life—to rescue her or kill her—he didn't know which he wanted more. But he did know that any interference in her fate was dangerous—akin to suicide, really.

Any Envoy foolish enough to admit they were infected with human emotion risked death. Asher knew this because not even a century ago the Envoys had shredded one of their own for just such an offense: for loving a human. It was an assassination, an abject slaughter, borne of intolerance for the corruption they all felt clawing away at them...the human emotion that was driving the Envoys insane.

Also, the girl—this one girl—had to die. For when her soul and body parted, her energy would open the Aether, and the Envoys trapped on Earth could finally go home. This design was centuries in the making. Asher wanted this. He wanted her to die.

At least, he should want her to die, and he shouldn't care that another Envoy moved to hasten her demise.

But he did.

And as he marveled at how his first tear slid between his finger and thumb, and how his second twinkled in the starlight, he realized he was not the only Envoy evolving. He was not the only one corrupted by feelings. All of the Envoys trapped on Earth were changing—going mad, perhaps—and these creatures who once valued balance above all else were now tipping the scales to one side or the other. While some experienced emotions, such as love, others chose behavior that was simply, as Woodfork had so eloquently put—evil.

Asher contemplated the fate that awaited his girl—the excruciating pain of having her soul ripped from her body, the hands of *another* Envoy touching her—

Asher felt his teeth gnash, and he resolved in that moment to go to her.

Chapter Two

A Guarded Girl

"Of all forms of caution, caution in love is perhaps the
most fatal to true happiness."

— Bertrand Russell

Hailey stared at the empty can on her tray, silently willing the
caffeine to kick in. The last thing she needed was to fall asleep,
dream of monsters, and have an "episode" in front of her 200 closest non-friends.

No way she'd let that happen.

Now if only her droopy eyelids would cooperate, because the
hard plastic chair under her butt sure wasn't. The dang thing was
teasing her and feeling mighty comfy, like a puffy armchair, and
she was sinking fast. Thankfully, though, just as her head bobbed,
the bell rang, jolting her into a wide-eyed, full-body spasm.

Great. Real smooth, she thought, rubbing her face with both
hands as a few gigglers shuffled past.

She groaned, rising with all the enthusiasm of a mushroom,
not at all looking forward to another two hours inside the social
torture chamber, or as everyone else referred to it, South Side High
School.

She was so intent on avoiding the students there for the rest of
her senior year that she rarely looked up from her books anymore,

and those last two hours dragged. When three o'clock finally rolled around, she bolted outside, took the first open seat on the bus, rested her head against the window, and let it bounce there. She was just about to make it through another day of school very happily unnoticed, when Tage Adams smacked her on the back of the head.

"Ah!" she yelled, startled from sleep.

The bus was waiting at their stop, like normal, and Tage was waiting for her in the aisle, politely—not normal.

Tucking a wayward strand of hair behind her ear, she hurried off the bus.

Tage followed.

"What's up with you today?" he said nonchalantly, adjusting his pace to walk next to her.

He'd never done *that* before.

"Nothing," Hailey said, surprised Tage was talking to her. They'd been catching the bus at the same stop for four years, and he'd never so much as looked at her.

"You're usually not like that, that's all."

"Like what?"

"Nodding off in class, falling asleep on the bus…you know, slacking off. It's just, you know, you usually have your nose in a book."

He watches me?

"Oh," she said, unsure.

"Guess you were working late last night…St. Paddy's Day…"

"Yeah." Of course she was working late. Her family owned the most popular Irish pub in Pittsburgh. Hailey pressed her lips together. Small talk was so not her thing. Especially not with him.

Her mind went blank.

Searching the pavement for a thought, she chewed her lip as too many seconds stretched the silence. Finally the pressure forced her good sense aside and she opened her mouth to say…anything.

"What's—"

"Well, see ya 'round, Dancing Queen."

She snapped her mouth shut and waved as he peeled off and trotted down Bridge Street. She tried to form the word, "bye," but all that came out was "buh—". Standing dumbfounded, she stared after him. She hadn't realized Tage knew she existed, let alone the fact that she waitressed. And danced.

Stunned, Hailey walked, then jogged, then stopped dead to puzzle over what had just happened. Then she jogged again until she finally reached the pub.

Nobody at that school "chatted" with Hailey. Not since the fourth grade, not since the day a particularly mean girl concocted a particularly ugly rumor—that Hailey had started the fire that killed her parents. The whispers and sideways glances lasted close to a year, and in trying to defend herself, Hailey only made things worse. By the time she figured out that nobody else believed in pyromaniac-nightmare-monsters, it was too late. She'd already earned the label, "weirdo," which, unfortunately, stuck.

When Hailey burst into the pub, Holly had already cleaned up most of the St. Patrick's Day mess but was still scurrying around the dining room, rag in hand. Hailey grabbed the rag from Holly, set it aside, and looked her sister dead in the eyes.

"You'll never guess who talked to me today," she said to Holly, though Fin, the new bartender, also looked up.

"Who?" Holly's sea-green eyes sparkled with curiosity.

"Tage Adams." Hailey stepped back, crossed her arms, and chewed her lip.

"No!"

Hailey nodded. "Yup."

"What did he say?"

"He told me I usually have my nose stuck in a book." Hailey paused for effect. "And then he called me Dancing Queen." Hailey raised her eyebrows as she waited for her sister's assessment.

"He knows you dance?"

Hailey shrugged, feeling as perplexed as Holly looked. Tage was hardly a regular at the pub. When he had come with his family for dinner—which was exactly twice—Hailey had reverted to her antisocial-school-self, stood in the shadows, and made Holly wait on him.

"He might like you." Holly pointed her finger at Hailey. "Isn't prom coming up?"

"What?"

Holly gave her the sister-ESP look, and Hailey recoiled.

"Oh, no. No, no, no." Hailey put her hand over her forehead. "Oh my God, I hope not." She didn't care how obscenely handsome Tage was—she'd rather be locked in a trunk full of spiders than attend a school function. Spider bites healed. Gossip stung forever. "I'd have to tell him no." She grabbed Holly's rag and wiped an already clean table.

"Oooorrrrrr…" Holly smiled, leaning casually against the bar, "You could suck it up and go to prom with the hottest guy in school."

"I'm sure he was just being polite," said Hailey wiping more vigorously.

"Oh, yeah," said Holly sarcastically. "I'm sure that's all it was. Football stars are typically *so* polite to the school's biggest introvert."

Hailey stared at her, full of dread. The very thought of prom made her ill. She was quite content to remain mostly invisible until she graduated and prayed that Tage had simply suffered a momentary bout of social amnesia in acknowledging her existence. More than that, she hoped he already had a date lined up—a perfect cheerleader or something.

She shook her head, pushing Tage and prom and excruciating, extremely public ridicule from her mind, but Holly wasn't done torturing her.

"Tage Adams," she marveled, and then she held up a white envelope. "And I thought seeing this would be the highlight of your day." She smiled brightly.

"What's that?"

"Another scholarship announcement—wait till you hear this one," she said, unfolding the letter. "A scholarship for the study of the mating habits of the arctic ice worm."

Hailey squinted.

"But wait." Holly held her finger up. "—requires a high tolerance for cold weather as well as an abundance of patience." She dropped the paper on the bar and stared at Hailey.

"An abundance of patience?" Hailey repeated, shaking her head. "Is it me, or do some of these seem…ridiculous?"

Fin let out a loud cough but then busied himself at the sink.

Holly studied the letter with her chin sticking out. Then she raised her eyebrows and shrugged.

"Seems legit." She eyed the return address. "It's Bear Towne University again."

The arctic ice worm was just the latest in a string of off-the-wall offers the girls had received for study at one very remote northern school, which neither of them had ever heard of. But they were desperate. Holly had already taken a year off to save money while Hailey finished high school, and they were willing to go to school as far away as Alaska if it meant they could go together, so they each completed and sent back one strange essay after another.

Bear Towne University also offered a grant for the study of bovine-induced personality disorders in the northern Yeti (lactose-intolerant individuals were discouraged from participating) and a scholarship for a degree in the care and feeding of carnivorous trees (current tetanus vaccine was highly recommended). There was even one for ParaScience.

"Remember the paranormal one?" Holly chuckled.

"Yeah," Hailey sighed. It was an essay application—only 1500 words, but the topic was "any personal supernatural experience." Both girls had written about the only bizarre event they knew—the fire that destroyed their childhood home.

Holly studied her little sister. "Wanna go see Mom before dinner?" she asked gently, but then she brightened. "You could tell her about Tage…"

"It's really not a big deal." Hailey scrunched her nose. "You think she'd care?"

"Are you kidding? This is huge—you're finally coming out of your shell."

"Blurting out a monosyllabic response is not 'coming out of my shell'." Hailey made a half-frown. "Besides, I like my shell. It's cozy in here."

Holly slapped her hands on the bar. "Come on. We'll go see them real quick. Grab some whiskey for Dad. I'll tell Uncle Pix we're leaving."

Fin was already holding out a bottle of Bushmills. "Here," he sighed. "And you better not drink any of that."

Hailey rolled her eyes.

Fin stared back at her, looking very annoyingly like the cover of a magazine: tall and ruggedly handsome with dark brown eyes; dark, disheveled hair; and always just the right amount of soft stubble on his face. It used to be hard not to gaze at him, but after two months of playful banter, a few broken pint glasses and an epic water-fight that ended with Uncle Pix punching Fin square in the nose, Hailey could see past his gorgeous face. And though he couldn't be any older than twenty-two, he was, as Uncle Pix had proclaimed, "way too feckin old" for her and Holly anyway.

"Thanks, Fin, I already have an overprotective guardian." She grasped the bottle, but Fin held it tight, and Hailey looked up at him.

"Let go." She grinned, and he shook his head.

"Ask me nicely."

Hailey huffed. "Let go of this bottle, or I'll tell Uncle Pix you kissed Holly."

"I never kissed Holly!" He dropped his cocky smile and the bottle.

"…but I bet you want to," Hailey teased.

"Want to what?" A smiling Holly appeared next to the bar, her chestnut ponytail still swinging.

Hailey giggled. "Come on. I'll tell you on the way."

She looked back at Fin just before the door closed behind her and in time to see him set his jaw. How she loved to one-up that man. If only it were that easy with all guys.

"What was that about?" Holly jabbed her thumb at the pub.

"I was just teasing Fin about kissing you."

Holly groaned. "I wish he would kiss me."

"You and every other girl that walks into Hullachan's."

"Don't you?"

Hailey shook her head. "Nope. I'm impervious to his immature charm." She turned to Holly. "I mean, it hits me, but it just ricochets off my shell."

"You and your shell—weirdo."

Chapter Three

Vanished

"Nothing fixes a thing so intensely in the memory as the wish to forget it."

— Montaigne

Hailey frowned, running her hand across the cold wrought iron as they passed through the cemetery gates. A menacing oak, abnormally large with octopus branches skimming the ground, squatted nearby. It groaned in the wind as they passed.

"You want to go first or should I?" Hailey asked as they crested the hill.

Holly opened the whiskey. "You go chat with Mom, and I'll raise a glass with Dad."

Hailey settled on her knees in the grass, pulling a few clovers as she gathered her thoughts.

Standing next to her, Holly held the bottle high. "Here's to you, Dad. *Sláinte*." She stared at the sky for a moment, and then she poured a healthy dose on the ground, took a swig and held the bottle out to Hailey.

"Amen." Hailey crossed herself and stood with her sister, taking just one molecule of the rusty nail juice and handing it back to Holly, who drizzled the rest over their parents' graves.

Hailey stared at their headstones, mentally willing an image that wouldn't come, wishing she had a photo—just one— of Mom and Dad, but the fire had taken those too.

"I can't remember what they looked like anymore."

"You were only five when they died, Hailey."

She looked up, frowning. "Do you ever think about that night?"

"Of course." Holly sighed, tipping her head at Hailey. She patted the necklace she always wore. "Every time I look at this."

"Mom's necklace." Hailey smiled. It was an heirloom charm— nothing valuable, just a shiny black stone in the shape of a heart. Hailey's mother had originally given the necklace to her. But on the night of the fire, Hailey had given the necklace to Holly for comfort, and Holly had worn it ever since.

Hailey drew a courageous breath. She hated to bring up the creatures that killed their parents—she felt like they were always listening—but she really needed to talk this out.

"Do you remember the purple eyes?"

"Don't tell me you still think the monsters from your nightmares started the fire. Hailey—"

"Envoys, Holly. They're called Envoys—you can say the name—and I know what I saw."

"A lot of people think they see things when they're scared." Now she sounded uneasy, and she was definitely giving Hailey the stop-talking-now stare, which, of course, Hailey ignored.

"I know you saw him too—"

"And if you keep talking about Envoys," Holly continued, "people are always going to think you're weird."

Hailey pressed her lips together and nodded, but the Envoys had been showing up in her dreams again—a lot. Lately, she'd seen quite a bit of one Envoy in particular—a very kind one, thankfully. Oh, she couldn't remember his name. That, like so many other details, evaporated as soon as her alarm went off.

Not that Holly cared. She was blank-staring at her Mom's marker, no doubt lost in her own thoughts. But then the church bells clanged, and she jerked her head up. She flicked her eyes at her cell phone.

"Oh, crap, the time! Hailey, we have to go, we're late for dinner."

Both girls took off running and barreled into the pub just as the cook, Mrs. Lash, placed the first plates in the pick-up window.

Holly shoved her hands under the faucet behind the bar, and Fin threw a towel playfully in her face.

"You're late," he droned, and Holly smiled, grabbing three plates from the window and hurrying them into the dining room. Hailey grabbed another three and followed.

Waiting tables at the pub was a cinch. Folks either wanted dinner or they didn't. The menu was a single line on a chalkboard—always traditional Irish fare served from 4pm until the food ran out. That day Mrs. Lash created a delicious beef and barley soup, which the girls served with a wedge of white soda bread, the perfect meal for a chilly spring day.

The mill workers coming off mid-shift loved the giant portions; the white collars loved the atmosphere, and the college students—they loved the three-dollar pitchers of beer.

About an hour into dinner, when every seat in the pub was filled and a throng of patrons stood at the bar, Holly tapped Hailey's shoulder as she rushed past, heading straight for the backroom, where the girls kept their Irish dance shoes. Hailey tore off her apron and followed, skip-dancing excitedly the whole way.

"We're starting with that new reel today," Holly called over her shoulder. "You up for it?"

"Of course!" said Hailey as she slid to a stop next to Holly. "As long as you're on that stage next to me, I'll dance anything."

"I was hoping you'd say that," Holly said as they grabbed their Irish hardshoes, plopped on the floor, and cinched their laces.

Holly hopped up and shook first one foot then the other to loosen her ankles. She turned to her little sister. "Ready?"

"Let's go!" Hailey followed Holly to the small wooden stage in the corner of the pub.

Holly stomped her foot in a rhythm and started clapping. "Welcome to Hullachan's, everyone!"

The crowd roared back, clapping in time with the girls. Hailey was stomping and clapping and smiling brightly back at them— until she saw a flash of purple.

She froze, and Holly, still clapping, shot her a curious glance.

Hailey was awake, she knew she was. She was dancing, so she couldn't have dozed. Swallowing hard, Hailey quickly scanned the pub. Then she blinked hard, forced a smile, and picked up the rhythm again.

Holly raised an eyebrow then counted down from four, three, two, one—both girls stomped their right foot and tapped out an a cappella hardshoe dance that sent their audience into cheers, hoots, hollers, and peals of applause.

The girls bowed and, still smiling brightly, threw their sneakers on and returned to running pints and plates and pitchers until happy hour waned and the dinner crowd thinned. During the evening lull Uncle Pix disappeared into the cellar to "count the whiskeys," and Mrs. Lash left to run an errand.

Holly bagged up the garbage. She threw a very large, very lime green St. Patrick's Day hat on top of the trash before tying the bag closed. Heaving it over her shoulder, she headed outside.

"Let's dance our slow hornpipe tonight," she called to Hailey from the doorway.

"I'll set it up," Hailey called back.

It was a super-fun rhythm, which involved a few dramatic pauses, lots of personality and, at least for Hailey, a full spectrum of facial expressions. The regulars loved it.

Hailey wiped her hands and went to the office, where she found the CD. Shoes in hand, she sat on the floor and set to tying and buckling the leather, which was old, ugly, and held together by duct tape—perfectly broken-in. She dressed them up with a pair of bedazzled trinity knots, very sparkly. It was like putting a chandelier in a haunted house, but at least it drew the eye away from the duct tape.

She was adjusting her shoe buckle when she heard a muffled commotion outside followed by the roar of an engine and a shrill screech of tires.

"What was that?" she shouted out the office door as she fussed with her left shoe.

No one answered.

She clippety-clopped down the hall, over to the sound system and placed her CD in the drawer. Leaning against the wall, she shook out her ankles.

"Come on, Holly!" she yelled.

Just then, Mrs. Lash bustled inside holding up a pink object.

"Hello dears," she announced with a huff. "Holly's dropped her cell phone outside, and now the screen's cracked."

Hailey's blood ran cold. Holly dropped her phone…and *left* it? No way. She loved that annoying thing—

Rushing to Mrs. Lash, she grabbed the phone and lit the screen. It was definitely Holly's.

"Holly," she breathed and bolted out the door. "Holly!" she shouted.

Blood rushed in her ears as she clutched the pink phone and snapped her head right and left.

"Holly!"

No answer.

She ran to the dumpster. Rounding the corner she saw a line of trash strewn across the pavement. Her heart pounding, she opened her mouth to shout again then stopped.

A very large, very lime green St. Patrick's Day hat quivered in the breeze. Next to the hat was a single shoe: green with pink laces.

Hailey picked up the shoe without thinking and wobbled.

Then she unleashed a scream so loud, she was sure it would reach her uncle in the cellar.

Fin and several patrons burst through the door.

Hailey stood wide-eyed and trembling in the middle of the parking lot, holding a green shoe with hot pink laces.

Fin rushed to catch her as her world went black.

Inside the shoe was Holly's severed foot

Chapter Four

The Search

"If you wish to discover the guilty person, first find out to whom the crime might be useful."

— Alexandre Dumas, The Count of Monte Cristo

"Hailey…" a wavering voice called.

Hailey rolled over and sat up, knuckling her eyes, and when she opened them, it was horror.

There was Holly—standing next to the bed, ashen-faced, shivering, and covered in dirt, blood oozing from a wide-open gash on her forehead.

"Help me, Hailey," she breathed, tears streaming down her face. Holly reached out, but when she did, her hands fell off as if they'd been lopped off by a pair of invisible blades. They landed in Hailey's bed, two muffled thumps against her quilt. Blood spurted from Holly's wrists as she raised them up. Gaping in horror, she flicked her eyes to Hailey and whimpered.

"Hailey, help me!"

"Holly!"

Scrambling out of bed, Hailey lunged for her sister, but Holly was yanked into the shadows before she could reach her.

Purple eyes flashed in the darkness, and Hailey screamed.

"NO!"

A heavy hand fell on her shoulder.

She drew a quick breath.

"You're awake now, Hailey, don't be afraid," whispered a gentle voice—his voice—next to her ear, and the room came into focus.

Hailey whipped around, furiously scanning the dark, but the room was empty, still. The silence only amplified her heartbeat as it hammered in her ears.

Uncle Pix burst through the door, and Hailey jumped.

"She's here, Uncle Pix, she was just here." Hailey darted to her bed and rummaged through the blankets. "Her hands fell off, they're—they're here...somewhere..."

Pix hurried to her side, grabbed her flailing arms, and pulled her into a tight hug.

"Shhh, Hailey, it was a dream. Just a dream, Hailey."

A dream? Hailey's shoulder still tingled where the Envoy had touched it. *THAT* was no dream. She buried her face into her uncle's shirt and sobbed.

Uncle Pix tucked Hailey back in bed, but that first night without Holly didn't get any easier. In between her nightmares, Hailey cried—cried and worried and wondered why someone would... would...

She shuddered, pushing the image of Holly's shoe from her mind and wiping her face on her sister's pillow. Then she hugged it tight.

She had to do something—go outside and search, post flyers... something.

As Hailey pulled herself up and through the house, things in her periphery quivered. More than once a shadow budged, startling her. After seeing three shadow monsters, she'd had enough and turned on every light in her path until she found her Great Uncle Pix sitting in the living room, staring at the door.

She sat on the couch and stared with him.

Uncle Pix, whose real name was Donald (but nobody called him that), looked like a grumpy old man and insisted he now stood a full five inches shorter than he did when he stepped off the boat from Ireland fifty years ago. To everyone else, Pix was a grouch, but to her and Holly, he was just a big teddy bear. Hailey remembered well the night they came to stay with him after the fire. He'd fixed them hot chocolate with whipped cream before rolling out the sleeping bags and camping with them right there, on the living room floor.

"Your grandfather's coming," Pix said suddenly.

Right now? Hailey looked at Uncle Pix then back at the door, half-expecting it to swing open. "Oh," she managed.

Hailey hadn't seen her grandfather in…well, ever. He'd gone back to Ireland 30 years ago and had been living with the silent monks ever since. The only thing Hailey really knew about him was that his real name was Seamus. Pix only ever referred to him as Wimp, though, which was a misnomer. In his heyday, he was a bare-knuckles fighter in the Navy.

"Your great uncles too," Pix added.

Uncle Pix had four brothers. In addition to Wimp, there was Dale, Skeet, and Johnny.

Hailey couldn't force words to respond, though she did wonder if Uncle Pix was keeping vigil for Holly for or waiting for his brothers. Whatever his reason, she watched the front door with him, biting her thumbnail and shaking her leg until dawn.

At 7:00 a.m., the coffee pot turned itself on, and Uncle Pix finally blinked. He rubbed his face with both hands and sprang to his feet. Hailey got up and followed him. Though she hadn't slept at all, she felt remarkably alert and ready to hit the pavement in search of her sister.

"I think we should call the hospitals again," she said as she moved to the phone.

Pix grunted his usual pre-coffee grunt and pulled six mugs from the cupboard.

"When are your brothers due in?" she asked as she dialed.

"Got in last night." He impatiently stared at the coffee pot.

"Last night?" She held the phone to her ear. "Where did they st—Yes, hello, I'm calling to find out if my sister was brought in overnight—Holly Hartley? Yes, I'll hold."

She placed her hand over the receiver.

"Where did they stay?"

"The pub, of course."

"What? They slept on the fl—Yes! I'm holding for the E.R.—" Hailey listened intently for a few seconds then sighed heavily. "No, Holly's nineteen years old," she explained, her voice half disappointed, half relieved, "—and thank you for checking," she added before hanging up.

She put her hand on her hip and turned to her uncle, who had shoved the pot out of the way and was holding his mug directly under the coffee dispenser.

"Why didn't they stay here?"

"Didn't want to disturb the house."

"We're already disturbed," she argued.

Just then the latch at the front door clicked.

"Holly!" Hailey sprinted to catch the door and threw it open.

Standing on the doorstep were four geriatrics, all of whom looked strikingly similar to Uncle Pix—short, gray-haired, and grumpy. Three stood solemnly, hands folded politely. One was naked, shoeless, shivering, and rolled up like a burrito in a rug Hailey recognized from the pub. She couldn't help but stare at the scrawny old man legs poking out of the bottom of the rug.

"Jesus, Mary, and Joseph, Dale," her uncle's voice boomed from the kitchen. "Where's yer drawers?"

"Didn't survive the flight," he answered.

"And took your shoes with'em," Pix concluded, as if these were normal casualties of commercial flight. "Well, get yerselves in here before the neighbors get an eyeful."

The brothers shuffled inside, each taking their turn to introduce themselves to Hailey.

"I'm your Uncle Dale," said the first with a hint of shame as he waddled past and into the kitchen.

"I'm your Uncle Skeet," said the next. He pecked her on the cheek and added, "You'll remember we met at your parents' funeral."

"Of course," said Hailey, not wanting to admit she didn't really recognize any of them.

"I'm your Uncle Johnny," said the next as he hugged Hailey so tight, her feet came off the floor. He was amazingly strong for a geezer.

Wimp came in last and simply kissed Hailey on the cheek.

Hailey closed the door and followed them into the kitchen where Pix was pouring cups of coffee and handing them around. When he got to Dale, who was still wrapped in his rug and using both hands to hold it closed, Pix grumbled.

"Well, go sort yerself out," Pix ordered. "Yeh look like a fool in a rug." He pointed to the laundry room.

Moments later, Dale emerged, fully clothed and motioning for coffee.

The brothers stood around the kitchen sipping from their mugs while Pix filled them in on Holly's disappearance. Hailey didn't care to hear the details again, so she left them to it, closing her bedroom door quietly behind her.

From her room, she heard a sharp knock at the front door, and a muffled Uncle Pix offered the greeting he reserved for all uninvited guests.

"Who are yeh?" he growled.

Hailey shook her head and went back to her internet search. Just as she found what she was looking for, Uncle Pix stuck his head inside her room. "May I come in?"

"Sure," said Hailey, untroubled by his tip-toeing. She looked up in time to see his lips press together and his eyes well.

"She'll need one of these when she gets back," said Hailey simply. She pointed to the screen and scanned the specs on a prosthetic foot with hydraulics.

"Alright, Hailey." Pix's voice was shaky. "The detective is here, dear. He wondered if you would talk to him and go and look at some photos at the department."

"Just a second," she said, waving him off as she studied a carbon fiber model. "I'm ordering information on this one now." She turned her head slightly as she read. "It's designed for dancers, and it takes four weeks to make. She'll have to have it fitted..." She looked up at Uncle Pix matter-of-factly. "Holly will want to start dancing right away when she gets home."

Pix nodded, his chin trembling, and he left her to her project, closing the door quietly behind him.

Hailey tapped the keyboard, nodded triumphantly, and joined the crowd in the kitchen, where a tall, broad-shouldered man, sporting a sandy blond flattop and wearing a suit and a badge stood in the middle of the brothers, who formed a half circle around him and took turns pelting him with questions. Except for Wimp, who stood quietly with his coffee, looking thoughtfully from brother to detective to brother and back again.

Hailey slid into the kitchen unnoticed and stood silently against the counter, safely out of the line of fire as the conversation heated up.

"I can assure you, Mr. Sullivan," said the badge in a loud, slow voice, "we will follow up on every lead that comes in."

Hailey cringed as her uncles exploded.

"Yeh feckin eejit!" Johnny bellowed over everyone, his face red with rage. "You wouldn't know a feckin lead if it bit yeh on yer arrogant arse, ya—"

Uncle Pix clapped him on the shoulder and took over in a more civilized but equally aggressive tone. "Detective Toll," he said, pushing his sleeves up as he moved into the man's personal space. "We want some information is all. Who are you lookin' at for starters?"

The detective shook his head. "Mr. Sullivan, even if we had a suspect, which we don't, I certainly wouldn't release a name—I know you'd go after him, and the last thing we need here is a band of vigilantes."

That was definitely the wrong answer. Even Hailey knew that.

There was an audible silence followed by another explosion.

Dale yelled and cussed; Skeet shook his fist; Pix grabbed a cast iron argument ender off the stove and held it high; Johnny threatened to kill the detective with his bare hands, and Wimp sipped his coffee, but with a white-knuckled grip on his mug.

Detective Toll seemed remarkably unruffled by all this.

"We will continue to use every resource available to find Holly. When we have new information, I will tell you, and—" He stopped when he finally noticed Hailey standing against the wall, and everyone turned to look at her.

It was like a bucket of ice water had hit her uncles. They immediately straightened up and adjusted their language to "lady-friendly." No more swearing. No more yelling. It was a whole new crowd in there.

"Hailey," said Pix in his fatherly voice, "come and meet Detective Toll. He's heading up the search for Holly."

Uncle Pix turned to the detective. "Detective Toll, my niece, Hailey...Holly's sister."

She didn't realize she was trembling until she reached to shake his hand.

"Hello, Hailey," he said politely, and she swallowed hard. "If you're feeling up to it, I'd like you to come down to the station with me and tell me about your sister...maybe look through some photos?"

"Of course," she said nodding. Finding Holly was the only thing on her to-do list.

"That's my Hailey," said Uncle Pix proudly. "She's a right strong young lady. Smart too. She could probably tell yeh the exact time Holly stepped out the door and the exact weight of the bag she was carrying."

Five fifty-eight pm and just under twenty pounds. She had looked at the clock over the door as Holly passed under it and had helped her stuff mostly paper into the bag with just a few scrapings from dinner.

Hailey followed Detective Toll outside to his car, which had a radio, a computer, a printer, a notebook, and a shotgun all mounted in the front seat. His lunch, coffee cup, gym bag, and some papers were piled on the passenger seat. Hailey had to slide his stuff over and be careful not to sit or step on anything when she got in.

Good thing I'm small, she thought as she closed the door.

"I'm sorry," said Toll. He rushed to move some things out of her way. "I should've moved this stuff earlier."

Grabbing up a stack of folders, he looked around for a place to put them, which he wasn't going to find inside that car.

"Here, hold these," he said, handing them to her.

Hailey took them without a fuss, setting them on her lap. She didn't really know what to say to a detective, so she just held on to his folders and looked out the window while they drove. Over and over, she picked up her sister's shoe in her mind, and as the scenery sped past, over and over she searched her memory for the critical clue that would lead her straight to Holly.

"Is one of these Holly's file?" she asked, surprising herself.

"They're… all… Holly's files."

Hailey looked down at them.

"All of this?"

Toll glanced at the files, pressed his lips together, and sighed without answering.

He was holding something back. And if he was going to keep secrets, she was just going to find out for herself, so she opened the folder on the top of the pile and started reading.

"You told Uncle Pix you didn't have any information," she said as she scanned the pages.

There was a ton of information—measurements from skid marks left in the parking lot, which they'd matched to a specific tire and wheel base. That narrowed their pool of suspect vehicles to seven possible models, three of which weren't even registered in the tri-state area.

"I told him I didn't have any suspects," he clarified.

"You lied." There were three names on a page labeled "Suspects."

"Close that file."

He made a quick grab for the papers and missed.

"Pay attention to the road," she shot back.

She pressed herself against the window, reading as fast as she could as they pulled into the station.

There were also some flecks of paint recovered from a smashed utility box at the corner of the parking lot exit. Hailey scanned the lab report, which included a list of manufacturers that used that specific paint.

She deduced that the police should be looking for a white Ford Explorer with damage to the passenger side.

Detective Toll put the car in park and ripped the pages out of her hand.

"Don't go getting the wrong idea about the stuff you just read," he chastised. "It's all preliminary. You shouldn't have read that."

"You handed them right to me."

"I didn't tell you to read them," he said, getting out of the car.

Detective Toll hugged the folders to his chest with one hand and opened the door to the station with the other, motioning Hailey to lead the way. As soon as they crossed the threshold, Toll dropped his folders and vaulted over a tall desk to assist an officer who was on the floor, wrestling with the biggest man Hailey had ever seen.

A pair of handcuffs swung from the man's wrist as he landed punch after punch. He was on top of the officer with one hand squeezing the officer's neck and the other tugging on his service pistol, which, thankfully, was stuck in the holster, when Detective Toll pulled him off.

Hailey watched them wrangle the giant's hands back into a set of cuffs. Then she stared at the folders on the floor.

This was too easy.

She fell to her knees, scanning each page, committing them to memory. There were interview notes and lists of names and locations as well as photos from the pub and a few of Holly's shoe (foot and all), which Hailey quickly covered.

One folder was particularly interesting. It was darker brown than the others and stamped CONFIDENTIAL in big red letters. Most of the pages inside had several lines of fat black marker running across them, obliterating a lot of the text. A visible word here and there indicated the pages had something to do with the fire that had killed her parents.

She knew she'd guessed right when she uncovered some pictures of her childhood home.

She puzzled over them.

One photo showed the house before the fire and one after—both from the same vantage point.

That's weird, she thought. *Why would they take a picture of her house* before *it burned down?*

Holding one of the papers up to the light, she discerned the outline of an acronym through the magic marker:

D.O.P.P.L.E.R.

Footsteps. Someone was coming. Hailey gathered the folders, put her butt in a chair, and folded her hands.

When Detective Toll came back out—not over the desk, but through a magnetically locked door—he carried a binder and found Hailey sitting in the lobby like an angel with the papers straightened and submissively tucked inside their folders.

He eyeballed her suspiciously, and Hailey looked innocently back at him.

"Bit of excitement," he said holding his hands out.

"Is everyone alright?"

"Mostly."

She handed him the folders, and he actually counted them. Right in front of her. Did he really think she would take one, she wondered, half offended and half amused that he'd underestimated her speed-reading skills.

"Hailey, I have to make a quick call, and it's a mess in there," he said apologetically. "Can you look through these mugshots out here for a few minutes? Make a note of anyone that looks familiar, okay?"

She nodded obediently as he waved a card in front of an invisible sensor. The door clicked open, and he disappeared inside.

As Hailey opened the binder, a television mounted to the ceiling in the corner of the lobby blared the morning news, which began with the channel logo flipping around on the screen with some bonging drums and a few dramatic notes from a shrieking horn. Enter the perfectly coiffed and annoyingly chipper morning news anchor.

Her voice was hard to ignore, and Hailey winced when she introduced their top story.

"Good morning, everybody. First up, a gruesome discovery in the parking lot of a local business last night has residents on edge, and just in this morning—a *second* local woman missing in as many days. Melissa has more."

Hailey leaned forward, breathless.

"That's right, Megan, you'll recall that workers at the Hullachan Irish Pub, a favorite watering hole for many in this area found the bloody shoe of one of their waitresses in the pub's parking lot last night. Since then, no one has seen or heard from the owner of that shoe—Holly Hartley. And this morning, another 19-year-old girl—vanished. The search for both South Side women continues. Take a listen."

The video cut to an interview with a woman wearing a suit and a badge, which hung from a lanyard around her neck.

"At this point, we have no reason to believe the two incidents are related—"

"That statement from the Pittsburgh Police only adds to the intrigue surrounding these vanishings."

Hailey was nauseous.

She felt like a four-year-old, plugging her ears with her fingers in the middle of a police department, but she couldn't bear to hear anymore.

Another girl missing?

Staring at the mugshots in her lap, she listened to herself breathe. She counted twenty-seven intentionally loud breaths before Detective Toll finally poked his head into the lobby and motioned her in.

"Sorry about that," he said, holding the door for her.

"Was it something to do with Holly? Or this other girl that's missing?"

Hailey pointed to the TV.

"No," he sighed as he led her through the squad room. "News can't get anything right. This other *disappearance* they're chasing is a 20-year-old known drug user with a history of near-fatal OD's. She's probably passed out in a motel again."

"Oh." Did that mean they weren't looking for this other girl? Hailey wasn't sure if she felt more compassion for the drug user or relief that the police weren't diverting any energy from their search for Holly.

"Anyone look familiar?" He pointed at the binder.

Hailey shook her head.

Leading her into his office, Toll motioned her to a chair facing his desk, which was a good old fashioned mess, piled with papers and photos and folders and notebooks with yellow sticky notes everywhere.

He sat down and blew his cheeks full of air.

"So tell me about last night."

"I already told the officer last night—there…it was…" Hailey sighed, her mind racing, her heart keeping pace. She shook her leg but resisted the urge to bite her thumbnail as she filled him in on everything from stuffing papers into the trash with Holly to preparing to dance.

"And then Mrs. Lash walked into the bar with Holly's cell phone—" Why hadn't she thought of this before? "Maybe Mrs. Lash saw who took Holly!"

Toll shook his head. "She didn't."

Hailey's shoulders fell. "Where do you think she is?"

She wanted to know what he knew. She wanted him to tell her exactly when Holly would come home. She wanted him to say that they knew where she was, that she was safe and sound and just waiting for the police to come and pick her up and bring her home.

He said none of that.

"I don't know, Hailey." He frowned. "We're working on it."

"What have you got so far?"

"Not much. We've got a timeline and some physical evidence, as you know."

Maybe she already did know as much as he knew.

"We're working on a suspect vehicle make and model…" Nope. She knew more. He obviously hadn't read the papers in his precious folders."…which we should have soon…"

Hailey couldn't stand it.

"You're looking for a white Ford Explorer with damage to the passenger side," she blurted, and the detective's mouth fell open.

The clock on the wall ticked twice, before he closed it again.

He grabbed up his notebook and pen. "Did you see the vehicle?"

"No," she said, pointing to his precious files. "I read the acceleration mark analysis and compared it to the analysis of the paint scrapings. That narrows your pool to one possible vehicle—a white Ford Explorer."

"I left you alone for five minutes," he said as he flipped through his stack of papers. "You read all that in here?"

"Didn't you?" she fired back. "And it was seven minutes." This guy was never gonna find Holly.

"No," he said, "I haven't read all this, yet. Just got most of it this morning on my way to your house."

At least he was honest.

"What else did you read in these files that you weren't supposed to even look at?" he asked, annoyed but interested.

Just then a uniform knocked twice on his door and poked his head inside.

"Sir, we finished that analysis you asked for," he said. "Looks like a white Ford Explorer."

"Thanks," he said sarcastically, and he turned back to Hailey. "Well? Anything else you'd like to share?"

"Why do you have a file from our house fire?"

"I just…" He pulled the confidential folder from the pile and opened it. "This is every scrap of info we had that relates to Holly. This file is…what…thirteen years old?" He raised his eyebrows as he thumbed through it, and then he closed it again. "I'm looking at everything," he said simply. "…anything that could point us in the right direction."

"What's DOPPLER?"

"Doppler?" He started flipping through the papers again.

"Never mind," said Hailey. He didn't know.

Toll clicked his pen and put his notebook on top of the chaos that was his desk.

"Does your sister have any enemies?"

"No. Everybody loves Holly."

"Boyfriends?"

"No."

"Anybody you can think of that wanted to hurt her?"

"No."

"Did she recently reject someone?"

"No." Hailey was feeling less and less helpful.

"Did you notice anything or anyone out of the ordinary at the pub, maybe paying extra attention to her lately?"

Hailey racked her brain, but no one stood out. She shook her head.

Toll licked his lips. "Anything...*strange* been happening?"

What the hell?

"You mean...stranger than finding Holly's—" That sentence punched her in the stomach and stole her voice. There it was, like she'd just picked it up again. Her throat aching, Hailey bowed her head so Toll wouldn't see her tears.

"I'm sorry," he said gently. He offered her a box of tissues and some water.

"You're gonna find her, right?" Hailey cried.

He dropped his eyes, drew in a breath, and looked directly at her. "I will personally keep looking until we find her, until the end of my watch on this Earth, I promise you.

Chapter Five

Denial

What peaceful hours I once enjoyed!
How sweet their memory still!
But they have left an aching void.
The world can never fill.

— William Cowper, Walking with God

Hailey let herself into an empty house, half expecting to find this was all just an elaborate prank, half expecting to see Holly, intact and unscathed, sitting in the kitchen.

She wasn't.

But a note from Uncle Pix was:

Hailey,
We're at the pub. "Search Headquarters."
Give us a call when you get home.
Love Pix

After making her obligatory phone call, she threw the note away and headed straight for her computer. She typed in "D.O.P.P.L.E.R.," and several websites came up, but they all had to do with radar or ultrasound or weather.

She sat back in her chair. That fire happened thirteen years ago. Maybe DOPPLER was defunct. In any case, it felt like a dead end, and Hailey's leg was shaking again.

It was nearly 3pm, and the kitchen clock with its tick-tick-ticking was driving her mad.

She had to get out of there.

Search Headquarters seemed like the logical place to go. Surely her uncle had opened for a reason—maybe he thought Holly'd come back there!

Hailey grabbed her keys and bolted out the door.

That night, customers were in and out of the pub as usual. The regulars offered their polite support, and after a few shots of whiskey (apparently, the Hullachan was serving the fight'n kind), they offered to light the torches, grab the pitchforks, and go after the "jag-offs" that took Holly.

Hailey found the five brothers sequestered in the back room with a map of the city, a bottle of Michael Collins, and a bodhrán, which Dale drummed in perfect jig rhythm. She left them to it. While they compared notes, Frog—the pub's giant bouncer—swore up and down to Hailey he'd never take another night off. He stood, arms crossed, jaw set, eyes fixed on the door; Mrs. Lash prepared dinner, and Fin tended bar. Hailey waited tables, avoiding eye contact as she ran pints and plates.

Sometime around 7:00 p.m., the college crowd trickled in and business picked up. The lion's share headed straight for the bar, especially the ladies, most of whom came to Hullachan's on a mission to win a date with Fin.

They could have him.

Holly might've found him—how did she put it—"genuine and engaging," but he was more like the big brother Hailey never wanted: slightly smug and more than a little overbearing. The one time she'd tried to flirt with a customer, Fin went all nuclear-Uncle-Pix on her and would've tossed him out, except Pix had beat him to it. Hailey never saw that kid again. The word "overprotective" always sprang to mind when Hailey thought of Fin. That and "man-whore." But the ladies of Pittsburgh loved him and pretty much threw themselves at his feet, and that was just fine by him.

A lot of students drank a few beers then went home, but some would stake out a booth and study there all night, drinking cups of coffee and eating the free pretzels. Hailey didn't care who came to drink what, as long as they kept her busy. Every time she slowed down, the image of Holly's foot caught up.

She was at the bar filling a carafe of coffee for a regular book-worm when *he* stepped through the door.

It was a bizarre moment for Hailey, who'd all but given herself whiplash from spinning around every time the pub door opened. But this time, she did not immediately turn to look, because she already, instinctively knew who it was, which was indeed strange, since she'd never actually met *him* in real life. She'd only ever seen him in her dreams, but she could feel him enter the room like the heaviness before a storm. She recognized this feeling.

So, when she did turn in his direction, it wasn't to see who was there, but to acknowledge his presence.

In her dreams, he was always shrouded in a tranquil, shimmer-ing light, a gladiator's silhouette under a cloak of moonlight. She had no idea what he looked like in real life.

But she did know he was an Envoy.

She also knew how crazy it was to think these things about a stranger who'd just wandered into Hullachan's, so as he moved through the pub, she moved to get a closer look. His face was smooth and clean shaven, and his tousled brown hair showed flecks of gold. Wearing loose blue jeans and a thin black sweater, which really showed off his physique, he strolled to a booth near the window, and like a prince who didn't give a damn, he sat with his back to her.

She needed to see his eyes. For the moment, though, she was perfectly content to stare at the back of his head.

Fin whipped her in the back with a rolled up a bar towel.

"Ouch!"

"Snap out of it," he said, and Hailey thought she detected a note of jealousy in his voice.

The table the Envoy chose was still dirty from the previous patron, and Hailey rushed across the room to clear it. In all her nervousness, she knocked over a glass, which was still half-full of beer and backwash. It spilled across the table and poured over the edge, right into the lap of the most handsome man she'd ever seen.

"I'm so sorry!" She opened her eyes wide and blinked furiously to keep from crying. Quickly, she wiped at the table and to her horror, ended up pushing another wave of beer over the edge and onto his legs. Mortified, Hailey froze, not sure what to say or do and bracing for an epic cuss-out.

But he never flinched.

Instead, he lifted his head slowly, very slowly, and looked up at her. With eyes so black they took on a blue sheen, he smiled his forgiveness. Then very briefly, a vertical line of bright violet bolted across his right eye then his left. It happened so fast, Hailey wasn't even sure it was real.

He stared at Hailey, his expression soft, and his eyes…his eyes after the flash, so gentle.

For several seconds, Hailey stared into those eyes. Strange, how comfortable she felt, locked in his gaze, as if she were seeing a good friend after far too long apart. She wanted to hug this man, but she also wanted to smack him for staying away for so long. It was a complicated emotion, compounded by uncertainty.

Hailey blinked. The stress must be getting to her. This man was probably just another college student. It was nuts to think he visited her in her dreams…and maybe rescued her from a burning house.

Remembering the spilled beer, she blinked again.

"I'm so sorry," she repeated. "I'll get you a towel."

Still he said nothing.

Hailey dashed to the bar but felt her lip trembling and decided mid-stride to go blow her nose instead. Somewhere between her exhaustion and anxiety was an ugly cry waiting to erupt, but she wasn't about to let it happen over something as meaningless as a spilled beer. She just needed a moment to breathe.

Bowing her head, she diverted to the ladies room.

"I'm sorry, Fin, I'll be right back," she called over her shoulder as she zipped past.

Fin grabbed a towel and strode to the booth. He did not offer the towel to the gentleman, who didn't so much as look at Fin when he reached the table.

"You're a long way from Alaska," said Fin to the stranger, as he bent to collect a shard from the floor.

The stranger looked down at Fin.

In a smooth, slow, slightly British accent, he said, "As are you, Pádraig." He bowed slightly then forced a quick cynical smile. "Taking the semester off?" he asked scornfully.

"Research project actually. For Dr. Woodfork." Fin answered in a brash voice, standing as he spoke and taking care to avoid eye contact. He glanced toward the toilets then back at the table and sighed heavily. "What are you doing here, Asher? Come to check up on me?"

Asher tilted his head and squinted. "Are you really so arrogant? Your life is meaningless, and my business here has nothing to do with you."

"Thanks," said Fin, sounding even more snarky than usual. "How 'bout I bring you a cold pint of 'kiss my ass'?"

"Mind your manners," Asher warned. "Or have you forgotten your debt to me?"

That deflated Fin, but only a little. "Fine," he said. "Just...stop creeping out the waitress, alright?" He threw a look at ladies room again. "She's got enough on her mind."

To Fin's surprise, Asher stood and turned toward the door, which encouraged him to beat his chest a little.

"In fact, stay away from the girls altogether, okay? That's why you're here, right? Morbid Envoy curiosity?"

Asher stopped mid-step, spun around, and put his face close to Fin's.

Fin struggled to avoid Asher's gaze.

"You forget your place, slave. Ever defiant, but you are no Guardian, nor will you ever be. You are far too selfish to be trusted with such a duty. And if Woodfork sent you here to protect the girls, I should inform him that you've failed." Asher turned toward the door again, took a few steps, and then he stopped and spoke sharply over his shoulder.

"I see only *one* girl, Fin." Asher's eyes erupted into an electrical storm, and Fin's face fell. He knew what that meant.

Holly wasn't coming home.

Chapter Six

The Hope

"Hope is the only universal liar who never loses his reputation for veracity."

— Robert G. Ingersoll

Hailey ran into the ladies room to recompose, but instead found herself trapped in a stall when two of Fin's scantily-dressed fans promenaded in and parked in front of the mirror.

Call it pride, but Hailey didn't want them to see her cry face, so she sighed and waited next to the toilet for them to leave. It sounded like they were just fluffing each other's hair anyway, which Hailey figured shouldn't take long, but then they started comparing notes on Fin—his clothes, his muscles, which of them he'd looked at first, which of them he was more likely to take home first...on and on it went.

Hailey was stuck.

She'd been so quiet in her stall, they obviously had no idea she was in there listening. And now it would seem like she'd been eavesdropping if she suddenly burst out. She weighed her options and decided to ride this one out...and eavesdrop.

"Did you see his tattoo?" said one.

Hailey didn't even know Fin had a tattoo.

"Oh. My. God. I bet it goes all the way up his arm," the other gushed. She smacked her lips. "Wonder how big it is." It sounded like she was putting on lipstick.

"You would, whore."

"That's not what I meant!"

"Whatever."

They both laughed.

Hailey felt like she was getting dumber as their babble continued—their makeup, their highlights, how their boobs fit into their tank tops, whether they thought Fin noticed their cleavage…it was never ending.

Hailey rolled her eyes. It was way too cold for a tank top.

"Seriously, he has got to be *the* sexiest guy I've ever seen," said one.

"Not as sexy as the guy that just walked in here," hissed the other. "Did you see him?"

"How could I not? That idiot waitress spilled beer all over him."

Hailey's jaw fell open. She wasn't the most graceful server in the world, but she thought "idiot" was going a little far.

"She's such a skank. You hear about her sister?" Hailey froze. "Somebody kidnapped her from the parking lot in broad daylight, and all they found was her bloody shoe!"

"Serves her right. She threw herself at every guy that walked in here."

Hailey's heart pounded in her ears. She felt sick. And angry.

"You're such a bitch."

Finally one of them was making sense.

"What? She *was*," the girl jeered. "I knew her in high school. It was probably her pimp that took her."

Well, that was all Hailey could stand. She kicked the metal door open, marched right up to the more guilty-looking of the two hairspray-monsters and put her finger in the girl's face.

"The only skanks in this bar just spent the past eight minutes picking bugs out of each other's hair and fussing over their over-painted, under-hydrated faces in front of this mirror, but none of your primping and preening makes a shit-bit of difference, because your soul is so ugly that no amount of lipstick and eyeliner can cover it up. No one is ever going to give you a second glance, and one day you'll see in that mirror what everybody else sees right now—a dried up, used up, shriveled up, pitiful shell of an STD-infected, loudmouth hag!"

The girl looked terrified. She shrunk away from Hailey and squeezed her eyes shut as if Hailey were winding up to punch her. The truth was, Hailey was no fighter, but she could sure shame someone into submission. She almost felt bad about that.

"And it's way too cold for tank tops!" she added as she turned to leave.

"She was talking to *you*," one of them said as Hailey strode out the door.

"Crabs is *not* an STD," the other argued before the door closed.

Gross, thought Hailey, and she scrunched her nose.

If Hailey felt bad when she walked into the bathroom, she came out feeling far worse. As she rounded the corner, she saw the booth where her dream man had been now sat empty.

"Hey Fin," she said, pausing near the bar, "where'd my customer go?" She jabbed her thumb at his booth.

"Oh… He was pretty pissed you spilled a drink on him. He just got up and left."

"Oh no, I didn't apologize properly." Hailey felt just awful.

"The guy was a jerk, Hailey. He didn't deserve your apology."

"Why? Did he say something?"

Fin pressed his lips together and busied himself with wiping an already clean part of the bar. She looked at him quizzically, wondering how bad it was—wondering if the stranger had used the word "skank" as he stormed out. Fin never answered and looked relieved when a customer asked him to refill a stout. She hated it when someone walked away angry. Just another worry to add to the pile of things eating away at her.

Holly would have smoothed things over in a jiffy. Then she would've grabbed her shoes, turned on the music, and got the crowd clapping and cheering and forgetting about one silly little spilled beer. Hailey looked longingly at the door, hoping she'd magically appear.

She didn't.

Fin's fans were back at the bar and back on the prowl in short order, fully recovered and completely unaffected by Hailey's tongue-lashing. Fin was eating it up, too, tossing glasses in the air and bottles behind his back, never missing one and never spilling a drop. The hags cheered and shimmied and smothered him with compliments.

It was revolting. Hailey didn't want to be anywhere near them. She was about to grab some whiskey and go talk to her mom, when an unshaven, sweaty little man burst into the pub. He strode past the bar and made a bee-line for the back room.

Hailey followed and watched as he disappeared inside with her uncles. She listened through the door.

"…at least two of 'em…skulking around…couple'a wretches to do the dirty work…" Hailey moved her ear closer to the door.

"Betrayal!" one of her uncles shouted, and Hailey winced.

"First Katherine. Now Holly!" Katherine was her mother's name. Hailey's heart pounded.

"The line is broken," said another. "Why would they do it? No, it's not them at all, at all."

"It makes no sense," agreed another.

"One's gone rogue, I tell yeh."

"And taken our sight! We're blind, all of us!"

"…could be a wretch, could be right under our nose—we wouldn't know it."

"And what can we do about it? Feckin nothing!" That voice belonged to Uncle Pix.

"We protect the ones that need protecting," one of her uncles answered calmly, "like we always have."

Someone slammed their fist on the table.

"We cannot protect against what we cannot see."

There was a long pause.

"Did you get a location, Tommy?" someone asked. Tommy was the man who'd just arrived, Hailey figured. He needed to talk louder. She could barely hear him over the high-pitched hag laughter coming from the bar.

"...on consecrated ground...still out there..."

She strained to hear more, but somebody grabbed her arm and yanked her away from the door.

"Ouch!"

"What are you doing?" Fin chastised, and Hailey wrenched her arm out of his grip.

"Eavesdropping," she said unashamed. "Obviously."

Just then a couple of chairs squeaked across the floor inside the room and some footsteps approached the door.

"Shoot!" she whispered, grabbing Fin by the arm. "Go-go-go." Fin let her turn him around and run him back to the bar.

"What did you hear?" he demanded.

She peeked over her shoulder.

"Nothing."

"Liar."

Hailey shook her head. "Bits and pieces. It didn't make any sense." Fin relaxed his posture, looking curiously relieved.

Sometime around 2am the brothers emerged from the back. Uncle Pix pulled Hailey aside as Fin closed up.

"We'll be out all night looking for your sister," he told her. "Fin will walk you home and stay with you until we get back."

All night? Hailey frowned, but nodded obediently. They couldn't know where Holly was then, but still she had a feeling her uncle knew a lot more than he was telling her.

"I'm coming with you," she said, her voice rising. Pix just sighed and shook his head. He hugged her tight, nodded to Fin, who nodded back, and he left the pub with his brothers. Hailey stared expressionless at the door as it closed behind them.

Fin grabbed his coat from behind the bar and met Hailey by the exit.

"Where's your coat?" he asked her.

"I didn't wear one," she said, still staring blankly at the door.

Throwing his leather jacket over Hailey's shoulders, Fin led her outside, hitting the lights as they left.

Hailey stuck her arms through the sleeves, which were several inches too long. She let them swish at her side as she walked. It was a chilly night, and she shivered when the wind blew.

"Zip your coat," Fin said with a smile.

Hailey lifted her arms repeatedly trying to get her hands out of the sleeves. Fin watched, chuckling.

"Come here, chowder-head." He pulled on her arm to break her stride, shook his head, and zipped his coat for her.

"Do you think they'll find her?" she asked him hopefully.

Fin seemed to be in cahoots with her uncles. So did Frog. In fact everyone seemed to know more than they were saying. It was like they were intentionally keeping her in the dark about something, and it was scary.

"I'm sorry, Hailey," he said softly. "I don't know."

It wasn't what she wanted to hear, but it sounded honest.

He put his arm around her shoulder and pulled her next to him as they walked.

"She's coming home, I know it," Hailey told him.

"I hope so too," he said, hugging her closer.

Asher looked on from the shadows. Seeing a human—that human—touch his girl stirred within him a new uneasiness. Now she was leaning into him, and Asher's hands tightened to fists. If she required comfort, Asher would provide it for her in the Aether—he'd instruct her to remember that.

As for Pádraig, though loyal and inherently good, he would do well to leave this place. His presence here was pointless. He could never protect the girl from an Envoy, he'd be shredded. And his interference with Asher's interest was troublesome. He had no idea the punishment Asher could inflict for his insolence. Perhaps he needed a reminder.

And perhaps Hailey needed a demonstration of Envoy power. Here. On Earth.

He'd rid her of Pádraig. And she'd look to Asher for comfort.

Relaxing his fists, Asher disappeared into the night.

Chapter Seven

Mistaken Identity

"Sorrow makes us all children again — destroys all differences of intellect. The wisest know nothing."

— Ralph Waldo Emerson

Everything inside the townhouse sat exactly as Hailey had left it. Sadly, there was no sign Holly had come home.

Hailey curled up in the chair, eyes fixed on the door while Fin made himself at home on the couch. Within minutes, he was fast asleep. A few times, he stirred, mumbling words that sounded German. At around 4am, after tossing and whimpering for several seconds, he bolted upright and yelled, "HAILEY!"

Feigning sleep, Hailey never stirred, though he'd shouted loud enough to make her ears ring. She figured she'd allow him the dignity of nightmaring with privacy. It didn't take long for him to settle back to sleep, and when his breathing fell into a regular rhythm, she got up to stretch her legs.

While she was up, she noticed Fin had taken off his shirt and lost his blanket to the floor, so she threw it back over him. His tattoo did indeed stretch all the way up his arm and over his shoulder, but in the dim light, Hailey couldn't make out the intricate shapes or intertwining letters, and she gently pulled the blanket over them.

Except for Fin's two bouts of sleep talk, it was another night spent staring at the door in silence until the coffee pot clicked on. Just as Hailey stood up, she heard some shuffling on the porch. Her heart swelled.

It was Holly—she was sure of it.

Hailey bolted down the hall and reached the entryway just as a key ground in the lock. She snatched the handle and flung open the door, smiling and thanking God, ready to hug her sister forever and ever and never let her go—

Morning sun bulldozed into the house, and her hand shot up to shield her eyes. Squinting around her fingers, she saw four people standing on the doorstep. She craned her neck to find Holly among them.

"Where's Holly?" she asked Pix.

He bowed his head.

"Uncle Pix…?"

"Oh, Jesus," he said, letting out a sob.

Wimp squeezed his shoulder and coaxed him inside.

"Where's Holly?" she asked again, more urgently.

Uncle Pix grabbed her hands and looked at her sadly, his eyes swollen, pink, and misty.

"Hailey, dear…" He cleared his throat and started again. "She's with your mum, dear," he said gently. "She's in Heaven—"

"No, she's not!" Hailey yanked her hands away from her uncle. "She can't be, she's coming home…"

It felt like someone was pulling her under water, and she stumbled back. Fin caught her just as her legs crumpled, and the world went dark.

Hailey woke up on the couch, which smelled like Fin's cologne. It was nauseating. With blood swishing in her ears, she desperately tried to blink away the blackness. Fin was sitting close and moved to steady her as she sat up.

"Take it easy," he said with a foreboding voice. "You look pretty pale."

"Where's Holly?" A pit opened in her stomach.

Wrapping his arms around her, Fin hugged her tight. "They found her last night," he said softly, and he held her tighter.

"Where is she?" She drew a sharp breath as her eyes welled.

He didn't answer, and Hailey pushed him away.

"Tell me where she is!"

Fin shook his head.

"Hailey…" he sighed heavily. "They… found her inside a mausoleum."

"Where is she now?"

"Hailey, she's—"

"Is she dead?"

Fin pressed his lips together and nodded, avoiding Hailey's eyes.

"Wha—" Hailey's throat closed and she struggled to breathe.

"I'm gonna be sick." She tried to stand.

"Whoa, whoa, whoa," Fin said. He threw her arm over his shoulder, gently rushing her to the toilet as she tried not to heave. Kneeling next to her, he held her hair back while she cried, retched, and spit. When she was spent, he handed her a cold washcloth.

"Where is everybody?" Hailey pressed it to her face and sunk to the floor.

Fin sat next to her. "They're at the police station. Left a couple hours ago. I'll stay with you until they get back." He patted her leg.

"Thanks," she said, staring at the floor. Tears were steadily dripping from her eyes, and she couldn't do a thing to stop them.

"What happened to her?"

Fin pulled her into a hug. She rested her head against his chest and tried not to snot all over him.

"Hailey, please don't make me..."

"Fin," she begged. "Please tell me."

"They..." He shook his head. "They stabbed her."

Hailey tried to inhale properly. She just couldn't suck in enough air. Every breath hurt, and she had to spit it out before it hit her lungs, because it was making her gut ache.

"Oh no," she panted as the room spun above her.

Fin cradled her in his arms as she drifted into unconsciousness.

"Hailey," he said gently, and she refocused on him. "You're hyperventilating. Breathe with me," he coached. "Slow breath in-one-two-three-four-five-six-seven-eight, and hold it." He counted to four then told her to breathe out, and he counted for her again. Several times he did this until she sat up on her own. "There," he said. "You're color's back. Come on, I'll make you some tea."

Hailey shuffled into the living room, where she sat on the arm of the couch, clutching the cuffs of her sleeves in tight fists and staring at the floor. The morning sun had long gone and taken with it the bright stripes of sunflower yellow from the entryway rug. Only a diffused glow pushed through the windows now.

Very carefully, Fin placed two cups of tea on the coffee table, and then he sat on the couch. He patted the cushion next to him, saying, "Decaf with a teaspoon of honey."

"Thanks," she managed, staring at the cup. He knew how she liked her tea?

Wiping her nose on her sleeve, she slid off the arm and joined him on the cushion, her shoulders drooped. Moving very slowly and watching the tea the whole way, Fin passed her a cup and scooted next to her on the edge of the couch.

Hailey's insides were heavy, the rest of her body numb, and she couldn't help but wonder if the police had made a mistake.

How were they so sure it was Holly they'd found? She could still be out there. And no one was looking for her. Without taking a sip, Hailey set her teacup down, stood suddenly, and walked briskly toward her bedroom.

"Hailey!" Fin dropped his cup and chased after her.

She had to get cleaned up and changed and go see this girl they'd found. She knew in her heart it wasn't Holly. She had to go tell them.

"What's wrong?" Fin asked when she closed the door on him.

"I have to change," she called through the door.

"Okay…"

Hailey could feel him waiting just outside her room as she hurriedly undressed and threw on some fresh clothes. She whisked the door open and shot across the hallway to the bathroom, where she combed her fingers through her frizzies and gathered them into a hairband.

"Where are we going?" he asked as Hailey quickly brushed her teeth.

"Coroner's office," she answered after she spit. "We have to see the body."

She scurried across the hall again, squeezing past Fin to grab a pair of socks from her room, which she'd forgotten. She zipped past him once more and headed for the door, hopping on one foot then the other as she pulled on her socks.

Fin followed.

"Hailey?" he said as she tied her shoes.

"Get your shoes on."

"Okay…"

"You have a car, right?" Uncle Pix was out with the only car in the family.

"Yes," Fin said, stepping into his sneakers. "It's at the pub…"

"Why did we *walk* home last night?" she asked him, and he followed her out the door. "Why didn't we take your car?"

Fin changed the subject as he chased Hailey down the street. "Pix wanted you to stay home today."

"Guess you'll be in trouble then. Where's your car?"

Brushing past her, Fin headed toward a black convertible with red racing stripes parked in a shady corner of the lot. Hailey had seen this car before. She thought it belonged to one of the regulars.

"This is *your* car?" she asked when he opened the passenger door for her.

"Yeah. Why?"

Hailey furrowed her brow.

"Uncle Pix told us this car belonged to an old fart with a—"

She clamped her lips together.

"With a what?"

She shook her head and tried to get in, but Fin threw the door shut. Then he leaned against it and crossed his arms.

"With a what?" he repeated.

"—with a small penis," Hailey blurted, and she covered her face.

She waited a few seconds then peeked through her fingers.

His nostrils weren't flaring. His face wasn't pinched. In fact he didn't look angry at all. Hailey's hands were sweating, but Fin seemed amused. He bit his lip to hide a smile and shook his head. Then he opened her door again, waving her in. Hailey couldn't look at him. She squeezed through and into the passenger seat with her head bowed, mentally berating herself for saying the word "penis" in front of him.

He shut her door, confining his laugh to a snort, and Hailey watched him walk way too slowly to the driver's side. Her leg started shaking when he got in the car. If he didn't start moving a little faster, she was going to snap at him.

"Fin," she said annoyed that he'd taken an extra three seconds to buckle his seat belt, "could you please move a little faster?"

"You got it." He pursed his lips, threw the car in gear, and stomped on the gas. The engine roared, and Hailey fell back in her seat as they shot out of the parking lot. She floundered around for her seat belt then dug her nails into the seat as Fin ran two red lights and weaved in and out of traffic at Mach one.

"Look out!" she shouted as he narrowly missed side-swiping a city bus.

"It would really help me concentrate," said Fin very calmly as he swerved into oncoming traffic again, "if you would please hold all yelling until the Shelby comes to a complete stop."

"Okay," Hailey mouthed. She pulled her knees to her chest and buried her face in her hands. Being in his car felt like a roller coaster, aside from the traffic noise. She heard more than a few horns honking, some squealing tires, and part of an expletive someone yelled at Fin.

He didn't respond.

"Was that fast enough for you?" Fin asked with more than a little hostility as he skidded to a stop next to the coroner's office.

They'd made it there in under five minutes.

Hailey uncovered her eyes and un-cringed. Fin's driving was... exhilarating.

He got out of the car and trotted to the passenger side. But when he opened Hailey's door, something in the alley next to the coroner's office caught his attention.

His smile vanished.

"Wait here, Hailey," he said in a voice so serious that Hailey actually did stay put...for a few seconds—long enough to see him disappear around a building. But, as soon as he was out of sight, she got out of the car, headed for the coroner's office, and asked to see the body.

An older lady with gray hair and shaky hands sat at the reception desk and answered Hailey in a painfully slow voice.

"That was Dr. Grabstein's autopsy," she said. "I'll see if he's available." She picked up her phone.

"Oh, he's expecting me," Hailey lied.

The old lady looked up at her, her hand hovering over the keypad, then the desk, then the keypad.

Hailey didn't have the patience to wait for this old dear. She needed to see Grabstein now.

"He told me to meet him in his office."

"...his office," the receptionist snickered. "He thinks that's so funny."

"Yeah," she agreed with an uncertain laugh. "Could you point me in the right direction?"

"Just push the 'down' button, and the elevator will do the rest." She motioned to the hallway on the right. "Dr. Grabstein's been at it all night. He should still be down there..."

Hailey pushed the button for the basement, which was very conclusively labeled, MORGUE. The doors clanged shut, shaking the entire platform, which dropped her off at the end of an underground hallway with harsh fluorescent lights and air that felt cool and heavy, smelled a bit metallic, slightly like bleach, and reeked of another pungent, synthetic yet rotting ick she couldn't identify.

Voices echoed in the hallway, and she made her way in their direction until she found a couple of men bent over a stainless steel gurney, each wearing scrubs under a black rubber apron.

Hailey opened her mouth to announce her presence, but nothing came out, so she cleared her throat, and one of the men looked up.

"Can I help you?" he said from behind a plastic face shield. He had a scalpel in one hand and a bloody glove covering the other.

"Yes. Could you tell me where I might find Dr. Grabstein?"

"You're looking at him." He held his arms out and smiled. "Please, step into my office." He bowed and still smiling, looked like he was waiting to see if she'd laugh. He really did think that was funny.

"Dr. Grabstein," she said using her most mature voice, "I'm here to see Holly Hartley."

Grabstein looked at her expectantly, and Hailey figured he needed more information.

"She came in last night... Detective Toll's case... A knife wound?"

"Knife wound?" he scoffed. "They took her head clean off, but not with any knife." He put his scalpel down and picked up a folder.

Hailey reminded herself it wasn't Holly.

He scanned one of the pages inside.

"Most of her injuries were consistent with tearing, except for the foot, which was removed with a large blade ..."

Hailey froze, but she clung to her theory: this was not Holly.

"Never seen anything like it, actually. Were it not for the spatter inside the mausoleum, I would have said she was drawn and quartered by a team of horses. I did find a couple of stab wounds, but they were mostly superficial...some defensive wounds on her hands...

"It was difficult to determine an exact cause of death with the body so heavily damaged, although I can tell you she was burned postmortem. You'll read all of this in my report, of course—should be ready this evening—eh—you did say you were with Detective Toll?"

"Yes," ...*in a manner of speaking...* "Could I see the body?"

"'fraid not. Mortician was here not half an hour ago to collect the remains. Not much to see anyway...just pieces really." He picked up his scalpel again. "And you'll have to wait until morning for an ID on these other two that came in with her."

Hailey sneaked a peek at them, but the pile on the gurney didn't even resemble a human. It looked more like mashed and chunky meat.

"Of course," Hailey said graciously. She didn't care about this crime, because it had nothing to do with Holly. She just needed to see the body to prove it.

"Which mortician, then?"

"Who was it that came for the female dismemberment?" he asked his colleague.

"Eh...Rising Sun, wasn't it?"

"That's right. On the South Side." Dr. Grabstein returned to his work, humming.

"Thanks!" Hailey hurried down the hall and inside the elevator, the stench of chlorine and death, sticking to her, making her nauseous. Rushing outside, she shook out her shirt, letting the sweet smell of city traffic and river water wash over her.

Fin's car sat empty in the parking lot.

When Fin rounded the corner into the alley, the cat with purple eyes, which he'd glimpsed from the parking lot, strutted next to a dumpster and sat itself down.

"Asher?" Fin said cautiously. "This is a new look for you."

The cat faded into the shadows and a tall, gaunt man emerged.

"Pádraig O'Shea," he said, and he bowed.

"Cobon," Fin replied coldly. "What are you doing here?"

"I might ask you the same," said Cobon.

Fin weighed his answer. The Envoy would know if he lied.

"Research. And you?"

"I hit a snag," Cobon replied, baring his rotting teeth and looking suddenly…amused.

Fin made a choking noise in his throat. "You…you got a little…" He curled his lip and pointed to Cobon's mouth. "I know a good dentist," he said, leaning back, wrinkling his nose.

Cobon's smile snapped into a grimace. "Mind your manners, slave," Cobon said slowly.

"Forgive me, your highness." Fin swung his arm with a flourish as he bowed mockingly in front of the Envoy.

Cobon drew a sharp breath as his violet eyes ping-ponged around the alley. "You were sent to protect her," he said in a high voice, "weren't you?"

Fin's cocky smile melted, and Cobon exchanged with him a knowing look.

"Don't make me laugh, Pádraig," Cobon jeered. "You? A Guardian?" Cobon put his face next to Fin's. "You would have ripped her apart if I'd asked you to, don't deny it."

"That's where you're wrong, Cobon," said Fin stepping back. "You're incapable of laughing—first of all." Fin rolled his eyes. "And second, you don't control me. Those days are over. I'm a free man."

"Are you so sure?" Cobon chuckled, and that chuckle morphed into a cackle, which turned into a maniacal belly laugh.

Fin eyed him cautiously. Cobon was clearly mad, and that was dangerous.

"Why didn't you ask me, then?" Fin said backing away slowly, and the Envoy straightened up.

"Asher's favorite pet?" he spat. "You would've run straight to him, and Asher...Asher the Benevolent!" Cobon raised his arms dramatically. "He still thinks he's so just. So...righteous. He objects to my..." He stifled a laugh. "...my...methods."

Fin took a few more steps away.

"So Asher made you a Guardian," Cobon taunted, and Fin wasn't about to correct him. "You're not a very good one. And now that you've failed in your duty, do watch your own back, Guardian. Asher does not very happily tolerate failure, and I find you insufferably annoying."

He turned toward the shadows, but then pivoted and lunged at Fin, thrusting his hand through his chest. Cobon wrapped his fingers around Fin's soul and tugged it just a little. He stared into Fin's wide open eyes.

"I would do it, you know," he whispered, "but why ruin a perfectly good servant?"

"You'd be doing me a favor," Fin grunted.

Cobon slammed him against the brick alley wall and vanished. Fin fell like a rag doll to the pavement and rolled onto his back, clutching his chest.

Hailey was calling for him.

He let out a moan as he hobbled to his feet. Leaning against the alley wall for support, he lumbered toward her voice.

Chapter Eight

Rising Sun

The greatest weapon against stress is our ability to choose one thought over another.

— William James

"Fin!"

Hailey was close to panic when he didn't answer straight away.

"Fin!" she hollered again as she stood next to his car. The whole block felt eerily quiet, and a lot like déjà vu. The last thing Hailey wanted was to walk around a corner in a parking lot, looking for someone who wasn't answering, see a dumpster, and pass out.

"FIN!" Her throat ached.

There was movement in the alleyway. *Someone dragging their feet, maybe*? Hailey lifted her shoulders, cringing away slightly, her heart pounding.

"Hailey…" a weak voice called out. It was Fin's. She sighed heavily and jogged toward the alley, rounding the corner just as Fin emerged.

"Oh my gosh, what happened?"

Bringing her hand to her mouth, she examined the broken man in front of her. Fin's eyes were bruised and bloodshot. In fact, his whole face looked bloodshot. A spider web of capillaries stretched across his cheeks; his nose was busted, and blood was leaking from his right ear.

Hailey looked over his shoulder for the gang of thugs that had done this to him, but the alley was empty.

"Nothing," he said shaking his head.

"Well, *nothing* sure packs one heck of a wallop. You look like you just expelled a demon." She hovered her hand over his cheek, afraid it would hurt if she touched him, but he tilted his head into her fingertips and closed his eyes.

"I'll survive." He turned his head so her fingers stroked his hair.

Reaching up, he took her hand and held against his cheek for a moment before he kissed it gently and returned it her.

Hailey didn't want her hand back. She looked up at him and then quickly away, weighing whether she'd tell Holly about this.

"Come on," he said. "I'll go inside with you."

"Oh, I already talked to the coroner."

"I told you to wait by the car," he said stiffly.

"I did." She shrugged. *For a good few seconds...*

Fin lowered his chin, looking very seriously at her.

"I couldn't wait any longer," she told him.

He placed a bruised hand on her shoulder. "Are you alright?"

"Fine," she answered, and Fin looked at her sideways. "The body they found isn't here anymore," she explained. "The mortician has it, so that's our next stop."

"Huh-uh." Fin shook his head decisively as he led her back to the car.

"What?" She searched his swollen eyes for some flicker of reason or at least an iota of loyalty as he opened the car door and motioned her in.

"The stakes just got a little higher, and I'm taking you home. Now, get in."

Hailey bowed her head and sat herself in the passenger seat without a word. She stared at her feet while Fin started the car.

"You smell like a corpse." He rolled down all the windows.

"You *look* like a corpse," she fired back.

Fin pressed his fattened lips together and threw the car in gear.

Hailey crossed her arms over her belly and stared out the window. She didn't need Fin or his stupid, fast car. She'd walk to the funeral home. She squeezed her teeth together with angry resolve.

"Don't even think about it!" Fin warned.

"What?"

"No funeral home is open this late. And you're exhausted." He fanned the air with his hand. "And you need a shower."

Hailey couldn't imagine confronting another night without proving Holly was still out there. Her stomach rolling, she slouched in her seat.

Fin patted her leg. "I'll take you first thing in the morning, okay?"

"What if she's still out there?" Her eyes flooded over.

Fin jerked the wheel and skidded to a stop. He threw his door open, slid across the hood and appeared at Hailey's side.

She was sniffling into her hands when he pulled her out of the car and hugged her tight. For several minutes he held her against him, rocking her gently, while she shook and sobbed with her hands over her face, and he never said a word.

Uncle Pix still wasn't home when Fin walked Hailey to the door. The windows on the house were dark, and Hailey hesitated before she put the key in the lock. There was a heaviness in the air.

"What's wrong?" Fin asked her.

"I don't…" Hailey felt a dozen daddy-long-legs crawling up her back. "I think there's someone inside," she whispered, backing away.

Fin checked the door then stepped back to survey the windows, his eyes studying one then another until something at one of the windows held his attention, and he squinted in the darkness. "Come on," he said, lazily pulling her to the door. "I think it's safe."

"How do you know?"

"No sign of forced entry." He yawned, pointing to the door and around to all of the windows. "I'll check the house before I leave."

"You're leaving?" Hailey didn't want to be alone in a big, dark house.

Fin stood, looking sleepy, his eyes glazed over.

"Fin!"

"Hm?" He blinked a couple times then furrowed his brow. "You want me to stay here again?"

"Yes!" She looked him up and down. *How could he even think of abandoning her?*

He put his hands on her shoulders. "Alright, I'll stay until your uncles get back, but…"

"But what?"

"You really need a shower." He wrinkled his nose.

Fin led the way inside, turning on every light, clearing each room with her, as they went, looking under the beds, in the closets, behind the curtains and doors and in the shadows. She even made him open the kitchen cupboards before she felt safe enough to leave his side.

"Happy now?"

Hailey shook her head, but, noticing something odd, she looked at him more closely. The wounds on his face were… gone.

"Your face is…is… It's all better…" she marveled, leaning close to study him. There wasn't even a scab.

Fin seemed to enjoy her new proximity and let her examine him for several seconds before he leaned even closer.

"I'm a fast healer," he said softly. He looked at her lips briefly then smiled proudly as he straightened up.

"Oh," she breathed. But then she blinked. "Wait, how is that possible? You had—"

"It was nothing, now go on." His tone was stern, but then his face softened. He patted her bum and pointed at the bathroom.

She opened her mouth to protest, but the fight in her was long gone. And seeing the patience evaporate from his face again, she bowed her head, ambled down the hall, and hopped in the shower. He obviously wasn't in the mood for questions, and she wasn't about to push it. The last thing she wanted was for him to get annoyed and leave. She'd just ask him later.

The blast of hot water beating against her head felt divine, and she felt safe closing her eyes and letting the shower's thunder fill her ears, knowing Fin was standing guard.

Steam was a funny thing. It had a way of evaporating all of her worries. As long as she escaped the shower before the steam re-settled, she could leave those worries to condense on the walls and trickle down the drain. That's why she always got out of the shower before she turned it off, which made a mess of the floor. It drove Holly insane, because she always seemed to find a puddle of water—and with a socked foot.

Hailey smiled, thinking of all the soggy socks she'd seen Holly peel off while barking Hailey's name out in two curt syllables. Wrapping her arms across her stomach, she pushed the ache from her belly. Oh, how she missed her big sister!

A door slammed inside the townhouse, and Hailey jumped. She cut the water off and stood soaked and slightly soapy inside the tub as she pulled the curtain back, listening.

"Fin?" she called, trying to hear over the drip, drip, drip of the shower head.

Dammit. Answer me. She shuddered as chilliness crept into the shower and chased her steam away, leaving her worries to settle on her back, two heavy, hairy-legged tarantulas creeping across her shoulders.

"Fin!" she called again. "Uncle Pix?"

Hailey grabbed Holly's towel from the rack, swatted her shoulders with it then wrapped it under her arms, tip-toed to the door, and cracked it open.

"Fin?" He should have heard that.

Opening the door enough to poke her head out, she looked down the hall, but all she saw was stillness. All she heard was silence. No kettle noise from the stove. No shadows moving on the wall. The house seemed hollow.

He went outside to get something from his car, she decided, and she traded her towel for her fluffy pink robe, tying it around her waist as she jogged into the entryway and peeked out the front window.

His car was gone! He'd left her!

Heading for the phone, she found two teacups on the kitchen counter, but the kettle sat half empty under the faucet in the sink. Obviously, he'd meant to stay and must've left in a hurry to move his car or fetch something quick. He must've figured he'd be back before Hailey was out of the shower. That was the only explanation for leaving without a word, and she could watch for him from the balcony on the second floor, which was precisely what she intended to do.

She'd give him three kinds of hell when he got back, she thought as she climbed the stairs and headed to the balcony.

Echoing her frustration, the neighbor's dog snarled then barked, just as the air on the balcony grew cold. Like icy fingers, the night air weaved through her hair, sending a chill straight to her core. But it wasn't uncomfortable enough to chase her back inside. She knelt in front of the railing, sat on her feet, and pressed her forehead against the bars, watching the road in both directions. Several minutes passed, and Hailey's exhaustion betrayed her resilience, squeezing her throat and hollowing out her stomach.

Just let go, she heard herself think. *Just let go, and let the darkness come. Why stay here when they've all gone? Holly is dead. Pádraig is gone. Nobody cares...*

Pádraig. She never called Fin by his real name...never called him "Pádraig." Clenching the iron bars of the railing in tight fists, she sobbed hard, throat aching as the image of a noose flipped through her mind like a cartoon, complete with instructions on how to tie one.

These thoughts weren't hers—

Subtle, she fired back at it in her head, but despair washed over her anyway.

"Holly," she sobbed, and she folded her hands, praying to God for strength but hoping for a miracle.

Just as she squeezed her eyes shut, she felt the air grow dense. She felt *him* approach—the kind Envoy, the one she trusted. He chased the intruder out of her mind, and Hailey's thoughts were once again all her own.

The kind Envoy stood on the balcony behind her— his proximity raising the hair on her back. But she couldn't bear to look at him. She re-gripped the iron rails, staring defiantly at the road, which looked distorted through her tears.

"Is Holly okay?" she squeaked.

"No," he said stoically.

"Did *you*—kill her?" Her sobs broke her accusation in half.

"No."

"Is she—dead?"

"Yes," he answered, again devoid of compassion.

"How do you know?"

His silence widened the gap between them, and Hailey squeezed her eyes shut. "Did an Envoy kill her?"

"Yes."

"Why didn't—you stop him?" she sobbed, enraged and still staring at the street, with no idea who "him" was.

The Envoy placed his hand on her shoulder and like a blanket, hot from the dryer, it chased her shivers away. She should have shrugged him off, but instead she raised her shoulder, tilting her head until his hand brushed her face.

"I could not stop him," he said, and he slowly withdrew his hand.

"Couldn't? Or wouldn't?" she demanded, shivering again and still refusing to look at him. She could feel him standing very still behind her, and when he didn't answer she fired another, equally wrenching question at him.

"Did she suffer?"

Silence.

And then he abandoned her too.

Hailey slid to the floor and curled into a ball, resting her head against the gritty concrete as she cried and ached and seethed.

An engine rumbled in the distance, growing steadily louder for a time, and Hailey recognized it immediately. Fin's car screeched to a halt in front of the townhouse, causing the neighbor's dog to go bananas. Bursting out of his Shelby, Fin sprinted toward the house, stopping midway when he heard Hailey sniffling on the balcony.

"Hailey!" he called to her.

She didn't answer. She didn't even look.

"Come and open the door, Hailey!"

She could hear him jiggle the handle to the front door, which was right under the balcony, but she just didn't care.

"Hailey!"

Something scraped along the outer brick wall, and the next thing she knew, someone lifted her up and was carrying her inside. It smelled like Fin, but her eyes were swollen, and she couldn't muster the energy to open them enough to see. Not that she cared.

"Hailey, I'm so sorry…" Fin was saying, but his voice faded in and out. "…freezing cold…in the house…" Hailey heard, but sleep thundered through her mind and claimed her for its own.

Chapter Nine

Hailey's Nightmare

"Reality is never as bad as a nightmare, as the mental tortures we inflict on ourselves."

— Sammy Davis, Jr.

Churning skies of violet greeted Hailey when she succumbed, still sobbing, to her dreams. Hailey's soul, like all human souls did, had wandered into the Aether in what humans call a dream, and *he* was there waiting. His voice came in the usual way—first as an echo, before it rang out loud.

"I'm very sorry," he said as Hailey approached. "I did not want to leave you tonight."

The Envoy was a muscular silhouette of soft iridescence. His eyes were exactly as Hailey remembered them—very kind and swirling with purple clouds. He still looked like an angel, but angels don't leave you in your time of need.

"Why did you leave me all alone?" She enunciated her syllables.

Talking to someone through the Aether was a lot like speaking across a giant chasm. You can't really touch each other, and you'd better not mumble or else the other person won't hear.

"The others were watching," he told her, sounding tortured. "I could not linger."

"But why? Why couldn't you stay with me?"

"I...*care* for you, Hailey, but if the others knew, they would tear me apart."

"Why would they do that?"

"We are creatures of balance, Hailey. We believe feelings are a perversion—a disease—one that should be eradicated among our kind."

Hailey shook her head. "I don't understand why."

A patient smile played on his lips. "We live by two laws," he said. "Never take a life before its time, and never extend one. Before we came to Earth, none of us were capable of...caring. Emotions don't exist in the Aether." He tilted his head. "But when we became trapped on Earth, we became infected with them. And those emotions, those *feelings*—they tempt us to break our laws...to extend some lives and end others."

"You're not allowed to care about me?" Hailey frowned and looked into the chasm between them. "There's so much space between us now. Where have you been anyway?"

He hadn't shown himself fully to her like this in ages...well, not that she remembered.

"I never left you, Hailey. I've been watching you...through the Aether."

"Was it you in the pub?"

"It was."

"Why did you leave?"

"Because you ran from me."

"I didn't run... I didn't run from *you*," Hailey stammered. "I ran, because I spilled beer all over you, and I was embarrassed. I'm really sorry. I didn't want you to go."

He closed his eyes and heaved a great sigh, looking suddenly very content.

"Will you walk with me, Hailey?"

He held out an incandescent hand.

Hailey looked at the chasm between them again.

"I can't reach you."

"You have to jump," he said, hand still extended.

"Will you catch me?" she asked as she pushed a pebble over the edge with her foot, listening as it bounced and ricocheted for several seconds, never hitting the bottom, and then she looked up at him.

"Or will you let me fall?"

"I haven't let you fall, yet," he told her, and Hailey pushed another rock over the edge, swallowing hard and trying to convince her legs to jump.

Stepping back, she shook her head and took a deep breath. It's just like dancing, she told herself, and then she went for it, leaping off the edge as hard as she could and reaching for Asher's outstretched hand. But she was way short and fell, arms flailing, grasping for an Envoy who didn't catch her. Down, down, deeper and further into darkness she sank, unable to catch her breath to scream and dropping for several agonizing seconds until finally a powerful yank jerked her up and over the wall again.

"I thought...you were...going to...let me fall!" she tried to yell, but it came out breathy as she steadied herself on shaking legs next to him.

He blinked, looking confused and a little injured. "I will not let you fall, Hailey. I will never let you fall."

"It felt like I was falling." Hailey was catching her breath and waving her hand at the canyon behind her.

"Where did the canyon go?" What had been a giant crevasse for Hailey to jump was from the other side nothing more than a hairline crack in the sidewalk.

"In the Aether, time and space move differently. I took your hand in the moment you stepped toward me."

Very slowly, Hailey wiggled her fingers inside his hand and marveled at how his light wrapped around them. It was like holding hands with the air. Her hand looked exactly like a hand should: covered in skin and not emitting any light at all, but his was bright and beautiful and felt like...nothing.

"Why do you look like a flare?" she asked him.

"I am an Envoy, made of energy." He lifted his hand to her cheek, where it tingled against her skin.

Oh, the Aether was frustrating! It was hard to remember anything that happened there.

But more was coming back to her. She remembered now. His name was Asher, and he and several others had fallen out of the Aether long ago, and now they could only visit the Aether, as a human does in a dream, but the Earth always pulled them back.

And they hated it.

It was driving them insane. It was driving them to...

"What happened to Holly?" Hailey asked in a whisper so faint she wasn't sure he'd heard. But when she looked up, she found a heartrending longing in his eyes.

He placed his hands over her shoulders and moved them down the length of her arms then beckoned her to stand with him under a great sycamore on a hill overlooking a clear river.

"Cobon killed her," he said, his voice gentle but strained, "just as he killed your mother."

"Cobon... Is he an Envoy too?"

Asher nodded.

"But why?" she asked, her voice rising. "Why is an Envoy killing the people I love? What did I do wrong?"

Asher moved his hand to Hailey's shoulder, which instantly calmed her, and he took his time in forming his answer.

"You did nothing to deserve this." He stroked her cheek, and Hailey pressed her head through the warmth he emitted. "Cobon believed that Holly could tear open the Aether so that we could go home," he told her.

"Why would he think that?"

"Holly came from a line of women who have for centuries, collected your family's energy."

Hailey shook her head, confused.

Asher studied the violet skies for a moment. "When someone dies, their energy is released from their body along with their soul. An Envoy's duty is to ferry that energy across the Aether and then back to Earth and into another human at the very moment of their birth. That energy fuses the soul and body together. It's life energy, and it's powerful."

With a wave of his hand, he drew a bright streak in front of them. Hailey reached out to it, smiling.

"It's beautiful. What happens to someone's soul after they die?"

"I don't know," he said faintly, and the band of light he'd painted crystalized, hung for a moment in the air, and fell to the ground. "Cobon fashioned a stone to hold your family's life energy on Earth," he continued. "As the generations passed, the energy in the stone grew, until he believed there was enough stored inside to split open the Aether."

This story sounded familiar.

"The legend of the black rock. It's a fairy tale." Hailey's mother had told her this story when she'd given her the necklace.

"It's no fairy tale, Hailey. It's Cobon's experiment. We all have them…our own theories, our own research, our own…obsessions." Asher paused here to gaze at Hailey, and she met his purple eyes, hungry for more information. "We all just want to go home…" he told her wistfully.

She held his gaze, unable to fathom being pulled away from her home.

"But it failed." Asher's voice boomed, and Hailey jumped.

He seemed suddenly angry—as if he cared more about a stupid experiment than he did about her sister.

"Why didn't you stop him?" Hailey demanded.

Asher, looking wounded, moved toward her, but she backed away. "Don't run from me, Hailey," he warned, and Hailey planted her feet to the ground, her heart thumping.

"Asher," she said more gently, "why didn't you stop him?"

"I very well might have stopped him from killing your sister," he said, his voice cold, "but only if I'd told him he had the wrong girl. In his madness, he may have killed Holly anyway and then taken you as well. I could not rescue Holly and protect you."

He tilted his head and continued more forcefully. "*You* were passed the black rock, Hailey. It is *your* energy the stone has lassoed, *your* energy Cobon must sever from *your* body. It's your death that will complete his experiment, only he doesn't know it. His obsession ended with Holly's death, she being the first born daughter. For now he believes the stone is a failure, and that will keep you safe."

"My mother gave the necklace with the black rock to me," said Hailey, realizing Cobon's mistake. "I gave it to Holly—" Her eyes filled with tears. "—I marked her for death!"

Asher moved to embrace her, but she swatted his light away. "It's my fault!"

"You mustn't tell anyone, Hailey. Do you understand?"

Hailey nodded, her lip trembling.

Asher studied her fearful expression.

"Don't be afraid," he whispered. "Cobon will not hurt you."

"You're protecting me. You're always protecting me." She looked up at him with a new understanding. "Was it you? Did you pull us from the fire?"

"I was there," he said simply, and then he cupped her face in his hands.

"I'm sorry, Hailey," he told her tenderly stroking her cheeks. "You're waking up, and you won't remember all these things we spoke of."

He fixed his intense stare at Hailey's eyes as he gave her his instructions.

"You *will* remember to keep your secret. You *will* remember that Holly did not suffer, that I would have saved her if only I could have, and you will remember that Cobon has gone, and I am watching over you…"

Asher's voice filled her ears in overlapping echoes, growing louder and louder, hurting her ears when it reached a roar and only dying when Hailey opened her eyes.

As she woke in Holly's bed to the smell of bacon and coffee and the sound of muffled voices in the kitchen, Hailey twitched her crusty nose. Her head was pounding and full of snot from a long night of uncontrolled sobbing, which she thought ended with a visit from an Envoy, but now she wasn't sure. She felt her shoulder where she thought he'd touched her, and something quite unexpected happened.

Her heart leapt.

She wanted to see him again. *Him*—the one who pulled her and Holly from the house fire; the one who would have rescued Holly if only he could have; the one who watched over Hailey now, even though she couldn't see him, protecting her from the evil Envoy—Cobon—who killed Holly...though, why he killed her, she couldn't quite remember...

Hailey staggered into the bathroom and twisted the sink faucet before looking in the mirror.

"Ah!" she yelled.

"Are yeh alright?" asked Pix through the door, and Hailey had to think about that.

"I think so..."

She surveyed her reflection. She had to do something, good lord, she looked a fright. Her eyes were red and swollen, her face was unevenly puffy and her hair—her hair was a physics experiment. It defied gravity, standing almost straight up and out like she'd been electrocuted. She knew better than to let it dry uncorralled. Still, it almost looked as if someone had teased her hair with a comb and hairspray while she slept.

She cranked on the shower and climbed inside.

By the time she got out, her puffiness had gone down, her headache had faded and her hair was in a more natural state.

When she joined the others in the kitchen for breakfast, they each greeted her with hugs and kisses, except for Fin. He sat in the corner and merely nodded as he wolfed down a piece of toast.

"Did you sleep well, dear?" Uncle Skeet asked as he pulled her chair out.

"I think I did."

"Sorry we were so late in getting home. We didn't wake you, I hope?" Pix said as he set a plate of breakfast in front of her.

"I didn't even hear you come in." She took a bite of bacon and suddenly realized how hungry she was. *Did she even eat yesterday?*

She finished everything on her plate and drank two glasses of water before she said another word, and those words stunned the table into silence.

"Why did an Envoy kill Holly?"

The brothers froze, most of them mid-bite, and they looked at each other in shock. Then they all shot their anger at Fin, who looked just as surprised as everyone else. He shook his head and shrugged as if to say, "Don't look at me!"

Hailey looked patiently at each of her uncles, her grandfather, and Fin, but they each looked to someone else expectantly, and in the end, nobody answered her.

"Somebody…" Hailey said. "Anybody?"

"Where did you hear that word?" Uncle Pix finally said in a horrified voice, as if Hailey had just dropped an f-bomb.

"I don't know." That was the God's honest truth—she had no idea where or even when she'd first heard it. "In a dream, I think."

The brothers exchanged worried looks.

Perhaps now was not the time to mention the Envoy on the balcony last night, she thought.

Hailey drummed her fingers on the table. Suddenly, everyone was too busy pushing food around their plates to talk to her. One revelation was sufficient for the day, she determined. If she delivered another shock, one of her uncles might have a coronary and keel over. She decided to just let the dust settle and changed the subject.

"Fin said he'd take me to the funeral home today to see the bod—" Hailey cut herself off and took a deep breath. "—to see Holly," she corrected, as her chin trembled.

The brothers turned angrily to Fin again, who was acutely and completely engrossed in reading the wax paper cover on the butter and refused to look up.

"I'll drive you myself," Pix grumbled. He pointed his finger at Fin. "And *you*," he ordered, "you stay away from Hailey. She's not one of yer *innumerable* conquests!"

"You just told me this morning to look out for her," Fin said, dropping his fork and holding his palms up.

"You can look out for her from a distance—arm's length or further!" Pix's face went red when Fin rolled his eyes.

"Fine." Fin sat back in his chair and gazed at Hailey.

Hailey didn't feel like she needed Fin looking out for her at all. She had an Envoy watching her back. What could be more secure than that? However, there was nothing in the world more soothing than riding in Fin's car.

"Uncle Pix," Hailey said timidly, "may I please ride with Fin today?"

Pix looked like he was going to blow a gasket. He opened his mouth to say no, but as soon as he saw Hailey cringing away, he sighed and dropped his shoulders.

"You may," he said smiling at her, but then he shook his fist at Fin. "You keep yer hands to yerself!"

Fin, sitting safely out of Pix's reach, winked at Hailey.

"I saw that," Pix hollered from the kitchen.

Fin pushed back from the table and helped Hailey with her chair.

"We'll meet you there," Hailey called as she and Fin walked out the door. "We have to make a quick stop along the way," she informed Fin when they reached his car.

"I'll take you wherever you want, Hailey," he said, sounding distressed as he opened her door.

Hailey froze and looked up at him.

"Are you alright?"

His eyes bounced around the ground a little before he looked at her. "I'm sorry about last night," he said softly, his head slightly bowed. "I don't even know why I left, and I didn't even realize I was driving 'til I hit the tunnels..."

Hailey didn't know what to say, but she did know she wouldn't try to conjure her feelings from last night. Never had she been as low as she was when she realized Fin had abandoned her, and that was the last place she wanted to dwell. The muscles in her throat pulled, and her eyes stung as she looked at him.

"No worries," she said, taking his hand and smiling through her tears. She trusted he had a darn good reason for leaving, and she believed he regretted it. "Thanks for coming back," she added and patted his hand before she got in the car.

Fin held onto her hand for several seconds after she was seated, so long that she looked up to see if he had something else on his mind.

He only gazed at her.

"Fin?" Her cheeks heated. "Can I have my hand back?" She smiled but couldn't look him in the eye.

He let her hand slide out of his and closed her door.

"Could we stop at the church?" she asked with misty eyes after he started the car. "I want to light a candle and say a prayer for Holly."

"Woman," he said, "I would drive you anywhere.

Chapter Ten

The Girl Who Died

"Never interrupt your enemy when he is making a mistake."

— Napoleon

The candle wick sparked briefly before it took the flame, which rose up, trembling. Hailey closed her eyes as Holly's favorite song rang in her ears.

"...a candle in the night outshines the sun..." a serene voice sang in her head.

Fin placed his hand on her shoulder, and Hailey looked up at him—her candle in the night.

"She really wanted you to kiss her."

"What?" Fin asked, smiling down at Hailey.

"Yeah," Hailey nodded, returning her gaze to the candle. "Holly was crazy for you. She thought you were—how did she put it—the paragon of hotness," Hailey chuckled, stealing a glance at Fin, whose mouth twisted as she spoke.

"The...paragon...of...*hotness*..." he whispered as if he were thoroughly enjoying how those words sunk in, and a giant smile spread across his face.

"But she never heard you snoring like a chainsaw," Hailey said, trying to banter, but it came out sounding sad. "Will you pray with me?"

His face hardened, but then he knelt down with her, made the sign of the cross and folded his hands as she whispered.

"Father God, please make a place in Heaven for Holly to dance. Help her find Mom and Dad. Please forgive me for being angry with You. And please help me accept that she's gone, because my heart keeps telling me she's alive, and I'm afraid she's still out there, hurting and waiting for someone to find her." She sniffled softly. "Please bless Fin. Thank You for bringing him into our lives. Without him, I'd be lost. Amen."

She wiped her cheeks and stood, but Fin remained penitently on his knees, and Hailey strolled outside.

"Sorry," he said when he caught up to her.

"Don't be," Hailey said kindly, and Fin hurried to get her door.

"There were some things I had to…straighten out with the Big Guy," he explained as he pulled away from the curb, and Hailey felt somehow comforted by that.

The House of the Rising Sun was a beautiful, polished stone building with vaulted ceilings and stained glass, stretching at least twenty feet high. It sat on a hill overlooking the Ohio River, just a few blocks from the church. Hailey's uncles were already inside with the mortician when she and Fin arrived.

"I wanna see her," Hailey blurted as soon as she saw Uncle Pix. She didn't mean for it to come out like that and quickly remembered her polite words. "I'm sorry," she said dropping her eyes. "Could I please see her now?"

"Of course, dear." Pix motioned to the mortician. "This is Mr. Tod. He's prepared Holly for the service."

A kind-looking man in his forties waddled over and shook her hand.

"Miss Hartley," he said gently but not at all hesitantly. "There are some things I'd like to tell you before we go see your sister."

Hailey gave him her full attention.

"There was substantial damage to her head and to her face, which may make it hard for you to recognize her. Her body was too badly damaged for us to embalm, and she also had some burns, which has made her skin color very dark. There's also some charring on her face and head."

"How do you know it's her?"

"The coroner made the identification using her dental records," Mr. Tod said, but Hailey still needed to see.

"I'm ready," she breathed. Her heart slammed against her throat.

Mr. Tod led the family toward a room with long, heavy curtains, hazy light, and a polished wooden casket, which sat, lid closed, against the far wall. Uncle Pix stopped Mr. Tod in the hallway, mumbling something about a list of people who had access to Holly's remains, but Hailey never broke stride and in fact quickened her pace. The casket was so close. She had but to open it, and then she could see—they all would see.

One of the brothers shouted, "Wait!"

Hailey threw open the lid and staggered back.

A charred, skeletal head wearing Holly's hair gaped at her. The rest was pieces.

Hailey saw the ceiling and the dim light fixtures spin above her before she hit the floor. Fin fell beside her, cradling her next to him.

"That's not Holly," she managed, the room swinging like a pendulum under her.

On the night before the burial, there was a gathering at the pub. Nobody called it a wake.

Someone sang a sad, slow tune in old Irish, which Hailey understood perfectly even if she didn't know what the words meant. The song ended, and hush dropped like a heavy curtain over the Hullachan.

Holly was dead.

The church held a Requiem Mass the next day. Every seat was filled.

Hailey sat down, blinked once, and it was over.

The next thing she knew, she was standing over Holly's open grave. Numb.

Squatting down, she wrapped her fingers around some loose Earth, red clay she squeezed into crumbles against her palm. She buried her sister at 2pm on a windy Sunday. She dropped a fistful of dirt onto the casket.

And just like that, Holly was gone.

Cobon waited for the last human to leave the cemetery before he revealed himself to Asher.

"Lovely service, wouldn't you agree?"

Strolling with his hands clasped leisurely behind his back, he approached Asher, who stood unmoving in the shade of a giant oak, facing Holly's grave.

"I especially liked that bit about perpetual light," he continued, taking his place at his brother's side. "Though," he said, rocking back on his heels then forward again, "I doubt that even the temporary light of this wretched planet could ever find *all* of her pieces…"

Asher said nothing.

Cobon pressed his lips together. "Well, not in that mausoleum anyway." He leaned closer to Asher. "Too many cracks and crevices."

Asher remained lost in his own thoughts, uninterrupted and quite obviously unamused.

"In fact, I think some of her is still stuck in my fingernails." He scraped a bit of dried blood from his thumb and flicked it away.

When Asher still took no notice of him, Cobon dropped his hands and impatiently quickened his cadence.

"Magnificent soul, though—pity I had to shred it, what a waste."

He looked for a moment with Asher at Holly's fresh grave.

"Simply exquisite that one, even my wicked humans thought so. Oh, they were happy enough to ravage her, but they just couldn't bring themselves to kill her—I had to wait hours for her to bleed out." He shook his head in short, minute bursts and muttered almost angrily, "Lucky I found a black widow to ensnare the girl—chop her foot off. Otherwise, those two buffoons would've failed to even get her into the car."

Asher was unaware of a third human involved in this scheme, and he tried not to show it...tried hard not to show a sudden, intense concern for his girl, but Cobon might've sensed it. Asher's jaw had tightened, ever so slightly.

But still he said nothing, and Cobon spoke even faster.

"Oh, but she's not the one you care about, is she—not the one you protect. I saw you, of course, *touch* her." Cobon looked as if he'd just bitten into a lemon. "Resilient, that one...downright uncharmable—" he gulped some air "—of course, you interrupted me on the balcony—and she shut me out of her mind anyway. Tell me, how will you control her?"

"I will not control her," Asher said slowly.

Cobon leaned back, drawing a deep, cleansing breath and letting it out with a smile.

"I hate it when you ignore me."

"I ignore your madness."

"It's not mad to dispose of a few wretches, is it?"

"The girl was no wretch. You took a life before its time, brother. Again."

Cobon shrugged.

"Maybe, but only just. Call it an act of mercy—collateral damage, if you like," he reasoned. "And you're the only one who cares."

"The others grow intolerant of your—"

"The others grow desperate," Cobon spat. "And in their desperation, they grow more tolerant. This place..." He brought his hands to his head and clenched them into fists. "This place is driving us all mad. We don't belong here, Asher, we have to go home!"

Asher searched Cobon's eyes, and Cobon let him.

"You were there, Asher. You saw them all, watching and waiting."

Cobon looked him up and down.

"Even you stood by as I ripped her apart."

Asher dropped his eyes. He had stood by and done little more than watch as the girl endured unspeakable atrocities. She'd cried out several times and once even looked Asher dead in the eyes.

And he'd looked away, ashamed.

He hadn't looked again until it was over, until her final thoughts evaporated. She'd projected quite a beautiful image as she'd suffered, of dancing with her little sister, and he had thoroughly enjoyed it.

That bothered him.

"Why do you linger here?" Asher asked.

Cobon frowned. "I've lost my rock," he said, kicking the ground. "I've looked for it everywhere. I even tore those two buffoons apart, but I just can't find it."

Asher knew perfectly well where the black stone was. After a doorway into the Aether *didn't* open, Cobon had flown into a rage and flung his precious rock onto the cemetery grass. Asher had seen it, and he had very stealthily taken it. The rock was in his pocket, and he wasn't about to tell Cobon that.

"Your experiment failed," Asher said flatly. "The passage is shut. Your rock is finished."

Cobon shook his head.

"No...no, I'd know if it were finished. I can still..." Cobon raised his shoulders. "feel it, I just can't find it."

Asher returned to gazing at Holly's grave.

"And you?" asked Cobon. "Why do you linger? Amused by your female? You do so adore your pets," Cobon said, frowning. "I might have claimed dear Hailey for my own, you know, but..." Asher squinted, and Cobon continued with some hesitation "... well, what good is a human who won't obey?"

Cobon tapped his chin then waved his arm at the rose in Asher's hand. "For the girl?"

"For her suffering," Asher said simply.

"You are brave. I don't think this one killed Adalwolf." He flung his hand toward Holly. "Not much fight in her at all."

He looked at the rose and then again at Asher, and his face softened into sanity.

"Do be careful, brother," he said quietly. "I will not condemn you, but the others are watching, and you remember what happened to Kiya."

Of course he remembered. An Envoy never forgot. To his everlasting shame, Asher had destroyed Kiya.

Her demise had unfolded in short order. She had fallen in love with a human and openly displayed her affection. When the others noticed, they were appalled. Their rage came on swift wings, and Kiya had come to Asher begging for protection. But instead of protecting her, Asher handed her to the mob, and then he joined them in shredding her into scraps of energy, which dissipated into the void.

Only Cobon had tried to help her, a futile attempt at a rescue. The others shunned him after that, which likely hastened his spiral into lunacy. Insane and genius and unrelenting, Cobon would tear Hailey apart if he knew he'd killed the wrong girl.

And now Cobon was possibly Asher's only ally—the only Envoy that would tolerate his feelings for the girl—the only Envoy that might stand with him, should the others attack him as they did Kiya.

"Strange how fate weaves us apart and together again," Cobon remarked, as if his thoughts had followed the same course as Asher's. He narrowed his eyes at the rose.

"Do enjoy your little pets, Brother. I so hope they don't bite you in the end, but perhaps you'll buy a muzzle for Pádraig or Fin or whatever the humans are calling him now." Cobon continued muttering to himself as he faded away. "I do find your *feelings* for that girl utterly despicable…"

Asher returned to his thoughts, letting his mind drift into the Aether. It was becoming more and more difficult to exist there. Where three thousand years ago, he'd spent most of his time in the Aether and was pulled away to the Earth only sporadically, now it was the other way around.

How he missed his home. And how he weighed once again whether he would remain on Earth and love Hailey for the rest of her natural life…

Or tear her apart tomorrow and end his torment.

Chapter Eleven

The Vanishing Rose

"And then there stole into my fancy, like a rich musical
note, the thought of what sweet rest there must be in
the grave."

— Edgar Allan Poe, The Pit and the Pendulum

Hailey tossed and turned, worried into insomnia about her return
to school after her sister's burial. At 3:13 a.m., she flopped on her
side and decided to watch as each minute flipped a digit on her
bedside clock, and she kept watching until 5:30 a.m., when she
decided it was finally late enough to rise. And rise she did, like a
drone, inching toward the bathroom, point-focused on her next
task and thinking of little else.

Brush teeth. Done.

Turn on shower. Done.

Get in shower. Done.

Wash hair. Done.

Grab towel—step out of shower. Done.

Turn off shower. Done.

Forget to wipe up a puddle so Holly can find it with a socked
foot. Done.

Catch glimpse of white-haired boy in mirror...

Hailey whipped her head around, a scream stuck in her throat. There was—there really was a white-haired boy of twelve or thirteen staring at her from behind the bathroom mirror.

She stared at him wide-eyed, unable to force air, and frozen in place, hoping that if she didn't move, he wouldn't see her.

Several seconds passed, and neither of them blinked.

The mirror took on the sheen of an oil painting, covered in thick strokes of washed-out tones which bled together to form a frozen face.

Breathing as quietly as she could, Hailey leaned in for a closer look. Then she pulled her face back, and the white-haired boy mimed her every movement. He now stared back at her slack-jawed with one eyebrow raised higher than the other.

Hailey closed her mouth, and the white-haired boy closed his mouth.

She squinted at him suspiciously, and he squinted right back.

Hailey sighed; he sighed, and then she threw her towel over the mirror and held it there. With both hands engaged, she wasn't quite sure what to do next, and she couldn't move without exposing the glass.

This was crazy.

She'd just decided she'd imagined the whole thing when a pair of albino arms jutted out from the mirror, through her towel and went straight for Hailey's head, pulling and twisting her hair this way and that, and Hailey fought against them, grabbing one and using all her might to pull it away.

It shook her loose. Then it slapped her hand and went back to work on her hair. Ducking and squirming, Hailey bunched herself into the corner. Finally, the hands stopped.

Hailey stood up, rubbing her head and finding her hair was pulled into a beautiful, ornate, albeit soaking wet, French braid.

The white-haired boy saluted her from the mirror then disappeared.

Hailey blinked, dumbfounded.

No way that just happened. No way anyone would ever believe her if it actually had happened. She probably braided her hair herself and from lack of sleep simply imagined the whole affair with the mirror. That's what happened.

Except, Hailey didn't know how to braid.

Eyes wide, she very slowly got dressed and went about her day.

With her hair gorgeously organized, she caught the bus to school, sat herself in the front seat, and avoided all eye contact.

Whispers erupted all around her, and they were hard to ignore. Some girls didn't even bother whispering their gossip about Hailey and her sister.

"—I heard when they were digging her sister's grave, her uncle poured a bottle of whiskey into it," gushed one girl in Physics class.

It was half a bottle, Hailey corrected her in her head. Her uncles drank the rest.

The girl sitting right behind her chimed in next. "At least she finally bought a brush for her hair," she giggled and a few others laughed with her.

Holy crap, I'm sitting right here.

Tage followed her off the bus that afternoon and fell in step with her as she moped home, walking so close, he actually brushed against her.

Hailey didn't really feel like talking.

"You've got a toothbrush in your hair," he said.

"What?!"

Hailey felt around and sure enough pulled Holly's toothbrush out of her braid.

"That albino little punk," she muttered. She glanced at Tage briefly then returned her attention to her feet. No wonder everyone was laughing at her...

"I missed seeing you in school."

Hailey pulled the corners of her mouth back in a weak smile.

"I never realized how nice it was to hear your feet tapping under your desk."

"I do that?" That was something Holly used to do. Hailey didn't know she did it too. It made her smile for real.

"Yeah, and it's always a pretty cool rhythm." Tage rubbed the back of his neck.

"Oh." Hailey dropped her head again and tried to hide behind some strands of hair that had come out of her braid.

"Wait," he said smiling. "Was that embarrassing?" He chuckled, and Hailey could feel her cheeks heat. "Actually, I'm glad you're so shy, otherwise I'd never have the courage to ask you to prom."

Hailey froze and looked at him in terror. Was he asking her to prom? She couldn't tell.

"So, uh...I mean, you don't have to answer right away," he stammered. "Just think about it for a couple days, okay?"

"I...I don't..." Hailey realized she had no idea how to turn down a date. Or accept one. This was all new.

"Just think about it."

Hailey sighed. She didn't need a couple days to think about it. She didn't even need a couple seconds. There was no way in hell she was going to prom.

"And, uh, you can come tapping in my direction with your answer anytime."

Hailey shook her head and tried to say, "no," but nothing came out. She was in the Twilight Zone. And Tage was clearly out of his mind. Maybe he'd recently taken a hit to the head...without his helmet. That would explain his craziness.

"I'll see you tomorrow," he said, and then he pecked her on the cheek and jogged away.

"Buh..." Hailey uttered after him.

Stunned, she stood on the sidewalk for several seconds before she turned and moped home, Holly's toothbrush in hand.

Detective Toll was at the townhouse waiting for her, and he was wearing his police-face.

Everyone stood up when Hailey stepped inside.

"Hi...?" she announced as she tentatively placed her backpack next to the door.

The clock in the kitchen spoke first. *Tick...tick...tick...*

"As you were," Hailey said, trying to lighten the mood as they all stared at her. She held up Holly's toothbrush. "Thanks for telling me I had a toothbrush stuck in my hair this morning."

Her uncles gave each other first quizzical then accusatory looks. All five of them had eaten breakfast with her. One of them should have said something.

She really missed Holly.

"Mrs. Lash is dead," Uncle Pix announced.

"And burning in hell," Dale added, and Holly's toothbrush fell out of Hailey's hand. She quickly picked it up and looked at Detective Toll for an explanation.

"Mary Lash hanged herself last night."

Hailey's hand shot up to her mouth.

"Oh my gosh," she breathed. "Why? Why would she do that?"

"There's uh...there's a little more," Toll said, and then Uncle Pix took over.

"She helped them kill Holly," Uncle Pix told her.

"What?"

"She confessed it in a note, and she left her weapon next... right next to it," Toll said.

"I just can't believe it," Hailey said, clutching Holly's toothbrush as blood swished in her ears. Blinking the dark away, she slowed her breathing, wishing Fin was next to her.

Where was he? she wondered, feeling the sting of abandonment. She hadn't seen or heard from him since Holly's funeral.

Sleep wouldn't come. Once the house went quiet, Hailey sneaked out her bedroom window and headed to the cemetery to visit Holly.

Shortly after she hit the street, the rain started, and the air went from chilly to downright frigid. Then the wind picked up. She realized too late she should have worn a jacket. As cold rain turned to sleet, icy needles pricked her skin, injecting their frost directly into her veins until she shivered in violent convulsions.

Still she walked, one shoulder raised to the wind, which still managed to blow ice crystals into her ear.

It felt good to hurt. She deserved it for abandoning her sister, for allowing Mrs. Lash, the bad men, and the Envoy from Hell to get her. In fact, she deserved far worse than a chill, she decided, as she trudged through the darkness, through the pouring rain-slush to Holly's grave.

Hailey's hands were numb, and she shoved them under her arms as she knelt on top of the mud that covered her big sister. Someone had left a single rose to weather the storm with her. Hailey didn't care that she was filthy. She didn't care that the wind sliced through her thin shirt. She just didn't care...

Very gradually, she felt tired, and she smiled, shivering as she laid herself down to sleep, hopefully forever with her sister. It was cold and colder, but then it was warm. In a little while she'd feel much warmer, and then it wouldn't be long. It was her time to go, she decided, and she rolled her face into the mud.

Death felt an awful lot like a dream, like being lifted and carried, wrapped in a warm cloak. Snuggling against its softness, Hailey moaned a great exhale and let herself go.

Holly's voice vibrated in tune with a fiddle playing in the distance. When Hailey tried to open her eyes, they slammed shut, gritty and burning something awful.

Somebody *was* playing a fiddle. Inside the townhouse.

And Hailey was in her bed, crusted with mud, wrapped in a dark wool blanket, and waking up to a muffled Rakish Paddy. The bed was filthy with flecks of dirt and clay stains on the pillow. A plug of solid Earth stoppered her right ear.

Swinging her feet onto the floor, she untied her sloshy sneakers. Her water-logged feet were grateful when she released them from their prison. As she peeled off her socks and wiggled her toes, she noticed, on her bedside table, a single red rose with a piece of parchment folded like a tent over it. She reached for the note.

Solitude stalks the lonely soul
that walks with isolation
hand in hand, Hope's greatest fool
and thoughts of death's temptation.

God's knot a weeping cesspool
that's fraught with devastation
band on band, Faith's golden rule
this Rose's hesitation.

Who else but you, so graceful
Could stand my adoration?
Who else but me, so gullible
(and God's abomination)
Would hope for love from you, my dove
Your hand — my soul's salvation.

Hailey read it several times. The last stanza pulled on her heart, but the rest seemed a bit cryptic. Poetry wasn't really her thing. It always felt like more of a riddle than anything, and this was no exception.

Squeezing her eyes shut, she set the note next to the rose and rubbed her face. She hated riddles.

Hope's greatest fool? A weeping cesspool? What did that even mean?

Just as she decided to read it again, both the note and the rose began to fade.

No, no, no!

She made a grab for them, but all she came up with was a fistful of air, and when she looked again, they were gone. Vanished.

She stared wide-eyed at her nightstand for several seconds. Then she sank into her bed and pressed her hands against her heart, wondering if she was losing her mind and hoping she hadn't just imagined that maddeningly cryptic poem-puzzle. It was the closest thing to a love letter she'd ever seen.

Chapter Twelve

The Silver Envelope

"Being ignorant is not so much a shame, as being
unwilling to learn."

— Benjamin Franklin

Hailey stepped into the shower fully clothed, peeling her garments off one piece at a time as she rinsed them free of graveyard dirt. Twenty minutes later, she was finally down to her skivvies and able to hear out of both ears again. By the time she turned the water off, there was enough clay at the bottom of the tub to make a pot.

As she wiped a swath across the mirror, it instantly re-fogged and there, written in neat letters through the steam was the word, "Tomas."

"Tomas?" she said thoughtfully. "Is that your name, you little trouble-maker?" she said into the mirror, but he didn't answer. Gathering her wet clothes inside her towel, Hailey peeked into the empty mirror one last time before opening the bathroom door and scurrying across the hall.

Very nervously, very hesitantly, Hailey joined her uncles for breakfast, not at all looking forward to the stern lecture, the tsk-tsk-tsk'ings and expressions of utter disappointment, which surely awaited her for sneaking out in the dead of night.

Her uncles stood and nodded their good mornings as she slid into her seat at the table, and then they went back to their coffees and papers and morning banter, behaving as if the world were still spinning normally. Nobody looked very seriously at her at all or even hinted at her late night jaunt to the graveyard.

Could it be they hadn't noticed anything out of the ordinary during the night? Hailey slowly relaxed into a more innocent posture and munched on some bacon.

She shouldn't be surprised. After all, they hadn't noticed a toothbrush sticking out of her head—why should they notice that she ran away to die or that someone or something had chucked her back into her bedroom, soaking wet and caked in cemetery dirt?

Absently, she flipped through a stack of mail on the table, stopping suddenly at a large silver envelope.

"To Holly and Hailey Hartley," it read in shaky lettering, and the return address was printed in two lines:

Bear Towne University
The Middle of Nowhere, Alaska

Ever so lightly, Hailey ran her hand across Holly's name, smiling as she remembered the hours they'd spent at the kitchen table, writing wild scholarship essays for Bear Towne.

Very carefully, she tore an opening along the edge of the silver paper and with trembling hands, pulled out a letter.

Dear Misses Holly and Hailey Hartley,

Congratulations on your full scholarship to study ParaScience at Bear Towne University in the Great White North.

Upon your arrival in The Middle of Nowhere, you will have already completed the course requirements for ParaScience 101,

An Introduction, which is a 3-credit course conducted during your 10-hour flight aboard the Bear Towne Luftzeug.

All incoming ParaScience freshmen are required to attend this course, and should be advised not to panic.

Please arrive at the Pittsburgh Executive Airport no later than 1000 on the first of August to board your flight, and hold all questions until your arrival on campus.

Enclosed with this letter, you will find important information regarding your move to Alaska and life in general at the Bear Towne campus. Follow the enclosed instructions and please adhere to the packing list. As a reminder, percussive instruments are expressly FORBIDDEN at BTU.

Once again, congratulations,

Simeon Woodfork
Dr. Simeon Woodfork
Dean of the College of ParaScience
Bear Towne University

Hailey turned the letter over then shook the silver envelope, looking for the promised information, but all she found was a note scribbled on parchment and folded asymmetrically, which advised her to bring no more than one piece of luggage—purse size.

Not much of a packing list.

"How am I supposed to fit everything I need into one small bag?" she wondered out loud, deciding on the spot that she was going to Alaska in the fall, without panicking, and by way of Luftzeug, whatever that was.

Why not? She hadn't received any other offers of scholarship or even admission from anywhere else, and there was no way she'd spend another year waitressing at the pub.

"Did you say something, dear?" Uncle Pix asked from the kitchen, and everyone turned their attention to Hailey.

"We got accepted to a college in Alaska."

"Alaska?" said Wimp, his voice full of foreboding, and Hailey looked at her letter again, her chin poked out in a half frown.

"Yeah, Bear Towne University. Full scholarship."

The brothers exchanged worried expressions.

"Holly won a full scholarship too," she said, smiling sadly.

"Let me see that letter." Uncle Pix strode across the floor and snatched it out of her hand. He skimmed the page and squinted at the signature on the bottom.

"What's up?" she asked.

Her uncles chatter-answered at once—the same message but in vastly different tones, some sad, some proud, and one very anxious, which rang through the others:

"We're worried about you going to Bear Towne," Wimp said with a frown, and she looked up at him in confusion.

"You've heard of Bear Towne University?"

"Sure, that's a feckin mad place."

"What does that mean? Is a 'feckin mad place'…is that good or bad?" She looked from Wimp to Pix and then to Dale, who had suddenly found a hangnail on his thumb which was very conspicuously demanding his full attention. Hailey honed in on him.

"Uncle Dale," she said. He grimaced before he looked at her. "Have you been to Bear Towne?"

He shook his head, sighing heavily. "I have."

"…and?"

"Well, you'll be safe there," he said with a strong, conclusive nod.

"Safe from what?"

"Everything," Pix answered her, very clearly indicating that would be the end of the conversation.

Hailey shook her head. She was getting tired of these riddles, half-answers, and cryptic talk.

"You guys and your secrets are killing me."

Leaving the table in a huff, she turned her back on them and plopped on the couch with her arms folded.

From the kitchen came a flurry of whispers and hisses, which culminated in a hushed, but very defined, "FINE!" and the sound of many feet scurrying down the hall and up the stairs.

Pix joined Hailey on the couch.

"Hailey," he said, "we've decided you should know some things about your family."

Hailey uncrossed her arms, anxious to hear whatever her uncle was about to share.

"You see, dear, a long time ago—a very, very, very long feckin time ago," he said with clenched teeth, but then he relaxed, "my brothers and I met a…a man, who asked us to watch over…eh… you and your sister."

"How long ago? Who asked you? And…and why?"

"Long before you were born," he said with a dismissive wave, but she furrowed her brow at him until he expounded. "It's been a few generations now. Started with our sister in Ireland. Then her daughter and her daughter's daughter and so on."

"How…old are you—wait" She held up her hand. She didn't want to know. "Just tell me you're my uncle." She left off the great-'s, because, honestly, at this point she didn't know how many to add, and she didn't care how distant his blood was anyway. She still had family. That's all that mattered.

Pix nodded, his eyes softening. "And it was more of a 'what' than a 'who,' dear."

"You mean an Envoy." Finally some information on her nightmare monsters!

"Monsters, all of 'em," he said angrily as if he could read her mind. "They don't belong on this Earth, dear, but they're trapped here. They want to go home, and you girls were...eh...helping them by living a good, long life."

"How does that help them?"

"That's a story for another day."

He patted her leg, and then he pointed to her letter.

"One exists at Bear Towne, and most of us think he meant to keep you and your sister safe."

This sounded vaguely like something Hailey had dreamed, but she couldn't quite remember.

"What do you think, Uncle Pix?"

"I think that we can't protect you here," he said, looking at her sadly, "but this one in Alaska... I think this one might be friendly, might want to protect you."

"Protect me from what?"

"I think you already know what killed your sister," he said ominously. "I don't think it will bother you, especially not at Bear Towne."

"What do you know about Bear Towne?" she asked.

He drew a great breath.

"Eh..." He shook his head and crossed his arms. "Strange place, for sure, and cold—feckin cold in the wintertime and swarming with bloodsuckers in the summer. Couple'a earthquakes and an explosion here and there, too."

Hailey's face fell.

"But," he said more cheerfully, "eh...the staff are very, very knowledgeable. You'd learn a lot studying under them. And Woodfork is a good man. We've known him for...well, for quite a while," he concluded with an exaggerated nod, which Hailey recognized. Uncle Pix was done talking about this.

Sighing, she leaned back into the couch and caught a whiff of cologne.

"Where do you suppose Fin is?" she asked.

"Who the hell cares?" was her uncle's response.

"I thought you liked him."

"He's a pain in the arse, and he's probably off chasing women and getting into trouble."

"Oh."

It was probably no use asking if Uncle Pix was worried about him. She was pretty sure she already knew his answer. Hailey stared at the floor, but caught a glimpse of white flit through the reflection on the coffee table.

She pointed at it excitedly.

"Did you see that?"

"See what?"

She debated whether she should tell him about the albino hairdresser living in their bathroom mirror.

Vanishing roses, disembodied hands and ghosts in the mirror...? He might think she was losing her mind.

That night, Hailey collapsed, heavy-hearted next to Holly's empty bed with more questions than answers about her sister's murder, about the Envoy that killed her, and about the creature that anticipated her arrival in the great White North.

Asher stood, eyes fixed on the horizon and seemingly deep in thought when Hailey emerged in the Aether. He made no move to greet her, which was strange.

"What is it?" she asked as she approached, and he finally turned to her.

"In your dreams, you belong to me and only me," he said almost angrily.

Hailey stopped dead in her tracks.

Whoa.

Asher started toward her, and she knew not to retreat even though her legs shook.

"I'm no longer content in the Aether, and I wish to see you on Earth again," he said in a far more gentle voice as he closed the distance between them.

Hailey heaved a great sigh of relief.

"For a moment I thought you were angry."

"I'm not angry...not with *you*," he said looking away and with a not-so-subtle emphasis on "you."

Hailey swallowed hard.

"One of your human friends touched you yesterday, and I find his demand for your attention...troubling."

Hailey wrinkled her brow as she searched her memory.

"You mean *Tage*?" Tage was hardly a friend, and..."Asher, are you... jealous?"

"I don't know," he said with genuine confusion. "You're mine, and when that *boy* put his lips on you, I very nearly tore him apart."

Asher pulled his hands into tight fists, and his whole glowing body pulsated.

"Is that...jealous?" he asked.

She nodded, her heart pounding. "I think so," she breathed. She had to concentrate on not running away. "You really shouldn't want to kill someone just because he touched me, Asher—that's crazy," she scolded him, her voice quivering.

"Is it?"

"Yes," she said, leaning away. "And frightening."

"Then I won't kill him," he said thoughtfully. He raised an incandescent hand to her cheek. "I didn't mean to frighten you," he murmured, and a soothing flush of warmth spilled across her face.

She drew a breath to tell him...something...

What was it? What was he saying just now? Something about a boy...or lips...something...

Hailey looked up at him, her mind blank.

"I'm sorry, Asher, what were you saying?"

He smiled slightly.

"I'd like to see you on Earth again."

"Oh."

Hailey pulled her brow down, unable to shake the feeling she was forgetting something. Whatever it was—it was gone. She shook her head and looked up at Asher.

"Does that mean you're real? You don't just exist here…in my dreams…?"

His smile widened.

"I am real," he said.

They stared together at the sparkling river in front of them.

"Hailey," he said gently, "will you tell me what you're thinking?"

"I feel so forgetful here. And I can never remember these dreams."

"Aether amnesia," he said. "All humans forget."

"Forget…" she repeated, and her lip twitched sadly.

Asher blinked in confusion.

"What is it?"

"I was just thinking about Holly," she said as a tear dropped to her cheek. Asher raised an angelic hand to it. "I don't want to forget her like I forgot my mom and dad." Another tear fell from her eye. "I miss her so much."

She sniffled for a time and continued.

"We just got accepted to a college in Alaska. I'm gonna go, but she won't be there with me. I never thought I'd go anywhere without her." She looked up at Asher. "Uncle Pix says I'll be safe there…in Alaska. He says there's an Envoy there that will protect me."

She held his gaze, hoping he'd answer her unspoken question.

Asher closed his eyes and smiled again.

"I am the one, and you won't be alone."

She smiled through her tears.

"Then I'll see you—I'll see you, Asher. I can meet you and shake your hand and have a conversation I'll actually remember—" Asher's wistful expression cut Hailey off. "What's wrong?" she asked.

"I'd like to hold you in my arms, Hailey. Ever since I left you on the balcony, it's all I think about."

Hailey froze. That was exactly what she wanted—comfort. From the one creature powerful enough to protect her. Her heart beat in her ears, and she finally exhaled.

"Asher, why do you like me?"

He pondered this for so long, Hailey figured he wouldn't answer. Heavy silence forced her blurt. "I wouldn't—"

"I should kill you."

Hailey's breath caught.

He fixed his mesmerizing eyes on her.

"But you will forget this conversation."

Oh, I very seriously doubt that.

"I should kill you and go home," he said, "but the thought of facing existence without you makes me feel…sad."

He turned in time to see her hug herself.

"Does that frighten you?" he asked.

"Yes," she said, meeting his gaze. "But only a little."

Chapter Thirteen

The Doppler Effect

"A lie which is a half truth is ever the blackest of lies."

— Alfred Lord Tennyson

Fully rejuvenated, Hailey awoke strangely excited about leaving her home and everything she'd ever known to go to a college in The Middle of Nowhere. She stretched and stumbled into the bathroom, where she showered, dried and grabbed an elastic, fully intending to go "bun" for the day, but Tomas had another idea. He shot out of the mirror, scissors in hand.

"Ah!" she yelled, throwing her hands over her head and squishing herself against the wall.

Tomas was fast. Pulling her hands away, he snipped and fussed. When he was finished with the scissors, he pulled out of thin air an otherworldly hairdryer, bigger than the sink.

"Are yeh alright?" came Uncle Pix's voice from outside the door.

Tomas clicked the gigantic hairdryer on to answer him, brushing and drying and studying Hailey's head until he was finally satisfied and disappeared.

Standing up with her hands on her head, Hailey hesitated to look in the mirror, but when she did, she was happily surprised.

He'd given her bangs that swept to the side, leaving some longer tendrils, which perfectly framed her face. It looked both dainty and edgy.

"YOU'RE WELCOME," came a word printed in frost on the glass.

"Why are you here?" she said.

"CURIOUS," was the next word he made, and then it disappeared.

"What are you curious about?"

"HAILEY-KHU"

"Hailey-khu? What's that? What does khu mean?"

"SCHATZ," it wrote.

Hailey opened her mouth to speak but was interrupted by a loud crash coming from the kitchen, and she zipped down the hall to see what it was. Uncle Dale was on the floor gathering up pieces of a plate and sang out to her. "Morning, Hailey!"

"Morning," she answered with hesitation. "Everything alright out here?"

"Sure." He dumped a handful of broken porcelain into the trash. "Just a bit of poltergeist shenanigans," he said, as if it were as normal as a comment on the weather, so she went with it.

"There's an albino ghost living in our bathroom mirror," she blurted, pointing to her hair.

"An albino?" he repeated, and Hailey realized how ridiculous that sounded. After all, weren't all ghosts albino? She shook her head and changed the subject.

"Do you know what a Luftzeug is?"

"Sure. Hopped on one to travel to Pittsburgh. Why do you ask?"

"I'm supposed to ride on one this fall when I go to college. What's it like?"

"It's interesting for sure," he said, "and a little bumpy. You'll want to hold onto yer clothes," he advised with his eyebrows seriously raised.

Only one month to go, she kept telling herself that day, and a horrific day it was, with the latest gossip centered around her. She couldn't help but overhear it—that Tage Adams had asked her to prom as a sympathy gesture.

Mina was a loud whisperer and a cheerleader who used to date Tage. Even though he'd asked Hailey to prom, Mina fully expected him to snap out of his craziness and escort her to their senior dance. She hissed to her horrible friends the reason behind his sudden madness.

"His dad *made* him ask her to prom out of pity for her dead sister, but Tage knows Hailey won't go—she's so weird—and so he's planning to go with me."

Great, Hailey thought, trying to bury her attention in world history, but no matter how she tried, she hadn't been able to *not* hear the buzz, and Tage followed her off the bus that day, wanting an answer.

"So," he said as soon as the bus pulled away, "are you going to let me take you to prom?"

"Oh, uh…" Hailey threw him a half smile then studied the sidewalk. "I'm not really up to it, but I am really flattered you asked me."

"Look, Hailey, I know what they're saying at school." He pulled her to a stop, and she instinctively looked up at him. "I didn't ask you to prom because I felt sorry for you or because my dad made me. I asked you because I like you."

He tried to look her in the eyes, but Hailey avoided him.

"I just don't want to go," she finally said, blinking back her tears. Tage wrapped his arms around her, backpack and all. Unsure what to make of this, she went rigid. Tage let her go.

"I don't really want to go to prom, either," he said as they continued down the street. "Can I take you out to dinner on prom night?" he asked, smiling excitedly. "You'd be saving me from an evening of hell…"

Hailey scoffed, doubting very much that being crowned King of Prom could really be classified as "hell."

"No, Tage. The cheerleaders of Pittsburgh would never forgive me if I stole you from their spring fling." Unexpectedly, her eyes welled with tears. She bowed her head so Tage wouldn't see.

"No worries," he said gently. Then he brightened. "Hey, I'll swing by the pub tonight for dinner to say hi."

Hailey shook her head. "Dinner service is cancelled," she said, and an image of Mrs. Lash resurfaced in her mind.

"Then I'll be by tonight at five to pick you up."

Hailey snapped her misty eyes at him.

"What?"

"I'll take you out to dinner tonight," he shrugged, and before Hailey could protest, he pecked her on the cheek and trotted off down Bridge Street.

How did that just happen? she thought, standing slack-jawed in the middle of the intersection as she watched Tage disappear around the corner.

True to his word, Tage appeared at the pub a few minutes before five o'clock, red rose in hand.

Pix eyeballed him as soon as he stepped through the door.

"Who are yeh?" he grumbled, pushing past Hailey and winding up to "welcome" Tage, but Hailey stepped between them.

"Uncle Pix!" she yelled with her hands up. "This is Tage Adams. I go to school with him. He's here to pick me up for a dinner… uh…date."

She turned to Tage, who held the rose out to her, looking absolutely terrified.

Hailey smiled as she accepted it, saying, "Tage, this is my uncle, Pix."

The two shook hands, Pix grudgingly and Tage hesitantly, while Frog looked on with his arms crossed.

"Well," said Hailey, quickly ushering Tage out the door. "Tage will bring me straight home after dinner," she said, already guessing her uncle's orders.

Pix grunted as the door closed behind them.

"I'm sorry about that," she said as Tage led her to his mother's car. He didn't open her door.

"It's alright," he said, settling behind the wheel before he unlocked the passenger door. "Did I look scared? Cause I was. Your uncle's sort of a pugilist legend."

"He's harmless," Hailey laughed as she scooted inside, relieved to find a hard plastic console separating them…and surprised Tage knew the word "pugilist." "So, where we going?"

"Station Square. I booked us a dinner on board one of the clippers."

"A river cruise?"

The night suddenly got longer as Tage drove at a snail's pace to the north.

"You're not afraid of the water, are you?"

"No." *It's not the water that scares me*, she thought as she looked out the window, wondering what she should say next.

"I didn't know if you'd let me take you out again, so I wanted to do something special," he said quietly. He sounded nervous, though she didn't understand why. Every teenage girl in the area wanted to date him.

Every girl except Hailey. She didn't want to be at the center of anyone's attention—not without her dance shoes, not without Holly. She certainly didn't want to be associated with the most talked-about boy at school. She could already hear the next day's gossip.

As the car crept north, her belly flip-flopped, and after an uncomfortably long pause, she tried to strike up a chat. She drew in a breath to speak but then snapped her mouth shut.

Don't say that, that's stupid—he can't be nervous.

"Why are you nervous?" she asked, saying it anyway as they pulled up to the docks.

"I'm not…do I seem…I guess I am a little nervous. You're just different from anyone I've ever dated—"

We're not dating.

"—and I guess I just really want you to have a good time tonight," he said shrugging as he got out of the car.

Hailey put her rose on the dashboard and followed him.

"Otherwise, you won't let me take you out again."

When they got to the ramp, he finally offered his hand, and Hailey took it, glad to see him remember at least some of his manners as they boarded the triple-decker ship.

He led her to a table on the top deck near the rail and pulled her chair out for her. Breathing in the river air, Hailey closed her eyes, enjoying the moment as music from the live band on deck filled her ears.

Maybe this won't be so bad after all, she thought.

Then Tage's phone beeped, and he actually pulled it out of his pocket at the dinner table—without excusing himself. He then read a message, half-smiled, typed one in response, and staged his phone face-up next to his plate.

Hailey bit her lips together, resisting the urge to toss his phone overboard.

"What were you saying?" he asked, and she opened her mouth to answer but was cut off by another beep.

Taking his phone with both hands, Tage sat back in his chair, fully engrossed in whatever message was flashing across his screen. He didn't even notice when Hailey got up with her arms crossed and strolled along the railing as the boat pushed away from the dock.

Watching the river as it gushed against the hull of the ship, ducking instinctively when a bridge flew overhead, Hailey was having a great time without Tage. In the background, a local band played a lively tune, and, to Hailey's delight, when they finished their version of a popular rock song, they switched to all Irish music.

Still holding onto the rail, Hailey turned to see them and caught a quick spark of violet, rather like a camera flash, coming from the shadows underneath the canopy.

She glanced at Tage, who was still busy with his phone and not missing her at all. *I'll just take a quick stroll across the bow and check it out,* she decided. She made it halfway across the deck, before a booming voice stopped her dead in her tracks.

"Hailey!" Tage shouted it as if he were calling a play on the field. Several couples turned and stared. "Oh my gosh, I'm so sorry—that was my recruiter blowing up my phone."

"Your recruiter?" Hailey said grudgingly. She was curious but not wanting to excuse his rudeness whatsoever.

"Yeah," he said brightly. "I'm going to West Point. I'll be studying physics—and playing football," he added with a wink as he led her back to the table. "Look," he said, and he ceremoniously turned his phone off and tucked it away, just as the appetizers appeared. "I got a scholarship from DOPPLER to—"

"What did you say?" She cut him off more harshly than she'd meant but recovered quickly. "I...I mean... What was that about DOPPLER?" In all her grief, she'd completely forgotten the confidential folder.

"DOPPLER? It's a research group. They're sponsoring my scholarship, so I'll go work for them, as an Army officer after I graduate."

"What do they research?" she asked, trying not to sound as interested as she actually was.

"Weapons. Some psychological warfare, I think." His face twisted in confusion as he picked up a piece of bread. "Actually, I'm not really sure. My dad said they do a lot of sleep studies. They didn't give me a lot of information, and what they did say was pretty cryptic. They only work with the military, so it's all secret-squirrel, hush-hush."

He took a massive bite, and Hailey nodded politely while he chewed.

"I saw that acronym recently," she said, studying his reaction.

"Where at?" he asked through a mouthful of sourdough.

"It was on one of the police files...one of Holly's files."

"That's weird," he said after he swallowed, looking away with a curt chuckle.

"Do you know what it stands for?"

"No. You really saw that on Holly's file?" he asked, pulling his chin back, and then he shook his head. "I'll ask my dad. He's been working for them forever. I think that's why I got the scholarship. Where are you going to school?" he asked.

For a moment, she wondered if he was changing the subject to throw her off, but he seemed genuinely interested.

"Alaska," she said. "It's a small school, called Bear Towne."

"Ah," he said. "I heard you might be going there."

"How?"

Hailey hadn't told anybody aside from her uncles, and she doubted any of them were spreading the word around the high school.

Tage shifted in his seat.

Hailey watched him suspiciously.

"Honestly, Hailey, I don't remember where I heard that."

"But you've heard of Bear Towne?"

"Yeah, it was one of the schools I could've gone to with my scholarship. It's a great school, but they don't have a football team, so..." He shrugged and dug into his mashed potatoes, and they finished eating in silence.

Following dinner, the mood changed dramatically. Tage walked the perimeter of the deck with her, staring over the railing and chatting about all things from football to Irish dance to school and the structural integrity of the bridges over the Monongahela until the boat docked and surprised them both.

By the time Hailey got into Tage's mother's car, she'd forgotten the uncomfortable start to the night and had almost slightly enjoyed herself on her first date.

She stole a glance at him. He really was handsome. And smart. And kinda fun. If dating him didn't come with the added joy of incessant attention from the gossipmongers, she might like to go to prom with him.

But Tage was no Fin. He was driving slower than Uncle Pix.

At least the conversation was quick.

"By the way," Tage told her, "I think your hair looks great like that. You look like one of those California girls."

"Which one?"

"The one every guy dreams of," he said, throwing her a wink and a cocky smile.

She scoffed loudly. "Sure, the dream girl that no guy ever looks at or asks out or kisses?" *Oops.*

"Never been kissed?" Tage said with surprise in his voice, and Hailey sank into her seat, going three shades of crimson.

"I don't know why I said that," she mumbled. "You should watch the road."

"Maybe you want me to kiss you."

This was unbearable. Hailey couldn't stop herself from babbling and gesticulating wildly as she spoke.

"No, that's not it at all, Tage, I just…I don't…well, I certainly don't want to hear all about it in history class tomorrow, and even if the galloping gossipers didn't find out about it directly, they'd sense that something juicy was afoot with their hag antennas—not that you were going to kiss me in the first place, or that I was day-dreaming about it on the boat, because I only thought about it for a second when you told me how much you enjoyed seeing Holly and me dancing…" Hailey slapped both hands over her face to make it stop, and Tage stifled a laugh.

Watching him through her fingers, she wished he'd drive faster. They were only half-way home.

"I really did like watching you guys dance," he said, checking his side view mirror. "It's amazing. The sound is incredible."

"Thanks," said Hailey, smiling slightly as they pulled up to the curb.

He stared at her for more than a few seconds, and Hailey scooted toward her door.

"Well," she said, grasping the handle, "I sure hope you can run faster than you drive, quarterback," she told him, laughing as she opened her door.

Tage sprinted from the driver's side in time to catch it before it opened all the way. He offered his hand and helped her out.

"How's that for fast?" he asked, keeping her hand as he walked her to the door.

"You may just survive college football," she said when they reached the landing.

"I was driving intentionally slow, you know." He leaned into her, pulling her hand so it touched his waist.

Her heart pounding, Hailey held her breath as he brought his lips close to hers, but right before he kissed her, he stopped. Frozen in an unnatural lean, Tage stared dreamily into Hailey's eyes, his lips partially puckered, as if he were stuck in some sort of trance.

Hailey shrunk away from him.

"Tage!" she barked.

He blinked several times, dropped her hand, and straightened up into a great stretch.

"Well," he said yawning as he turned away from her, "I'll see ya tomorrow, Hailey."

With that, he shuffled down the walkway and left.

Once again Hailey stood slack-jawed as she watched his departure, trying to figure out what just happened.

And to think—she left her rose on his dashboard almost completely unintentionally.

Chapter Fourteen

Stolen

"Soul meets soul on lovers' lips."
— Percy Bysshe Shelley, *Prometheus Unbound*

Shoulders hunched, Hailey unlocked what she thought was an empty house. All was quiet, and according to the note Uncle Pix left in the kitchen, he and his brothers would be at the pub all night, and she shouldn't wait up.

She folded the note away and trudged into her bedroom, heavy-hearted and wishing her big sister were there to talk to her. Slumping onto Holly's bed, Hailey stuck her face in the pillow and breathed, wondering how long Holly's smell would stick around, before it, too, disappeared.

As she breathed it in again, a shrill crash rang out—breaking glass—and Hailey shot upright, catching her breath, staring rigidly at her closed bedroom door.

An image of Mrs. Lash holding a hatchet zipped through her head. Her eyes bounced around the room in search of a suitable weapon. Holly's hairbrush on the dresser, pillow, shoe, stuffed dog—*how come everything in her room was fluffy?* Hailey grabbed the only sharp object she could find (a pencil) and crawled out her window, closing it behind her and crouching low in the shadows as she listened. Heaviness and hush flowed across the lawn and into the darkness where Hailey hid.

The neighbor's dog, which should have sounded the alarm at the crash of breaking glass, looked down at Hailey in silent curiosity from the second-floor window next door.

It cocked its head at her.

If he's not barking, it's probably safe, she thought as she crept toward the front of the house and peeked around the corner.

Wielding the pencil with two hands, like a sword, she searched the darkness. Seeing nothing out of the ordinary, Hailey took off toward the pub and didn't look back until she reached the door.

Frog snapped to attention as soon as she burst inside.

Panting, Hailey leaned against the jamb.

He eyeballed her briefly. Then he moved her out of the way, puffed his chest out, opened the door, and surveyed the streets.

"Somebody bothering you, Hailey?" he asked in his breathy voice.

"I don't know." She swallowed as she caught her breath. "I thought I heard glass breaking, so I dove out my bedroom window and ran here."

Frog continued looking outside as he stood in the doorway.

"Your uncles are out," he said.

"What? Where?"

"They didn't say," he told her, coming back inside the pub. "I can't see anybody out there right now, but you should probably stay here till Pix gets back."

Hailey nodded and waited at a booth next to Frog for over two hours before her uncle Pix limped through the door.

"What happened to you?" she demanded as he hobbled across the floor, and he spun around.

"What are ya doing up so late?"

"I got scared," she sighed. "I thought I heard some glass breaking, and I bailed out of the house through my window and came here, but now I'm not sure what I heard, and I'm afraid to go home."

"We'll walk you home." He threw a nod to his brothers, who had followed him into the pub and turned right back around to escort Hailey to the townhouse.

Intact with no sign of broken glass or anything else out of the ordinary, the house sat, looking rather innocuous and tired on the corner, exactly as a house should. The gang filed inside, and Hailey's uncles performed a sweep of each room, finding nothing more nefarious than a missing bathroom mirror.

"Get some sleep, dear," said Pix. He kissed her cheek then shuffled off to bed.

As she fell asleep that night, she felt strangely at ease and could've sworn, just before she drifted off, she saw a tiny spark in the darkness...

"Asher?"

A dark figure emerged from the corner.

Hailey sat up in bed and blinked several times, trying to discern whether she actually saw something there.

"I don't want to frighten you," said a soft voice from the shadows, but still Hailey couldn't see much.

"Too late," she breathed. "Step into the light," she told him, and she swallowed hard.

A shadow floated toward the window, where illumination from the half-moon oozed in and revealed a familiar silhouette.

"Am I dreaming?"

"Not quite," he said in his soothing voice. "You were just dozing."

"I can hardly see you." She swung her legs to the floor, and he extended his hand to her.

"You're only half awake, Hailey, your eyes are barely open."

"What are you doing here?" She took his hand, solidly in her own and smiled up at him. This was the first time she'd actually touched his skin. It felt so soft.

"I wanted to see you, and..." He hesitated as Hailey ran her fingers across the top of his hand. Lifting his free hand to her cheek, he stroked it gently as he leaned closer. Ever so lightly, he brushed his lips against hers.

A cascade of darkness and warmth enveloped her mouth and tumbled through her body.

"Hailey," he said against her lips, "will you be mine?"

She smiled as he gently kissed her again.

"I always have been, haven't I?" she answered against his lips, her eyes fighting to stay open. But she was exhausted, and a full sleep snatched her away from Asher's solid arms, which caught her body as her soul fell into the dreamland of the Aether.

When Hailey woke, snuggled and warm in her bed, her heart swelled. She brushed her fingers across her lips.

Asher had kissed her! And she remembered it! A giant, silly grin spread across her face, and she let it go from ear to ear.

Until she saw the clock.

Crap! She scrambled out of bed and threw on her clothes. Zinging out the door, she rounded the corner just as the bus pulled up to her stop.

Tage hopped on board without looking back, and Hailey was out of breath when she fell into the first seat. Hailey rested her head against the window, ticking off another calendar day of school in her head. She only had twenty-three more to endure, and ever since Tage decided that she existed, those days were becoming more and more unbearable.

This day was no exception.

Positively bursting at the seams, Mina could hardly wait for Hailey to come within earshot so she could spew the latest news to her fellow cheerleaders. When Hailey sat down at her desk in

History, Mina gave the signal, and no fewer than four girls galloped over to her to receive their daily gossip.

"You guys," she said, her fingers spread out in front of her, "Tage would *not* stop texting me last night. He was on a horrible date with you-know-who..." Mina shot a sharp glance at Hailey. "...which his dad totally made him do, and so he spent the entire evening on his phone with me," she said, very pleased with herself, and her friends giggled.

In a few years, these hags would fit right in with Fin's skanky fans, Hailey thought, though she didn't know if she or the pub or even the city of Pittsburgh would ever see Fin again.

Where the heck is he?

As she wondered, she frowned.

Mina seized upon it immediately, no doubt convinced her gossip forced Hailey's sad face. "Hailey," she jeered. "How was your date with Tage last night?"

Hailey sighed, wishing she could go back to being the invisible girl. "Not bad."

"Did you guys talk about your dead sister?" Mina hissed behind her.

Hailey thought about throwing a punch, but decided Mina already felt threatened enough and simply shook her head instead. At the end of class, when Hailey stood to leave, Mina, who was a good four inches taller than her, stood in her way with her hands on her hips.

"He doesn't even like you," Mina spat. "Why don't you just tell him you're not going to prom and get it over with?"

Hailey looked up at her, waiting patiently for Mina's nostrils to stop flaring before she spoke.

"I already did, Mina." She said it loud enough for her hag friends, who waited in the hallway, to hear, leaving them to fabricate a new reason why Tage hadn't yet asked Mina to prom.

Mina's jaw fell open, and Hailey brushed past her, out the door, and onto the bus. Five minutes later, Tage stepped on board and walked past Hailey as if he didn't see her, which felt strangely comforting, like the way things used to be—normal.

But as soon as he stepped off the bus behind Hailey, he found her suddenly and inexplicably visible again and threw his arm around her shoulder.

"What are you doing tonight?" he asked.

Hailey stopped walking.

"Why do you only talk to me when your friends aren't around?"

Tage's eyes went wide. "What do you mean?"

"I mean," Hailey said walking again and at a brisk pace, "you've ignored me for three and a half years—which is how I like it—but then you asked me out, and you must have told somebody, because I'm sure not spreading rumors, and now the whole school is flabbergasted, because you haven't asked Mina to prom yet, and she's having a conniption and blames me, of course, and then I have to sit through History and pretend I can't hear her telling all her friends—which is everybody, though I don't understand why—that you spent the whole night texting her because you can't stand me."

She drew a deep breath and heaved a great sigh. *Wow that felt good.*

"I wasn't…that…I can't stand Mina. And I was texting my recruiter, Hailey, I don't know what Mina's trying to pull, but… She's a manipulative bitch," he said, mostly under his breath, and Hailey laughed.

"I don't know why that's funny," she told him.

"Because it's true?" he said as they reached the intersection. "When can I come see you dance again?"

Hailey shook her head. "I've never danced without Holly," she said, her lip quivering. "It hurts to even think about it."

"Oh, man, I upset you again." He rubbed Hailey's arms. "I'm so sorry," he whispered. "I really do like you."

"It's okay," Hailey said sniffing loudly. "You didn't know."

He gave her a quick hug, and then he waved as he strolled away.

That was the last day Tage took the bus. Hailey heard his dad had given him a car that night. Since he no longer saw Hailey during the privacy of their walk home, he made a complete recovery from his social amnesia. He remembered Hailey didn't exist and never spoke to her again.

It was strange behavior, for sure. But considering the events of the past few months…Holly's murder, Fin's disappearance and—oh, yeah—the revelation that Envoys were indeed real, Tage's sudden personality shift seemed in order.

Whatever his malfunction, he finally asked the girl he couldn't stand to prom, which greatly improved Hailey's standing among the hags. She no longer had to endure their passive-aggressive, behind-her-back hissing and sputtering during History, and the rest of her senior year flew by.

Chapter Fifteen
The Luftzeug

"Love is a fire that burns unseen."

— Luís Vaz de Camões, Rimas

When Hailey approached Tage on graduation day to offer him congratulations, he looked straight through her as if he couldn't even see her. Then Mina appeared and like a kid in kindergarten, she poked her tongue out at Hailey as Tage wrapped his arm around her.

Tage wasn't the only man snubbing Hailey. She hadn't seen or heard from Fin in over two months, and her dream man, well, he was giving new meaning to the phrase "keeping a low profile." Hailey was starting to think he was just a figment of her imagination after all.

And then there was Tomas. When her bathroom mirror disappeared, her phantom hair-dresser had disappeared with it.

Thankfully, Uncle Pix clapped her on the shoulder, startling her out of her trance before disbelief turned to self-pity.

"Congratulations, dear." Pix lifted her off the ground in a great hug.

"Thank you," she said with a bittersweet smile, imagining Holly standing next to him as he put her back down.

She didn't feel much like celebrating—or existing—without her. Hailey needed a change of scenery.

August first couldn't come soon enough.

Hailey laid out all the things she wanted to take to Alaska and set her little purse next to it, scratching her head.

What she really needed was a stuff-shrinker, she thought as she surveyed her pile. There was no way she'd fit all this into one purse-size bag.

Shaking her head, she picked out the absolute necessities.

When it was all said and done, she barely got her micro-duffel closed over: one hand towel, a bar of soap, a bottle of shampoo, a comb, a toothbrush, one pair of jeans, three t-shirts, one sweatshirt, socks, undies, and her laptop.

That's one strong zipper, she thought, deciding she'd just have to buy everything else she needed once she got to Alaska.

She grabbed the only picture she had of her and Holly dancing together from her bedroom mirror, tucked it in her back pocket and left.

After the thirty-minute drive to the airport Pix hugged her like he was never going to see her again.

"Uncle Pix, are you alright?"

"Right as rain, dear," he said with a hoarse voice. "I'm so proud of you." He gave Hailey her "luggage."

"Bye," she breathed with a brave smile, waving as he drove off.

She turned around, took a deep breath and walked inside the terminal.

There were several trembling and ashen-faced travelers about Hailey's age standing inside, but they each had a pile of luggage next to them. Some had several clear plastic bins, which were filled with sheets and blankets, pillows and comforters, parkas and boots, hairdryers and curling irons; others had giant duffle bags and snowshoes and skis.

Hailey's jaw fell.

Nobody had "one piece of luggage—purse size." Her heart splashed into her stomach. What's worse—all of them carried a winter coat and a sleeping bag separate from their bags.

This was bad.

She looked around for a sign or airport worker or anything that could direct her to where she could find a Luftzeug representative.

As she scanned the area, her eyes fell on a young man with multicolored hair and trendy eyeglasses, who was standing in front of a mountain of luggage, clutching a large silver envelope in one hand and holding onto a bulging duffel bag with the other. He looked exactly how Hailey felt: absolutely terrified.

Hailey crept up to him.

"Are you heading to Bear Towne?" she said, and he started. Loudly.

"Oh God, why?" He retreated away from her, clutching his swollen bag against his chest as if she were going to steal it.

"I just...I'm going too, and I was wondering if you knew where we were supposed to wait to board the Luftzeug."

"No." He looked at her like she had warts, and then he turned his back on her.

That worked well to chase her bravery away.

With her mouth clamped shut and her one, small bag, which held absolutely nothing, she strolled to the window and surveyed the tarmac. Shining like a new penny in the summer sun, a glittering, bronze-colored private jet sat next to the terminal with the words, "Bear Towne" emblazoned in silver lettering on the side.

This was going to be the best 10-hour flight ever.

Hailey smiled, breathing a sigh of relief just as a terrible racket screeched behind her. A troop of tall, thin men, all wearing gray flight suits and full-face gas masks marched through the terminal, pulling several pallet jacks behind them. Stopping at each terror-stricken student, they loaded pile after pile of luggage onto a cart, shrink wrapping their load as they went. When a cart grew to six feet high, one of the flight suits would wheel it out of the terminal. They did this several times before they approached Hailey.

"Luggage?" one of them asked her in a muffled almost mechanical-sounding male voice, and Hailey saw he wore a Bear Towne patch on his shoulder.

"This is my luggage." She held up her purse.

The flight suit made no move to take it and seemed to be staring at her, though she couldn't tell because of the gas mask.

"Where's the rest?" he asked her in a voice laced with static.

"This is it—this is all I brought."

Despite the instructions in her letter, she suddenly felt an irresistible urge to panic and run home to pack a footlocker. She checked her watch.

"I think I have time to run home and pack a footlocker." She turned to leave, but another flight suit grabbed her by the neck and squeezed. Hailey made a choking sound, and the gas mask that held her cocked its head. The other gas mask clapped the one holding her on its shoulder, waving his finger slowly at the offending crewmember until it let her go.

Hailey fell to the floor, doubled over and gagging.

"There's no time," the first one spat. He snatched her bag. "The Luftzeug will leave in twenty minutes."

He popped to attention, did an about-face, and marched outside.

"Thank you," she called through a bruised throat.

Through the window, Hailey watched as they pulled their pallets past the Bear Towne plane. She turned around to see if anyone else noticed and saw the kid with the multicolored hair disappear through a jet-way door along with a gaggle of others. Hailey ran to catch up and tugged the rainbow-headed boy's sleeve as they emerged outside.

"They took our bags right past the Bear Towne Luftzeug," she said, pointing to the luxury jet in front of them.

"That's not the Bear Towne Luftzeug." He pointed to an ugly gray shape behind the beautiful jet. "*That's* the Bear Towne Luftzeug."

"That's our airplane?"

"It's not an air*plane*—it's an air *tool*. The Gulfstream is for the Pre-Med students," he explained with disgust, as if Hailey should already know this, but he was clearly pleased to tell her. "It makes stops in Chicago, LA, and Seattle before heading north."

"Oh." Hailey hadn't realized Bear Towne had a Pre-Med program. She drew a breath, but the rainbow held his hand up.

"I know, I know... Now, you're wondering about the geology students..."

Geology?

"They left from Columbus last week on the bus, geez, didn't you read any of your handbook?"

"There's a handbook?"

He scoffed. "You're in for a few shockers," he said like a brat, and he turned his back on her.

No use asking if she could borrow his copy to read during the flight, she figured. She walked behind him on her tiptoes, trying to get a full-on look at the gray blob that was the Bear Towne Luftzeug. To her, it looked like a modified military cargo plane. Barely visible on the side of the hull, faded letters read: Bear Towne Luftzeug: *Traumzeug*.

When they reached the mobile stairs leading up to the Luftzeug's entry hatch, the rainbow stopped suddenly with wide eyes, grabbed Hailey by the arm and shoved her ahead of him. At the top of the stairs stood the source of his angst—a gangly, contorted-looking man-thing, clad in a gray flight suit and elephant-nosed gas mask. It leaned unnaturally on the platform at the entryway door. If they were at an amusement park, Hailey would have sworn she was looking at a reflection from a fun-house mirror rather than a real man.

Reluctantly, she lifted her foot and climbed the steps.

"Not scared, are you, dear," the contort-incarnate crackled when she reached the top. He handed her a heavy metal lunchbox.

"Not at all."

That was a lie—she was scared to death. And she probably wouldn't have the courage to actually open the metal box he'd just handed her. Who knew what was inside? Raw brains, maybe? Spiders?!

She tried her best to project an image of calm as she thanked him and stepped on board.

Inside, the Luftzeug seemed like a large, oblong tuna can: cold, cavernous and empty with a high ceiling, bare metal, no carpeting—in fact nothing soft whatsoever—and something inside literally smelled fishy. Folded jump seats lined the hull in the front, and shrink-wrapped pallets were anchored to the floor in the back. There were no windows in the Luftzeug, but there was a galley near the nose of the plane with a coffee pot and several other metal doohickeys as well as a ladder, which Hailey was guessing led to the cockpit.

Scampering all around the fuselage—ALL around the fuselage, even zip-lining across the ceiling, though Hailey couldn't actually see the zip-line—were gas-masked contort-men, who were examining each rivet in the hull. They gave Hailey an immediate and chilly case of the creeps.

She found an empty jump seat near the back of the plane and folded it down. Next to her and in the very last seat sat a student, who upon her approach raised his newspaper higher and, like everybody else on board, pretended not to notice her. But Hailey had already caught a glimpse of his handsomely rugged face, and she knew exactly who it was.

"Fin?" she asked excitedly.

He dropped his paper.

"Hailey!" he said with a forced smile.

"Wha...you..." Hailey didn't know where to begin. "You go to Bear Towne?" *There. That was a good question.*

"Yes," he answered, sounding annoyed.

She leaned her head toward him, turning it slightly with her eyes open wide as if to say, "...and...?"

Fin shook his paper and raised it again.

"Where have you been?"

"You know, it's none of your business what I do," he said from behind the Times.

Ouch.

Shrinking back into her place, Hailey noticed the other students pulling a small plastic bag from under their seats and putting whatever was inside into their ears then strapping themselves in.

She felt around under her own seat and found a bag labeled: indispensable. Inside was a set of earplugs, which were easy enough to figure out. The seatbelt, however, involved no fewer than seven straps and two buckles, and it took until the Luftzeug roared to life for her to put it in order—with no help from Fin.

The engines of the Bear Towne Luftzeug spun up to an ear-splitting screech, leaving Hailey to wonder why the heck she even bothered with the indispensable "ear protection." Weirdly, nobody else seemed disturbed by the continuous, painfully shrill thunder and in fact, everyone seemed quite at ease, so much so that as soon as the plane took off and despite the incredible turbulence, one by one, each passenger unbuckled, got up, rolled out a sleeping bag on the floor of the plane and climbed inside. Before long, everyone on board, except for Hailey, Fin and just one other student sitting near the front of the plane, was stretched out and ready for bed— in the middle of the afternoon.

How anyone could relax with such a blaring racket and inside the coldest airplane in the world was beyond Hailey. Though, as she began shivering, she did wish that she, too, had a cozy sleeping bag to keep her warm and wondered if there were any blankets on board.

She stared at Fin until he acknowledged her.

"What?" he said, dropping his paper. It looked like he'd said it sharply, but Hailey couldn't hear a thing over the scream of the Luftzeug's four engines.

"I'm freezing!" she shouted to him, and everyone on the airplane—everyone except for the only other student not bundled up inside a sleeping bag, turned to look at her. Hailey's cheeks burned.

Fin lowered his brow and cocked his head to the side as his jaw jutted out.

"You didn't turn on your Buzzdoodles," it looked like he said.

"My what?"

"Earplugs, dummy." Fin reached over and flipped a switch above her head. It was an off-switch for the engine noise in Hailey's ears, which apparently, everyone else had already activated.

"This was all in your student handbook," Fin said rubbing his forehead. "Why didn't you read it?"

"I would have read it, if I had gotten one," she said in a voice of normal volume but increasing hostility. "There was no mention of earplugs in the letter I received, Fin, I would have remembered reading the word *Buzzdoodle*," she told him, lifting her chin. "There was nothing about a Buzzdoodle or cargo plane or sleeping bags or packing lists or the incredible coincidence that you're also a student at the most remote school in world."

Fin gave her a half smile and leaned toward her, playfully bumping her shoulder with his own.

"Buzzdoodles are new technology out of BTU. Noise canceling earplugs," he told her kindly, and Hailey sighed, loving the sound of his friendly voice. "So you don't have to yell at me anymore," he said with a wink.

Hailey wasn't sure if she was done yelling at him and debated the tone she wanted to use for what she said next.

"One second you're holding my hand next to Holly's grave, and then you were gone," she said sadly, her eyes boring into his. "No explanation—you just disappeared. You left me."

Fin bowed his head, biting his lip. "I'm sorry," he said, meeting Hailey's eyes. He pressed his lips together, and she could tell he wanted to say more but for some reason, he didn't.

He raised his hand to touch her but then made a fist, shook his head and dropped his arm. "I'm sure Pix told you where I was…"

"Out chasing women and getting into trouble?"

"I wasn't chasing women."

"Did you get into trouble?"

"A little," Fin told her, and he glanced briefly at the student still sitting in his jump seat in the front of the plane.

"Who is that?" Hailey said.

"That," he said, studying Hailey's reaction, "is Asher."

Chapter Sixteen

ParaScience 101: An Introduction

"Those who believe in telekinetics, raise my hand."

— Kurt Vonnegut

Hailey's breath caught.

That's Asher? The Envoy?

She didn't mean to, but she couldn't help but stare at him.

"He sort of works at the university. Like me."

Why wouldn't he look at her? He sat like a statue, his hood hiding his face. She silently willed him to turn so she could see him.

But he never moved. And Hailey's heart sank. Why was he ignoring her?

Maybe he's not interested in you, silly girl, her good sense told her. But he had kissed her, hadn't he? Now she wasn't sure. Maybe he was suffering from "Tage Adams Syndrome" and could only see her when no one else was around.

Frowning, she shook her head, knitted her fingers together in her lap and studied them. *Did Fin know Asher was an Envoy? And—wait a second…*

"You work at the university?"

"Yeah," he said stiffly. "I'm a teaching assistant. For Dr. Woodfork."

"I didn't mean for that to sound condescending." Now Hailey couldn't stop smiling. It felt good to have a friend again. "Dr. Woodfork is the dean of the university, right?"

"He's the dean of the College of ParaScience," he corrected, his voice was much kinder now. "There are three colleges at Bear Towne: ParaScience, Pre-Med, and Geology. You'll get all of this during your campus tour," he said with a wave. "Did you check out your lunch?"

"Not yet..."

Feeling brave, she opened her metal lunchbox and, peeking inside, she sighed happily. *Good! No brains.*

She certainly wouldn't go hungry. Hailey started nibbling through the contents: two giant sandwiches, a bag of chips, an apple, a banana, an assortment of cheeses, crackers, two candy bars, a bottle of water, and a can of pop.

"Do all the teaching assistants leave from Pittsburgh?" she asked as she polished off her first sandwich and looked around the cabin floor.

"No," he smiled sarcastically. "I drew the short straw this year. The others are on flights leaving from LA, Chicago, Frankfurt, and Moscow."

"Well, I'm glad you got the short straw. What's Alaska like?"

He drew a slow breath, humming as he formed his answer. "It's not Pennsylvania."

"How so?"

"Well, for starters, there are only three seasons in Alaska: butt-ass cold, break-up, and mosquito."

"Mosquito...oh..." Hailey sang. "Uncle Pix said Alaska was full of blood suckers." She looked at Fin shamefaced. "I thought he meant vampires," she admitted with a self-deprecating cringe. "And with the way things have been going lately..."

Fin only stared at her in response, and Hailey cocked her head as she contemplated the other seasons. "Why would Alaska reserve a time of year for ending relationships?"

Fin straightened up and looked at her sideways. He licked his lips, shook his paper very loudly, cleared his throat, and went back to reading, just as one of the gas masks slid past them carrying a giant wrench on his shoulder.

Hailey tugged Fin's sleeve. When that didn't get his attention, she barked a whisper. "Hey!" she hissed as loud as she could.

Fin peeked around his paper.

"Why are these guys wearing gas masks?"

They both watched the wrench wielder disappear behind a pallet. "So they stay awake."

"Oh." That didn't make much sense to Hailey. Most folks drank coffee, but whatever. Different strokes for different folks, she guessed, and she imagined how nice a steaming cup of coffee would feel as she shivered in her seat.

It was getting colder inside the Luftzeug, and Hailey didn't have hats and coats and blankets and puffy sleeping bags like the other passengers. Fin unbuckled and unrolled a mummy bag while Hailey hugged herself and watched.

"Are you going to sleep?" she asked him.

"Yes. So are you."

"I'm not tired."

"You will be when they turn the gas on."

"What gas?"

Fin shot a glance toward the front of the plane and lowered his voice. "Come on, chowder head," he said almost under his breath. "You can use my bag. I'll grab a blanket from the crew."

Hailey still wasn't sleepy, but she was hovering around hypothermia.

"Thanks," she said, kicking off her shoes. She wiggled inside the most comfortable sleeping bag in the world. "Fin?" she said as he settled down next to her, wrapped in a navy blue wool blanket.

"What?"

She scooted closer to him, and he smiled. Not wanting to admit that she only wanted to hear his voice and didn't really have a question, she only closed her eyes and enjoyed her contentedness.

"Fin?" she said again, as sleeping gas hissed through the cabin.

"Mm."

"I really missed you…" she told him, as she drifted to sleep.

"I missed you too," he said, but she wasn't sure it was real.

Gas filled the airplane and knocked everyone out.

In the Aether, Hailey emerged on board the plane next to her jump seat. The Luftzeug: *Traumzeug* looked the same as it had when she was awake, except the roof was wide open, and sunlight poured in through it. The turbulence had stopped, and the plane sat parked in the clearing of a bright forest. In the distance, Hailey heard songbirds and a waterfall.

"Welcome to ParaSci 101," a familiar voice announced. Fin stood at the front of the plane and held in his hand a CB-looking microphone connected to the plane's PA system.

"My name is Pádraig, and I'll be your course instructor. If you didn't already figure it out, you're asleep, and this is a dream. Right now, our souls are in the Aether, which is what you see and hear and smell and feel all around you. Pay attention, because you'll never share a dream with a living soul again, unless, like me," he said in a voice laced with cynicism, "you're lucky enough to ride on board the *Traumzeug* over and over."

A hand went up among the students.

"What?" Fin said to the boy in a way that let him know it was not the time for questions.

"I can't feel my hands!"

"You just *raised* your hand, doofus," Fin told him, and another hand shot up.

Fin dropped the microphone, closed his eyes, and pinched his nose. "No more questions," he said stiffly. Then he looked up. "In fact, everybody shut your mouths."

When there was silence, he proceeded without the mike.

"Normally, the Aether messes with your memory. You don't always bring all you know in, and you don't always remember everything you've experienced here once you leave.

"This Luftzeug is a special piece of equipment used by the college and the US military to study the Aether. It allows those on board to share a common dream space, to take data, and most importantly, to remember our observations."

Fin paused and looked around at each student until his eyes fell on Hailey. Smiling at her, he continued.

"Now, all of you listen up," he barked. "It is very important that none of you panic."

He looked directly at the guy who couldn't feel his hands.

"If you do panic, you risk dragging us all into your own personal nightmare. If any of you think you feel a panic coming, just close your eyes and count to eight, alright? I don't want to see your zombies or watch your teeth fall out...and I certainly don't want to see any of you naked."

His eyes found Hailey again.

"Most of you, anyway," he said, and he winked at her.

Hailey's chin dipped and her ears burned, but to her relief, nobody paid attention. The others wore expressions ranging from concern to alarm. Looking around, she noticed at least three students wide-eyed and close to hyperventilating, but Hailey felt perfectly at ease.

Until the man-eating spiders crept in through the ceiling.

"Ah, shit," she heard Fin mutter, and a pandemonium inside the Luftzeug ensued.

Trying to stay calm, Hailey watched the spiders with increasing interest. They seemed more confused than aggressive, she told herself, though one had lifted a student with its hairy legs and another was scampering in Hailey's direction.

She closed her eyes and had counted to three when a powerful clamp gripped her shoulders and jerked her aside.

When she opened her eyes, she was standing in a forest outside the Luftzeug, listening to the muffled chaos coming from inside.

Turning around, she realized she stood in the woods of her favorite childhood place and collapsed on the soft grass, breathing in the crisp mountain air and watching violet skies swirl above her.

"How did you escape the *Traumzeug?*" An Envoy tilted his head as he appeared in the grass next to her.

Hailey bolted upright and stared at him speechless for several seconds.

"Asher," she breathed, as his name dawned on her, and her belly fluttered. Taking a moment to gaze into his gorgeous eyes, she smiled uncertainly. "I would have guessed that you pulled me outside."

"If you hadn't disappeared, I might have. It is exceptionally rare for a human to find its way out of the *Traumzeug*." His gaze fell on her right eye for a moment and then her left.

"I find you..." he drew a sharp breath. "...surprising and... lovely," he said as if he struggled to find the right words.

"Asher," Hailey repeated. "You're on that plane with me, aren't you?" She pointed at the Luftzeug, which suddenly tilted into a steep nose-down attitude.

Hailey jumped up and stumbled back.

"What's happening in there?"

Asher closed his eyes for a moment.

"Panic," he said, rising up and once again trapping her in his gaze. "One of the students is afraid of falling, and though she doesn't mean to, she's about to send the *Traumzeug* into a nosedive."

"Will they be alright?" Hailey was thinking about Fin.

"It's only a dream, Hailey. It will be uncomfortable, but they will wake up soon, and they will no longer be aboard the *Traumzeug*. They will be back inside the Luftzeug," he explained, and Hailey finally realized the airplane was the Luftzeug on Earth, an airplane making its way from Pittsburgh to Alaska, but in the Aether, it was the *Traumzeug*, which looked like something out of a Salvador Dali painting.

"I'm going to remember this," she said, her eyes fierce with determination. "And I'll remember you, right?"

Asher hesitated.

"You're outside the *Traumzeug*. It's hard to know. You may indeed remember—"

She held her arms out, throwing her head back.

"Finally!" she said with a laugh, and then she collapsed onto the grass once more.

"It is good to see you smile again," he told her, and her smile widened. "I'll see you very soon, Hailey."

"It'll be a dream come true, Asher."

In front of her eyes, the eddying skies of the Aether morphed into the cold metal ceiling of the Luftzeug. She squeezed her eyes shut and opened them again, finding herself tucked warm and snug inside Fin's sleeping bag, while he snored with one arm draped lazily across her. As he stirred, he curled his arm and pulled her into a tight cuddle as if she were his own little teddy bear.

If she could have moved inside that mummy bag, she's not sure she would have. She woke up feeling like she was in love, so instead of shrugging Fin away, she relaxed and let him hug her, enjoying every second until he woke and let her go.

Groaning, he raised his arms in a great stretch. As he sat up and rubbed his eyes, Hailey feigned sleep and listened to him struggle against the turbulence to make his way to the front of the plane.

The PA clicked and made a brief feedback howl before Fin's voice rang through.

"That was absolutely pathetic," he said, as lumps of sleeping bags stirred to life. "I should fail all of you. But the shame of walking into Chinook Hall in your current state should be punishment enough, so you'll all receive a C."

A chorus of groans rose up.

"Everyone except for Hartley did exactly what I told you NOT to do, and now look at you." Fin threw his hand up, and several students gasped and whimpered, clutching their sleeping bags. "It'll be a cold walk to campus if you lose your sleeping bag," he warned.

Hailey saw many naked shoulders poking out of the floor. She wiggled her own shoulders out and was relieved to find herself still fully clothed. But she was one of few.

"Where are my clothes?" one of the female students cried.

"Probably in the Aether where you left them." Fin answered her in his most caustic voice as the plane descended. "Be thankful none of you dreamed of losing your teeth."

"My teeth!" another yelled, showing a gaping hole where two incisors should have been, and Fin pointed at him in reprimand.

"I told you not to panic. The school will fit you with falsies, so calm down. Now everyone get ready for landing."

Fin dropped the mike, which swung on its cord like a pendulum, and he staggered to the back of the plane, where Hailey helped him stuff his sleeping bag into his backpack.

"Where'd you go?" he asked her, and Hailey looked up at him. "What?"

"While we were in the Aether. You were here. And then you were gone, Hailey. Where'd you go?"

"Oh, I went outside," she said nonchalantly.

Fin studied her eyes. "How?"

Hailey shrugged and went back to packing his sleeping bag. "I don't know. I was getting scared, so I started counting to eight like you said and then I was outside lying in the grass, looking at the sky with…"

"With what?"

She stole a glance at Asher.

"With *him?*" he spat with a scowl.

"Keep your voice down," she whispered with wide eyes. "I think so."

Honestly, she hoped so. Her memory was a little fuzzy.

"Hailey—" He jerked his backpack out of her hands.

"What?" she demanded, but the only response she got was an angry glare and noisy breathing. Fin threw the backpack zipper closed with enough force to tear the fabric. Out of a separate compartment, he pulled a pair of goggles then strapped himself into his jump seat.

Hailey followed.

"What's that for?" she asked as he donned his eye protection.

Fin let out an edgy laugh. "You'll see."

As Hailey fumbled with her harness, the floor opened under her, and she slipped out of her seat and out of the Luftzeug, swinging her arms at Fin, who made a frantic grab for her and missed.

Before she could scream, she was falling through the sky, plummeting to Earth, and the ground was coming up fast.

Chapter Seventeen

Whipped

"It may be he shall take my hand.
And lead me into his dark land."

— Alan Seeger. I Have a Rendezvous with Death

Down Hailey fell for several seconds until a painful jolt stopped her descent at about 3 feet above the ground, where she hovered briefly with very wide eyes before landing with a giant splash in a cold, marshy puddle.

She sat shivering in that puddle, which came up to her waist, holding onto her face with trembling hands, saying over and over, "Am-I-dead-am-I-dead-am-I-dead…"

"No." A soothing voice rang through her panic.

Slowly, she uncovered her eyes to find an outstretched hand. The hand was connected to an arm and that arm belonged to *Him*. Staring up at his purple eyes, she tried to think of something intelligent to say. Were it not for those purple eyes, he might pass for a regular grad student, looking slightly standoffish and oozing authority. Though his outstretched hand seemed more like an order than an invitation, Hailey trusted him immediately, as if she'd known him for ages, and she placed a quivering hand in his.

"Didn't I spill a drink on you?" she blurted. It was the only thing that came to mind.

He smiled as he helped her stand on wobbly legs on the spongy ground.

She was shaking all over—mostly from fright, but also from the chill. Frigid, marshy Alaskan bog water soaked her from the chest down. Asher took her other hand in his, but when she lost her balance, he snaked an arm around her waist and pulled her close. An incredible, gorgeous heat radiated from him, which hurried her chills away.

"I'm really sorry about that drink—whoa," she said as her legs tried to crumple again, but he caught her and hugged her closer. "I wanted to apologize properly, but when I came out of the ladies room, you'd already gone." There. She'd been waiting months to get that off her conscience.

Asher simply held her by the waist with one hand, caressed her hand with the other and gazed adoringly into her eyes.

"So, you're Asher," she said, and her stomach tied itself into a knot.

"You remember me then."

Hailey nodded. "Of course." How could she not, he was her first kiss. At least, she thought that was real. Biting her lip, she tilted her head down. She could feel herself blushing and hoped he wouldn't see.

He dipped his head and lured her eyes once again into his.

"Will you tell me what you're thinking?" he asked.

I want you to kiss me again.

She felt a moment of unnatural courage and seized it. "Did you kiss me, Asher? I mean, was that real, or was it a dream?"

She couldn't believe she'd said it.

"It was both," he said.

Hailey waited, holding her breath to see if he would kiss her again, but he made no move to close the gap between them.

"It is good to see you," was all he said, and Hailey's face fell. Her pocket…her photo!

"Oh, no—Holly's picture!" Stepping away from Asher, she cautiously pulled it out. "Oh no...no..." It was wet and ruined and barely holding itself together in Hailey's hands.

Very carefully, Asher took the picture from her and held it between his hands. When he gave it back, it was—dry. Completely restored.

Hailey smiled. "Would you carry this for me until I dry off?" she asked as she closed his hand on it. If she put it back in her pocket, it would just get ruined again.

"Of course." He tucked it away and took her hand again. Leading her through the alders and around patches of Jurassic jagger bushes and giant puddles, Asher kept hold of Hailey's hand, lifting her with ease over downed spruce trees and across rocky streams. Every move he made appeared effortless, and Hailey honestly couldn't tell if his feet actually made contact with the ground.

She couldn't say the same for her own feet. At least twice, she had to ask him to stop and help extract her shoe from a mud hole after it got sucked off.

While Asher dug her right sneaker out again, Hailey stood balanced on one foot, though she didn't know why she bothered— both of her feet were already filthy and water-logged and numb, and she doubted the one pair of shoes she'd brought with her to Alaska would still be wearable in the morning.

"Would you like me to carry you?" Asher asked as she struggled to tie her soggy laces with freezing fingers.

She didn't know what to say. Of course she wanted him to carry her. But even more so, she didn't want to be a wimp. "How far is it?" That seemed like a fair question.

"Two hours at this pace. Five minutes if I carry you. Three seconds if I whip you."

"That sounds...painful?" She was fairly certain she didn't want to be whipped, but...three seconds. And she wouldn't arrive on campus in Asher's arms like a damsel in distress—it sounded like a good compromise, though she wasn't sure what "whip" meant, and it sure didn't sound pleasant.

Smiling slightly, Asher removed a mud blob from Hailey's forehead.

"It won't hurt you. I can…propel you so that you'll land close to the others. They're ahead of us and less than a half mile now from campus."

"You mean, like, *throw* me?" Even though it sounded cold, scary, and painful, after surviving a fall from the Luftzeug, Hailey was willing to take Asher's word for it and try a whip.

She heaved a decisive sigh and said with a shrug, "Okay, Asher. Whip me."

Asher wrapped his arm around her waist and pulled her against his side. "I'll see you soon," he whispered against her ear, and with a crack that sounded more like thunder than a whip, the air at Hailey's back pressed in, and a familiar heaviness enveloped her, static electricity, raising her hair.

What happened next felt an awful lot like a gigantic shock—like she'd moonwalked across a winter rug and bumped into a metal shelf. She arched against the jolt of Asher's throw, squeezing her eyes shut as the foliage rushed past, her body hurtling through the air. Only when her feet hit the ground did she open her eyes again. Sure enough, there she was, holding her arms out as she regained her balance and standing in the middle of a gaggle of students, who looked even soggier and muddier than she did. Several trudged along naked and shoeless, clinging to their sleeping bags, and one of them had a leafy twig tangled in his filthy rainbow hair.

Hailey tried not to laugh, thinking of Holly's toothbrush.

"You've got a twig in your hair," she told him as she partially weaved it out.

"Don't touch me," he snapped, and Hailey started.

Jeez, she was just trying to help the kid.

Asher appeared at her side, and the rainbow waddled hurriedly away.

"I have that effect on people," Hailey said, and Asher glared after him.

"He won't bother you again," he said darkly.

"Oh, he wasn't bothering me." She looked down to brush herself off, and when she looked up, Asher was gone.

"I've never seen Asher actually talk to a student before," a soaking wet and filthy Fin said, stumbling over to help her. He had a clean spot in the shape of goggles around his eyes, and looking dead serious, he added, "You know he's not human."

Raising her eyebrows, she mouthed the word, "Oh." Of course she knew. But she didn't know Fin knew. She thought for a second, and then she baited him. "Well, what is he?"

"Don't care," was his answer. He quickened his pace.

"You don't care?"

"No..." he sang, sounding highly irked.

Hailey tripped over an alder bush, struggling to keep up with him.

"Oof! How can you not care about what Asher is?"

"There are a lot of 'not humans' here, Hailey."

Hailey stopped and gawked after him. Then she ran to catch up. "Wait! What other 'not humans' are there?"

Ignoring that question, he fired one back at her. "Why didn't you land with the rest of us?"

As if she'd planned to fall out of the Luftzeug!

"The floor opened under me," she said, her voice rising, "and you didn't grab me!"

"Oh," he said in a slightly more casual, yet still heated tone. "Well, where'd you land?"

"On my bum."

"Did you get hurt?"

"No," she told him, "but it was scary, and I really have to pee now."

Fin went from irate to highly amused, instantly. "You're a goofball," he said chuckling. "We're less than a minute out. When we get to Chinook Hall, throw your shoes and socks in the mud room, grab a pair of house-shoes off the rack and head straight to the back of the hall for the toilets."

"Thank you," she breathed.

"I'll be heading that way too," he told her with raised eyebrows. "Leech-check."

"Leeches?" She tried not to think of slimly little worms crawling all over her. "How was your landing?" she asked quickly to get her mind off Alaska's creepy-crawlies.

"Rough. But that's normal. The pilots are a lot gentler with the women," he said. "Most of the men ended up in the lake this time—hence the leeches. Thankfully everyone splashed down near shore, so no drownings this year."

Hailey's mouth fell open. "Students have died?"

"Yeah," he said indifferently, "but only temporarily."

Hailey opened her mouth to ask what the heck 'only temporarily' meant, but Fin cut her off. "Chinook Hall." He pointed to a giant log building in a clearing up ahead, and Hailey's bladder coaxed a sprint.

She had her shoes and socks off before she opened the door to the mud room. Snatching a pair of booties from a rack next to the door, she zipped inside, passed by a four-story stone fireplace, ran under seven wrought-iron chandeliers, down the central hallway and all the way to the back, where the restroom doors were marked with moose silhouettes—one with antlers and one without.

She picked the one without antlers, crossed her fingers and opened the door, finding (much to her relief) two female... humans, she guessed—parked in front of the mirror.

"I guess the parafreaks are here," one said after Hailey closed her stall door.

Hailey wondered what a parafreak was and if that was a bad thing.

"Let's get out of here before they muddy the place up," the other answered, and Hailey listened to the bathroom door shut behind them. When she stepped up to the sink to wash her hands, she recoiled at her reflection in the mirror.

"Good lord," she whispered as she turned on the water. "Definitely a bad thing," she murmured.

With the exception of her booties, every part of her was covered in dirt, bugs, and other unidentifiable ick. The whites of her eyes really stood out. She looked like a mud monster.

Did I really meet Asher looking like this? Hanging her head and squeezing her eyes shut, she gripped the sink, torturing herself by rethinking every word she'd said to him.

Oh, it's no wonder he didn't kiss me again, she whimpered inside. At least she could wash her hands and face now. If only Tomas were around to put her hair in order.

She tapped her finger on the sink.

"I wonder..." she said out loud as she peered into the mirror. "Tomas," she called softly. She peeked over her shoulder to make sure no one was watching her speak to her reflection.

"Tomas?" she said again, but the only supernatural thing in the glass was a crazy-haired mud monster. "Oh, if only you could come here, Tomas," she begged quietly.

"HIER" came through in frosty letters on the mirror.

She perked up.

"Tomas? Is that you?"

"SCHMUTZIG" followed in bigger letters and a familiar set of hands shot out of the glass and shoved Hailey's head into the sink.

"Gently," she told him, and he actually handled her with a little more finesse as he rinsed her hair. It took several minutes and a whole bottle of ghost shampoo, but when Tomas was done, Hailey had a neat, clean, delightfully perfumed and trendy bun.

"Thanks," she said, and Tomas frantically waved his hands at her through the glass.

"What is it?"

"D.O.P.P.L.E.R." frosted across the mirror.

"What about them?"

"Gefahr"

Hailey mouthed the word, but she didn't know what it meant and shook her head, adding "Gefahr" to "Schatz" on her mental list of Tomas-words to look up. She was pretty sure they were German.

"Tomas, I'm sorry, that's way beyond the German I know. I have to look it up. Is there anything else?"

"bin entwichen" appeared briefly but long enough for Hailey to take a mental picture of it, and then Tomas saluted and disappeared as another mud monster waddled through the ladies room door wrapped in a wet sleeping bag.

Hailey nodded to her and exited.

Other ParaScience students were shuffling into Chinook Hall from the porch. Falling in step behind them, she entered a large banquet room opposite the fireplace, finding inside no fewer than fifty round tables, each set for fifteen people. Near the door, she found one occupied by only five students, all soggy and dirty.

"May I join you?" she asked with her most friendly smile.

Nobody answered.

Instead, they all stiffened and stared, either at random objects around the room or at their place setting. One whispered something sharply to the student on his left. That student looked over his shoulder and whispered to the student sitting on his left. Then without a word, without even glancing at Hailey, all five of them slid their chairs back, got up, walked away, and sat down at another table, leaving Hailey, shoulders drooped and sitting alone at the giant table for fifteen.

A sudden pang for her big sister pushed a lump into her throat. This was not how she'd envisioned her college experience.

Drumming her fingers on the table, she looked around. It was easy to see the students had divided themselves up. The filthy ones sat together, as did the clean, yet scruffy-looking ones in tattered flannel shirts and denim overalls. In one corner of the room, a large group of very attractive, very clean, very well put together students in name-brand outdoor wear sat with their noses in the air. She guessed those to be the Pre-Med students.

Except for the filthy freshmen, she couldn't tell the difference between the students of geology and ParaScience.

In the back of the room and also at a table by herself sat a clean student with long gray hair. Her head was bowed, and it looked like she was reading something. The other students gave the gray-haired girl a wide berth.

At least I'm not the only outcast, Hailey thought as a murmur ran through the crowd. A few of the students began to chant, which grew into a roar with some of the larger men standing and clapping in time.

"O-SHEA-O-SHEA-O-SHEA," they cheered, and they all looked toward the door. Hailey glanced over her shoulder to see what the hubbub was, and her jaw dropped.

Swaggering into the room, freshly showered and wearing a victorious smile, Fin high-fived almost everyone he passed, and the hall erupted.

Chapter Eighteen

Welcome to Bear Towne

Fame is no plant that grows on mortal soil.

— John Milton, Lycidas

Fin joined the group of large men, who took turns clapping him on the back and hugging him.

Trying hard not to stare, Hailey wondered what else she didn't know about her favorite bartender. Clearly he'd left more than a few things out of their conversations in Pittsburgh.

A microphone crackled through the hall.

"Is this on now?" a man with a bow tie said as he stood at the front of the hall. "Uh, I see the last of our ParaScience freshmen have finally sloshed inside."

The Pre-Med group tsk'ed and shook their heads while the flannels chuckled.

"Let's all extend to them a warm welcome, I'm sure they'd appreciate it. By the looks of them, it was a lake landing again this year, am I right?" The man looked at Fin, who pressed his lips together and nodded. "Well," the man said, "no drownings, then?"

Fin shook his head. The man clapped his hands together.

"Wonderful. The food will be out shortly. Welcome to the Terquasquigenary anniversary of Bear Towne University's move to Alaska. Freshmen—be sure to pick up your welcome package from the tables on the west wall. Inside you will find your room assignment and orientation schedule for the week ahead as well as a campus map, a can of Yeti spray, some tree repellant, and a canister of fuel for your dormitory room ghost trap."

Hailey hoped there'd be a written explanation of all this inside her welcome package as well.

"And here's dinner," said the man, as a troop of uniformed ladies carried tray after silver tray of delicious-smelling fare to the buffet table.

It was then Hailey noticed Asher standing next to the man with the bow tie, leaning toward him and speaking. The man with the bow tie nodded, and Asher stepped away as the man picked up the mike.

"Uh... Please help yourselves, everyone, and if I could just see Miss Hailey Hartley up here quickly, please..." Her face flushing yet again, Hailey dipped her head.

Oh crap, why is he singling me out?

As Hailey tentatively stood, Asher spoke to the man again, watching Hailey's every move, which only made her more self-conscious. Thankfully everyone else was far more interested in the food than they were in her, and none of the students seemed to notice when she stubbed her toe on an empty chair and doubled over. When she righted herself, Asher was gone again.

"Ah, Miss Hartley," said the man with a bow tie, holding his hand out as she approached.

Hailey extended hers expecting a handshake, but like a gentleman of old, he bowed and kissed her hand.

"I'm Professor Simeon Woodfork, and it is a delight to meet you."

"Likewise, Professor."

"Well," he said, stepping back, "let's see your flail-beat."

Hailey blinked.

"I'm sorry, sir. My what?"

"Your flail-beat. Didn't you read my instructions?"

"I read your letter, sir, but there was no mention of a flail-beat in it."

"Hartley received a tampered package," Fin said through a mouthful of fried chicken as he made his way to Woodfork.

"Really," said Woodfork with great interest. "What was in it?"

"Two letters," Hailey told him. "One signed by you and the other was..." She shook her head. "The other was one sentence long."

"One sentence?" Woodfork wrinkled his forehead and looked at Fin then back to Hailey. "How was it written?"

"It looked like scribble. Like a five-year-old wrote it."

"Thick letters?"

Hailey nodded.

"I believe you've attracted a poltergeist, Miss Hartley."

"Oh." She already knew she had a poltergeist and wondered if that little trouble-maker, Tomas, was responsible for sabotaging her silver envelope.

"In any case," the professor said, clapping his hands together, "Pádraig here will find you a handbook, and everything else you need is in your welcome package. But before you leave this hall, I must advise you, Miss Hartley, to ready your flail-beat."

"Okay..."

"You see, due to the random breaks in the veil here at Bear Towne, we recommend all students practice their extraction technique should they stumble upon an unmarked in-between and become accidentally trapped there."

Pinching her face together thoughtfully, she replayed Woodfork's sentence in her head, but she literally had no idea what he was talking about.

"I'm sorry, I didn't understand one word of that."

Woodfork smiled brightly at Fin who gnawed the last sliver of meat off a chicken leg then left to fetch another.

"Ah, what a delight you are indeed," said the professor. "Most students would try to bamboozle me. Nobody admits when they don't know something anymore—this is so refreshing." He drew a breath and continued. "The veil is a barrier that separates Earth from the two other realms—the Aether and the Heavens. An in-between is a partial opening through the veil—not large enough to travel completely through, you see, but still sufficient in size to pull one partially across. It leaves one trapped and somewhat vulnerable—it's a bit like stepping into deep, sticky mud."

That, Hailey understood.

"Every in-between is fraught with danger. One never knows what to expect inside. Any new student would be fortunate to escape unscathed, only...well, given your...er...*status* here, one might try to harm you irreparably or even kill you completely if you fell into such a hole, you understand?"

"No. What's my status?"

Woodfork waved his hand, dismissively. "No need to fret about that now. What's important is that you leave here ready and able to pull yourself out of an in-between, and the only way to do that is to perform a flail-beat."

"Okay." Hailey nodded, ready to learn how to flail-beat.

"It's quite simple," he told her kindly. "All you have to do is use your hands or your feet to produce a regular, recurring percussive noise by striking them against whatever surface you find inside the in-between. That's very important, to find a surface, as clapping usually doesn't work. Of course, you already know that a regular percussion repels most non-humans," he said, but this was all news to Hailey. "So it repels an in-between as well. With your background in percussive dance, it should be fairly simple for you, yes?"

"You mean you just have to...to dance your way out of an in-between?" Surely it couldn't be that simple.

"Ah, then you understand. Alright, if you would please—just this once—demonstrate for me your flail-beat?"

Not since the day Holly vanished had Hailey urged her feet to dance. Glancing around, she made sure nobody was watching. Then, with a heavy heart but eager feet, she tapped out a simple reel beat.

Woodfork clapped her on the shoulder after two short seconds. "That will do. Can you do the same with your hands?"

"Yes."

"Very good. Now, should you find yourself trapped in an in-between, you tap out a beat precisely like that, and you'll pop right out," he said with a reassuring smile. "And I may ask you to assist the other students with their flail-beat inside the in-between studio, but," he said shaking his finger at her, "that is the *only* place on this campus where you may produce a regular percussive noise, do you understand?"

"Yes, but, Professor…why—"

He held his hand up. "No more questions today, you'll learn everything about in-betweens and the veil and the Aether and everything else in class. For now, go and eat, pick up your welcome package and meet your fellow classmates," he said, patting her on the back to hurry her away.

The eating part went well, as did the picking up of the welcome package, but the meeting of the fellow classmates—that went nowhere.

While Fin worked the room like a movie star, Hailey literally repelled people. No one would come within five feet of her, and she was starting to wonder if she smelled bad.

For almost two hours, Hailey sat alone at a table for fifteen, eating her smoked salmon and exploring her welcome package, which thankfully came bundled inside a Bear Towne backpack—another item she hadn't brought. As students began filing out, she looked over her orientation schedule for the next morning and pulled out her room assignment:

Dorm: Eureka Hall, 3rd floor, Room 333
Roommate: Giselle Goarhausen.

Just as she found Eureka Hall on her campus map, a friendly voice rang out from inside her invisible five-foot demilitarized zone.

"Come on, I'll help you with your bags," said Fin.

Hailey looked up from her map.

"Can you tell me how to get to Eureka Hall from here?" She folded her papers and placed them inside her backpack.

"I'll do you one better and show you."

"Really?"

"Yeah. I'm heading that way too," he said as they walked into the grand hallway, where the other ParaSci freshmen had already removed the shrink wrap from the pallets and were picking through the luggage.

"Which ones are yours," he asked, and her eyes searched the piles.

"That one's mine."

She pointed to the smallest bag on one of the pallets, and Fin grabbed it.

"What else?"

"That's it."

"That's it? This?" he said, shaking her small bag. "This is all you brought to Alaska?"

"Well—" Hailey let out a curt sigh. "Yes! My letter said to bring *one* purse-size bag, and there wasn't any packing list or anything else inside the envelope, and it said not to ask any questions until I got here, and…"

Hailey threw her hands up then dropped them in a huff, and Fin stared at her, unamused.

"Why didn't you just ask me?" As if this would have been the logical thing to do.

Hailey let him have it.

"I haven't *seen* you since the day we buried Holly. You never came back to work, you never even *called* to say you weren't coming back, you just disappeared. You left me!" She turned to stomp away but turned on him again. "And you never mentioned *anything* about going to school in Alaska. What the heck were you doing in Pittsburgh anyway?"

Fin dropped her bag on the floor at her feet and grabbed her by the shoulders. "I *never* left you," he said forcefully, and then he pushed her away, turned around, and left her.

"Clearly, Fin," she muttered to herself as she grabbed up her bag, "you and I differ greatly in our idea of what it means to leave someone."

He threw open the Chinook Hall door and looked back at her.

"Well?" he said grudgingly. "You coming?"

"Yes," she said, snapping out of her grudge and trotting to the door. "Hey, what's a parafreak?"

"It's you," he said in his normal, slightly caustic tone as he took Hailey's "luggage" from her. "And me too. It's anyone lucky enough to study ParaScience in the Last Frontier state. We are definitely the redheaded step children of the university."

"I certainly am, but you seem to have a lot of friends here," she told him while she tied her wet shoes.

"There's only one friend I care about."

He winked, and Hailey froze, her belly tightening. Then she shook her head and laughed.

Holding the door for her, he followed her out, and they headed toward Eureka Hall.

"Really, though, Fin, what were you doing in Pittsburgh?"

"Chasing women and getting into trouble," he answered without hesitation as their path opened into a giant square.

Several buildings dotted the campus, some log, some stone, and one that looked like a giant igloo. Each bore an ornately carved wooden signpost with large, bubonic-looking knots.

"Eureka Hall is here on the north-east corner." Fin opened the outer door for her and showed her inside.

"I'm on the third floor," she told him.

"I know."

Up the stairs they went, and Fin explained Eureka's layout.

"So, this is the only co-ed dorm on campus." The stairway opened onto a large landing that split the building in two. "To the right are the boys' rooms and to the left are all the girls' rooms. The girls have their own showers, which are conveniently located almost directly across from your room, next to the laundry closet. In front of us is the Spruce Room, which is a community study hall slash TV room slash kitchenette."

He opened the door to the Spruce Room and turned on the lights. "Nice," she said, taking in the giant TV, five fluffy couches, desks and tables.

"This," he said pointing to a large presidential-looking suite adjacent to the Spruce Room, "is where your Resident Assistant lives."

"Okay," Hailey said with a nod.

"If you have any problems—you get locked out of your room, you have an issue with your roommate, you need more Yeti spray—any problems, Hailey, you come and knock on this door, okay?"

"Okay."

"And I'll answer."

"O—what?"

Fin smiled.

"You're my RA?" Hailey said brightly.

"Yup."

Yes! He'd be right down the hall and could help her get her bearings and explain these in-betweens and answer her questions, and oh crap! What about Tomas and these ghost traps? She had to disable them.

"I need to go to the library," she blurted.

"Of course you do." Fin threw a confused hand in the air.

"I need a German dictionary and a book that explains these ghost traps," she continued very seriously. She did not want Tomas getting stuck. "The campus map shows the library, but it doesn't give the hours and—"

"Stop. The library is closed. Besides, you need to unpack all your stuff," he said holding up her bag.

She took it and frowned.

"Go check out your room, make sure your key works, meet your roommate, take a shower, et cetera, et cetera. I'll swing by later with a German dictionary."

He unlocked the door to his giant room.

"And don't worry about ghosts," he said over his shoulder. "You're not gonna get any ghosts in your room."

Hailey wrinkled her brow.

"Oh?"

"They're afraid of your roommate," he said quickly through the crack in his door, shutting it before Hailey even had a chance to gasp.

Chapter Nineteen

The Roommate from Hell

"One skeleton said to another - If I had any guts I'd get the hell out of here."

— Anonymous

Hailey stood in the hallway with her one piece of "luggage" and stared at the door to room 333—her room, wondering what kind of monster could scare a ghost. Whatever it was, its name was Giselle; it waited on the other side of this door, and Hailey would have to live with it for the entire year. Unless of course she fell into an in-between, and someone killed her completely…

As she raised the warped, wrought-iron skeleton key from her welcome kit to the lock, she straightened up and put on her friendly face. The lock clicked, and Hailey pushed open the door.

The room was larger than she'd expected, with a built-in desk, stretching almost the whole length of the left wall. Two chairs were pushed against the desk at opposite ends and in the middle, the desk was divided by two sets of drawers. The wall above the desk was mirrored from end to end. On the wall opposite the door was a large window. In the window hung a golden decoration, which resembled a dream-catcher and had a tiny motor, causing the thing to vibrate and twist back and forth.

There were two closets and two beds. Just inside the door and to the right was an empty, undressed bed—Hailey guessed that would be hers. The other was in the far corner opposite the door and occupied by a girl who lounged with her legs outstretched, her feet crossed, and her face hidden behind a beauty magazine.

She didn't stir when Hailey tentatively stepped into the room.

"Hello," Hailey said, but the girl ignored her. "I'm Hailey," she tried again, but the girl never acknowledged her.

Frowning, Hailey set her bag and backpack on her bare mattress. She opened her empty closet and sighed.

She should just shower and wait for Fin, she decided. Tomorrow morning, she would tour the campus and hit the bookstore, where she could hopefully find clothes, shoes, sheets, blankets, pillows, and towels. And somebody to talk to…

Giselle stirred in her bed and Hailey jerked her head around, but she still couldn't see the girl's face behind her magazine, which boasted "5 New Makeup Tricks to Make Him Notice You."

Hailey rolled her eyes and unzipped her luggage. It took less than a minute to unpack, and as she gathered her hand towel, soap, and shampoo, there came a sharp knock.

"Hi!" Hailey said brightly as she opened the door to Fin.

"Here's your handbook," he said, holding it up before passing it to her.

"Thanks." Hailey looked at his empty hands. "Where's the dictionary?"

"Right here." He held his arms out.

"You speak German?"

"Yeah," he said stepping inside her room. "I grew up there once."

Hailey cocked her head.

"What do you mean, you 'grew up there once'?"

Fin answered with a half-smile. "What do you need translated?"

She grabbed a pen and tablet from her welcome bag and scribbled down her Tomas words.

"Khu isn't German, at all, it's...ancient...Egyptian, I think." He shook his head. "Sort of means soul. Schatz is treasure; Gefahr is danger; bin entwichen is 'I escaped'—Hailey..." With a concerned look he handed her the tablet. "What's the context of all this?"

She tried to think of a quick way to sum things up. "How much time do you have?"

"None," he told her, checking his watch. "I'll swing by tomorrow morning for breakfast," he said, and then he leaned over and pecked her on the cheek.

"Goodbye, raging bitch," he called to Giselle, and without moving her magazine, she flipped him the bird as he walked out the door.

"Whoa," Hailey breathed, clutching her stomach after the door closed. "That...was..."

"Gross," her roommate finished for her, and Hailey looked up. Giselle had moved the magazine, stood up, and was scowling hatefully from beside her bed at Hailey, who smiled excitedly back.

This roommate was no monster. She was just the girl with the prematurely gray hair. Hailey blew a sigh of relief, and as she marveled, Giselle fell like a feather back onto her bed and lifted her magazine again.

She certainly was aptly named, moving with the grace of a ballerina. Though her eyes were a mesmerizing crystal blue—the rest of her seemed a bit horrible, with slightly frizzy gray hair reaching down to her hips and a couple of facial wrinkles that belonged to a crotchety, 80-year-old bat.

Otherwise, in the face, Giselle looked...at least in Hailey's eyes...somewhat similar to Holly. Were it not for her six-foot stature, corpse hair, and permanent look of disgust on her kisser, she could have been Holly's doppelganger. Maybe she just missed her sister. In any case, and despite her grumpiness, Hailey liked her immediately.

"Stop staring at me," Giselle said from behind her magazine.

"I'm sorry." Hailey diverted her eyes. "You just remind me of my sister."

"She must be ugly," she said in a monotone, and Hailey shook her head.

"She was beautiful." Hailey reached for her back pocket. "Oh," she whispered. "Asher still has Holly's picture, or else I'd show you."

"I don't want to see it," Giselle droned, and Hailey ignored her indifferent tone. So far, Giselle was the only student to talk to her, and even if that "talking" amounted to a string of grouchy insults, Hailey was delighted.

"So, where are you from?" she tried.

"Hell."

"Oh, come on, Giselle, Cleveland's not that bad," Hailey laughed, trying to coax a smile, but Giselle flicked her magazine down to show Hailey her pointy teeth.

"It's a village in the Alps," she said through them. "The literal translation is Hell," she sputtered, and then with a loud tsk, she pulled herself back behind her magazine.

Hailey rubbed her forehead. "I actually have a roommate from Hell," she muttered. "What country would that be?"

Giselle didn't answer.

"Well, I'm from Pittsburgh," Hailey said as she arranged her things inside her closet—all on one shelf.

"I don't care," said Giselle with more than a little hostility, but that didn't discourage Hailey. Since small talk wasn't working, she tried flattery.

"I think your eyes are really pretty, and…" Hailey swallowed hard. "I saw you at the welcome dinner. You and I must be wearing the same student repellant," she laughed, and a puff of steam literally rose out of Giselle's head.

"Nobody will talk to you," she snapped, ripping her magazine as she threw it down, "because Asher told us all to stay away from you."

"What? When?"

"This summer. And he already killed one student as an example, and I'm not supposed to tell you that or anything else about him, but I'll probably be dead in a couple months anyway, so who cares if he rips me apart?"

Hailey's jaw fell. "That can't be, Asher's—"

"Asher can be terrifying, little girl."

Hailey stared at Giselle, the horror of her words a great weight against her chest.

"Why are you telling me this?" Hailey murmured.

"Not because I want to be your friend. I'm telling you this so you'll stop talking to me. I don't want to know you, Hailey."

"I had no idea," she said quietly, her insides gone cold, and she didn't bother Giselle again.

Lying on her bed in utter silence, much like Giselle, Hailey read her student handbook from cover to cover, struggling to focus on the strangest and most fascinating subject matter she'd ever seen. Her guilt kept distracting her, gnawing at her insides like a White Forest Yeti or Man-Eating Tree, neither of which she ever wanted to happen upon. Both of which had their own section in the Bear Towne Handbook's glossary of lethal beasts.

The handbook divided White Forest hazards into two types—summer and winter.

Summer hazards included familiar things, like mosquitos and black bears, but the list ended with tips on avoiding carnivorous trees. Apparently, they only ate during waking hours and had a taste for non-Alaskan humans. The handbook advised anyone from Outside to travel through the White Forest only when escorted by a non-human.

Yetis were another hazard. According to the handbook, most of them hibernated until winter, though some seemed to enjoy warm weather, and all Yetis preferred human meat. The book recommended students carry Yeti spray and cross their fingers when venturing into the White Forest.

An asterisk next to the chapter on Bear Towne's three active in-between zones noted a warning: small, unmarked in-betweens tend to appear and disappear here and there around campus during the spring months especially, but not exclusively.

Bewildered, Hailey closed her book and sulked. It was like reading another language.

Grabbing her shampoo, she hoped a hot shower would steam away her guilt and make things make sense. But when she walked into the shower room, the three students inside, who were in mid-shower and still soapy, all finished suddenly and scattered like cockroaches. The same thing happened in the hallway when she emerged from the showers, with the added happiness of slamming doors to punctuate her misery.

Hailey sighed and shuffled into the laundry room, wearing her other jeans—the clean ones—and a fresh t-shirt (she didn't have pajamas). In she tossed her Luftzeug clothes and shoes for a spin, using a community bottle of detergent and a healthy dose of hope that Alaskan muskeg mud would wash out.

As she closed the laundry room door behind her, she turned her attention to the giggling coming up the stairwell. Walking up the stairs with his arm around the waist of a stunning brunette and his tongue in her ear was Fin.

Hailey stumbled backward inside the laundry room and peeked through a sliver in the door.

Her heart plummeted into her stomach.

Fin fumbled with his room key as he passionately kissed this girl. She had her shirt nearly off by the time they swayed inside his room.

Hailey's throat tightened.

Slowly, dejectedly, she slid down the door and sat on the floor of the laundry room, staring at her hands until the washer clicked, unsure why she should even care that Fin had a girlfriend. Of course he had a girlfriend—why wouldn't he?

But he kissed my cheek...

Disgusted by her own jealousy, Hailey shook her head and collected her wet clothes. She'd just hang them in her closet to dry and not think about Fin. Nothing else was in her closet, and Fin didn't matter to her anyway. Her shoes might even be dry before morning, and Fin was...was...

Hailey threw open her room door and barged in, forcing Fin out of her mind by wondering if Giselle would ever speak to her again. More than that, she wondered if Giselle was even human— *sharp teeth...probably not.*

In stocking feet, she stepped in front of her closet, when something sloshed.

"What the...?"

Hopping on one foot, she followed a trail of little puddles leading all the way from the door to Giselle's bed, which lay curiously empty. Someone inside the room was snoring softly. Somewhere...

Crouching down, Hailey peeked under Giselle's bed then lifted her gaze higher. Pressed against the ceiling above her bed and sound asleep, Giselle snored and moaned, her long, kinked gray hair hanging down like a gossamer web.

Definitely not human, Hailey thought, and she stepped in another small puddle of water with her other socked foot. Giselle must've skipped the whole drying-off part of her shower. Now she knew how Holly had felt. This was annoying.

Unable to take her eyes off her roommate from Hell, Hailey fell asleep worrying about Giselle and whether she would get in trouble for telling her Asher was a murderer. She hoped not. Giselle might hail from Hell, but she was Hailey's only friend, and that was a slice of heaven.

That night, Hailey sat on a mossy boulder in the Aether and wept. Asher approached her cautiously.

"Hailey," he called softly, "why are you crying?"

She looked up at him through slow-motion raindrops, irides-cent flecks of light that shimmered when they graced her face, mix-ing with her tears before tumbling away.

"I'm afraid for my roommate," she said with pleading eyes. "Is she in trouble?"

Asher tilted his head. "Why do you ask me this?"

Maybe he didn't know what Giselle had said. Or maybe he was testing her. Or had Giselle been testing her? Had she just betrayed her roommate? Hailey shook her head. All this busi-ness with Fin—she was definitely projecting her mistrust onto Asher, onto Giselle...plus all that talk of murder had her head swimming...

She trusted Asher. Since childhood, she'd trusted him. She couldn't bear to think he'd hurt anyone, and she didn't want him angry at Giselle. She had to tell him the truth.

"Giselle told me you killed a student, and she's afraid you'll... kill her, too...for telling me."

Raindrops landed steadily on the rocky landscape in gentle *plops* exploding in tiny bursts of squiggly flashes as Asher consid-ered her, and Hailey continued her plea.

"I feel so alone here, and Giselle's the only student that's talked to me. I feel awful, Asher, I just... I don't want her to get in trouble for talking to me."

"You ask a lot of me, Hailey. There is much you don't understand."

"Then explain it to me."

Asher closed his eyes, and a peal of thunder, sounding more like breaking glass rang out.

"Giselle disobeyed me. If I don't punish her, I'll quickly lose control of the other Earth dwellers, and you will not be safe here."

Hailey shook her head.

"Nobody will know what she told me. Nobody talks to her. They all avoid her like they avoid me. I need a friend, Asher. Please."

"Giselle is an abomination, and if she threatens you, I will kill her. But I will overlook this one instance of defiance because you wish it."

Smiling her relief, Hailey wiped her face.

"I think she's warming up to me." She tried to touch Asher's hand through the sheer light surrounding him, but of course, there was no hand, and Hailey sighed with frustration.

"There's so much I want to ask you, but I won't remember any of this, will I?"

"Ask me, Hailey. Ask me anything and I'll answer. But we are in the Aether, so you may forget all this when you wake."

"Is it true, then? Did you kill a student?"

"I've killed several."

Hailey's lungs failed, and for what seemed like too long, she stared at him, heart hammering until she finally breathed her worst fear. "You're a… a murderer…?"

"It is not murder to dispose of a wretch," said Asher quickly, reaching out to her.

She side-eyed him, and he dropped his arm.

"I've never ended a human life before its time. Where I come from, such an act is unthinkable."

"What about the Envoy that killed Holly? What about Cobon?"

"He did not kill her before her time. He influenced a few wretched humans to injure her until it was her time."

"That's splitting hairs, don't you think?"

"Many of the Envoys no longer follow our laws," said Asher forcefully, and he turned away.

"Are you alright?" Hailey asked.

"Not at all," he said without facing her. "I'm sorry I—I'm sorry I could not help Holly," he said with shame in his voice. "And… I'm afraid. I fear that you will hate me. I fear that I'll lose you," he whispered.

Still the rain tinkled, teeny crystals shattering against the rocks, and Hailey drew a deep breath.

"Uncle Pix taught us that all things can be forgiven," she said, her voice wavering, and Asher turned his head slightly.

Hailey stared straight ahead, eyes wide to hold in her tears, unable to actually say, "I forgive you" because she didn't. She didn't forgive him. Or herself.

"I don't blame you for what Cobon did." Her tone was flat, and that was the best she could do. "Asher, I understand why you didn't save her, but I wish you had. I'm angry and sad, and I wish he had killed me instead, I—"

"Don't say such things."

But it was the truth. She'd trade places with Holly in a heartbeat. She searched Asher's eyes, trying to convey her anguish, but seeing his own anguish broke her heart. It wasn't Asher's fault that Cobon was a monster.

Her throat went tight and she pressed her arms to her belly.

Asher watched her closely.

"I'm not going anywhere," she resolved, and she wiped her eyes. "You're not going to lose me. But I still have so many questions, Asher. They can't wait."

"What would you like to know?"

"For starters, what is a wretched human? And…wha…" Hailey shook her head, befuddled, but she wanted to know exactly what killed Holly.

"A Being living on Earth without a soul is a wretch," Asher explained. "Anyone who seeks redemption will find it. However, those who live a wicked life slowly kill their soul. To save itself, such a soul will abandon its body here on Earth, leaving behind its life energy. The body lives on as a wretch, and a wretch is fair game for any Earth dweller to dispose of."

"You can live without a soul?"

"Not very well."

"But why don't they die? Who decides when it's someone's time to die?"

Asher shook his head. "I don't know. Any Envoy can see it, though. It's as obvious as a flickering light bulb."

"Giselle said you killed a student to make an example…to warn the others to stay away from me. Was he… flickering…?" she prodded as she sat on the soft grass, beckoning him to join her.

"He was a wretch, Hailey," said Asher, his voice rising even as he sat next to her. He seemed angry, but not with her. "And I killed him to remove him from the Earth. He not only disturbed you, he brought the spoils of his wickedness onto my campus."

"The boy with the rainbow hair? What did he bring?"

"A severed human head."

"What?" Hailey breathed. "I tried to befriend a murderer?"

"And a cannibal."

"Oh my God."

Bringing her hand to her head, Hailey stared at a beautiful waterfall, shocked. There was no easy way to wrap her mind around her first day at Bear Towne. She wanted Asher to say that everything would be alright. She wanted Asher to touch her.

"Asher?" she asked when she felt the pull of morning.

"Yes, Hailey?"

"Will you ever kiss me again?"

Asher closed his violet eyes and smiled. "Yes, Hailey."

Chapter Twenty

The Breakfast

"Believe nothing you hear, and only one half
that you see."

— Edgar Allan Poe, The System of
Dr. Tarr and Prof. Fether

Still smiling at the thought of Asher kissing her again, Hailey groggily rolled out of bed and into the shower. She returned to her room after making some effort to look halfway decent, which, given her lack of supplies or a change of clothes, was a challenge. At least she had Tomas.

Somewhere around 6:00 a.m., Giselle floated down from the ceiling and landed on her bed with a barely audible crush. Then she grabbed her morning reading material, reclined with her legs outstretched, feet crossed, and ignored Hailey completely.

Returning students were still arriving, steadily filing in and out of the dorm, carrying big boxes, bins, and suitcases. Hailey regretfully watched through her window as student after student trudged inside with towels and robes and clothes and blankets and sheets and everything else under the sun that she wished she'd known she could bring but didn't thanks to some cranky poltergeist.

All that paled in comparison to what she was really missing—Holly.

And what if Holly is still out there?

Sighing heavily, she shook her head. She needed to stop this. Dental records didn't lie. Right? Holly was dead, and she wouldn't want her little sister frowning and ruminating her university days away. She closed the blinds to sulk as Giselle sat silent and motionless behind the same beauty magazine.

Biting her lip as she paced the room, Hailey stole a glance in the mirror. Tomas had done a grand job with her hair that morning, twisting and teasing small locks that he'd secured with shiny gold pins in a relaxed half-up do.

Hailey was waiting for Fin, though she wasn't sure if he would show up and if he did, she wasn't sure he'd be alone. If he weren't the only person on campus that would speak to her, she would have fled her room already and avoided the awkwardness of seeing him for the rest of forever.

Finally, there was a knock at the door.

"Morning, Hailey," Fin sang, metal coffee cup in hand. Of course he was happy this morning. "Good morning, Medusa," he called into the room, and Giselle gave him the finger again. "She hates me," he told Hailey with a mischievous grin as they walked down the hall.

Hailey nodded.

"What's up with you?" Fin said, eying her suspiciously.

"Nothing." That was a lie. She couldn't get the image of Fin and his girlfriend out of her head, but she had no intention of even hinting that she'd seen him grope her in the hallway the night before. He might think she was jealous. And of course she totally wasn't...

"You're a horrible liar." He sipped his coffee as they made their way to Chinook Hall and through the breakfast buffet. "And you're very distracted today—usually means you're up to something."

He took her tray for her and led her to a corner table. "So, tell me about these German words. Where'd you come across them?" he asked, pulling Hailey's chair out.

"My phantom hair dresser frosted them across my mirror?" She shrugged with a slight cringe, and Fin choked on his coffee.

"What?" Screwing up his face, he surveyed her hair.

She turned her head for him. "Nice, huh."

"It is actually. But, you shouldn't encourage a poltergeist. They feed on attention."

"This one seems helpful. And I'm pretty sure someone from DOPPLER kidnapped him from our house, but he must have escaped, because he's here now. And he says DOPPLER is dangerous." Hailey looked to Fin for his assessment of all this.

"This is troubling, Hailey," he said with a thoughtful expression. "Only an Envoy can catch a poltergeist. You'll see—the ghost traps don't work very well. Anyway, DOPPLER funds a lot of research here. If they're monitoring you without the university's permission, Woodfork and Asher need to know. It sounds like there's another Envoy involved in this."

Hailey sighed. "I need to find Asher anyway." He had her picture of Holly and answers to a thousand questions…and maybe another kiss… "Do you know where I can find him?"

"Asher?" he said bitterly. "Asher can't be found, Hailey. If he wants to see you, he'll find you."

"You don't like him, do you?"

"He's a monster," Fin said almost angrily, and Hailey bit her lip, trying to remember anything monster-like about his kiss. Fin slapped his hand on the table. "What are you all moony-eyed about?" he asked with a definite note of jealousy, and Hailey startled out of her daydream.

Lately, Fin was sending a whole lot of mixed signals.

Biting her lips together, Hailey almost blurted a thought she'd regret, but the perfect Pre-Med student from the night before saved her the trouble by interrupting them at the breakfast table.

"Hi Pádraig," she cooed as she danced over to him, and he looked up at her as if he'd never seen her before.

"Hello?" he said through a mouthful of sausage gravy.

"Last night was fun," she told him, twirling a strand of hair as she sat down next to him.

"Was it?" he asked, looking like he was ready to duck and cover, but she threw her head back and giggled.

Hailey grabbed her handbook and flipped through it, moving her eyes as if she were reading, but she was way too distracted by the show in front of her to comprehend the words.

"Yes," she chastised him. "It was fun three times," she whispered loudly in his ear, and Hailey peeked over her book in time to see him scowl and lean away from her.

Shrinking into her seat, Hailey pulled her handbook over her face. She didn't want to hear this.

"Don't act like you don't remember, Pádraig," she said, and Hailey detected a shrill note of warning.

"This is no act." Fin was using his irritated voice, and she matched it. Then she brought it up a level.

"You're such an asshole!" It sounded like she slapped his face pretty hard, scooted her chair out, and stormed away.

Very cautiously, Hailey lowered her handbook. "Who was that?" she asked once the cafeteria resumed its normal hum of activity.

"Uh…Joanne," he said, looking bewildered. "I caught up with her last night at the LOED meeting." He looked at Hailey, still blinking rapidly from the slap. "I honestly have no idea what the hell that was all about," he said, lobbing a pointed finger in the direction of Joanne's retreat.

Hailey looked at him sideways. "Really?"

"Really," he repeated.

"Maybe she's pissed off because she was naked in your room last night, and now you're acting like nothing happened." She took a thoughtful bite of toast.

Fin dropped his spoon and fumbled with his napkin. Clearing his throat, he sat up in his seat, and Hailey stool a glance at him.

"That—" He sat back, licked his teeth and continued. "No," he said definitively, and he looked her dead in the eyes. "I don't know what you think you saw, but don't believe it. I don't do that."

"Maybe you were drunk or something?" She knew what she saw.

"Yeah…or *something*," he said emphatically.

"Anyway, what's a 'load' meeting?" she said, letting him off the hook. At the end of the day, she didn't care what he did as long as he didn't leave her again.

"It's actually pronounced LO-ed, like co-ed. It's a club—the Legion of Earth Dwellers," he said dismissively. "Come on," he said checking his watch. "You're gonna be late for your tour."

Fin hurried her out of her chair, grabbed her tray, and pushed her out the door even as she was itching to ask him about LOED, about her roommate from Hell, about DOPPLER, what the heck ParaScience was, and what, if anything, he knew about Asher and the other Envoys.

"Don't forget your flail-beat," he said, straightening her shirt like a parent putting his child on the school bus for the first time. "And don't talk to strangers," he added with a smile.

Hailey turned her back on him and walked toward a gaggle of freshmen who stood in front of a girl holding up a Bear Towne flag.

"ParaFreak!" Fin called after her.

Running with her hands over her ears, she caught up with her campus tour just in time to see her orientation leader step back, fold in half, and disappear.

Chapter Twenty-One

Campus Tour

"Shallow men believe in luck or in circumstance.
Strong men believe in cause and effect."

— Ralph Waldo Emerson

The southern belle, who had opened her mouth to greet her freshmen ParaScience orientation group, took a small step backward; her body pleated like a skirt, and then she vanished, leaving behind the echo of a guttural yelp.

Leaning over her vanishing spot, the group murmured and exchanged worried expressions.

"I think she fell into an in-between," one of the students whispered.

"She should have come out of it by now, right?" worried another.

"Come on, we have to help her!" Hailey yelled. She plowed through the group and jumped, head first into the in-between to rescue the orientation leader, fully expecting somebody to jump in with her.

Nobody did.

Hailey found herself all alone, between Earth and someplace else, suspended in goo that reeked of ammonia.

Surprisingly, the in-between wasn't a hole in the ground, rather a wall of thick air, which sounded and felt an awful lot like plunging head-first into a pool of clear Jell-O. Only it seemed to have reverse pressure and was sucking Hailey further from her tour group, like quicksand, only horizontal.

Even as jelly oozed into her ears and stung her eyes, she could still see her fellow freshmen on the other side of the barrier. They all looked warped, their voices muffled. It was clear from their dancing eyes and wringing hands—they couldn't see her. Turning her back on them, Hailey searched the gelatin landscape for their orientation leader, finding her nearby, white-eyed and flinging her arms as if she were drowning.

Air inside the in-between rushed out of Hailey's lungs just fine, but breathing it back in against the vacuum wasn't easy. Gooshing her way through the thickness took every ounce of power Hailey could summon, and the jelly in her right ear especially began to ache.

With burning lungs and a great stretch, she finally reached the girl and grabbed a fistful of bleached hair.

Then she stopped. For the briefest instant, her mind went blank. She knew how to get out—Professor Woodfork had taught her...something...

A flail-beat!

Feeling around for a solid surface, she found a tiny one, and through the throb of suffocation, she tapped her foot with great difficulty in a slow then fast treble. Twice she did this and on the third treble, a long foghorn bellowed out, the gelatin twisted, and the in-between heaved Hailey onto the sidewalk. She was still clutching a fistful of tour guide hair, which was pulling her back in. Hailey stood up, feet slipping on the goo as she braced against the cement, and with a mighty yank, she pulled a bleach-blonde, gelatin-covered, gasping and choking orientation leader from the in-between.

As Hailey spit out chunk after bitter chunk of jellied ick, the girl faltered briefly, looking at Hailey with a mix of sheer terror and brief gratitude. Then she scrambled closer, grabbed Hailey by the head like Tomas and wrenched a foot-long, shrieking worm out of Hailey's right ear. Flinging it to the ground, she stomped on it with both feet while Hailey choked and sputtered.

"What was that?" Hailey managed between coughs.

"That was a tunneling earworm, those bastards…" the girl said in a thick southern drawl. She stamped on it again.

"A what?"

"A tunneling earworm," she said louder as Hailey pulled on her ear lobe.

It felt like she had water in her ear. "What? Are they dangerous?"

"Yes. Lethal." The girl's foot once again came down on the grease spot that used to be a tunneling earworm. "Painfully lethal," she qualified with another stamp, and Hailey was pretty sure that one was for good measure. "They dig through your ear, and as they chew into your brain, they hum an annoying jingle that resonates inside your head until you die."

Hailey stared at her blank-faced. The girl extended her hand to Hailey with a megawatt smile.

"Hi, I'm Jaycen Mae, and you're Hailey Hartley, aren't you?"

"That's right," Hailey said, shaking the girl's hand. "There was no mention of earworms in the handbook."

"Ha! There's no mention of a lot of things in the handbook." Her smile faded but only a bit. "You know," she said quietly, "for a second, I thought you wouldn't come in after me."

Hailey blinked.

"I'm really sorry about the earworm," she added in an anxious voice, turning away and raising her Bear Towne flag.

Still dripping gobs of in-between jelly onto the pavement as she moved, Jaycen launched into her campus introduction with a slightly shaky southern charm, and Hailey had the strange sensation she'd just been pulled on someone's string.

"Welcome, freshmen ParaScience students, to Bear Towne University—proud home of the snarling Yetis," Jaycen said excitedly, her composure now completely restored.

Hailey was not as refined and continued coughing, wiping her nose, and flinging globs of goo off her hands even as the southern belle sang the Bear Towne alma mater with several highly motivated freshmen joining in:

Break down the Barrier,
Build up the Ferrier,
Breathe in the eerie air,
Pierce the veil. Pierce the veil.

A legacy of light,
Benevolence is right,
For righteousness we fight,
Old Towne we hail. Old Towne we hail!

"Great job, y'all!" Jaycen blared. "Now, Bear Towne campus is laid out like a warped four-leaf clover, but don't count on luck to get you out of any 'hairy situations'," the jellied blonde laughed. "ALWAYS carry your Yeti spray anytime you venture into the White Forest, which lies inside the north-west leaf," she said, motioning toward the path Hailey had walked the day before—after she'd fallen out of the Luftzeug. "I'm sure you've all read your handbook and know to also carry your tree repellant? Nobody likes stepping in freshman-shaped tree poop, am I right?"

The group chortled politely, though Hailey could almost smell the fear in the air.

"Let's begin our tour with the Campus Bowl, or THE Bowl, which is where we are standing…

"Y'all will eat, sleep, and do most of your living here in the Bowl," Jaycen drawled. "This is the safest place at Bear Towne. In fact, until today, there had been no known in-betweens here, but now we know there's at least one," she giggled, "which the In-between Management and Extraction Team, or I-MET," she made big air quotes, "will survey later and mark if it endures.

"In addition to operating worldwide Luftzeug service and performing numerous other functions, I-MET is Bear Towne's search and rescue squad. If you ever get stuck in an in-between or lost in the White Forest, I-MET is the team that will find you and bring you back, hopefully alive and in one piece, but as you saw on the Luftzeug, sometimes I-MET can be a little rough."

A hand went up among the group.

"Do they always wear gas masks?"

"No. But they always cover their faces. Trust me, you do NOT want to see the face of an I-MET member. There's a reason only dead people do that job. You just never know how you're going to look after an in-between spits you out," she said, striking a Vanna White pose, and the group giggled.

Another hand shot up.

"How do we call for I-MET?" asked an anxious boy in wrinkled clothes.

"Oh, you don't have to. I-MET will know if their services are needed. The big building at the center of the Bowl—no more questions about I-MET—is Trinity Square, where you'll find the Bear Towne bookstore, the campus chapel, your mailboxes, and The Bruised Moose Café. The café serves grilled food, sandwiches, pizza…" Jaycen eyeballed one of the boys in the group. "…as well as an array of metallic and sulfurous fare for you non-humans. The chapel holds Mass daily and twice on Sundays—DO NOT neglect your soul here, y'all. If your soul jumps ship while you're at Bear Towne, you won't last three seconds. Too many scavengers here, am I right?"

Jaycen pointed to a very human-looking kid, in Hailey's opinion. "You're one, aren't you, cutie pie?" Jaycen said to him, and he grinned bashfully.

"The second most-important building on campus is Igloo Arena, which is the dome-looking structure on the north end of the Bowl."

Several of the female freshmen gasped and swooned, and Hailey peeked around the group to see what the all the fuss was. Making their way inside Igloo Arena was a group of muscular and fearless-looking men. One of them carried a hockey stick.

"What luck!" Jaycen twanged. "There they are, Freshmen— the Bear Towne Yetis hockey team, reporting for practice. I think everyone is excited to see some W's this year after last season's dismal finish, huh?"

After the last hockey player disappeared into the Igloo, Jaycen waved her flag and beckoned the group toward a carved stone and wood gazebo near the ParaScience leaf.

"The Chattering Gazebo will immediately strike up a conversation with any non-human, other-worldly or supernatural creature that passes under its eaves," she explained. She stepped under its roof.

"Well, well, well, well, well!" the gazebo gushed. "If it isn't Jaycen. Long time no see. In fact I haven't seen you since Alexei caught you smooching his teammate, what was his name?"

Jaycen jumped back, frowning.

Aha! Hailey knew Jaycen was far too chipper to be human.

"Y'all get the point," Jaycen said abruptly without looking at the group as she trudged under the iron gate of the ParaScience College leaf.

"Percussive instruments—"

Somebody raised their hand.

"—such as *drums*," Jaycen said looking squarely at the kid with the stupid look on his face, "are forbidden here. There are three— check that—four known, active in-between zones on this campus," she laughed. "Olde Main is an active in-between zone." She motioned to a haunted house, which stood leaning at a physically impossible angle. "It always leans into the wind. Looks like it's out of the northeast today—I'd say twenty knots right now," she called, and Olde Main groaned, screeched, and tilted even further as the wind picked up.

"You'll have most of your classes in Olde Main, but don't worry, the dangerous zones of the building are clearly marked, and all the exits have been fitted with an Indispensable Out-Between, which you'll learn all about in your first class. Trust me," she said emphatically, "you'll be in and out of that place enough that by the end of the year, you may even land on your feet when it spits you out."

Jaycen tipped her flag at a rough-cut stone castle.

"The observation tower and attached stone building are off limits to all students, and—" The smiling guide cut herself off, and Hailey craned her neck to see why.

Standing at the base of the observatory tower with his hands in his pockets, Asher watched the group of freshmen with great interest.

"We're moving on," the guide said urgently. "Quickly, now. Chop-chop, everyone."

"Who was that?" one student whispered as they followed Jaycen at a near run.

"That's Asher," said another secretly. "He's the head honcho. He's like the president of the school or something."

"More like a tyrant," chimed another. "And I heard he's got a nasty temper—"

"Shhhh!" hissed yet another as he jabbed his head at Hailey, and he wasn't even trying to be discreet.

Looking hopefully in Asher's direction, Hailey lingered behind and tried to catch his eye, but to her dismay, he ignored her, fixing his stare on Jaycen as she all but sprinted from the observatory.

Hailey bowed her head and chop-chopped away with the rest of the freshmen, trying not to feel wounded.

"On your left is the library—"

Finally.

"—which will reopen at oh-eight-hundred this Monday—"

Rats.

"—in time for the start of semester. Entry into the library is tightly controlled by the librarian, Mrs. Spitz. You must ask for her permission prior to setting foot in the stacks. Once she lets you in, you may access the library any time, day or night. If you have trouble gaining Mrs. Spitz's favor, try bringing her a new book—oh, and avoid mentioning sharp objects around her."

Jaycen led them back out to the Bowl and pulled Hailey aside.

"All y'all can go and check your mail and buy your books. Buh-bye, now," she called as she held tight to Hailey's gooey sleeve.

"Listen, Hailey," Jaycen said, looking grave—almost frightened. "I sure didn't mean for you to get hurt with that in-between. You know that, right?" She looked pleadingly into Hailey's eyes. "I'll take you shopping for new clothes—I mean, as long as it's alright with The Benevolent." Now she was trembling.

"Jaycen," Hailey said, peeling her hand from her sleeve. "It's not your fault that I jumped into a jelly mold."

Jaycen's lip trembled.

"Is it?" Hailey asked. "Is it your fault I jumped into that thing?"

"I'm so sorry," Jaycen said, and her eyes ran over. "It was supposed to be a benign in-between, only made to look dangerous. I had no idea it was a vacuum-glaze with tunneling earworms."

"A what?"

"A killer—and the worst kind," she said, wiping her face. "A vacuum-glaze sucks the air out of you and traps you like a spider's web so you can't do a flail-beat." Sniffling loudly, she straightened up a bit. "Maybe since I pulled the earworm out of your head, The Benevolent won't shred me," she whimpered.

Jaycen threw a glance toward the ParaScience leaf. "Well, I'll come find you later to take you shopping in town, okay?" she said with a voice full of hope, and Hailey nodded uncertainly.

"Alright. Thanks, Jaycen."

"Don't thank me, Hailey." She lingered for a moment, wearing a haunted expression, and then she scurried away. Watching her until she disappeared behind a building, Hailey swallowed hard then headed for the mail room with an upset stomach.

Instead of her class schedule, Hailey found inside her mailbox a folded note.

My Dearest ParaFreakazoid,
Your schedule's not done yet.
I'll get to it later. Maybe.
Yours, Fin

How was she supposed to buy her books if she didn't know which classes she had? Fin was going to get her schedule done *now*, and Hailey stormed out of the mail room, across the square, and up the stairs of Eureka Dorm to tell him so. She couldn't believe it! He had plenty of time to entertain the beautiful LOED girl, but he couldn't take five minutes to scribble out her schedule…?

After taking the stairs two at a time, Hailey still had a head full of steam and pounded on Fin's door with the side of her fist.

"Enter," he called, but Hailey pounded again, insisting he answer the door like a gentleman.

"What!" he yelled as he threw open the door. "Ew." He wrinkled his nose at her. "You look sticky."

"Do you have my schedule?" Hailey said in voice way nicer than she intended.

"Mmm—maybe…" He smiled with his nose in the air as he pulled an envelope out of his back pocket.

Hailey made a grab for it, but missed when he pulled it out of her reach. "That's not funny," she told him, trying to sound more mature than irritated, and Fin shook his head with a mischievous smile.

"Ask me nicely."

"Give me my schedule."

"You're funny when you try to be angry."

"I *am* angry."

"Really?" he said pointing at her chest. "They why are you still hugging my note to your heart?"

Hailey whipped the note down and stuffed it in her back pocket. She hadn't even realized she'd been holding it that way, which made her even angrier.

"I wasn't—"

"—you were," Fin sang, smiling and nodding and overly pleased with himself. "This isn't your schedule," he told her waving the envelope, and Hailey sighed.

"When will you finish it?"

"Come see me tomorrow morning," said Fin, and before Hailey could protest, he slammed his door.

As she sulked toward the stairs, Giselle popped into the hallway out of nowhere, and Hailey ran right into her.

"Watch where you're going," Giselle spat, but Hailey didn't hear her. She was too distracted by a gorgeous, dark-haired girl, who'd just passed them in the hallway, swishing her hips as she walked up to Fin's door.

"Why do you care?" said Giselle, snapping Hailey out of a very unbecoming stare just before Fin invited the belly-dancer-walker into his room.

"What now?" Hailey smiled brightly at her roommate. "Are you actually talking to me?" she asked excitedly. Then her smile vanished. "What are you talking about?"

"That's Aida," Giselle informed her. "Pádraig sleeps with her a lot—she's one of his favorites, and she's in love with him, but he could give a shit."

Hailey didn't know what just hit her, and she stared with a blank face at Giselle. "Wha—I don't—"

"—don't lie." Giselle grabbed her hand and pulled her down the stairs. "I saw you clutch your stomach. And all he did was kiss your cheek. But I don't know why you entertain him—you clearly belong to Asher, and Pádraig only touches you to piss him off."

"Belong...?" Hailey pulled her chin back, shaking her head. "I don't—"

"You think you have something special with Pádraig, but that's just his talent. Pádraig O'Shea makes every girl feel like they have something special with him—that's why so many end up naked in his room. He's just an asshole."

Hailey suddenly missed the time when Giselle wasn't talking to her and stared at the ground as they both walked outside.

"I thought you didn't want to talk to me," she said as Giselle turned toward the bookstore with Hailey.

"I don't, but Asher scares me."

"I don't understand," Hailey said, stopping mid-stride. "Did Asher tell you to talk to me?"

"No, he told me to make sure nothing happens to you."

"What does that mean?"

"It means," Giselle snarled as she plucked Hailey's shirt away from her skin with her finger and thumb, "if somebody decides to kill you or maim you or scratch you or...or..." Giselle grimaced at Hailey's sticky shirt. "Or coat you in goo, Asher will punish *me*."

Giselle scowled, releasing Hailey's shirt as they approached the Trinity Center.

"Why would anybody want to kill me?"

"You're annoying."

Hailey waited for the rest, which didn't come. "...and?"

"There's a price on your head, Hailey," she said, rolling her eyes as if Hailey should already know all of this. "A lot of non-humans hate Asher for various reasons, but mostly because they're afraid of him. They think they can wound him through you, and they'll risk his wrath, though I don't know why—Asher knows immediately when someone here does something evil, and he never forgives."

Hailey opened her mouth to ask about Asher, but Giselle cut her off.

"Oh, and humans just hate you because they're lemmings, and they see the non-humans avoiding you like the plague, so they avoid you too. Humans are idiots—why are you glazed?"

"I jumped into an in-between."

"That was stupid. Where do you think you're going now?" Giselle sounded like an irked mother.

"To the bookstore," Hailey said, for the first time realizing that Giselle was following her. "I need clothes and…" she sighed and kicked the ground. "…everything. Jaycen—the orientation leader—said she'd drive me into town later for some shopping, but…" Hailey sighed. "I have nothing here, and I want to get settled in, but I can't even get my books, because Fin never finished my schedule."

"I wouldn't count on Jaycen," Giselle said with a dark grunt. "And you don't need your schedule," she went on like a snob. "All ParaSci freshmen have the same classes. They'll have your list of materials at the bookstore, dumbass."

"Are you a ParaScience student too?"

"No."

"Are you a freshman?"

"No."

Conversations with Giselle just didn't flow, so Hailey tried another topic. "Do you know if Fi—if Pádraig is human?"

Giselle scoffed. "Barely."

"Do you know what LOED is?"

"It's a club for those who are stuck here."

"Where?"

"Earth!" Giselle barked, and Hailey could tell she was approaching her chat limit for the day…maybe the week.

Wait. Is Fin "stuck here"? What does that mean anyway? She hesitated to ask Giselle about Fin again.

"Are you stuck here?" What Hailey really wanted to ask was, "What the hell are you?" but she didn't want to be rude. Giselle shot her a dagger anyway.

"Stop asking me stupid questions."

"Okay," said Hailey, biting her lip, but she still had one more important one she just had to spit out. "What did you mean when you said I belong to Asher?"

Giselle stopped and grabbed Hailey's shoulder.

"You're joking, right? Don't you know anything about anything?"

Hailey blinked. She liked to think she did, but Giselle made her feel terribly...naïve.

"You *are* naïve," Giselle said, and Hailey gasped.

"Can you read my mind?"

"No," she said impatiently. "I can tell what you're feeling, though. It's written all over you." Giselle looked her up and down. "You're intrigued by Asher, but Asher doesn't care about you. He *possesses* you. And if you don't behave the way he wants, he'll kill you."

Looking away, Hailey shook her head in protest or denial—she wasn't sure which. Asher couldn't be the monster Giselle painted. He was strong and good and...and he was protecting Hailey from the real monster—the one that'd killed Holly. Hailey trusted him. He was just being...authoritative at Bear Towne. It was his university after all.

"You know, I've hardly seen him since I got here," she told Giselle reluctantly as they continued walking.

Giselle curled her lip. "Don't get all swoony over him because of the way he looks—any Envoy could look like that."

Hailey stopped. "What?"

"You didn't think it was weird that Asher looks an awful lot like James Dean?"

"Who?"

"Really?"

"I—"

"Stop. Listen." Giselle held her hand up, drew a loud, nasal breath, and put on her serious face. "Envoys can make whatever body they want. Most are so socially clueless they end up looking like death. Why should they spend their energy to keep an attractive body? They don't give a shit what people think, and they only see each other as balls of energy."

"Asher looks normal—better than normal, he—"

"That's the point. He shouldn't. Two decades ago, he didn't."

Giselle fell to her knees.

"What are you doing?" Hailey asked with a confused chuckle as she bent to help her roommate up, but instead of standing, Giselle fell onto her hands and pressed her forehead to the ground in a full-on grovel.

"Hello, Hailey," said a familiar, velvety voice.

Hailey turned to find Asher approaching. And he looked angry.

"Hi," Hailey breathed, and Giselle whimpered.

Chapter Twenty-Two

Tied in Knots

"It's necessary to have wished for death
in order to know how good it is to live."

— Alexandre Dumas, The Count of Monte Cristo

Asher flicked his stormy eyes at Hailey. "Would you excuse us?" he asked. It was more of an order than a request.

Hailey swallowed hard and nodded. "Of course," she said with a shaky voice, and Asher grasped Giselle by the arm, pulling her to her feet.

"Asher!" Hailey cried, her heart sinking horribly, and he hesitated without breaking his gaze at Giselle. Hailey shook her head, desperately searching for the words that would spare Giselle from his wrath.

"It's my fault! Giselle didn't do anything," Hailey begged, as a tear rolled down her cheek, and Asher shoved Giselle to the sidewalk.

Very slowly, he turned to Hailey, his eyes squinted and churning, and Hailey knew not to run from him, even as terror washed over her. She stood her ground and met his eyes as he squared up with her.

"Are you well, Hailey?" He gently brushed the tear from her cheek.

Hailey nodded, relieved he didn't direct his anger at her. "I'm just afraid for Giselle."

"You care for her, but she doesn't deserve your affection," he said tenderly. Then he smiled briefly and turned to Giselle, again snatching her up, this time by her ugly gray hair. "I'll return her in one piece," he promised, and then they both disappeared into thin air.

Asher sensed Jaycen's anxiety before he opened her door. Sure enough, Jaycen was there, wringing her hands inside her dorm room as she nervously paced in a three-foot square, no doubt rehearsing her petition. When Asher and Giselle stepped across the threshold, Jaycen fell to her knees at the Envoy's feet. She quivered there, all but dry heaving in terror until he addressed her.

"You've betrayed me, Jaycen. You've been consorting with the wicked humans. What do you have to say?"

Asher waited for her to regain her composure. He would hear her petition before he destroyed her. Seeing Hailey covered in plasma had ignited his rage, and though he yearned to rip Jaycen to shreds, he would honor the agreement he had with all non-humans at his university and give her a chance to defend herself.

"Jaycen," he said gently, "I've allowed you to remain here under my protection from them, and this betrayal is how you repay my kindness? You lured her into a place that would have killed her before I even knew she was in danger."

"I'm so sorry," Jaycen cried without looking up. "Those DOP-PLER men—they lied to me—they tricked me—it was supposed to be a benign in-between, I swear—they said they just wanted to get a bug on the girl—they just wanted to listen, that's all—she wasn't supposed to get hurt! It almost killed me too—please don't punish me…"

"I have no intention of punishing you, witch," Asher said calmly. "Your time on Earth is done."

"No!" Lifting her head, Jaycen glanced at Asher. "I can't leave my sisters with DOPPLER—they torture witches, Asher, please!" Jaycen looked to Giselle, who stood with her head down.

Asher shoved Jaycen's face to the floor. "Your sisters are wretches, and your soul is as black today as it was the morning you came to me on your hands and knees, begging for my protection."

"Hailey would understand," she sobbed. "She wasn't hurt— I pulled her earworm out—I saved her life, Asher—and you would have known if I meant to hurt her—you would have seen it coming," she tried, and though she was correct, Asher remained unimpressed, and Jaycen babbled on in desperation. "It doesn't make sense, they didn't want her dead—they wanted her alive and bugged so they could spy on you." She shook her head against the floor. "Someone... Someone changed the plan—switched the barrier breaker," she breathed. "I can find out who did it—I can find out who tried to kill her," she offered quickly, and Asher lifted his head.

Finally she'd said something he found valuable. The humans at DOPPLER would not have provoked Asher with such a blatant attack—Jaycen was correct, and they risked much in recruiting her to spy for them. Someone undoubtedly leveraged that risk to harm his girl. Such a scenario reeked of Cobon, but Asher had to be sure before confronting his oldest friend.

"You will find out," he told Jaycen through clenched teeth, "and then you will go to the cage. If you disobey me, if you even look at her, I will finish what I started here tonight."

"Thank you," she said eagerly, and Asher grimaced.

"Don't thank me, wretch."

"I'm not a wretch," she argued. "I still have my soul."

"Your soul barely clings to your body. Your wickedness has not abated; you've done nothing to rehabilitate yourself. Soon, your soul will flee, and you'll be a wretch like your sisters."

Jaycen listened unmoved, and Asher turned to Giselle.

"You know what to do, demon."

Giselle gnashed her sharp teeth, plunging her hands through Jaycen's chest and holding her soul down while Asher broke it and bent it and twisted it until it resembled something like a square knot.

And Jaycen screeched until she couldn't force air. Her soul writhed in agony that threw black bruises across her skin and pinpricks of blood through her pores.

"You will live in agony," he told her as he moved to the window. "Maybe in a few centuries, your soul will work itself loose, and if it does, I will—I promise—tie it tighter."

When he was through listening to Jaycen's intermittent sobs, he grasped Giselle by her stringy hair and left Jaycen lying on the floor of her room, alive but just barely.

Hailey left the bookstore with an armful of books, a lump in her throat, a box of vibrating crystals, a knot in her stomach, a pair of wellies, heartburn, Bear Towne sweat pants, and a horrible feeling that Giselle was being tortured. Aside from needing clothes, bedding, and every toiletry except for soap, she was ready for her first day of class.

Walking painfully slow and trying not to stick her tongue out as she moved, she managed to carry her stack up the Eureka Dorm stairs without dropping a thing. Even when Fin's latest concubine accidentally bumped her as she sashayed up to Fin's door, Hailey recovered and rebalanced her leaning tower of school books. She did however divert some of her concentration to survey his second girl of the day. This one had bright blue eyes and foot-long eyelashes. After the girl disappeared inside Fin's room, Hailey could hear her giggling through his door as she lingered in the vicinity, pretending to read his whiteboard, which showed:

Dinner then LOED – Back at 8pm

Balancing her stack of books on her knee, she freed a hand to unlock her door then bumped it open with her bum, scooting carefully inside as her crystals teetered precariously on the edge of the heap in her arms. Smiling proudly as she turned into her room, she was enormously relieved when nothing had fallen. It all looked so breakable.

"Oh my goodness!" Hailey jumped back and dropped the whole mess on the floor. In the corner of the ceiling over Giselle's bed hung a thick cocoon of spider webs. The blob inside stirred when Hailey's crystals shattered, and Hailey yelled louder, "Oh my goodness!"

Fin slid to a stop at her side almost instantaneously, while the eyelash girl waited several paces away, twirling her hair with her finger.

Hailey pointed to the web.

"L-Look!" she said, backing away in alarm. Surely the spider that created this web was huge and probably still inside her room, but Fin rolled his eyes.

"It's just Giselle," he said over his shoulder as he swaggered off. "Take a shower, Hailey, you smell like cat pee."

"My roommate's a giant spider," Hailey whispered to herself as she watched every step Fin took. *Giant spider*. He offered his arm to the eyelashes, which she of course took—*giant spider*—and he escorted her toward the stairs. Giant spider. Hailey stepped back and craned her neck—*giant spider*—to watch him walk for a half-second longer. *GIANT SPIDER!*

Hailey whipped her head around and looked at the cobwebs inside her room.

"Giselle?" she said, wrinkling her nose. "You alright?"

"No," came a stuffy-nosed, unalarmed voice from the corner, and Hailey hesitantly stepped over her broken, but still vibrating crystals, ducking and checking the ceiling corners as she crossed the threshold.

"Wha…ummm…" Hailey breathed heavy, her heart racing as she looked around the room. "Is there a giant spider in here?"

"No!" she answered loudly, and Hailey heaved a great sigh of relief as Giselle wriggled inside the cocoon.

"Do you need help getting out of that?"

"No!" Giselle yelled, becoming more agitated as Hailey lobbed questions at her.

"What did this to you?" Hailey asked, half-expecting her to say "Asher," and Giselle thrashed angrily inside her silky shroud until it ripped open. Coming loose from the ceiling, she floated gracefully down and sat, shoulders hunched on her bed.

"*Nothing* did this to me," said Giselle irritably with her back to Hailey. Then she sniffled.

"Are you crying?" Hailey moved to Giselle's bed. Tentatively, she reached her hand out, only hesitating for a moment before she softly patted her shoulder.

Giselle angrily shook her off and jerked her head up. "Don't touch me," she barked, and Hailey gasped.

"Are you crying cobwebs?" she said with a mix of shock and horror.

Giselle pulled a long string of silk from her eye, balled it up, and threw it on the floor.

"Oh, Giselle," Hailey breathed, stepping back. "You're crying cobwebs."

"Duh!"

"Sorry," Hailey said quickly. "I've never seen anyone cry cobwebs before," she told her roommate apologetically, and then she plopped on the bed beside her and threw her arm around Giselle's shoulder. "You want me to find you a hanky? …or one of those cobweb dusters? We'll need a big one," she said lifting her eyes to the ceiling, and she could have sworn Giselle let out a single giggle.

"Get away from me," she said, but not in her angriest voice, and Hailey slouched back to her own bed.

"I was afraid that I got you in trouble," she told Giselle.

"You did worse than that."

Hailey's heart sank. "What happened? Where did you guys go?"

"To punish Jaycen—he made me hold her soul down while he tied it, so I could feel her pain and her fear—he thinks it keeps me in line," she told Hailey, pulling another string from her eye. "He makes me help him with all his punishments—that's why everyone's afraid of me."

"How do you hold down a soul?" Hailey asked, mortified. "How do you *tie* a soul?" she said, with her hand to her heart, unable to imagine the agony.

Giselle didn't answer.

"I'm really sorry, Giselle," Hailey told her. "Is Jaycen alright?"

"Jaycen?" Giselle spat. "Who cares? She deserved it—she almost killed you, Hailey." Giselle wiped a ribbon of web from her chin and threw her hand out. "She's been here for years, and she doesn't even try to rehabilitate herself." She put her nose in the air and sniffed.

Hailey had no idea what she meant by "rehabilitate herself," and she wasn't sure she wanted to ask.

"She didn't try to kill me. I jumped into that in-between, and she actually helped me get rid of a tunneling earworm."

"She lured you, dumbass. She used a barrier breaker—

"What's a barrier breaker?"

"It's a bomb, you idiot. It tears the veil a little—it creates a temporary in-between. She opened a lethal one, knowing you'd come in after her. She only pulled out your earworm, because she's dead scared of Asher."

"Oh," said Hailey, clutching her stomach. "Why would she do that to me?" Taking a great breath, she tried not to think about suffocating inside a jellied in-between.

Giselle studied Hailey.

"I know why Asher claimed you," she said, her face softer than Hailey had ever seen it. "You ring with goodness. I can hear it over your broken crystals. It must remind him of the serenity inside the Aether—and you can't even imagine the wickedness inside Jaycen," she told her almost kindly. "Anybody can pretend to be a good person some of the time, but to rise like you do with nothing but good in your heart—it's very rare, Hailey. Even though everyone here avoids you, they all want to know you."

Giselle's crystal eyes sparkled beautifully, and Hailey could have sworn her hair showed flecks of gold.

Expecting the insult that was sure to follow all that, Hailey sat in silence for a good ten seconds before she realized that Giselle had just paid her a compliment.

"You stink," Giselle said, wearing her normal look of disgust again.

There it is, Hailey thought, and she shuffled off to the shower, careful to avoid the shards of vibrating crystals spread across the floor. Before bed, she gathered the pieces back into their box and pushed it into her closet. Giselle was already snoring on a bed of silk—on the ceiling—when Hailey reclined on her naked mattress. She shivered twice and drifted off.

In the morning, on the floor at the foot of her bed, Hailey stepped on an envelope someone had slipped under her door. Inside, she found her schedule and a note.

M-W-F 0800 ParaSci 110 – An Explanation of Strange—Olde Main Auditorium

M-W-F 0930 ParaSci 120 – Weights & Measures in 3 Realms – Olde Main R210

M-W-F 1100 ParaComm 100 – Human/ Non-Human Interaction – Trinity Ctr R3

Tues 0800 ParaSci Laboratory – First Year – Olde Main Lab 1

Section Lead: Asher. Office Location: Observatory

Thurs 0800 Music 101 – Harmony and the Aether – Edge Labs R1

That liar, she thought as she read her schedule. Fin knew exactly where to find Asher—he had an office inside the observatory. It was written in black and white on her schedule. Not that she would ever venture there without an invitation, but she wanted her photo of Holly back. She hastily unfolded the note:

My dearest Chowder Head--
Come find me in the a.m. Jaycen is asking for you.
Yours, Fin

She thought about what Giselle had told her the night before—that Jaycen was wicked and had tried to kill her. It would have been great to ask Giselle if she knew why Jaycen would want to see her, but she'd already gone. She must've tip-toed—or floated or maybe she just crawled across the ceiling for all Hailey knew, but she never made a sound when she left the room that morning before Hailey woke up.

She'd just have to rely on Fin's assessment.

Hailey had slept in her Bear Towne sweat pants, and after she opened her closet, she decided she'd wear them for the rest of the day too. There was no other option.

Her jellied jeans popped up to attention as soon as the closet door opened, and then they began pacing back and forth as if they were on patrol. Her jellied t-shirt had folded itself into a swan and cooed sleepily on its shelf. Meanwhile, her other pair of jeans, which had fallen into Alaskan bog water, had come out of the washer and dried into otherworldly cement. They now resembled a stone carving, and they were just as flexible as one too. Hailey couldn't bend them enough to get a foot inside and left them standing against the wall. She was afraid to put on her muskeg-jellied shoes, which quivered in the corner.

Thankfully, rain poured on Bear Towne that day, and Hailey grabbed her wellies while Tomas fixed her hair.

Outside Fin's door, Hailey listened for any suspicious giggling before she knocked. He answered straight away and closed his door quickly behind him, before Hailey could see inside.

"Morning," she said more like a question, and he nodded, grabbing her by the hand and practically dragging her down the stairs.

"All the clothes that went into the in-between with me have come to life," she told him right before she tripped down the stairs.

"Careful!" he yelled as he caught her.

"You're pulling me too fast, Fin, my legs can't keep up with your lightning speed," she said, smiling brightly as he held onto her.

Fin laughed heartily and shook his head. "I'm sorry."

"What are we running from?" she asked as he steadied her back to her feet, and then her face darkened. "Did your clothes come to life too?" Maybe he knew what to do about autonomous jeans.

"No, goofball. There's just an angry woman in my room."

"Oh," said Hailey, her playful smile vanishing.

Fin looked at her sideways, smiling as they made their way out the door and across the Bowl to Chinook for breakfast.

Neither of them said a word until they sat down to eat.

"Was that your girlfriend?" Hailey blurted, bursting the silence, and then she imagined slapping herself in the forehead.

"Who?" Fin asked, looking mighty smug as he shoveled a spoonful of scrambled eggs into his mouth.

"The girl..." Hailey sighed, dipping her head. "You know, the girl you were...with last night..." She couldn't even look at him as she said it.

"No, Hailey," he said sounding highly amused. "That was my dinner date. You're not jealous, are you?"

"What?" she said, scoffing loudly with *almost* believable disbelief. "No." She was absolutely jealous. "So, why is there an angry woman in your room?" she asked, trying to look convincingly focused on her pancakes.

"She wants a new roommate."

It was RA business. Hailey tried not to sound as relieved as she felt.

"Oh."

"Badly."

"Oh?"

"Apparently you're impossible to live with…"

"Oh!" Hailey's jaw dropped. She thought she and Giselle were getting along fine!

"'Impossibly annoying.' I think that's how Giselle put it," he said, chewing his bacon. "Probably because you talk to her—she can't stand humans. And when I told her she'd have to ask Asher, she went all exorcist on me."

"I do talk to her a lot," Hailey pondered, pushing the food around on her plate.

"Yeah, that would do it."

"And then I hugged her last night…" Hailey said, ducking her head, and Fin choked on his coffee.

"Gross," he muttered. "Well, congratulations, Hailey," he said, getting up. "Your roommate hates you."

Hailey stared at her plate.

"Let's go," Fin said impatiently. "And I hope you washed your hands after you touched that thing."

Hailey hung her head. She actually liked her roommate from Hell.

"Where are we going?" she asked, almost absently, as she imagined the loneliness of living without a roommate.

"To see Jaycen."

"Oh, I don't know if I should go see her," she said, shrugging one shoulder. "Giselle said she—"

Hailey couldn't bring herself to say Jaycen tricked her into jumping into a glazed in-between, so she stared at her plate instead.

"Relax," said Fin standing over her. He rubbed her shoulders and brought his head next to hers. "She just wants to apologize," he said softly, and his cheek brushed hers.

Hailey turned slightly, and he didn't move away. His lips were so close to hers, it made her heart pound.

"Huh?" she said dreamily, and Fin stood up, smiling and very obviously pleased with himself.

"Come on," he said, kicking her chair. "Let's get this over with."

"What if she gets into more trouble for talking to me?" Hailey dragged her feet as Fin pulled her toward the door.

"I don't think that's possible."

Chapter Twenty-Three

Orientation

"The less we deserve good fortune. the more we hope for it."

— Lucius Annaeus Seneca

Fin used his master key to unlock Jaycen's door. They found her lying on the floor, covered in a film of blood and writhing in agony.

"Oh—thank goodness—you came, Pádraig—you have—to help me," she breathed, her voice hitching. She pulled her knees to her chest in a tight hug and wailed.

Hailey stood by the door, wringing her hands as they spoke.

"I brought Hailey, Jaycen," he said unmoved by her pleas. "… so that you can apologize…" he added when she didn't respond.

"I will," she moaned. "After you untie my soul…okay?"

"Are we forgetting you drove a wooden stake through my heart?"

"That was so long ago, I can't even believe you're bringing it up," Jaycen muttered into the floor, as she heaved and arched. Then she curled herself into the fetal position.

"That was two years ago," Fin corrected. "You know how long it takes a heart to work a splinter out? I'll give you a hint. It's longer than two years."

Jaycen let out a howl. "Pádraig, you have to help me."

"Alright," he said sarcastically. "Go to church and learn how to be a good person."

"I am a good person," she said sharply, rolling onto her back and letting out guttural moan.

"No," Fin countered. "You act like a good person. You need to learn how to actually *be* one. And when you figure that out, your soul will untie itself."

"I can't," she cried. "It hurts too much!"

"Then I guess you're screwed," he said, devoid of sympathy. "Bye-bye, Jaycen."

Fin took Hailey's hand and pulled her out the door.

"Well, that was a colossal waste of time," he told her. "Sorry—I should've known, but I thought I'd give her a chance to help herself by confessing and apologizing." He squeezed Hailey's hand. "Alright, let's go."

Hailey stood frozen outside Jaycen's door. "Fin, I'm just not sure she lured me into that thing," Hailey said. "I mean, I jumped in all by myself to help her. She couldn't have known I would do that."

"Look, Hailey," Fin said, taking her hands and looking her in the eye. "Jaycen is a very manipulative person, and she's a skilled student. She should've extracted herself immediately from that thing."

Hailey still wasn't convinced, and Fin could see it in her eyes.

He pointed emphatically at Jaycen's door. "Jaycen is a monster. She saw you coming, and she knew you'd try to save her—Hailey, she told me all this, and she deserved what she got."

"You don't think Asher was a little hard on her?"

"I actually agree with Asher," Fin said, reluctantly.

"What?"

"Hailey, Jaycen's soul is black. She's lucky it's still with her. Asher saved her life by tying her up. Now, she has no choice but to tend to her soul. He's saving her from an eternity in Hell."

"It's just..." Hailey shook her head. "If Asher punishes everyone that talks to me, I'll never have any friends here."

"You got me," he suggested.

"You talk to me all the time," she observed. "How come he doesn't punish you?"

Fin cast a half-smile at her and winked.

"Oh!" Hailey's hand flew to her lips. "He does!" she gasped. "Only you heal fast—oh, I'm so sorry!"

"No worries, Hailey," he said with an air of someone who truly didn't care. "Totally worth the searing pain. Besides, Asher is an ass, and it pisses him off royally when I don't do what he says." He laughed, and Hailey tried to smile as they made their way back to Eureka, but she was just sick.

"I'm surprised you still talk to me."

"Don't worry, Hailey," Fin said coolly. "Asher and I have a gentleman's agreement now—so, no more punishments for talking to you."

"What's the agreement?"

"We agreed not to tell you," he said mysteriously.

"Why?"

"Don't worry about it, okay?" he said soothingly. "He does still get into my head sometimes, though," Fin continued, more seriously.

"What do you mean?"

"I mean, I'll be doing something he strongly disapproves of, and then before I know it, I'm driving through Montana wondering why I left you after Holly's funeral." He opened Eureka's door and waved her in.

Pausing in the doorway, Hailey looked at him with an openmouthed frown.

"He made you leave me?"

Fin shrugged. "I told you. He's an ass."

"Did Asher ever tie your soul?" asked Hailey heavily, and she pressed her hands to her stomach.

"No, actually," Fin said, raising his eyebrows. "He untied it—well, he taught me how to untie it—it was years ago—probably sorry he ever did too," he said, his eyes sparkling with mischief. "Don't get me wrong, Hailey, he's a monster, but he has done a few good deeds during his time on Earth," he said grudgingly.

Still Hailey held her stomach.

"Hey," he said, bumping her shoulder as they came to Eureka. "Why so glum?"

"Who tied your soul, Fin?"

"Adalwolf," he said simply. He opened his mouth to say something she couldn't wait to hear, but he snapped it shut again when they reached the third floor landing. Jaw set, he surveyed his broken door and glanced inside his room.

Stooping to peek under his shoulder, Hailey saw what looked like the aftermath of a grenade blast where Fin's room should have been.

"Giselle!" he yelled, his face going red, and Giselle sulked, arms folded into the hallway to meet him.

"What?" she barked.

Fin pointed at his door, which hung crooked, attached to the frame by one hinge.

"Fix that door," he said to her through clenched teeth, and then he pointed inside his room. "And clean up that mess."

"No," she said, crossing her arms again like a spoiled brat.

Fin grabbed her by her ear, and she whimpered.

"Do you want to spend another semester in the cage?" he threatened.

"No!" she yelled back at him, still sounding slightly petulant.

"Then fix that mess, go to your room, sit on your bed, and read your magazine."

"Fine!" she spat, and Fin let her go.

Giselle stomped inside Fin's room, and Hailey had no idea how, but she created a small tornado. Standing in the center of it, Giselle lifted her arms as her gray hair whipped around in all directions. When she dropped her arms again, the wind died, and Fin's room was back in order. On her way out, she kicked the door, which creaked and cracked and righted itself onto its hinges.

"Good job," Fin said like an impatient father. "Now get the hell out of here, Satan."

He turned to Hailey as Giselle stormed off.

"Holy crap," Hailey breathed.

"I know. She's a pain in the ass."

"What the heck is she?" Hailey demanded. "And what's the cage?"

"She's a bitch," he said, angrily, "and there's a cage in the White Forest for non-humans who act like animals. It's literally a metal cage. They hate it. You know," he said, looking apologetic, "I tried to get you a normal roommate, but Asher thought it would be safer for you to room with a monster than a human. And by the way, he wants to see you."

"Really?" Hailey asked.

"Yeah…" Fin's voice trailed off, and he looked past Hailey to the stairwell, smiling warmly.

Turning, Hailey found yet another beautiful woman making her way toward Fin's room.

"Melody," he said, pushing past Hailey to hug a voluptuous redhead.

"Pádraig," she sang, thrusting her chest out when he stepped back.

Hailey cleared her throat, but they both ignored her and started down the stairs, chattering like little old ladies.

"Oh, but…" Her words dissolved into a sigh as Fin moved out of earshot, leaving Hailey with no idea if she was supposed to go find Asher or if he would come find her or what. But she sure didn't want to wait. Her list of questions about Bear Towne and the Envoys and ParaScience grew by the second, and Asher held answers to all of them.

Remembering the observatory was off limits to students, she figured she'd better just stick to her orientation schedule. That way, she wouldn't miss any important Bear Towne information, and Asher would know exactly where to find her.

When Hailey opened her dorm room door, her one pair of sneakers—which had tapped out a flail-beat and secured her escape from the vacuum-glazed in-between—stood waiting. As soon as she stepped inside, the sneakers jumped up, ran into the hallway, pattered down the stairs, and fled out the door.

Looking longingly after them, she sighed heavily and closed her door. Now she had to wear sweat pants and rubber boots until she found a ride into town. Hopefully, Asher wouldn't mind seeing her dressed like a clown.

"Oh…" she moaned, cringing inside as she imagined it.

Checking her closet, she found her glazed pants still on patrol, while her glazed t-shirt played solitaire on a tall shelf.

"Where'd you get a deck of cards?" she said, and the t-shirt shrugged.

Her box of broken crystals had gone—who knows where—and Giselle sat, reclined on her bed in silence behind her magazine.

Hailey reviewed her orientation schedule for the day. Even if she didn't see Asher, the afternoon promised to be interesting with a group lunch scheduled at the Bruised Moose Café following a slew of bizarre orientation seminars at the Trinity Center, which she couldn't wait to hear.

Hailey made her way into the seminar room and sat in a back corner just as the sky over Bear Towne opened up and unleashed a torrential downpour. Other students filed in. Some she recognized from the ParaScience campus tour, but they all sat at least five seats away from her in all directions.

The Pre-Med group began the day's seminar with a presentation on staying healthy and a stark reminder that Hailey wasn't in Pittsburgh anymore.

"Remember," said the too-groomed man at the front of the room, "Bear Towne hospital is a teaching hospital that treats humans and non-humans alike, which sometimes leads to inadvertent mix-ups. Now," he said holding up a superior finger as his nose also went in the air, "despite the rumors, we haven't had an accidental transmutation in almost a decade."

"Thank you, Professor Starr," said an equally well-groomed, but younger man, who ushered the professor out of the way and took over the presentation.

"Bottom line—" he told them, "I've got three reasons to NOT end up at Bear Towne Hospital. Dr. Starr already mentioned the transmutations," he said holding up his thumb. He added a finger at each increasingly horrific reason to stay away from campus health care.

"Second—and this is no rumor—the hospital has a resident banshee, who doesn't always follow the prescribed treatment plans—if you know what I mean," he said with a nervous laugh to a roomful of crickets.

Hailey tried not to look as shocked as she felt. Honestly, Professor Starr had her at "transmutation." Everything after that was fodder for nightmares.

"Also," he continued, "there has been an increased incidence of flesh-eating Zombitis among patients treated in the emergency room."

"So, do what you need to do to stay healthy, because there's no telling if you'll come out of the campus hospital in better or worse shape than when you entered."

Campus safety for humans was next. The student handbook laid out most of the information on Bear Towne's predators, but Hailey did take a few notes from the I-MET worker, who marched to the front of the room wearing a presidential mask—Reagan it looked like. For instance, she had no idea you could use a shotgun to kill mosquitos. Also, the colored flag atop the Trinity Center indicated the mosquito climate for the day, with green meaning a low concentration of blood suckers (usually due to high winds); yellow meaning no amount of DEET will protect you, and red meaning grab the shotgun.

Things wrapped up with the campus priest blessing the freshmen and reminding everyone to tend to their soul—go to church, be nice, and don't kill anyone, was his advice.

Seemed easy enough.

With that, a very hungry Hailey collected her notes and headed to the Bruised Moose Café for lunch, where she was delighted to find Giselle sitting alone at a table next to the windows.

"Hi," Hailey beamed, having forgotten completely that she'd vowed to keep to herself.

Without even looking at Hailey, Giselle pushed her chair back and bolted out of the café. A mass exodus of every patron followed. And then the cooks dropped their spatulas and hurried away, leaving Hailey in the middle of a very large, very empty Bruised Moose.

Suddenly, she didn't feel like food. Not that she could have ordered a delicious-smelling cheesesteak anyway. The place was deserted. Shoulders hunched, and head low, she slouched toward the exit. Only after taking a few steps did she realize someone stood just inside the café door.

"Asher," she said, smiling—mostly because she was glad to see him, but partly because it wasn't she who had emptied the Bruised Moose.

"How are you enjoying my university?" he asked in his very kind way, unfazed by the sudden emptiness of the entire café.

"It's great," Hailey answered with zero enthusiasm, and Asher tilted his head. "Actually," she said, looking away, "I'm an outcast—you've made—" She sighed, motioning to the emptiness. "Everyone's afraid to talk to me."

Asher closed the distance between them and lifted Hailey's chin. "Those who look for a reason to fear will find one, and those without reason will follow," he said. That was what Giselle had told her. Kinda. Asher put things much more eloquently. "I believe you'll feel at home once you've met my more seasoned students."

He held Hailey's gaze, and she felt he was searching for something.

"What is it?" she said, and he broke his stare to look at her lips.

"We must talk," he said darkly, and Hailey's smile vanished. He placed her photo of Holly into her hand, moving his thumb against her skin in a gentle caress before stepping away.

"Thank you for holding this," she said, her voice uncertain. Then she turned to the window and wondered how she'd get it back to Eureka without ruining it in the rain.

Asher must have sensed her distress, because he gave her a knowing grin. "There's a better way than through the rain," he told her. "I'll show you, but you must eat, Hailey. I can see you're weak with hunger."

Whatever Asher had to say must be pretty bad if he didn't want her to hear it on an empty stomach, she figured, frowning.

"Mitch," Asher called, and a tall, bug-eyed man tottered from the shadows. "Would you prepare your signature sandwich for Hailey?"

Mitch grabbed his spatula, twirled it in the air, and smacked it on the grill.

"You got it, boss."

Hailey's stomach growled. It sure looked and smelled like a cheesesteak. Wrapping it in foil, Mitch handed it to a delighted Hailey.

"Thanks, Mitch."

"Anytime, Miss Hailey," he answered, pointing his spatula at her and winking.

"This way," said Asher, taking her by the hand. He led her to a stairwell, and down they went until they reached an underground landing.

Tapping a switch on the wall, Asher lit four corridors leading away from the stairs at 90-degree angles. They were so long, Hailey couldn't see an end to them.

"Many of the buildings here are connected by an underground tunnel system," he told her, and her face lit up. "It's especially popular in the winter."

Carved wooden signs with arrows indicated which corridor a student should take to get to the hospital, for example. Olde Main, the Library, and Eureka showed on another sign, which pointed down the tunnel in front of them.

After nervously walking hand-in-hand with Asher for too many quiet seconds, Hailey decided to break the ice. "Has Giselle asked you if she could have a new roommate?"

"She hasn't," he said with curiosity.

"She doesn't like me very much…"

"Yes, you have made quite an impression on her, but I don't believe it's negative," he told her. "Giselle fears rejection above all else. She's never known the sisterly affection you show her. I believe she's rather fond of you," said Asher, and Hailey pulled her brow together.

"If she is fond of me, she hides it well," she said. "What is she?"

"When she's ready, she'll tell you."

Hailey turned her attention to an unmarked side passage, slowing her gait to peer curiously into it.

"Dangerous things lurk in the darkness of these tunnels, Hailey," Asher said. "Always turn on the lights, and *never* stray from the main corridors."

A low growl rumbled from the blackness inside that passage, and Hailey's breath caught.

"Keeping you safe requires much effort," Asher sighed, gently tugging her hand. Then he paused to study her. "I wonder if I shouldn't lock you away," he said, his eyes tracing Hailey's hairline as he ran his fingers across it. "I would put you someplace where no one could touch you."

Hailey yanked her hand from his.

"Lock me away?" she said, her voice rising. "Asher, I'm not your prisoner here--and you don't own me—I'm not your possession—I'm your…your student," she said more offended than angry…and a little scared. Now that she was at Bear Towne and thousands of miles away from her uncles, no one would help if Asher went all *Beauty and the Beast* and locked her away. She gave him a good old-fashioned, angry, Irish stare.

"You provoke many things inside me, Hailey," he said, his eyes flashing, and she could tell he struggled to keep his voice even as he clenched his fist.

Hailey's heart raced, but she stood her ground, betting that despite what Giselle had told her, Asher would never hurt her no matter how she behaved. She could probably prove it.

"I will protect you, but you mustn't defy me," he warned, and she met his intimidating gaze.

"I *will* defy you, Asher. If I need to."

Asher squinted briefly, but then the fire inside his eyes died.

Dipping her chin, Hailey studied her feet as her heart rate came down.

"I can handle this place. I've already proven that I can escape a killer in-between, right?" she said, her eyes dancing around the tunnel. "I mean, I've survived for eighteen years. I think I can handle four more."

"You had five Guardians for eighteen years," he told her.

She furrowed her brow for a moment before realizing he must mean her uncles.

"And now I have you," she countered.

That made him smile.

"Don't ever lock me away, Asher," she said slowly, stealing a glance at him as they approached the stairwell to Eureka, and he seemed to be thinking about it.

"You would forgive me in time," he concluded without looking at her.

Hailey shook her head. He needed to stop this. Now. There was no way she'd ever belong to anyone.

"No, I don't think I would," she said, sounding appalled. She looked him up and down as she gathered her courage. "And I would *never* love you."

Nauseous, she turned on her heel and trudged up the stairs.

Asher stared after his girl, furious, remorseful, alarmed, and altogether unsure if he would allow her the freedom to defy him again. It was as if he had had her in the palm of his hand not ten minutes ago only to let her slip from his grip.

He wanted her back. He wanted her happy. And he had no idea how to manipulate her—she simply would not obey him.

These circumstances—these *feelings*—required a keen understanding, which he did not possess. But he knew who did, and he appeared inside the office of his friend, Simeon Woodfork, hell bent on finding answers.

"Ah, Asher," Simeon said as soon as he noticed the Envoy standing pensively at the window inside his office. "How can I be of service?"

"The girl is…" Asher struggled to choose the proper word. "…difficult," he decided.

"Hm? Yes. All the good ones are," Simeon remarked in an offhand way.

"Explain this to me."

Simeon straightened up. "I'm sorry, Asher, what would you like me to explain?" he asked, and Asher left the window, preferring instead to peruse the professor's collection of books.

"I cannot control her, Simeon," he said flatly and his eyes found the title they'd sought. Pulling it off the shelf, he skimmed a page near the center of the book.

Simeon clutched his chest.

"Good Lord. Are you in love?" He pointed to *The Indispensable Collection of Love Poems*, which Asher held in his hands.

"I think of little else," he realized. "And I fear I've lost her affection even as others compete for her favor."

"Good Lord," Simeon breathed again, holding tight to his desk as he watched Asher with bulging eyes.

Ignoring Woodfork's display, Asher concentrated instead on the literature in his hands. Humans had loved for thousands of years. Surely one of them had written down the methods and techniques required to win a woman's affection.

After several seconds of shocked silence, Simeon cleared his throat. "Tell me, Asher, why is it you believe you've lost the girl's affection—I assume you mean Miss Hartley?"

Asher looked up from his book. "She pulled her hand from mine in anger and walked away," he recalled. "She told me she would never love me."

"Oh, dear," said Simeon. "Surely something preceded this sudden departure...?"

"I offered to lock her away...to keep her safe," he reasoned, and Simeon raised his eyebrows.

"Forgive me, Asher, but are you so willing to lock her away because you wish to protect her from harm? Or is it because you wish to hide her from another suitor?"

For a moment, Asher considered this, but then he returned his attention to the book.

"I see no difference," he said.

Woodfork drew a breath to speak but seemed to rethink his words and pressed his lips together.

Asher scowled at the book.

"There are no instructions in here," he said with a level voice, even as he furiously flipped and scanned the pages of poetry. Stopping at one, his finger traced a passage.

If love were what the rose is,
And I were like the leaf,
Our lives would grow together—

"These are nothing more than riddles," he concluded and slammed the book shut.

"I'm afraid there are no great answers in any of these," Simeon said, waving at the shelves. "Just a collection of hopes and laments…and some joys."

With that, the professor turned away and pulled from the shelf a well-worn copy of *The Hunchback of Notre-Dame*. Placing it in Asher's hands, he said, "Read this one, my friend. In it, you may find some enlightenment."

Asher studied the professor. "You once loved a woman who adored you, I remember her well. How did you win her heart?" he asked, squinting slightly as he searched Simeon's mind.

"That was long ago," the professor sighed, turning to the candle he kept lit on his desk. "I'm afraid there's nothing I can tell you. Besides, we both know how that ended." Pinching the wick between his finger and thumb, he snuffed out the flame, wiping his eyes before turning again.

"If I may be so bold," Simeon said politely. "Perhaps you should ask Miss Hartley out. On a date."

Chapter Twenty-Four

Locked Out

"God is the supreme humorist.
and it is his divine sense of humor that we
men call fate."

— Evan Esar

As Hailey grabbed her tiny towel, soap, and shampoo (she didn't have any fresh clothes to change into), Giselle brushed past her and glided out the door without uttering a word or even glancing in her direction.

At least she's a quiet snob, Hailey thought, as she stepped across the hall and claimed the corner shower.

The stall was divided into two parts with a partition separating the actual shower from the changing section. Hailey undressed and hung her towel on the hook nearest the shower. Grabbing her soap, she turned on the water and let a high-pressure blast of warmth envelope her.

She showered fast, but when she opened the shower door and reached for her tiny towel all she felt was an empty hook.

Her clothes were missing, too.

The steam from her shower lifted quickly, and Hailey shivered as droplets of water fell from the ends of her hair, trickling down her back.

Panic-stricken, she peeked out the stall door. The whole room was empty. No sign of students or towels or clothes or shoes or *anything* she could use to cover herself. It took at least a minute of shivering inside the stall to work up enough courage to venture out.

Covered in goose bumps, she wondered if she should just throw an arm over her boobs and make a run for her room.

She poked her head into the girl's hallway. It was empty, and her room was only a couple of steps away. Hugging one arm across her chest, she bolted across the hall and slammed against her door.

"Giselle," she called as she jiggled the handle. "Unlock the door!"

She twisted the knob again, but it didn't budge.

Crap.

When the door on the ground floor screeched open, Hailey pinged back to the shower room, only to find that door locked too. Feet, lots of feet were trudging into Eureka, and the laundry room door wouldn't budge either. As the hollow chatter of at least five students entered the stairwell, Hailey felt a panic brewing and was running out of private time.

Swimming across the ceiling and wearing Hailey's Bear Towne sweats, a wispy, Picasso-faced female poltergeist pointed and laughed.

"Oh, you little brat," Hailey sputtered.

Dripping and shivering, she made a mad, naked dash for Fin's door and stood pressed against it, knocking frantically. He'd have a towel and the master key that would open her room.

"Fin!" Hailey hissed against a vibrating door.

Guitar music, so loud it reverberated in her chest, answered.

She looked over her shoulder and tried beating his door with an open palm.

"Fin!" she begged. "Open the door!"

More students were coming upstairs, and they were getting closer.

She pounded on the door with her fist.

"Fin!"

The music stopped abruptly.

The latch clicked, and the door flung open just as a gaggle of students reached the third floor.

Hailey fell into Fin's room, head-first, buck-naked, and soaking wet. Trying to cover her body the best she could with her tiny hands, she scooted out of the doorway and pressed herself against the inside wall.

"Well, hello, Hailey," Fin announced in a smooth voice as he pushed the door shut.

"Avert your eyes!"

Stifling a laugh, he turned around. "To what do I owe the pleasure of your nakedness?"

"A poltergeist. Little brat took my towel, locked me out of my room, and then it locked me out of the shower—could I borrow a towel, please?"

He reached for one off of the top of his dresser, balled it up, and flung it under his arm without looking.

"Thanks," she said, wrapping it around herself. "May I please borrow a shirt?"

He picked up his closest shirt and threw it. It was some sort of hockey jersey, and it had his name on it.

She pulled it over her head and stuck her arms through the sleeves. The thing was huge on her, coming down to her knees like a dress. And it was itchy.

Squirming inside his shirt, she cracked his door open. "How long do you think they'll be out there?" she asked, closing it again.

"All night?" he guessed in a way-too-hopeful voice.

"I can't go out there like this! They'll think I was naked in here." She gave him a condemning glance over her shoulder. "And from what I've gathered, a lot of naked girls come in your room, Fin."

He swallowed a laugh in his throat.

"What?" Hailey insisted. "Oh," she said, disapproving of him. Of course his mind went straight to the gutter. "You're a juvenile."

Plopping on his recliner, he put his feet up.

"You're welcome to stay here," he said, smiling widely with his hands laced behind his head.

"Right," she muttered, her eyes desperately searching for another way out.

His room was huge. One of the perks of being the RA was that he lived in a suite with a private bathroom. In addition to the recliner (Fin looked extremely satisfied sitting there), there was a couch facing a giant TV. In the corner sat his bed, neatly made with a fluffy blanket on top. He had a big desk and a book shelf against the wall next to his bathroom. Another door, a closet maybe, stood closed beside the bathroom. Everything was neat, clean, and orderly. Surprisingly, he was a good housekeeper.

"I didn't know you played," she said, pointing at the Fender next to his bed.

"Yeah," he said, "have for many, many, many years." He was smirking and stifling yet another laugh, but at least he wasn't looking her up and down. She hadn't shaved her legs in months and was desperately embarrassed he'd notice. Hailey tugged the hockey shirt down as far as she could get it, but it wasn't far enough to cover her tarantula legs. "Hand me your pants," she said, nodding to a stack of laundry on top of his dresser.

Jumping up, Fin popped the button on his jeans.

"Don't be a jerk!"

"Relax, woman," he said, holding his hands up, and then he lobbed a pair of sweats at her. "I was kidding."

Hailey caught the giant sweats with one hand and pulled at the collar of the jersey with the other. It was really itchy. And the emblem was a bear—the university's team, maybe?

"Why do you have this?" she asked.

"It's my hockey jersey."

"You play hockey?"

"A little." He looked at her as if she should already know all this.
"You any good?"

"I can hold my own," he said, sounding offended.

"You worked in the pub all spring," Hailey brought up as she handed him back his towel. "Will they let you play this season?"

"Uh...yeah."

"You must be pretty good."

"I'm phenomenal."

"And humble," Hailey pointed out.

Fin poked his tongue into his cheek, and Hailey peeked out the door again.

Without warning, Fin grabbed the door from her grip, threw it open, and pushed her into the hallway using both hands.

She grabbed at the sweatpants, which were way too big to stay up without help and fell off her hips as she shuffled unwillingly into a gaggle of her classmates.

Fin lowered his chin and pointed at Hailey. "When you're all done cuddling with my jersey," he said loud enough for the whole floor to hear, "you can bring it back." Then he slammed his door.

Hailey looked around, mortified...and still locked out of her room.

Curling up on the floor against her door, she hoped her roommate would reappear before morning. Class started at 0800, and it wasn't until ten minutes before the hour that she heard footsteps approach.

She didn't look up as she sat with her knees pulled to her chest, head resting on them, until the feet stopped right in front of her.

And it wasn't Giselle. It was Fin. With Hailey sitting directly under him, he pulled a skeleton key from his pocket, shoved it in the lock, and pushed open the door. He looked down at her without backing up, and Hailey had to wrench her neck to see him.

"I'll have my jersey back now," he said.

She scooted away from him on her bum and stood slowly, unbelievably stiff after spending a very cold, very itchy night crunched up on the hard wooden floor. Hobbling into her room and without uttering a word, she closed the door in his face.

He could wait for his impossibly itchy jersey.

Giselle's bed and the ceiling above it lay empty, but Tomas greeted her by urgently tapping the back of his wrist.

"I know, I know," said Hailey as she frantically searched her room. "Where are my books?" Not only were her books missing, but her backpack was gone too, along with her boots.

Tomas shrugged. He flew out of the mirror and did his best to wrestle her crazy hair into a braid while she pulled on her socks. He'd only just finished pinning back a stray frizzy with a sparkly barrette when she dashed out the door in stocking feet, using both hands to hold up Fin's sweat pants.

Bounding down the stairs three at a time, she slapped the switch in the tunnels and sprinted across the rough-cut stone floor toward Olde Maine, arriving only a minute or two late and just as Professor Woodfork was writing "Envoy History" on the blackboard.

Holding onto her gigantic pants and breathing way too loudly to sneak into the auditorium unnoticed, she snapped her mouth shut and went to all nasal huffing as she nudged open the auditorium door. The latch was silent. The hinges, however, unleashed a screech that Uncle Pix probably heard all the way in Pittsburgh.

Everyone, human and human-looking non-human alike, turned to see who dared come late to the first class of the semester.

Slinking inside with her head ducked, Hailey put her butt into the first open seat in her path, shamefaced and still panting. It wasn't until she sat down that she realized she'd stepped on a wasp, or at least that's what it felt like.

As discretely as she could, she pulled her foot onto her lap and found it bleeding through her sock. Pushing her sock down, she surveyed the damage. It looked like a pretty good gash. Hoping to stop the bleeding, she pressed her sock against it. What else was she going to do with her hands? She didn't have a pen or paper or a book to occupy them.

"Uh...continuing," said Dr. Woodfork once Hailey was seated and the class once again turned their attention to the front of the auditorium.

"Over three thousand years ago, a man with no unnatural powers tore a hole in the barrier between the Earth and the Aether—no one knows how he did it, but we do know why. He, like all men, coveted power. He sought to steal the energies of the Aether and wield them as one might a nuclear weapon. What he didn't know was that the energy in the Aether was not there just floating freely, waiting to be plucked like a flower from a garden. Rather, the energies were kept by beings called Envoys.

"Now, an Envoy's purpose in the universe is to shuttle life energies out of those who die and in to those who are born—" Dr. Woodfork paused when a hand went up.

"A question. Yes, Mr. Lorn."

"What about God? Where does God fit in?"

"Good question. Your life energy is not the same as your soul, you see."

He slid a chalkboard out of the way to reveal a clean one behind it. There he drew three circles and connected them with lines to make a triangle.

"There are three realms," he said, and he pointed to one of them. "One realm is the Earth, where physical things, like your body, exist. That's where we are right now, we're on Earth, obviously. The second—" he moved his hand over another circle, "—is the heavens, a home for your soul. This is where your soul comes from...and where your eternal soul ends up. It is God and Heaven, if you behave, or fire and brimstone if you don't. The third realm—" he moved his hand to the third circle, "—is the Aether, home of life energy—the energy which binds your soul..." He pointed to the Heavens with his right hand. "...to your body." With his left hand he pointed to the Earth.

"Does that answer your question? Yes? Good."

He slid the three realms out of the way.

"When the barrier between the Earth and the Aether was breeched, energy flowed from the place of high concentration—the Aether—to the place of low concentration—the Earth. In effect, the Earth was a giant suction and the Envoys who were near the great tear, were sucked through the barrier and flung onto Earth. No one knows how many Envoys crossed over, but there were at least seven and maybe as many as a hundred.

"For the remainder of the term, we are going to talk about the history and science surrounding this phenomenal event and come up with our own theories as to how a man with no unnatural charms, did the impossible and tore the barrier. Any questions?"

A hand went up.

"Yes, Miss Watters."

"Does my soul leave my body when I dream?"

"No. Your body and soul are bound. It's also a phenomenon, really, but try to think of it as your soul's mind wandering along the border between realms."

Hailey's hand shot up.

"Yes, Miss Hartley."

"What happened to all these Envoys after they came here? Where do they all…live?" If that's what you called it.

"Anywhere they want. Anybody else? No? Continuing, then—"

"Well, Professor," Hailey persisted, "where are they all?"

Dr. Woodfork sighed heavily.

"A good question for your laboratory period, Miss Hartley. Continuing then…" Dr. Woodfork flicked the switch on what looked like a document camera.

Nothing happened.

He flipped it again. And again. Then he tapped it with his pen, and when the thing jittered, half the class cringed, with several students letting out a whimper.

Hailey giggled. This was nothing compared to life with Giselle. And the thing merely threw an image on the screen anyway.

Woodfork cleared his throat.

"There is a theory," he began, "that if a man had a sufficient amount of energy, from a very large stick of dynamite, for example, he could force the flow of energy to reverse in case of another tear in the barrier, so that an Envoy might escape the pull of the Earth and return to his home in the Aether."

He drew a picture of a crude cartoon explosion, and some of the students snickered, but Woodfork continued unabashed.

"Over the centuries, many of the Envoys have attempted to tear the barrier to get back home, but none have succeeded. In fact, this university was founded with the express intent of piercing the veil between the realms."

Woodfork clapped his hands together and turned on the lights. "Now then, let's hear some of your theories on how a man did the impossible and tore the barrier in the first place. Who wants to start?"

The room went dead silent.

Looking at his watch, he sighed his disappointment. "We're almost out of time anyway. Questions anybody? Yes. Miss Hartley."

She couldn't believe nobody'd asked the obvious and winced slightly as she shifted her foot.

"Dr. Woodfork, could the tear still exist?"

The professor blinked. "What did you say?"

"The original tear in the barrier—you said it's impossible to tear the barrier. Could it be that nobody *tore* it? Is it possible that this man simply found a flap or a...a door that already existed? And if so, wouldn't there still be a flap in that very spot? Maybe it's more a matter of precision than explosive force..."

Dr. Woodfork's jaw opened, and he stared at her thoughtfully for several uncomfortable seconds.

Hailey shifted in her seat.

"Now, well, that's very interesting…" his voice trailed off as he gazed into the distance.

"Ah, here they are," he said, blinking rapidly as four gentlemen made their way to the front of the auditorium. Woodfork nodded to them.

"I would like to introduce your Section Leads. Overseeing Section Two's practical lab is Rakesh."

Looking far too young to be a grad student, a man with jet black hair and flawless bronze skin waved unenthusiastically from the aisle.

Behind him, walking with a familiar swagger and holding his metal coffee cup, Fin turned to face the class when he reached the front of the room.

"Of course, this is Pádraig, who will head up Section Three."

An excited murmur rose from the audience with some students clapping and others proudly gushing that they were in his section.

There were five sections in all with a stern-looking Boris standing to represent Section Four and a smiling Zhang Wei heading up Section Five. Professor Woodfork didn't introduce Asher, who had somehow snuck in and was sitting in the front row, stock-still with his head down.

"ParaScience 110 will teach you the theory and history you'll need to complete your experiments and write your reports on paranormal observations. Rest assured that these five gentlemen will ensure you survive your first year, and they will prepare you for your second year responsibilities."

He held up an instructive finger.

"Now, I'd like for you to spend the remainder of today's class divided into groups and meeting with your section leads. They will help you choose your term project and prepare you for your first lab tomorrow morning… I believe Boris will be conducting a field trip and extraction exercise into an in-between, for example, and Rakesh will be leading a journey through the White Forest," he said as four of the gentlemen dispersed to separate corners of the auditorium.

Deeply engrossed in reading a book, Asher remained seated.

A flurry of auditorium seats swung up, and students sorted themselves into their respective corners, while Hailey and only Hailey made her way toward Asher, limping slowly down the stairs on her right heel, each step a red-hot nail through her foot. Half-way down the stairs, she met Professor Woodfork.

"Miss Hartley, you're limping—are you hurt," he asked, adjusting his glasses, and Hailey shook her head dismissively.

"It's—it's just—it's just a tiny cut," she lied. "I stepped on something sharp."

"Where are your shoes?"

Hailey looked at her feet and sighed.

"They—uh…they're gone. Along with my books. And my clothes," she added. "That's why I was late, Sir, I'm really sorry."

"The joys of living with poltergeists," he said, smiling kindly. He patted Hailey on the head, re-gripped his briefcase, and continued up the stairs.

Hailey continued hobbling down the stairs. Asher never looked up from his book.

"Where's the rest of our group?" she asked, nervously sitting on the edge of the seat next to him, idly wondering whether her first lab with him would involve a set of bars and a sturdy lock.

Asher flipped the page of his book.

Biting her lip, Hailey tucked an invisible strand of hair behind her ear.

"Asher?" she said, her heart racing.

When she quietly cleared her throat, Asher's jaw tightened.

"Leave now, Hailey," he said in a condescending voice, still staring at his book. "I don't want to see you."

She blinked, her stomach twisting as she stared at his back in disbelief…wondering if he was mad at her because she didn't want to be his prisoner.

"But..." she said hesitantly. "We're supposed to discuss tomorrow's lab..."

When the gash in her foot sent a bolt of pain straight into her bone, she drew a sharp breath, which provoked an equally sharp tone out of her section lead.

"Go to the hospital—your foot requires attention."

She tilted her head to see his eyes, hoping he'd at least look at her, but he didn't.

"Leave now, Hailey," he repeated, barely opening his mouth.

She stood up with her head down, biting her lip, her eyes stinging as much as her foot. Very gingerly, she hobbled up the stairs, frowning and trying not to grunt as her foot screamed with each step. Thankfully, everyone else in the room seemed absorbed by their lab preparations and didn't notice when Asher kicked her out. Her lip trembled, but she made it up the stairs without the pressure of a hundred eyeballs following her, and that was the only reason she didn't cry.

In fact, she made it all the way to the door in stealth mode and was about to sneak out when Fin decided to humiliate her.

"Hailey!" he yelled, causing the whole place to turn and look as she froze next to the door.

Fin bounded up the stairs.

"You alright?" he asked, but Hailey knew if she tried to talk, she'd just cry, so she stared at the door with wide, misty eyes and shook her head.

Fin sighed in disapproval.

"Asher's an ass. Lemme see your foot." Stooping down, he pulled her shin, lifting her foot as if he were shoeing a horse. Balanced on one leg, Hailey looked back at him then to the center of the room where Asher had been sitting. He'd left...thankfully.

Fin peeled her sock back and scrunched his face. "You need to go to the hospital right away," he told her. "This looks really bad."

"It's just a cut," she said, able to speak now that Asher was gone.

"It's not just a cut," Fin scolded, giving her back her foot. "And where are your shoes, Hailey? You can't tramp around Bear Towne in your stocking feet."

"My shoes are gone," she told him, her voice wavering horribly. "My books are gone. My clothes are gone…"

Fin hugged her tight. "Go get your foot fixed, knucklehead."

She rested her head against his chest. "Thanks," she breathed.

When he let her go, he tilted her chin up and gave her an encouraging smile. Then he headed back to his lab group, who behaved more like groupies than students. They smiled and swooned and watched every move Fin made. As did Hailey.

"By the way," he called over his shoulder as he bounded down the stairs, "you look good in my jersey."

Chapter Twenty-Five

The Splinter

"Many are stubborn in pursuit of the path they have
chosen. few in pursuit of the goal."

— Friedrich Nietzsche

Hailey had no intention of going to the hospital, partly because
it was just a cut and only needed a Band–Aid; partly because she
didn't want to contract flesh-eating Zombitis; but mostly because
Asher had ordered her to go there, and she had no intention of
doing anything he said.

So, instead of heading directly to the hospital like a good little
Envoy's possession, she headed to room 210 for her next class in
weights and measurements, walking stubbornly on her heel so she
didn't leave bloody footprints in her wake.

Room 210 had a wall of windows, and she found a seat next
to one of them, watching as the scenery swayed with the wind.
Olde Main leaned and tilted under her feet, but something about
the in-between made it feel as if it weren't moving at all…most of
the time. Every now and then a piece of chalk would slide off the
tray under the board at the front of the room. For the entire class,
Hailey watched the chalk slide back and forth, trying and failing
to will the throbbing pain out of her foot. In fact, the only thing

she succeeded in doing was missing the lecture as the ache spread to her ankle.

Hopping into her third class of the day several minutes early, she was delighted to see the un-friendliest face she knew. She limped directly over to Giselle and collapsed in the chair next to her.

"You look like hell," Giselle said, her hands folded on the table they shared. "Where're your shoes?"

Hailey shook her head, feeling too sluggish to answer, and Giselle stared at Fin's jersey.

"Tell me you did *not* spend the night with Pádraig." She grabbed Hailey's shoulder. "I told you, he's an asshole."

"I didn't," she almost yelled. Then she rolled her eyes. "I got locked out of our room, locked out of the laundry room, and a poltergeist stole all my clothes and all my books and my boots." Hailey huffed loudly. "Plus, I think Asher's peeved at me, and nothing is going right today."

Giselle's jaw fell open in jagged-toothed disbelief. "You did *not* see Asher wearing those clothes." Her head pulsated; her nostrils flared. She grabbed a fistful of Fin's jersey. "He thinks you woke up with Pádraig, you idiot. Why else would you be wearing his clothes—his JERSEY." She flung the jersey away. "You better go explain this to him like five minutes ago. I'm surprised he hasn't had you removed already—or worse."

Hailey dropped her head into her hands and moaned. *Of course! That's why he didn't want to look at her.*

"Ouch!" Hailey yelped unintentionally. It was like a hot knife pushed through her foot.

"Are you hurt?" Giselle asked incredulously.

"I—no—it's just a scratch," Hailey breathed, shifting her foot to hide her bloody sock.

"Let me see that." She bent down and snatched Hailey's foot up, ripping the sock off, and pulling the wound open.

"Ahhhh!" Hailey yelled.

"Shut up." Dropping Hailey's foot on the desk, Giselle ran to the corner of the room, grabbed an Indispensable first aid kit, and returned looking like a woman on a mission.

"You have a carnivorous splinter," she said as she pulled a lighter and a large pair of tweezers from the kit. "You have to get it out before it takes root around your bone, or else you'll lose your entire leg."

"What? Well, get it out!"

"I will. Hold still," she said grabbing Hailey's foot again. "It's already burrowed pretty deep." Giselle looked up. "You need to go to the hospital—you need a painkiller," she said, slamming the tweezers on the desk and crossing her arms.

"I am not going to the hospital."

"Whatever. It's your leg."

"Giselle," Hailey pleaded irritably. She shoved the tweezers back into her roommate's hand. "Just yank it out."

Giselle studied her for a moment.

"Fine. Hold still. It'll probably latch onto a chunk of muscle, and they usually spaz and barb when they're threatened. This is going to hurt. Don't pass out."

Holding the tweezers in one hand and Hailey's foot with the other, Giselle went to work. First, she ripped Hailey's foot in two—at least that's what it felt like, and Hailey let out a screech that made the whole class stare. Then Giselle plunged the tweezers through her foot until they hit her bone, whereupon she clamped onto the bone and ripped it out along with a tendon that broke loose from the back of Hailey's heel, rolled up like a blind and dragged the arch of her foot out with it.

Holding the teeny wooden stake up triumphantly, Giselle whizzed a roll of gauze at Hailey.

"Hold pressure on your foot—I have to burn this thing." She held a lighter to the carnivorous splinter, which screamed like a boiled lobster.

Hailey held her breath to stop the agony inside her foot. It didn't work. And as she lost consciousness, she heard Giselle cussing her out.

"Oh no you don't, I told you—shit!"

"...why you won't just heal her foot..." A familiar voice trailed in and out as Hailey opened her eyes.

"She must ask for such a favor," Asher answered sharply, and Hailey blinked, recognizing the naked bed under her as her own.

"Well, you're a real gentleman, Asher," Fin said in a voice dripping with sarcasm. And then he proceeded to mock the Envoy in an overly dramatic and holier-than-thou voice. "*Beg for forgiveness, and I shall heal you.* You're such a romantic. Make sure you tell her she'll be your slave for eternity."

The next thing Hailey heard was a choking noise, and she turned her head to see Asher holding Fin up by his throat, pinning him against her closet.

"It's nice to see you two getting along," she mumbled.

Dropping Fin, Asher turned to face her.

Fin stood up and cleared his throat.

They both glared at her.

"I told you to go to the hospital!" they yelled in unison, one pointing at her foot, and the other in a southern direction.

Looking from one angry face to the other, Hailey scooted back from them in her bed. Then she surveyed her foot, which was still attached and nicely bandaged.

"I didn't need the hospital," she shrugged. "Giselle got the splinter out just fine."

She looked at her roommate's bed and the ceiling above it then the floor in front of it, but Giselle wasn't home.

Asher stepped toward her, looking angrier than she'd ever seen him, his eyes letting off flashes of dark violet.

Looking up at him, Hailey frowned as she imagined his smooth voice full of scorn. But he said nothing. Instead, he simply turned and walked out, leaving Hailey with all of the guilt and none of the balancing anger she would've had if he had chewed her out.

Fin sat on the bed, and Hailey scooted next to him.

"He's going to lock me up," she said objectively, "or expel me."

Fin patted her leg. "I don't think so." He nodded at her desk. There, in a neat tower, sat all of her books, a box of vibrating crystals, a pair of Indispensable Magnoggles, a vial of gold dust and next to that, a stack of Bear Towne sweats. A new pair of wellies stood on the floor in front of it all.

"Did you find my books?" she asked excitedly.

"No," he answered in a long, drawn-out monotone. "Asher brought you new ones." Fin threw his arm out, looking thoroughly one-upped. "Tell you what," he said turning his charming smile to her. "I'll drive you into town on Thursday after your music class, and you can do some shopping."

Closing her eyes, Hailey smiled and threw her arms around him.

He held her close, resting his forehead gently against hers for a long moment.

"Try to be more careful, okay?" he whispered, and then he kissed her cheek, got up, and left.

After the door closed, Hailey clutched her chest and stared at the floor.

He's an asshole. Giselle's voice grated inside her head, abruptly ending her swoon.

Rubbing her forehead, Hailey turned her attention to the pile of goodies on her desk and hobbled over to check them out.

Not only had Asher replaced all of her class materials, he'd added a book on mountaineering in Columbia with a note:

Take this with you to the Library. Mrs. Spitz will like it.

He'd also left an Indispensable flashlight, a first aid kit, and a vase full of wildflowers. Hailey shook her head at all of it, smiling sadly as she puzzled over Asher's quirks.

Why was he so…so…grumpy? Clearly he cared about her, she thought as she gently touched some thistle in the bouquet.

For the second night in a row, Giselle didn't come home, and Hailey had no idea if she should be worried as she got ready for bed. There was nothing normal about Giselle. There was nothing normal about Bear Towne.

Unhooking the ghost trap from her window, Hailey carried it into the shower, hoping to snag the little brat that had stolen her clothes. With her foot wrapped in a plastic bag and her senses on high alert, she moved her head under the faucet, and just as the spray hit her face, a slight vibration disturbed the air.

Pivoting on her bad heel, Hailey lunged into the changing stall, ghost trap in hand and clobbered the would-be brat over the head with it—which did absolutely nothing. In fact, the polter-geist paused only momentarily to point and laugh, and then it grabbed Hailey's sweat pants and took off.

"Tomas!" she yelled, limping as fast as she could out of the stall. She didn't care that she was naked—she was going to catch that little trouble-maker.

Tomas appeared in the mirrors, looking confused.

Hailey pointed to the brat on the ceiling, which taunted her by waving her sweat pants. "That urchin stole my pants again. Can you get them back?"

"Jawohl" materialized on the mirror, and Tomas flew to the ceiling. A polter-scuffle took place there, which looked cartoonish, and after a few seconds, her sweat pants popped out and fell to the floor. The brat wailed and flew away, and Tomas reappeared in the mirror, smiling victoriously.

"Great work, Tomas," she told him, holding up her pants. "Listen, I'm designing a new ghost trap, and I'll need a test subject. Wanna help me?"

Tomas tapped his chin thoughtfully then nodded, saluted, and disappeared.

That night, Hailey made it half-way through her new copy of *Balance and the Aether: The Lessons of the Seven Envoys*, before she fell asleep with Asher on her mind (one of the seven mentioned in her textbook). She had a thousand questions and found him waiting for her in the Aether.

"Asher," she called as she hobbled near.

He stood on a bluff, facing a breathtaking view of snow-draped mountains and turned only slightly to greet her.

"I find it very difficult to talk to you on Earth," he said.

It shouldn't have been a surprise, but hearing it so plainly sort of hurt Hailey's feelings.

"I'm very quickly frustrated with your defiance," he went on, and Hailey pressed her lips together.

"Asher. You threatened to lock me up. How am I supposed to respond to that?"

He stepped away from the bluff, and Hailey shambled behind him.

"I really like the flowers," she offered, trying to keep up.

"They remind me of you—*wild*flowers." he said sharply, but then his mouth twitched. Hailey wasn't sure how to take it.

"You're doing it again. You make me so nervous—it seems like you're always mad at me, I—"

He spun around. "Hailey, I wish to heal your foot."

"You can do that?"

"Yes," he said, looking apologetic. "But not here. It has to be done on Earth. May I come see you?"

Hailey beamed. "Of course!"

She reached out to him, and he moved his translucent hand over hers.

"Then I will see you soon."

Hailey woke just as Asher was leaving her room.

"Asher. Wait," she said groggily, and he hesitated at the door. "Won't you stay and talk to me?"

His eyes glowed warmly when he turned to her. She swung her feet over the side of her bed and wiggled them excitedly.

"Did you fix my foot?"

"I did," he answered even as Hailey unwrapped the bandages.

"This is amazing," she said, pirouetting and laughing her relief. "Thank you!"

Without thinking, she danced to the door and flung her arms around him, hugging him tight—something she'd always longed to do when she'd seen him in the Aether. It felt good to feel him close; it felt warm and safe.

But when Asher didn't embrace her, she slid her arms off him and stepped back.

"Why did you do that?" he asked.

"I guess I was happy to see you," she said, cringing inside. Clearly, she'd invaded his personal space. "I'm sorry."

"Don't be." Asher took her hand and pulled her back into him. "I can never predict you," he said, stroking her back, and Hailey melted into his powerful arms.

"Clothes," she blurted, leaning slightly away. "I was only wearing Fin's clothes because a poltergeist stole mine. I wasn't—"

"I'm aware," was all he said, and Hailey studied his eyes.

"So, you're not going to kick me out of lab tomorrow?" she teased.

"No."

"What are we going to work on—crystals?" Sliding out of his arms, she pranced to her pile of school materials, unable to hide her curiosity as she held up the vibrating box.

"Or…" She put those down and pulled on her Magnoggles, which reminded her of something the Red Baron would wear. "What do these do?" she asked when she found him looking perfectly normal on the other side of the lens.

"They allow you to view the Northern Lights."

"Oh." Pulling them off, she turned them over in her hands. "You can't see the Northern Lights without goggles?"

"Not properly," he told her. "I'm afraid we won't be using them until November."

"What about this?" She held up her vial of gold dust and shook it.

"For calibrating a ghost trap," he said striding toward her.

"You have to calibrate them…oh…" Hailey said thoughtfully.

Very gently, Asher took the vial from her hand, pausing to brush his fingers across her skin. "You remind me of the wonder I felt when I first came to your world. And I very much look forward to working with you." He gazed into her wide eyes for several seconds before placing her vial of gold dust back on the desk.

"Tomorrow, we'll discuss DOPPLER," he said with a somber tone, but Hailey was still transfixed by his swirling eyes—so adoring, so kind.

"DOPPLER…" she repeated dreamily. Then she blinked several times, remembering Tomas.

"Why did they kidnap my poltergeist?"

Asher nodded, seeming to already know what she was talking about. "The men there are ambitious. They seek information and leverage in their dealings with the Envoys, and they know that you're…important…to me."

"Am I?"

Asher trapped her in his piercing stare again. "I would reorder the world for you," he told her softly, and Hailey caught her breath.

Hailey-Khu and Schatz—that's what Tomas meant—she was Asher's treasure—he protected her soul. She dropped her gaze, not sure she rated such a compliment even as Asher pulled her close and moved his lips to her ear. "I promise you, Hailey," he whispered, "I'll never lock you away. Forgive me for suggesting it."

As he looked her in the eyes again, Hailey held her breath, convinced he was about to kiss her.

Instead, he stepped back and surveyed her room.

"How are you adjusting to Alaska? Do you require anything?" he asked, and Hailey breathed again.

"No, I don't think so." She waved her arm at her school books. "Thank you for bringing me all this. You're a life saver. And Fin's driving me into Anchorage on Thursday for some…shopping…"

Hailey's voice died when Asher flicked his eyes at her. They erupted, and without explanation, he stormed out of her room, slamming the door behind him.

If she had a pillow, Hailey would have screamed into it.

In the morning, Fin caught up to Hailey as she bounded down the stairs, heading purposefully toward Olde Main for her first lab with Asher.

"Why are you wearing your wellies? It's not raining," was how he greeted her.

"My sneakers ran away." She pointed at his feet. "It's forty degrees out here—I can't believe you're wearing flip-flops."

"This is Alaska, Hailey. It doesn't matter how cold it is—if there's no snow on the ground, it's flip-flop weather."

Hailey nodded, impressed.

"How's the agony of the feet this morning?" he asked.

"Great! It's completely healed," she said brightly, and Fin stopped her.

"You didn't ask Asher to heal your foot, did you?" he said, his eyes narrow.

"No," she said defensively. "He just showed up in the middle of the night and fixed it." Hailey's stomach dropped. "Why?"

"Because," he cautioned her, "if you ask for a favor from an Envoy, it's like handing them an eternal free pass into your head. They basically make you their immortal slave forever and ever amen."

"Well, I don't think I asked him... I mean, I remember talking to him in my dream, but I don't remember what we said."

"Oh, you'd remember."

"He's mad at me again, anyway," Hailey said glumly. "I told him you were taking me to Anchorage, and he just left. He slammed the door."

Fin laughed out loud.

Hailey shot him a sharp look. "It's not funny."

"Ohhhhh," Fin sighed heartily. "Sorry," he said, still tickled.

"Do you know where Giselle is?" she asked to change the subject. She hadn't seen her roommate since the carnivorous splinter incident.

"I don't know—sharpening her demon teeth?"

Hailey rolled her eyes, and Fin held his hands up as they approached Olde Main.

"I have no idea what that thing does," he told her, opening the door. "You're in Lab 1, which is down there." He pointed to a hallway that was stretching and compressing like a horizontal slinky. "I'm upstairs, so I'll catch up with you later," he said, walking backwards as he spoke, and Hailey waved.

Wearing her wellies, Bear Towne sweatpants, and a "Where the heck is The Middle of Nowhere" sweatshirt, she shuffled into Lab 1 a full ten minutes early. It would have been fifteen, but she'd stopped in the girl's bathroom to fuss over her hair, which Tomas had insisted she wear down.

After thirty minutes of staring at the door, waiting for Asher to arrive, Hailey gave up and decided to pay a visit to Dr. Woodfork, whose office was also on the first floor.

She found his door slightly ajar and heard the unmistakable boom of Asher's voice coming from inside.

"Get rid of her, Simeon, or I will," he almost roared.

Shoot. Is he talking about me?

He stormed into the hallway but stopped abruptly when he saw Hailey. His mouth turned down, and he tilted his head away from her.

"You will leave this place," he said with ice in his voice.

Her heart fell. Eyebrows squished together, she glanced at Dr. Woodfork for an explanation, but he avoided her.

She swallowed hard. "I...no. I will *not*," she said, looking Asher up and down.

When he put his face in hers like a drill sergeant, she pulled her head back slightly but refused to back away, even as her throat tightened. She stared at him defiantly, and he stared back, a thunderstorm of dark violet clouds rumbling to life inside his eyes.

Then, as suddenly as the storm in his eyes erupted, it dissipated, and his face softened.

"It's no longer safe for you here," he said gently, and he dropped his gaze then walked out, leaving Hailey stunned into silence and staring after him.

She turned to Professor Woodfork, following him into his office as he retreated. "What was that?" she breathed, struggling to keep her voice steady.

"Oh, dear," said the professor, sighing deeply as he sat pensively at his desk. "Ah, don't worry," he said brightly. "I don't believe he truly wishes for you to leave. Come," He motioned her to a leather armchair near a woodstove. "I'll conduct your first lab. Let's have a short discussion about Envoys, shall we?"

Standing, he plucked a book from his shelf and placed it into Hailey's hands. "He'll probably know that I've given you this—he can see into my mind, but he doesn't always look. Still, best if you didn't mention it to him," he warned, and Hailey nodded.

She ran her hand over the gilded leather cover. It was obviously an antique, an objet d'art in remarkable condition, and a book he'd written himself—a chronicle penned in an elegant old script. She hungrily scanned the first couple pages, picking out the gist of the story of the Envoys.

During the seventeenth century B.C., a king among men became obsessed with the Aether, the realm, which holds life energy, as he believed he could harness and wield its power. What few records survive, indicate the king conducted barbaric experiments in his effort to understand the Aether, oftentimes slaughtering his slaves while they slept.

Through a series of increasingly larger explosions, the king suc-ceeded in tearing the barrier between the worlds. It remained open for several seconds, during which a vortex pulled many Envoys from their home in the Aether and hurled them onto the Earth.

Fascinated, Hailey flipped to the center of the book.

Seven of the Envoys pulled across the veil made contact with humans: Theon the Loyal, Asher the Benevolent, Cobon the Clever, Kiya the Serene, Adalwolf the Veracious…

Flipping again, she found what she was looking for.

An Envoy is devoid of emotion, incapable of experiencing what we call "feelings."

Chapter Twenty-Six

A Dark Tunnel

*"There are more things in heaven and earth. Horatio.
Than are dreamt of in your philosophy."*

— William Shakespeare. Hamlet

Hailey stood, staring at those lines, lips parted as some mix of disbelief and horror bubbled in her stomach.

…devoid of emotion…

That…couldn't be right. Could it?

Asher certainly had at least anger figured out. And he cared about her—he'd said so.

"You'll read this then and return it to me once you've finished," Woodfork instructed, and Hailey nodded slowly, unable to tear her eyes from those words.

"But…Professor," she said in a small voice, "this can't be…" If Asher had no emotions, he could betray her tomorrow and never think twice about it. A twinge of fear in her belly robbed her breath.

She looked up at Woodfork, shaking her head.

"It's a long story," he said. "You'll read the rest, yes?"

"But—"

"And return it to me once you've finished." Woodfork turned his back, gathering some objects into a bag as Hailey stared, slack-jawed and unable to spit out a thought.

"That'll do for an Envoy discussion for one day."

"But—"

"And now…" He spun around, smiling. "Let's go explore a dark tunnel."

"Asher told me to stay out of the dark tunnels."

"Huh," he grunted. "He does worry after you. But! You'll be perfectly safe. All we need is a robust spirit of adventure." He dug around inside one of his desk drawers. "Aha! And some portable light." He held up an Indispensable flashlight. "Our back-up will be the Indispensable Never-Fail Lighter," he said, handing her a small bronze object.

"What is…how does it work?" The whole thing was smooth. She couldn't even tell where the flame would come out.

"With breath," he said, and Hailey frowned. "As if you're blowing out a birthday candle, like so." He took the lighter, and holding it out from his mouth, he blew a puff of air against it whereupon a giant flame popped into the air over the professor's head, as if it belonged to an invisible torch. He handed the lighter back to Hailey, and the torch-less flame floated over her head.

"How do you put it out?" she asked, never taking her eye off the fire above her. "And where's its fuel source?" She turned all around, still looking up at it, trying to figure it out.

"Simply hold your breath," he told her, which she did with one eyebrow raised. To her astonishment, the flame snapped out.

"How is that possible? I mean, where's the fuel?"

"Oh, you are a delight! A healthy dose of skepticism is always in order when one studies the science of the paranormal," he told her. "After you," he said as he opened his door.

She adjusted her backpack, and—

Wait. He was trying to distract her from asking about Asher. And she was falling for it!

Well enough of that.

She opened her mouth to speak but hesitated a bit too long.

"The fuel source is the Sun," said the professor. "The Indispensable Lighter is simply a precision barrier breaker—a bomb of sorts."

"A bomb?"

And once again, her curiosity betrayed her.

Woodfork nodded, indicating her to lead the way down the stairs of Olde Main.

"Indeed. It opens a discrete in-between, which doubles back on itself, effectively folding our dimension so that a bit of the fires from near the surface of our sun come through. And it attaches its position to the breath of the one holding the lighter—quite a feat of para-engineering. That was Pádraig's project when he first arrived here. He's been a very productive student for the Indispensable brand."

"Indispensable makes a lot of things I've never heard of," Hailey remarked as they reached the tunnels.

"Yes, well, of course it's the University's brand. Not much demand for it outside of the paranormal world, but our devices are wildly popular among the supernatural creatures of Earth. They sell very well in the hidden places of this world," he said proudly. "Let's try this one." Professor Woodfork pointed down a dark tunnel to the right, which emitted a low, mournfully spooky cry.

Hailey peered into the darkness. "What do you think is down there?"

"Let's find out, shall we?" He clicked on his flashlight, and Hailey blew a puff of air onto the lighter, igniting the nuclear suntorch above her head.

Down the tunnel they went. As the moaning grew louder, it took on a more pathetic tone, like a cry for help. Soon they were right on top of the noise, but Hailey saw nothing that could be causing such a racket.

"Aha!" said Dr. Woodfork. "A moaning bookworm. Well, this isn't normal."

Hailey side-eyed him. Nothing about Bear Towne was normal, and she wondered if the professor knew that.

"You see," continued the professor as Hailey squatted next to him, "he's bookless…and it appears…" With his thumb and forefinger, the professor touched what looked like a fat inch-worm and raised a tiny object. "Yes. You see, it appears his eyeglasses are broken," he explained, showing Hailey a teeny pair of spectacles. "We'll get these straight over to I-MET for repair, and then we'll bring them back along with a book."

He handed the tiny glasses to Hailey. "Otherwise, if we were to neglect this little guy, he'd morph into a tunneling earworm— I believe you're familiar?"

Hailey nodded.

"You see, the dark tunnels are where various creatures come when they have…issues. Second-year students spend an entire semester sorting out the ones they can, and of course avoiding the ones that are too far gone.

"Those," he said, waving his finger in the air, "are the ones that become killers." He held up his flashlight. "They hate the light. As you can see," he told her as he shined a light on the bookworm, "our little friend here does not shy away from the light, and so he's still redeemable."

"What do bookworms do?"

"Read, mostly. And drink tea."

"Out of tiny cups?" Hailey tried to imagine it.

"Actually—and you'll find this in the library—they can suck down a normal size cuppa in less than a second—it's remarkable to witness. It does make them swell, though, and some of them swell to an enormous size. But, they are very gentle creatures," he said as he started down the main corridor.

Soon they'd be topside again, and Hailey would miss her chance to ask what she really wanted to know. Or not know. Truthfully, she didn't want to confirm what she'd read, and he'd probably just shut her down again anyway, but it was now or never.

"Professor," Hailey said, gathering her courage, "you wrote in your book that Envoys are emotionless…" She drew a breath but chewed her lip, rethinking this whole line of talk as she envisioned Asher listening in through Woodfork's head.

"You want to know if Asher is capable of love."

"Yeah…" she sighed, feeling exposed. "I mean, he seemed to want me here yesterday, but now it seems he's just kicked me out of the university."

"As you'll read in my chronicles, the Envoys came to this Earth devoid of emotion, but as the centuries passed, they became infected with feelings. It's new to Asher—to feel. In a lot of ways, he is emotionally like a child—very easily injured. Be patient with him, Hailey. I believe his feelings for you are genuine."

The tunnel opened to the Olde Main stairwell, and Dr. Woodfork led them into the darkness behind the stairs, where a large, rusty door hung with the letters I-MET painted in bright white.

Inside sat a crooked reception desk and a few tattered chairs under dim light, like the waiting room of a haunted doctor's office. The professor tapped a "ring for service" bell, which called forth a shrouded figure, who held his hand out as if he were expecting them.

"This won't take long," the professor told Hailey after the ghoulish figure disappeared.

"Do you know where I can find Asher?" Hailey couldn't stand it when someone was mad at her. Mostly, she wanted to straighten out her expulsion and find out why it was suddenly "unsafe" for her there. Honestly, she thought she'd handled things pretty darn well so far. In fact, the more she thought about it, the more her Irish blood boiled. He had a lot of nerve expelling her!

"The Observatory, I believe," Woodfork answered as I-MET presented a repaired set of teeny eyeglasses. The ghoul also handed the professor a paperback book.

Hailey frowned as they made their way back to the dark tunnel. "The Observatory's off limits to students, isn't it?"

"Yes, and I would *not* disturb him there." He handed her the glasses.

Very gently, she placed them onto the face of the bookworm and set the paperback in front of him. Immediately, the groaning stopped—the worm flipped open the book—and both the book and the worm vanished.

"Where'd he go?"

"The library, most likely." Woodfork beamed at Hailey. "Well done."

Following her successful rehabilitation of the moaning bookworm in a dark tunnel, Hailey had every intention of disturbing Asher at the observatory, and headed out the doors of Olde Main via the red-buttoned out-between with quite a bone to pick.

Marching to the Observatory with an increasingly quickened pace, she swatted all thirty-five species of Alaskan mosquitos as she went, trying but failing to reach a particularly hungry one attached to the middle of her back. By the time she reached the off-limits building, she didn't hesitate to barge inside to escape the hungry swarm of bloodsuckers.

"Asher!" she called.

She got no answer from the Envoy at the top of the mezzanine, who looked through a telescope in the middle of the day, undisturbed by her yells.

"You've got a lot of nerve—ignoring me now...after..." She had to catch her breath. "...if you...think I'm leaving this... place..."

The room swayed a bit, and she staggered.

"...I'm not...afraid of you... You're..." She couldn't believe she had to catch her breath again. "...I'm not..." She forgot what she wanted to say and blinked hard before falling to her knees.

Asher landed with a metallic clang on the grating in front of Hailey, and she squinted to see him. Fingers of blackness crept around her eyes as Asher helped her crumple gently to the floor.

"Asher..." she breathed. "...I don't...feel..." As numbness spread down her legs and pins and needles jabbed her hands, Asher pulled a quill from Hailey's back.

"It's poison," he said with no emotion, and then he paced away from her, looking thoughtfully skyward.

"Asher..." Hailey cried between gasps. She tried reaching out to him, but her arm didn't budge. "Asher?" she called again, but he didn't budge, either, and darkness caved in over Hailey.

Chapter Twenty-Seven

The Quill

"Love must be sincere. Hate what is evil;
cling to what is good."

The Bible. Romans 12:9

Asher held the deadly quill. But what he saw in his hand was the end of his suffering on Earth; he saw a way back into the Aether; he saw his home.

As Hailey convulsed and struggled for breath on his observatory floor, he pulled from his pocket a shiny black stone. That such a small trinket could slice open the great barrier between realms seemed fantastic. He had but to hold onto it for another minute to find out if it would work. That's all it would take for the poison to rob the Earth of his girl. And while she writhed in agony against the floor, no doubt silently pleading for his assistance, Asher hesitated to give it.

The Envoy yearned for his home almost as much as the man he had become yearned for Hailey's affection.

Asher replaced the stone in his pocket and knelt down next to his love. The comfort inside the Aether tempted him still, but the temptress before him commanded his heart. Taking her into his arms, he placed his lips against her forehead and repaired her delicate body, compelling beads of poison to drop from her eyes like tears.

Gradually, her breath came in an easy rhythm, and her heart beat in a slow, effortless cadence. She slept in his arms, and in holding her there, Asher found his home.

Hailey's college career was off to a fantastic start, she despaired as she woke up with a misty-eyed giggle.

At the world's premier school of paranormal studies, she'd already managed to fall out of a Luftzeug, survive a vacuum-glazed in-between, experience a tunneling earworm, live with a roommate from Hell, lose her clothes to a mal-tempered poltergeist, step on a carnivorous splinter, rehabilitate a moaning bookworm, and be shot in the back by a poisonous quill.

And she was only two days into her freshman year.

Before she opened her eyes, a tear escaped, and as it coursed across her temple, she imagined her bedroom in Pittsburgh, with Holly sleeping peacefully in her bed near the window and Uncle Pix cooking up the breakfast bacon. She could almost smell it.

Wait. She did smell it.

Hailey opened her eyes and confronted a splitting headache. Letting out a curt moan, she snapped them shut again and pinched the bridge of her nose to keep her brains from leaking out.

"This will help," said Asher, who sat next to her.

"If I open my eyes, the light is going to crack my head open."

Asher tenderly kissed Hailey's forehead and an electric tingle enveloped her face. It was like he'd hit a release valve on her cranium and let the pressure out of her skull.

"That's much better," she said when he moved away. "Where am I?" As her eyes adjusted to the light, she realized she was in a strange, but richly beautiful house. She sat on a large, plush couch under a vaulted ceiling, facing a grand stone fireplace.

Asher set a plate of fresh fruits, bacon, eggs, and toast on the ornately rough-cut coffee table in front of her.

"You're in my home next to the observatory," he explained with low volume, which Hailey greatly appreciated. "You're still weak from the poison, but some food will help."

With arms of lead, Hailey reached for the bacon and nibbled it slowly.

"I must leave you for a while, but I'll return soon," Asher said getting up. He turned to go but turned to her again with pleading eyes. "You're free to leave this place while I'm away, but I wish you wouldn't. Stay and eat and rest. I'll escort you back to your room when I return."

"Where are you going?"

"To tend to the one who hurt you."

"You know who did this?" she asked, and Asher dropped his eyes.

"I knew before the quill hit you," he confessed.

Hailey dropped her bacon, waiting on the edge of the couch for his explanation. She only spoke when he moved to leave without giving one. "What? How? Why didn't you stop it?"

Asher stood with his back to her. "The human soul is not naturally evil," he explained. "When a man or a woman begins down a path of bad behavior, it causes a disruption in their energy. It's a lot like discord in music or clashing colors. An Envoy can hear and see it right away if one cares to. I'm always listening to my campus for such evil." He faced Hailey as he continued. "Joanne had been plotting this for days, and she encourages others with this malevolence."

"Joanne?" she said skeptically.

"Do you know her?"

"No, not really. I was sitting with Fin when she slapped him…"

Asher studied Hailey for a moment. "I've delayed confronting her to see you wake, but I must go now. She will tell me her motivation before I destroy her."

Before Hailey could process the word "destroy," he was gone—vanished into the shadows.

"Asher?" she called to the emptiness, but she was alone in his gigantic Alaskan mansion. She finally stood upright and walked twenty paces on shaky legs into his dining room. A chandelier of a thousand sparkling crystals hung over a long oak table with totem-carved legs.

That room shared an all-glass wall with what looked like an atrium of giant trees and lush greenery. Mostly hidden behind an ivy-draped tree sat a tall marble fountain.

"Whoa," she marveled as she took it in.

On the other side of the dining room, Hailey found a long, window-lined hallway, which led her into another great room. Set up like a gallery with a large, upholstered bench in the center of it, the room also held an oft-used violin and bow on a stand next to the bench.

Lining the walls of that room from floor to ceiling hung pieces of glass masterfully painted and illuminated from behind so that they glowed warmly—one of a beaver dam over a stream near a serene grove of mighty oaks; one of a bluff overlooking a river at the foot of white-capped mountains; one of a lush field in the clearing of a familiar forest.

Hailey recognized them all. They were scenes from her dreams—exact replicas, and Asher had gorgeously painted and illuminated over a hundred of them. As she studied each one, a torrent of memories washed over her...conversations in the Aether, confessions she'd made, revelations Asher had shared, and—the black rock. The Envoy Cobon had killed Holly because of it, but it was Hailey's death, not Holly's that would send the Envoys home to the Aether. That's why she was in danger. And Asher protected her from the other Envoys...because...

Interrupting her thought was a painting, which hung in the center of the largest wall—a piece of glass that was not an image from her dreams—one that transfixed Hailey: a six-foot tall image of two sisters dancing at an Irish pub—a perfect copy of the photo Asher had repaired and held for her on the day she'd arrived in Bear Towne.

Hands pressed to her chest, Hailey stared at it for several minutes until her chin quivered and a flood of tears filled her eyes.

Asher slid his hands around her waist, and she leaned into him. She hadn't even heard him return. When he brushed his lips over her ear, Hailey tilted her head to them.

"I miss her so much."

"I know," he murmured.

"Asher, I don't know who to trust here, and you... you were going to let Joanne kill me, weren't you?"

He stepped back, gently turning Hailey to face him.

"No," he whispered, and a single tear dropped from his beautiful eye. "Hailey, I would not harm you," he pleaded, and Hailey's heart broke.

She bowed her head, disarmed. She knew Asher wouldn't have done that, but still. There had to be a reason he didn't stop her. Maybe he wanted to find out if he had an enemy; maybe he was testing that stupid rock...

"But you let her attack me. Why?"

"Joanne attacked you, because she coveted the closeness you share with Pádraig," he explained, tentatively stroking her cheek. "She won't harm you again."

"That doesn't make any sense, Asher. She would've known that you'd...you'd..." She couldn't bring herself to say it. "Did another Envoy make her do it?"

Certainly Joanne would not have risked Asher's rage—and her very life—over simple jealousy.

"She believed she acted alone."

Believed. Past tense. Hailey swallowed hard. "Jealousy," she said.

"A savage motivator."

He would certainly know.

Asher moved to his violin, and Hailey watched him—not technically a murderer, but a killer just the same.

"Why didn't you stop her?" she asked. "And why... I watched you look at the black stone as I was dying. For a moment, I thought you wanted me to die." She hugged herself tight.

"For a moment, I did." Asher picked up his bow, twisting the tension screw.

"You wanted me to die," she repeated. "And you let Joanne poison me. And then you changed your mind...?" she said slowly, her voice quavering as she exposed Asher's darkness.

"I reconsidered."

"How can I trust you, Asher?" Hailey said over her shoulder.

"You shouldn't," he said, and his bow splintered in half.

"Are you jealous too?"

He stood in stiff silence.

"Don't be," she moaned throwing her hand out. "Fin is just a big flirt. There's nothing serious between us at all. He flirts with everyone."

Hailey turned to a painting of the river in Pennsylvania, where Uncle Pix had once taken her and Holly rafting. She'd shown that place to Asher after Holly had died, and he'd made her feel so safe there.

He'd always been there for her, in one way or another.

"You know, if you would've just let me go, you could've gone home. Your troubles would be over." She tried to gauge his reaction, but he revealed nothing. "Why did you save my life?"

"Because I would rather endure the hell of this Earth with you than spend an eternity in paradise without you," he replied without hesitation.

The fireplace crackled in the next room, and Hailey exhaled. But then she shook her head. "Most of the time, you mean," she said sadly, as she scratched at a mosquito bite on her neck.

Asher brushed her skin with the back of his hand, and like an eraser, it wiped away the itchy welt.

"I reconsider often," he confessed, still caressing her neck, and Hailey readjusted her arms, hugging herself closer.

"Should I be afraid of you?" Honestly, she didn't know if she wanted to scream and run or stay and find out if he'd finally kiss her again.

Stroking her arms, Asher coaxed them away from her belly. "I don't want you to fear me."

Hailey couldn't look at him.

"Fear the others," he told her. "If Cobon finds out he's killed the wrong girl, he and the others will tear you apart. But they won't touch you as long as I protect you."

"You mean as long as you favor me over your home," she corrected him. "And who knows how long you'll want me."

"Forever," he murmured.

Hailey bowed her head so he wouldn't see her tears.

"Even when you enrage me with your disobedience, I still choose you over the Aether." With the back of his hand, he brushed her tears away. "Hailey, you're weak from poison. You should sleep."

"Are you asking me to stay with you tonight?" she teased.

"I'm asking you to stay with me forever."

"Oh." Her heart pounding, she tried to read whether he meant "forever" literally. "In case you change your mind by morning, will you stay up all night and talk to me? Here…on Earth?"

"You're exhausted," he said with an amused half frown, "but I'll stay with you until you sleep."

"Tell me about DOPPLER. They've been watching us since we were kids," she said, recalling the photo of their childhood home from Holly's police file.

"They are curious about any human who has dealings with the Envoys. Because of the black rock, Cobon has guarded your family for centuries."

"Until recently, you mean. What happened the night my parents died? Who started that fire?"

"Adalwolf, I believe."

"Adalwolf," Hailey repeated, thoughtfully. That was the name Fin had said. That was the Envoy that had tied his soul. "Where is he now?"

"He's dead, Hailey."

"An Envoy can die?"

"Not in the sense that you know it. But, an Envoy can be torn apart, effectively destroyed."

"Who destroyed him?"

Asher studied her.

"You," he said simply.

"Me?" She shook her head. "No, Asher, I would remember destroying an Envoy. I can't even tear myself away from your gaze." She laughed, but he seemed quite serious. "Asher," she said just as seriously, "you're mistaken."

"It's no mistake. You were quite young, and you don't remember." Hailey opened her mouth to protest—but Asher cut her off. "DOPPLER is harmless," he said, steering her back to her original question. "They are an Envoy's pawns. They obey us, and they don't even know it," he said leading her back to the couch. "Your friend, Tage, for example."

"Tage?"

"The men at DOPPLER knew I protected you. I allowed them their curiosity for a while. But when they placed one of their agents close to you, I became…jealous very quickly." Asher flicked his eyes at the floor then back to Hailey.

"You stopped…" Hailey shook her head. "Did you make him forget me?"

Asher nodded, looking ashamed.

Hailey's head pounded. She sat on the edge of the couch. Tage really didn't like her after all—he was just spying. It made her sad and angry, because his stupid attention dominated one of the last conversations she'd had with Holly.

"Forgive me," said Asher.

"I'm glad you stopped him."

Asher sat next to her. "When I built this place," he said, his eyes tracing something in the distance, "it was with the intention of tearing the Barrier and finding a way home—I was never convinced that Cobon's rock would succeed. To function in the world of men, I made certain concessions… I shared bits of information with the government through DOPPLER, and in return they sent me great minds and stopped interfering with my work."

Though she hung on Asher's every word, Hailey stifled a yawn, struggling against the drowsy aftermath of a paranormal poisoning.

"Sometimes it's necessary to have dealings with those who are despicable—an alliance, even. The men at DOPPLER believe they operate as spies for the humans, gathering information about the Envoys. But they are our puppets. Many Envoys use them. Cobon has used them to watch your family for decades."

"Do you think he kidnapped my poltergeist from Pittsburgh?"

Asher tilted his head, squinting slightly.

"Tomas—he told me he escaped from DOPPLER…that they were dangerous…"

"Cobon," Asher said as if to himself then he looked at Hailey. "Call your ghost friend. I wish to speak with it."

Gleaning information from a poltergeist was no easy task, even for an Envoy. There was no mind to manipulate, and ghosts simply didn't care—about anything. Tomas had latched on to Hailey, though, and he eventually offered Asher a few details.

When Asher returned from his conference with Tomas, he was sure of two things. First, Cobon already knew he'd killed the wrong sister. Before escaping DOPPLER, Tomas had witnessed many things, one of which was Cobon's interference with Jaycen's pathetic attempt at spying. Jaycen had been telling the truth—Cobon had indeed switched her barrier breaker.

Second, Hailey fussed with her hair a lot, especially if she anticipated seeing Asher, which bolstered his confidence in her affection for him.

He found Hailey sleeping soundly on his couch and watched over her for several loving minutes. When it was clear she wouldn't wake to continue their talk, he gathered her in his arms and moved her into his bed.

She never stirred.

During the night, she shivered once. Very easily, he could have pulled a blanket over her. Instead, he warmed her with a gentle embrace, holding her tenderly through the night, wondering how much of his plan for her he would divulge.

"Thank you for the book for Mrs. Spitz," Hailey told Asher as he escorted her across campus to her dorm the next morning. "I can't wait to get my hands on some ParaScience data—I'm designing a new ghost trap. The one in our room doesn't work, and even if it did, it would require an escape hatch—I'd feel awful if Tomas got stuck," she gushed, feeling completely rejuvenated after a great night's sleep in a bed with blankets and a pillow—and Asher.

"Mrs. Spitz expects you this afternoon," he said. "She's a gifted clairvoyant, and she has a message for you."

Chapter Twenty-Eight

The Librarian

"A room without books is like a body without a soul."

— Cicero

"Want to come to the library with me?" Hailey asked her newly appointed conversation partner in her ParaCommunications class.

Giselle contorted her face. "I hate libraries," she grumbled. "Too many bookworms."

She only answered because she had to, otherwise she'd get a low mark in class participation, and she'd already failed the class three times. She made it clear that she wasn't happy about having a conversation partner, but then Giselle wasn't happy about anything. At least she hadn't asked Hailey where she'd slept last night...which reminded her...

"Giselle, where were you Monday night? You never came home."

"Working."

Hailey jerked her chin back.

"Really? Where?"

"I had the night shift at the hospital," she said airily.

Of course! That's how she knew about carnivorous splinters.

Hailey tried not to shudder as she imagined Giselle's bedside manner.

"And by the way," Giselle continued like a snob, "I wasn't home last night, either. Obviously, you weren't there to notice—where were you?"

Well, that backfired.

"Were you sleeping with Pádraig?" Giselle jeered.

"No—I didn't—it was—" Hailey sputtered, and then she huffed in frustration. "I got shot by a poisoned quill."

"Really. I didn't see you in the hospital."

"Asher fixed me up."

Giselle crossed her arms and bared her top teeth. "You mean he made you his slave."

"No, he just fixed me up."

"Envoys are all about balance. They don't just save people without getting something in return."

"Well, this one did."

"Then he must be losing his mind." As soon as she said it, she slapped her hands over her mouth and ducked. She looked around, terrified for several seconds before bowing her head, sniffling and pulling a string of silk from her eye.

"Are you alright?" Hailey asked.

"Asher scares me," Giselle answered softly, and Hailey gently patted her back.

"Remarkable!" trilled Professor Mum loudly as she clapped her hands and rushed over to the girls. "You two are a model of human/non-human cooperation." She beamed. "Everyone!" she called, and the whole classroom turned to see a frozen, wide-eyed Hailey patting the back of cobweb-faced, whatever-the-heck-Giselle-was. "Observe." Professor Mum motioned to the girls. "This is what a cross-creature friendship looks like!"

Hailey turned stiffly to Giselle, who turned to Hailey, looking as shocked as Hailey felt. Hailey stifled a giggle. And Giselle actually cracked a smile.

"Well, non-human *friend*," said Hailey at the end of class, "you sure you don't want to come to the library with me?"

"I hate you," said Giselle, but she was only mildly wrathful as she walked out.

"Hello?" Hailey called softly as she finally stepped over the threshold of the Bear Towne University Library. An impossibly large shadow-clock spanned the ceiling, hands silently twitching. "Hello…" Hailey sang again, though she wasn't sure why—it was a public library.

Some clairvoyant, she thought as she made her way inside, bribe in hand.

"Six hundred and eighty-seven," barked a female voice.

Hailey spun around.

There stood the librarian, hands planted firmly on her hips, foot tapping impatiently. Mrs. Spitz looked like she'd just stepped out of 1960. She wore pointy, wing-tipped glasses, a beehive hairdo, and a boxy jacket with large buttons.

"Excuse me?" Hailey said politely.

"Six hundred and eighty-seven." Mrs. Spitz articulated each syllable. Peering down her nose at Hailey, she thrust her hand out.

Hailey placed her offering into Mrs. Spitz's outstretched hand and stepped back.

Mrs. Spitz opened the book, read a few lines, tested the binding, sniffed loudly, slammed the book shut, and said, "Follow me."

Falling in step behind her, Hailey noticed a suspicious object protruding from the librarian's back. And it looked an awful lot like a knife.

"Uh…Mrs. Spitz?"

The librarian whirled around.

"You have a…a…" Hailey remembered she wasn't supposed to mention sharp objects.

"A what?" Mrs. Spitz demanded.

"There's something wrong with your jacket," Hailey said quickly, cringing as she nodded to it.

"Huh?" Looking over her shoulder, Mrs. Spitz tugged at the hem of her retro coat, which made the knife in her back wiggle up and down.

"I can never get this thing to lay right," she muttered. "How's that look?"

"That's much better," Hailey whispered, giving her a nervous thumbs-up and trying not to hyperventilate.

"Hmph. Still feels wrong." Mrs. Spitz placed her hand on a bookcase in the reference section. "You'll start on this shelf, here. Those books need to be shelved." She pointed to a stack on a wooden cart next to the shelf, and then she shook her finger at Hailey. "Exactly six hundred and eighty-seven books to a case."

Hailey gave her a blank stare.

"Oh, I wasn't looking for a job, Mrs. Spitz, I came to find some information, and Asher said you had a message for me."

"You'll finish these, and then you'll start on the Mysteries section in the 001's with the books on Atlantis." She shoved an armful of books into Hailey's chest. "Six hundred and eighty-seven books per case," she said again, and then she walked away.

Hailey wasn't sure what to do, so she started shelving and counting and making sure each case had exactly six hundred and eighty-seven books. So began Hailey's first day as a part-time library clerk at Bear Towne University.

It took her two hours to sort out one case in the reference section, mostly because every time she started counting, a poltergeist would shout numbers at her, and she'd lose her place. Over and over and over.

Finally, she gave up and worked on her original mission, which was finding a book on ghost traps. "And you're the first ghost I'm going to lock up!" she called over her shoulder as she marched to the circulation desk.

There she encountered a problem. The place was deserted. There was no card catalog and no computer. Hailey slapped her hands against her legs and looked all around. How was she supposed to find a book in that place? Slumping into a wooden chair at a desk near the stacks, Hailey plopped her head against the bare wood of the table and squeezed her eyes shut.

When she opened them, she saw, unnervingly close to her face, a tiny inchworm.

Hailey bolted upright. "You're a bookworm, aren't you?"

The worm nodded.

"You wouldn't happen to know where I could find a good book on ghost traps, would you?"

The worm nodded again, inched itself together and like a pebble out of a sling-shot, it flew off the table toward the stacks, skidding to a halt only moments later on the desk in front of Hailey with two books in tow—*Modern Methods in Poltergeist Procurement* and *Techniques in Crystallic Ghost Trap Calibration.*

"Perfect!" she said, and the worm bowed. "You got a name?"

The worm nodded and flipped open a stray book on the desk, tapping its nose against the name of the author—Matthew.

"Pleased to meet you, Matthew."

The worm bowed again and inched away as Hailey headed to Mysteries.

She'd only just climbed the ladder with an armful of books when Fin appeared.

"Too bad you're not wearing a skirt," he called up to her with a broad smile.

"Fin!"

"Hai—ley!" Mrs. Spitz called out.

She pumped her arms high as she took ridiculously long strides. Fin gave her a wide berth.

"There are only six hundred and eighty-*five* books on that shelf!" She pointed emphatically toward Reference.

"I'll add another two when I'm finished here."

"You'll add another two right now," Mrs. Spitz countered.

"I'll only be ten minutes longer here…"

"Fix it now!" She stamped her foot.

"But…I'm on the tenth rung of this ladder…"

Like a three-year-old in a tantrum, Mrs. Spitz gnashed her teeth and let out an ear-piercing screech until Hailey climbed down and headed to Reference.

Fin followed, smirking, his shoulders silently quaking.

"Sometimes with Mrs. Spitz, you just have to shut up and color," he said once the librarian was out of earshot.

"That woman is three kinds of crotchety."

"That happens to zombies," Fin said nonchalantly, and Hailey froze.

"Is she…?" Hailey couldn't bring herself to say the word.

"Yup. Mostly dead most of the time and all the way dead some of the time. She might be late to her funeral, but she's never late to work."

"Bear Towne has a zombie librarian?"

Fin stepped back, looking sly. "You know how hard it is to find a good librarian these days?" he asked, and Hailey shook her head. "It's a dying profession," he told her with a wry smile.

Hailey threw her arm out and pointed toward the circulation desk.

"Is she going to eat my brains?"

He shook his head. "You watch too much TV. You still wanna go into town with me tomorrow?"

"Yes, definitely."

"Alright, we'll hit whatever stores you need to pick up your … necessities. Like a razor."

Hailey gasped. He *had* noticed her tarantula legs!

"Oops," he said checking his watch. "Gotta go. It doesn't look good when the team captain's late for practice."

"You're the captain of the hockey team?"

Fink winked at her.

"Told you I was good."

When Hailey got back to her room that night, she found a note on the floor just inside the door. With Fin on her mind, she grabbed it up and tore it open.

Giselle tsk'ed loudly from behind her magazine.

The envelope twitched. Then it bulged. And something that resembled a corpse hand emerged.

Hailey dropped the envelope and by the time it hit the floor, an arm and part of a shoulder were crawling out of the letter too.

Scared beyond the capacity to scream, Hailey backed away as a decomposing, hair-covered head followed. The corpse said nothing as it pushed in jerky movements with both hands on the floor, wiggling its torso and legs out of the parchment. It yanked its head up and looked Hailey dead in the eyes as it wriggled across the floor.

"Gi—Gi—Giselle!" She finally breathed, wild-eyed and shaking as a horrible, Holly-looking carcass inched closer, scowling and oozing black juices.

Hailey backed up against the window.

"The ghost trap isn't working!"

"Not a ghost," said Giselle uninterested from behind her magazine.

"Wh—what is it?"

It slapped another hand on the floor and hauled its limp body forward.

"Ignore it, Hailey. It'll go away."

But it didn't go away. It crept closer, and Hailey pressed herself against the glass.

"I can't ignore it… It looks like my sister!" She pulled her legs up and curled into a ball on the window sill.

Giselle got up, stepped around the monster, snatched the parchment off the floor, struck a match, lit the paper, and watched with her hand on her hip as the Holly-corpse ignited.

"Didn't your mother ever tell you not to open a Nasty Gram?" she scolded as Hailey watched the burning Holly-corpse through her fingers.

The thing spun around, waving its arms wildly, flinging tiny crescents of flame in all directions. One struck the picture hanging above Hailey's desk.

"No!" Hailey lunged to save it, but the picture was destroyed.

"Give it to me," Giselle demanded snobbishly, holding out her hand as she rolled her eyes.

"It was the only picture I had of us dancing together," Hailey said.

Giselle snatched the half-burned photo.

"Don't—" Hailey stood wide-eyed as the picture healed itself in Giselle's hand, growing back to a whole image right before her very eyes. Giselle handed it back to Hailey and plopped onto her bed.

Hailey stared at the photo. "What just happened?"

"Oh, sometimes I can fix things," Giselle said in a bored voice from behind her magazine.

Hailey sat on the edge of her bed. "Who sent that thing to me?" she asked, dragging her sleeve under her nose and sniffing loudly.

"Somebody that hates you, though that doesn't narrow the pool of *student* suspects, does it?"

"Kick me while I'm down, Giselle."

"Someone who knows your sister," she added lazily.

Hailey turned away, covering her face with her hands and sobbing quietly.

"What are you doing—stop that." Giselle threw down her magazine and jumped up.

"Just give me a second," Hailey said in a muffled croak between sobs. When a weight pressed the bed next to her, Hailey looked up.

There sat Giselle, looking pensive as if she were balancing her tush on a bed of nails.

With her eyes darting around the room, Giselle sat stiff as a board. She drew a loud breath, stuck her jaw out, raised the shoulder nearest Hailey, and said, "She was really pretty." Then she stuck her hand out like a robot and mechanically patted Hailey on the back.

"Giselle, you're scaring me."

Giselle grinned as she stood up, looking wholly proud of herself.

"Next time you get a Nasty Gram, take it to the Dead Letter Office at I-MET—they can tell you who sent it." Giselle looked down at her roommate. "I'm sure you'll get more."

"Good evening, Pádraig," sneered a voice from shadows, as Fin trudged into his room. It'd been an arduous evening on the ice, and Fin was in no mood for Envoy lunacy.

He flung his door shut and flipped on the lights.

"What do you want, Cobon?" he asked, sounding drained as he dropped his duffel on the floor.

"Reciprocation. Is that too much to ask?" Cobon scowled as he emerged from the corner. "Three thousand years I've endured this place. I ferried energy for billions of you ungrateful humans—I was a servant before I was imprisoned here—"

"—try not to spit all over my room when you speak," Fin interrupted.

Cobon glared at him.

"All I ask is for a little obedience." Cobon leaned menacingly forward, but then he smiled cheerfully, straightened up, and shook his head.

"Let's not argue, Pádraig. I only came for a chat, you see, I was in the neighborhood delivering a personal message, when I had an epiphany." He paused as he surveyed Fin's room, wiping his finger across a bookshelf then rubbing it with his thumb before he continued.

"The Envoys don't belong here, Pádraig, you know that. They—we, I mean—have to go home, and that girl." He extended a flat hand toward Fin's door. "She must die."

"Why don't you just find a chump to kill her, then?" Fin said, detached. "You know…like you did Holly…" He threw his keys on his dresser and grabbed the remote.

"Didn't you know?" Cobon answered excitedly. "I already have!" Then he sighed. "Well," he said flippantly as he made himself comfortable on Fin's recliner, "in a manner of speaking. My brothers have grown weary of my methods. If I were to take another life before its time, they may very well turn on me. Besides, a wicked human would never make it past Asher, he protects her, you know."

Cobon stood and paced thoughtfully around the room.

"Oh, I tried a few round about ways to kill her already." He tapped his lip. "She just won't die.

"But! If she were to take her own life, then…" Cobon held his arms wide and shrugged gleefully.

"Suicide?" Fin scoffed. "Perhaps you haven't met Hailey."

"Oh, but *you* have, slave." He lowered his head and pointed at Fin. "You're my chump."

Fin shook his head, one eyebrow raised. "So, what—are you going to kill me, Cobon? Right in front of her? Make her think I'm dead…?"

"Oh, no. No-no-no…she's far too resilient for that, no, this requires something far more…destructive."

Cobon stood, tenting his fingers together, walking stiffly around the room.

"To destroy a house, you cannot simply crush it—it is too easily rebuilt. No…you must wreck the very foundation on which it stands. She trusts you, Pádraig. She loves you. And you know how to destroy one who loves you…"

"Go to hell, Cobon."

"Oh, why so squeamish? You'll destroy her sooner or later, why not just get it over with?"

Fin pushed his jaw out. "Listen, Oprah, I have no intention of hurting her. Ever. And this interview is over."

"...fuck them and bounce... Isn't that your modus operandi?"

"That was a long time ago."

"That was last year, Pádraig, have you forgotten?"

"That had nothing to do with me," Fin said, his voice rising as he turned away from Cobon.

"Really? Quite a coincidence, then, didn't she hang herself in your room?"

"It wasn't my room."

"Oh right, it was your lab, wasn't it? That was a nice touch, don't you think? I remember it well, *I was there*. Oh, Adalwolf and I go way back. He never could get you to take a life, though, could he? Well, not one that mattered anyway, but he did eventually figure out how to make you kill."

Cobon paced the room with his hands folded behind his back, looking thoughtful and hopeful and completely deranged. "And all he had to do was leverage your God-given talent!"

Cobon leaned toward Fin and raised his hand to the side of his mouth as if he were divulging a great secret. "...and maybe whisper a few words of encouragement into the heads of your concubines," he hissed.

Fin squeezed his eyes shut.

"Adalwolf showed me all of his little tricks and all of his little games he played with you. How many women have you sent to Hell for him? More than a dozen, I think. What's one more? We could make quite a homicidal team, you and I."

"Forget it, Cobon. I'm not your slave."

"We never forget," Cobon whispered through clenched teeth as he lurched forward. "She would let you, you know—she trusts you. You could very easily destroy her—drive her into despair and madness—just as you've done it before—drive her to…suicide?"

Fin bowed his head.

"You say, 'no,' but your wickedness says yes," Cobon continued. "You dream of her. You dream of the things you'd do to her, I've seen it."

"You little pervert," Fin said feigning incredulity. "Did you enjoy the show?"

Cobon grabbed Fin by the neck.

"You will obey us, Pádraig, whether you wish to or not."

"We've been here before, Cobon," Fin grunted, rolling his eyes. "I am not your slave."

Cobon's eyes flashed, and he set Fin back down on the floor.

"Besides," Fin coughed, "she's in love with Asher."

Cobon spun around and crushed Fin's face with powerful back fist.

Staggering back, Fin held his mouth and nose with both hands as a torrent of blood spilled out.

"No human could ever love an Envoy."

Fin grabbed a towel on his dresser and pressed it against his face.

"The sooner she rejects him the better. For everyone. He favors her, you know, his love for her grows—he may well make her immortal, and then what?" he asked, throwing both hands up. "We'd all be trapped here…she becomes his slave…you live an eternity without her…without love… She was made for *you*, I've seen it—I've seen her soul—you two are mates."

Fin raised his head slightly.

"Ahhh," Cobon cooed. "You know it too—you knew it the first time you saw her, didn't you? I couldn't use you for Holly, because you would've run straight to Asher, but I'm betting you won't be telling him about our little chat tonight, will you?" he said, watching the red as it fell from Fin's towel into little puddles on the floor. "Because if you did, I think he'd protect the girl from

you. Maybe he'd put you into permanent storage someplace…
underground maybe—or perhaps he'd seal you inside a sarcopha-
gus with a heavy stone lid—that would hold you. And you would
live your life over and over and over again—an eternity trapped
inside a coffin, does that suit you?"

Fin made a mostly nasal gurgling noise then coughed.

"Why don't you sleep on it? I'll help you, of course. Good
night, Pádraig." With that, Cobon walked toward a dark corner
and vanished.

And Fin sopped up the blood on his floor, using every second
of the next twelve hours to decide if he shouldn't leave Bear Towne
University and Hailey Hartley forever.

Chapter Twenty-Nine

Civilization Road

"Gravitation cannot be held responsible for people falling in love."

— Albert Einstein

Fin was a no-show, and Hailey waited a whole fifteen minutes past their rendezvous time before she pounded on his door.

"Enter," he called, sounding dispirited, and Hailey poked her head in.

"You alright?" she asked when she saw him sitting hunched apathetically over his guitar.

Without looking up, he strummed a familiar tune, singing coldly.

"His disguise is the black of night, and in your heart, he's darkness…"

He plucked a single, hard note and with his head still bowed, set his guitar aside.

"That's not how it goes," Hailey said softly, though his voice was beautiful and honest, and she wished he'd sing some more.

"For me it is." He showed his face, and Hailey gasped.

"What happened?" He had two black eyes and a crooked nose.

"Rough night. I was hoping it would heal a little more before our drive. Maybe by the time we get to town, you won't be ashamed to be seen with me."

Hailey rolled her eyes, smiling earnestly as Fin grabbed his wallet and keys.

"And here I thought you were standing me up."

Fin offered his elbow. "Never, my dear, you're the only thing in this world that matters to me," he said under his breath. But Hailey definitely heard it. She froze.

"You alright?" he asked.

"Yeah," she said softly. "Are you alright?"

Fin let out a curt laugh. "Right as rain, dear," he answered in his best grumpy Pix voice.

"I think you have a head injury," she surmised. "Do you want *me* to drive?" she asked coyly, and Fin's bruised face fell.

"Uh—no." He led her outside to a brand new, bright red, four-door pickup truck with big tires and decals boasting "off-road" and "4-wheel drive."

"What happened to your car?" Hailey asked, frowning her disappointment.

"Convertible-go-fast car in Pennsylvania," he said. "Sturdy-go-in-snow pickup truck in Alaska."

Civilization Road led out of Bear Towne University and away from The Middle of Nowhere like a stem on the four-leaf clover-shaped campus, and even traveling at warp-Fin speeds, it took more than three hours to actually reach civilization.

"Where should we start?" Fin asked as they came into Anchorage.

Hailey shushed him so she could concentrate on three small airplanes circling the pattern around an airfield, which she could only see out of Fin's side window. She leaned into his lap and craned her neck.

He shifted slightly, letting out a low groan.

"Cool, huh?" He spoke down to her as she stretched across his legs.

"They're so tiny. They look like toys, don't they? Oh, I bet it's a breathtaking ride!"

"Alright, sit up," he said, expelling a lungful of air as he nudged her with his knee. "Let's get some lunch."

As Fin pulled in to a fried chicken joint, Hailey grabbed her stomach, which was trained to growl at any mention of food.

"...and if you can hear me over that monster in your gut, I'll take you flying in the school's Super Cub this winter," he offered.

Hailey gave him a blank stare.

"You can fly?"

"There's a lot I can do," he said in his oh-so-confident way, and Hailey looked away. She could feel her cheeks burning as she all but fell out of the truck.

"Get your mind out of the gutter," he chided.

"I wasn't even thinking about sex with you," she blurted before she could stop herself and in a voice so loud another couple turned to stare.

Paralyzed by shame, Hailey wrapped her arms around her head.

Footsteps crunched against the gravel next to her.

"Yes you were," said Fin.

"No, I really—I wasn't—I never even..."

When she uncovered her head, a few tears of embarrassment sneaked out of her eyes.

Fin wrapped his arms around her and squeezed. Oh how she missed his hugs!

Even with a twinge of guilt pricking her heart, she didn't want him to let go, and she closed her eyes as she breathed in his cologne.

Then he kissed her on the head with a loud, "mwah!" and the moment was gone.

"Let's get some grub," he laughed, walking with his arm around her shoulder, pulling her in tight. "You're the biggest spaz…" he teased, and Hailey wiped her face.

"You stink," she chuckled with a sob. Jeez, not twenty-four hours had passed since her last break down, and there she was crying again. "Someone sent me a Nasty Gram yesterday," she told him.

Fin threw his head back and let out a groan. "Cobon."

"What?"

"He swung by last night…said he was out delivering a personal note."

"Is that what happened to your face? I thought Cobon couldn't come to Bear Towne—I…I thought Asher could keep him out—I thought…" Her heart pounded as her sense of security evaporated.

Fin pulled her into another hug, pressing her head into his chest, instantly quelling her panic. Just like with Asher, it was complete comfort…and Fin didn't want her dead.

"Don't worry about it, okay?" he said softly. "Asher can stop anyone from hurting you before it happens…"

Fat chance.

"…and Cobon won't come near you."

Hailey stepped back. "What do you mean? Why?"

"He's afraid you'll destroy him."

"Why? Why does everyone think I destroyed an Adalwolf—I didn't," she insisted with wide eyes, and Fin pursed his lip.

"Everyone *thinks* that, because Adalwolf went into your bedroom when you were a child… And then he exploded."

Staring vacantly at the pavement, Hailey wondered how long it would take Cobon to figure out she was harmless.

Fin patted her bum and led her inside, where he ordered a bucket of chicken.

"Why did Cobon come see you?" she asked after he paid.

"Because he's a perverted, psychotic maniac. Here." He shoved a fried chicken leg into her hand. "Eat."

Hailey nibbled her chicken leg, and with no further talk of exploding Envoys or her almost certain death at the hands of a perverted psychopath, they reached the bottom of the bucket and headed out.

"Where to first?" Fin asked, slapping her leg after he started the truck.

"Clothes, shoes, boots, pillow, blankets, robe, towel, toiletries, winter coat."

"Mall," he said, putting the truck in gear. "Don't worry about your winter gear. I'll take care of it while you get all your other stuff. And Hailey—do *not* forget..." He paused, shaking his head as he claimed a spot near the entrance, and Hailey's mind raced.

What? What could be dangerous about the mall? Unmarked in-betweens? Cobon? What?

Fin sighed. "—a razor." He smiled playfully, and she slugged his arm.

"Meet back here in an hour, okay?" he chuckled as they made their way inside.

Within forty-five minutes, Hailey had everything, including a razor, and she met Fin at the exit. He took her bags for her as they walked to the truck.

"You wanna do some skating while we're here?" he asked, tossing her things onto the back seat.

Hailey shook her head. "I've never been on ice skates. I wouldn't even know how to put one on."

"Then I'll show you," he said using his professor's voice, and he steered her back inside.

"I usually try to avoid embarrassing myself in public, Fin."

"No you don't," he reminded her as he pushed her into the ice arena. "You wait right here while I get our skates...and don't talk to strangers."

Hailey waited obediently with her hands folded in her lap for Fin to return with two sets of skates. One was already installed on his feet, and he fitted the other onto her little feet in a way that made her feel like Cinderella.

"Let's go." Grabbing her hands, he pulled her toward the rink.

"No-no-no-no-no-no-no-no," she pleaded, walking stiff-legged like the tin man, but Fin lifted her onto the ice anyway, wrapping his arms around her waist from behind and holding her tight against him.

"Come on little penguin," he sang as he skated across the rink with her. "Time to spread your wings and glide."

"Penguins don't spread wings and glide," she said on wobbly legs. "They flop and slide."

"Not if they're from Pittsburgh," he pointed out as he pivoted in front of her. "It's time you learned." He took her hands, pulling her along as he skated backwards.

"You know I really don't think this is a good idea." Her legs stiffened, her butt jutted out, and she almost lost it in a spastic cartoon-like pirouette. But Fin had good reflexes. He pivoted, turned, and caught her under her shoulders so gracefully it felt like a choreographed dance.

"Nice save," she breathed as he steadied her on her skates again.

"You should see me play," he offered. "Season opener in Anchorage," he said. "I'll even get you a backstage pass IF you can stay out of trouble until October."

Hailey wobbled dangerously but recovered with only a slight nudge. "Deal," she said confidently, holding onto his hands. "You know, I think I'm getting the hang of this," she smiled, slipping her hands through his until he held only her fingertips.

Then she let go altogether.

"Hey, look!" she exclaimed proudly. "I'm doing it—whoa!"

She faltered slightly, which threw her off balance, which caused her arms to circle like a windmill, and when she instinctively turned her foot out like an Irish dancer, her ankle crumpled with a wet-sounding CRACK! Down she went—like a flyswatter.

"Ouch," she mumbled into the ice, and Fin skidded to a halt next to her. As she rolled over and pushed herself up to sit, her ankle flopped to the side.

"Dammit," Fin said angrily.

"I'm sorry," Hailey gushed as he scooped her up. "I was doing great, and then I lost my balance, but I totally had it, but then my ankle quit, and…" She twitched her foot. "—ouch—I think I hurt something."

"Nonsense," he said, skating her off the ice. "You just wanted me to carry you, so you could feel my bulging pectorals." It sounded like he was joking, but his voice had a scornful edge, and Hailey didn't know what to say.

Setting her on a bench, Fin surveyed the damage.

"It's not your fault," he said throwing his hand up. "Your laces came loose."

Hailey looked down. Not only had they come untied, but they'd uncrossed themselves from the hooks, draped themselves under her bootie, and retied themselves into a loose bow.

"This has poltergeist written all over it. You must've pissed one off, if it followed you here."

When Fin pulled her skate off, her foot swelled past a comfortable fit-into-wellies size.

"I'm designing a new ghost trap—you know—one that actually traps ghosts," she said quickly as Fin touched her foot. "—ouch—it'll be my term project—ow—ow—ow—and I told the one in the library it would be the first to go."

"That would do it," he said woefully. "We should head back anyway."

The ride home to Bear Towne became too quiet. Fin stared through the windshield with his elbow propped against his door, head resting on his fist. For forty very uncomfortable miles, he said nothing, so Hailey decided to break the silence.

"That was a fun day," she said brightly.

He shot her a disgusted glance then turned his attention back to the road.

"You thought that was a date?" He asked in a way that told Hailey he sure didn't.

It took her a second to realize he'd misheard her.

"No! No-no-no, I—"

"That was not a date, Hailey."

"Oh, I…I didn't—"

"I don't want you to get the wrong idea about me. This was *not* a date."

Could this get any more awkward any faster? And more importantly, why wasn't this a date? They'd spent the entire day together. And Fin wasn't even remotely afraid of Asher. Whatever his malfunction, this was starting to feel like a rejection, so she mustered the best defense she could think of—denial.

"No, Fin, I… I know… I wasn't—that never even crossed my mind," she lied, trying not to seem as offended as she felt.

"It didn't?" He sounded either hurt or surprised.

Hailey was confused.

"No," she said uncertainly. "I—no. I said day. That was a fun day."

Fin stared at the road.

Hailey bit her lip.

Watching another milepost fly past, she decided she should just keep her mouth shut for the rest of the drive.

By the time they pulled up to Eureka Dorm, Hailey's stomach was in a knot. Fin was the closest thing she had to family for thousands of miles, and she managed to completely alienate him over the course of one night. He'd probably never talk to her again—the silly little girl Hailey, pining after the campus-heartthrob-muscular-captain-of-the-stupid-hockey-team, showing up naked at his door, throwing herself at him...

She couldn't wait to bury her head in her new pillow and never leave her room again.

Blinking back a few tears of embarrassment, she opened the passenger side door and hopped out on one foot.

"Wait for me to help you, Hailey!" Fin yelled, clearly annoyed as he hurriedly jumped out.

"I got it," she told him, her voice strained.

But she didn't have it. When she tried to push the door shut, her one good foot slipped out from under her and down she went, cracking her head on the pavement and sliding almost completely under the truck.

She let out a pitiful moan, a little from the sharp pain in the back of her head, but mostly from shame.

"Why is there ice in August?" she groaned.

"Hailey!" she heard a voice yell, but it wasn't Fin's.

Someone with warm hands grabbed hers and pulled her out from under the truck and back onto her good foot with one swift tug.

Fin ran from the driver's side, rounding the front of the truck and stopping dead to stare at Asher holding onto Hailey.

"I guess you don't need me," said Fin sourly, as Hailey clung to Asher. He unloaded her bags, and gripping them so tight his knuckles went white, he hiked toward Eureka.

"Fin!" Hailey called from Asher's arms.

Fin faced her with his jaw set.

"Thank you," she said, her heart sinking terribly as she limped a few feet in his direction.

Fin dropped his head for a moment, and then he straightened up and threw his chest out.

"Listen," he asserted, addressing Hailey and quite clearly only Hailey. "A lot of us are going to the hot springs this weekend. You wanna come along?"

"Oh, no… I—I don't think so. I don't have a bathing suit," she said uncomfortably.

"Oh, you don't need one." Fin raised his eyebrow at her.

"Oh! Then definitely no."

"Come on. It'll be dark. And…it's not like I've never seen you naked," he said loud enough for Asher to hear.

Hailey whipped around in time to see Asher's eyes explode.

"Um…that…I…" she stammered, hopping back to Asher.

"Come and sit," he said, his tone flat, expression unreadable as he guided her to a wooden bench. Kneeling in front of her, he stroked her wounded foot.

Hailey dug her nails into the bench, anticipating an awful prod or twist or jerk or something painful, but what she got was a delightfully cooling comfort, which spread from her toes up to her knee. When Asher stood, Hailey stood next to him—her ankle healed and the swelling gone.

"That's amazing," she said, cautiously hopping on it. Eyes shining, she tilted her head slightly. "I'm not going to be your slave forever, am I?" she asked with a nervous chuckle.

"Only if you want to be." A ghost of a smile played on his lips. "These are not favors I often bestow, Hailey."

She shook her head, all humor gone. "I wouldn't ever want that," she whispered, pulling her shoulders up and tucking her elbows in.

"No, you wouldn't. Still…" Holding his hand out, palm up, Asher conjured what looked like a ball of crystalized violet light. He held it out to Hailey. "I am tempted to give you this."

"What is it?" she said, transfixed by its beauty.

"Immortality. An eternity of youth and health. The Envoys call it a gift. But any human who has accepted it would call it a curse. If you were to take this from me, you would be a slave to the Envoys—all of us—forever. Such an infusion of energy leaves a scar, Hailey, through which any of us might see into your mind. And in some cases," he added darkly, "even control it."

Closing his hand, he collapsed the orb, which burst into a flash as bright as a camera's.

"As much as I want you on this Earth with me forever," he said gazing adoringly into her eyes, "I would not curse you with this burden."

Bringing her hand to his lips, he kissed her fingers then spoke against them.

"The Envoys are changing. They no longer respect each other's possessions as they once did, and I couldn't bear it if another touched you."

Possessions?

Hailey jerked her hand away. "I'm not your possession, Asher. I don't belong to you—I don't belong to anyone, and you need to—"

Asher stepped back, blinking as if she'd slapped him.

"I didn't…" Frowning, he shook his head, eyes wide as Hailey considered him, arms crossed. His lips parted, his brow wrinkled, and she couldn't stand seeing him hurt.

Finally she sighed. "You have to stop saying that," she said gently, and when he reached a tentative hand out to her, she took it.

Relief etched his voice, but it was still a plea. "I didn't mean… I only meant that I protect you. And the Envoys no longer regard each other as family. You're beautiful, Hailey. I'm not the only one who sees it, and one of the others would surely stalk your mind."

Instinctively, Hailey flicked her eyes to the ground, disarmed again as he nudged her chin up. He was so close she could feel his breath against her lips.

"I'm sorry," he whispered, planting a soft kiss on her mouth.

"I'm sorry too," she said, and he kissed her again. Then, sighing heavily, he pulled away, and Hailey studied his eyes, trying to imagine life on Earth for hundreds or thousands of years.

"Have you ever cursed anyone?" she asked.

"Once."

"It's Professor Woodfork, isn't it?"

Asher smiled. "He and I have known each other for a very long time. I try to stay out of his mind," he said, looking almost mischievously at her, "although sometimes I get bored and go see what he's thinking."

Hailey studied him. For the first time, he seemed relaxed and almost amused. "I don't really understand how any of this works." She looked down at her healed foot then around at the campus and back to Asher. "Someone told me it was dangerous to ask you for help with…things…"

"Giselle," he guessed. "She's always honest, but not always correct. Hailey, you're very dear to me. I healed your body, because I wanted to. I've asked for nothing in return."

Taking his hand, Hailey pressed it to her heart.

"I would like to see you more," he told her, using his free hand to stroke her cheek.

"You can start by showing up to lab," she teased.

"Yes," he said softly.

He drew an awkward breath. "Hailey, I would like to show you my observatory. This winter… If you'd like. I'm afraid it would have to be very dark for you to see…"

She watched him, smiling in awe as it dawned on her—he was asking her out, and he was nervous.

"I'd like that," she said quickly.

"And in December… The university hosts a Christmas ball. May I escort you?"

"I'd be honored," she said, though this was the first she'd heard of such an event and would have to find a dress and shoes and learn to walk in heels and figure out how to dance non-Irish and find Giselle a date, because there was no way she was doing this alone…

Hailey sighed.

"Go and rest," Asher told her, kissing her cheek.

Fin was playing his guitar when Hailey knocked on his door to retrieve her things.

"Enter!" he shouted. As she poked into his room, he began strumming softly.

"I love that song," she said, standing in his doorway.

"I know."

"How do you know that?"

"I know everything about you," he said, setting his guitar aside.

"Enlighten me."

"I know that roses are your favorite flowers—"

"Typical," she said with a flick of her hand.

"And that your favorite color is green—"

"Obvious," she yawned.

"And that you cry more out of your right eye than your left—"

"You noticed that?"

Fin nodded. "Seen you cry a lot—I know that you're afraid of Asher, but you won't tell him."

Hailey ducked her head.

"Listen," he said, leaning forward, "Asher's powerful. He can protect you from harm, from bad people, from other Envoys… But," he said emphatically, counting his points on his fingers, "he can't laugh." Searching Hailey's eyes, he extended another digit. "He can't love. He can't have children. And he won't tolerate your dancing."

Hailey furrowed her brow.

"It's the drumming," he explained. "It's like fingernails on a chalkboard to an Envoy."

Staring at the floor, Hailey chewed her lip. She didn't owe Fin an explanation. He wasn't even interested in her, so why did he even care? This was just his big-brother-look-after-Hailey thing, and she was sick of it.

"I put your stuff in your room already," he told her when she didn't respond. "You're not really building a ghost trap for your term project, are you?" he asked, adjusting to a much more agreeable tone.

"Yes," Hailey said sounding way more excited than she wanted, and he closed his eyes, tossing his head back.

"Hailey—" He sighed loudly. "You're gonna piss them off, and they're going to come after you again."

Chapter Thirty

The Trap

"Our pleasures were simple - they included survival."

— Dwight D. Eisenhower

For her term project, Hailey might have undertaken a jaunt into a dark tunnel, rehabilitated a needy creature, written her report, and been done in a few hours. Instead, she decided to build a better ghost trap.

And it was Giselle who'd given her an idea for how to do it. As the two walked from their ParaComm class, Giselle stepped a little too close to the Chattering Gazebo, which immediately recoiled, saying, "An acoustical nightmare as usual, Giselle. How I wish you'd keep your loathsome vibrations away. You really do know how to repel any creature, don't you? Oh, I suppose it comes naturally to a—"

Giselle jumped back before the gazebo finished.

"I hate that thing," she muttered.

After a whole class of forced conversation with Giselle without a single accidental insult, Hailey's foot jumped in her mouth.

"So, what kind of monster are you?" she asked in an innocent voice, and Giselle slowly scowled. "Insensitive…" Hailey mumbled. "Was that insensitive? I'm sorry," she said as fast as she could.

"You need a blurt filter. Maybe that should be your term project," Giselle growled. The day's ParaComm discussion topic had been "My Term Project," and Giselle thought redesigning a ghost trap bordered on suicidal stupidity. She hadn't been shy about sharing that opinion, either.

"Why did the gazebo say you vibrated?"

"Because I *do*."

Hailey frowned. She figured she only had one more shot at this before her roommate clammed up for the rest of the night and tasked her every last brain cell to contemplation. Finally, and with only another minute or two before they reached Eureka Hall, Hailey's gray matter came up with a humdinger.

She bit her lip, made a curt, confident nod, drew a breath and said, "Wha—"

"Banshee," Giselle burst out.

Hailey's mouth fell open. *No wonder she didn't have any friends.* "Why didn't you tell me?"

"Why would you need to know? It has nothing to do with you!"

"Sorry," she said quickly, her eyes wide. "Okay. No big deal. You're a harbinger of death, that's all."

In trying to wrap her mind around it, Hailey imagined Uncle Pix's reaction. He would never believe it. If he did, he'd probably blow a gasket. But Giselle wasn't a murderer. Matter of fact, she could warn Hailey if there was a murderer lurking about...

Giselle frowned. "I can't tell when someone's going to die," she snapped. "That's why I'm here—my family's ashamed of me, and this whole college thing is a huge joke to them."

A silver string flew out of her eye.

"They told me to study medicine and—*quote*, 'figure it out'."

Another thread of silk let loose and blew away.

"That's why I look like this." She uncrossed her arms and threw her hands up then hugged herself again.

"Don't all banshees look like you?"

"No!" Giselle yelled. "They only go 'hag' like this when they're about to die!" She pulled a cobweb from her eye, balled it up and let it fall. "I'm just an ugly, useless abomination that nobody likes." She cried softly as Hailey walked next to her.

"Well, I like you," Hailey offered, stroking Giselle's hair. "And look." She held a golden lock in her hand, staring at it with one eyebrow up. "Your hair's turning blonde."

Giselle rolled her eyes.

"And I saw David staring at you in class today. Like, staring in a good way."

"You're lying."

"Don't you remember, when you almost laughed...after I said the thing about Professors Mum, Loon, and Starr, and the whole class turned to see who the idiot was, only you were already staring at me with daggers, like normal—that's why you didn't notice— and then you stifled a laugh and everyone looked away, except for David. He kept looking at you not me, and he even moved his head a little to see more of you."

Giselle went silent, but at least she wasn't crying anymore.

"Anyway," said Hailey, getting to her point, "I think someone's being a little hard on herself," she peeped as if she were encouraging a three-year old. "You're not useless. In fact, I could sure use your help."

"How?"

"The gazebo gave me an idea. Tell me more about these vibrations."

Giselle shrugged. "Every creature has a death frequency, and I know it instantly—it vibrates inside me. A real banshee would know when someone was about to bite it and wail out their frequency." She looked tentatively over at Hailey.

"Do you get a vibe on ghosts, too?"

"Yeah. Ghosts are easy. They all have the same frequency. Why?"

Hailey pressed her brow down. "If there's a frequency that repels all ghosts, could there be one that attracts them?"

"How would I know?" she yelled.

"Can you control it—you know...the vibrations you give off?"

Giselle whirled around. "What good is it if I can control it? I can't tell when to wail—I'm useless," she spat. "Just ask my mother."

"If you can control it, I can measure it," Hailey said excitedly. "I know a friendly poltergeist we could use as a test subject. You throw different frequencies at him, and we'll observe his response...see if he's attracted to one. Then I could reproduce that very frequency in a crystalline matrix, so a ghost would be drawn into the trap, surrounded by vibration, stuck there forever, and there you have it—ghost trap," she concluded, looking sunnily to her roommate. "So?" she sang. "Whaddya say? Will you help me?" she begged, lightly touching Giselle's arm.

Stopping dead in her tracks, Giselle glared at Hailey's hand for what seemed like an eternity before she sniffed loudly.

"Fine," she snarled.

With Giselle's cooperation, it took less than a month to figure out which frequency to use for the new, Hartley Hook-a-Haunt (that was what she was calling it). Growing the crystals proved a bit more challenging, but with Asher's guidance, she was making great progress. And that progress did not escape the attention of the mostly free and healthy population of specters at Bear Towne, who quite liked the ineffective golden ghost traps currently in use.

As Hailey worked late into a chilly October night, alone inside Asher's lab at Olde Main, she got the feeling someone was watching her. More than once she got up from her work station to investigate, but the place seemed deserted.

After her third security check, Hailey threw down her goggles and rubbed her eyes, deciding it was time to call it a night.

It was just after midnight when she stood up to go. She didn't know Asher had left the campus. She didn't know the poltergeists knew that, and she sure didn't know that Asher kept in his lab no fewer than five desktop staplers and two staple guns.

But when she turned toward the door, she found, hovering in midair and blocking her path, all seven—locked, loaded, and unhinged.

She stared at them for a good three seconds as two of them flanked her left side and a roll of tape moved on her right. Poltergeists—too many to count—swooped across the ceiling, sharp wisps of wind-swept fog, and, ironically, they had her trapped.

Hailey broke for the exit, batting down one stapler as six others stung her in the back and arms.

The tape sprang to life and unwound with a shrill "ZZZZZ!" flinging itself around and around her wrist so tight it cut off her circulation. While she battled that, the six staplers hit her back and arms over and over while the seventh darted for her neck.

Hailey staggered for the door.

The tape caught her other hand, binding both together, yanking them up and away from the latch, as the staplers slapped against her with an unrelenting click-click-click-click-click and periodic ka-chonk of the staple gun.

"Tomas!" she yelled, looking desperately into the glass of the door she couldn't reach. "Help me!"

Immediately, Tomas appeared, raised his eyebrows, shot into the room, and created enough of a distraction for her to high-tail it out of there.

Hoping to find Asher, Hailey punched the out-between, and with her hands bound tightly with Scotch tape, stumbled outside and headed straight for the observatory, moving her torso as little as possible…trying not to think about a thousand staples lodged in her skin, especially the ones from the gun, which felt like they'd splintered bone.

Asher will help, she told herself, but when she reached the tower door, she found it locked.

"Asher," she called, but he didn't answer.

After shivering and bleeding for thirty seconds on his doorstep without a response, Hailey spun around stiffly and walked as gingerly as she could toward Eureka Hall. The temperature hovered around ten degrees that night, and Hailey's breath came out in curt, painful puffs.

Shaking violently and holding her arms as still as she could with her hands still painfully bound, she trudged up the stairs, trying not to disrupt her shirt, which, along with her bra, was pretty much sewn into her back and glued into place by dried, frozen blood.

At last she reached the third floor, and thankfully, Fin's door was wide open; his light flooded the hallway. When Hailey stepped onto the landing, he shot out of his room.

"Where have you been? It's past midnight—where's your coat—"

He cut himself off and rushed across the hallway, ripping the tape off her wrists and rubbing them gently. Hailey sighed as blood returned to her fingers.

"I got stapled." She turned rigidly around to show him.

"Oh, Hailey," he breathed. "Come in here." He led her to the community room opposite the stairs.

"Wait here a sec," he told her. "I'll go get the tweezers."

Hailey stood still until he returned.

"Oh, man," he said as he looked at her back again.

"How bad is it?"

"There's several hundred," he estimated, and when she pivoted to look at him, he gave her a half-frown. "Surprised you didn't run to Asher."

"I did," she grunted as she sat on top of a table. "He wasn't home."

Fin's face tightened, and he curled his tongue as he yanked the first staple out of her neck.

"Ouch! They're all over me," she breathed, remembering to count to eight before she exhaled.

"...lucky staples..." Fin muttered softly, as he removed another one from her back.

"Ouch!"

"What are you doing?" Giselle demanded, appearing in the doorway.

"Removing staples...?" He jerked a big one out of Hailey's arm.

"Ouch!"

"You know what I mean," Giselle spat.

"Shouldn't you be in the lab getting your bolts tightened?" he jeered.

Huh. Giselle actually did bear a striking resemblance to Frankenstein's bride. Really. She was only a couple of black hair streaks and some stitches away from moaning, "Fire—Bad."

Giselle glared at him for a beat before spinning on her heel and gliding out of the room. "I'm bringing the first aid kit," she grumbled over her shoulder.

"Why are you so mean to her?" Hailey asked him.

"Because," he said as he drew one from her scalp, "she deserves it."

"I wish you'd be a little—ouch!—nicer. I think it hurts her feelings that everyone's so mean."

"Clearly you don't know your roommate." He made a third attempt at a staple that embedded itself near Hailey's underarm. "Come 'ere," he said under his breath as he tried to grab it again.

Hailey looked over her shoulder to see how things were going, and that was a mistake. Among the sea of bloodied staples strewn across the table, one still had a chunk of flesh attached.

"Uh-oh," Hailey said, woozy. Darkness crept into her periphery and her ears felt like they were full of water. The whole room tipped like a canoe, and she fell forward.

"Whoa!" Fin lunged to catch her before she hit the floor. The tweezers clanged against the table, and Fin grabbed her by the shirt, ripping at least twenty staples out at once.

That was enough to put her the rest of the way out.

When Hailey came to, she was sprawled, belly-down, shirt-less, braless, and mostly skinless on Fin's bed—she recognized the cologne. A soft and peaceful *Moonlight Sonata* vibrated through Fin's guitar. His humming joined it in perfect pitch as she stirred.

"Giselle dressed your wounds. Your clothes were ruined, but on a brighter note, I found you a new roommate." He tossed her one of his t-shirts.

"What?" She groaned as even the slightest movement stretched the raw skin on her back. "I don't want a new roommate."

"You're still out of it."

"No, I'm not. I like my roommate." Hailey turned away from him as she sat, painfully lifting the t-shirt over her head.

"*Nobody* likes your roommate," he told her. "She's a raging bitch."

"She's not…" Hailey heaved an aggravated sigh. "She's not… raging."

"Yeah, she is."

"Well, I like her," she said decisively, and Fin cocked his head, studying her for a moment.

"How come you came here instead of waiting for Asher?"

"I would have waited—I *did* wait…long enough anyway, outside the observatory," she told him, and he looked away. "It was weird," she continued. "I called his name, and he never showed. I mean, the other day, I tripped going up the stairs in the Trinity Center, and he caught me before I fell—he got to me instantly, coming all the way from Olde Main," she told him forlornly. "Guess he must be pretty busy tonight, huh."

"Maybe he's bored with you," Fin said with an edge. "…or maybe he's dead," he added in a way too hopeful tone.

Hailey rolled her eyes, but inside she worried. She'd just lost half her skin in his lab. She'd cried out for him, and he'd ignored her. Maybe Fin was right. Maybe Asher changed his mind again and now wanted her dead. She felt guilty for thinking it, but maybe he was off conspiring with Cobon.

"Can I just sleep here?" she sighed, falling forward onto Fin's pillow.

"Sure," he said. When she turned her head to him he was smiling. He pulled a blanket from his cupboard, curled up on his recliner, and stared lovingly at her until she fell asleep.

"To what do I owe the pleasure?" Cobon asked rather anxiously as Asher appeared in his home uninvited.

"I cannot help but imagine your interest in my girl," he answered coldly. "Do you wish to kill her?"

"Straight to the point, as usual," Cobon observed as he gazed out his window at his home near Pittsburgh. "I should return the favor, but I enjoy your conversation too much to skip the pleasantries. I've grown quite fond of this place," he said, sounding more content than he had in decades. "See here, Asher," Cobon said, pointing out a tall window. "One can hardly see civilization through the autumn leaves. Is it not beautiful here?"

"There is much beauty in this world."

"How right you are, and yet..." Cobon flicked his hand at the breathtaking landscape. "It is not this beauty that interests you— and certainly not the beauty of our home in the Aether. It's that girl, isn't it?" Cobon sneered. "But she must die. And you know this as well as I do."

"She *will* die. When her time comes. But that time is *not* tonight at the hands of the poltergeists."

"Time…" Cobon repeated with a far-off gaze, "a mortal creature's enemy, but what do we care of time until the absurdity of love grips us, eh brother?"

Cobon turned a knowing eye to Asher and wiggled his finger at him in time with the pendulum of a grandfather clock in the room. "How is your little romance with that skinny Irish cow going—a hopeless endeavor, if you ask me. Borders on desperate, does it not?"

"You cannot understand it, Cobon."

"I understand more than you think," he scowled, but then he smiled brightly. "If I were you, I would disembarrass myself from such a bauble. A human cannot love an Envoy—we are…" Cobon drew a great breath. "…too powerful, too wise."

"I will protect her from any that would harm her, brother, even to my own demise."

Cobon pursed his lips. "I admit, I've tried to hasten her death—the ghosts in the lab—that's why you're here, isn't it? There was the fall from the Luftzeug, a deadly in-between, a splinter, a poisoned quill—none of it worked," he shrugged, laughing. "She is resilient—and of course you keep rescuing her, though you haven't given her the gift…yet." Cobon narrowed his eyes. "—a good thing, and I'll tell you why, but first you must know I have protected the Sullivan line for centuries. In the end, her energy belongs to me. But you can keep her body and soul—I have no use for them." Cobon paced the room with his brow furrowed. "You keep her at your zoo in Bear Towne, but I cannot figure out how you hold her there—I saw no cage, no chains, no rope…? Will you tell me?"

"She is free to leave."

"And yet she stays. Why hasn't she run from you? Is it because she fears the others?"

"She stays not from fear."

Cobon grimaced. "Really? You believe she stays because she loves you, but does she know you stood by while her dear sister perished… No?" he taunted. "I thought not. And what of your challenger, that mutt Pádraig? How did you win her away from him?"

Asher ignored him.

Cobon paced with long strides across the room.

"You are a fool, Asher. You mistake your girl's fear for love, but what does it matter? As long as the others are here on Earth, you will never be free to love her. The others would destroy you and the girl if they knew." He faced the great clock, staring hatefully at it. "There is a way, though. You could complete the black rock with her energy without killing her completely—send the others home but remain here on Earth...with her…"

Asher shifted his gaze, and Cobon grinned. "You are intrigued by the idea—why else would you ignore her now, as she cries for you. Even I can hear her."

"It's not possible," said Asher.

"Oh, but it is! Simply remove her soul—gently, of course— separate it from her body, but keep hold of it," he told him raising an instructive finger. "Let her energy out, and then rebind her to her body—it's a simple energy swap. Be sure to fling the rock away, far away—the others will follow it. Open the Aether, and send them home. You'd be free to love her…"

Asher straightened ever so slightly, and Cobon smiled gleefully. If his brother weren't insane, Asher would have found Cobon's sudden good humor suspicious.

"Bring the girl here, Asher, she needn't fear this. We'll talk… the three of us. Over dinner—she'll like that," he rambled. "And I'll try not to kill her in the meantime—she'll like that even more, I suspect."

"I will choose the time, Cobon," Asher commanded. "And you will not touch her."

"I promise you nothing, brother, you know my impatience. Make it soon," Cobon stressed, "and she'll be safe."

With that, Cobon bowed, and Asher reappeared in The Middle of Nowhere in time to watch *his* girl fall asleep in another man's bed.

Chapter Thirty-One

Neglect

"Better never to have met you in my dream
than to wake and reach for hands that are not there."

— Otomo No Yakamochi

Hailey woke up and made it back to her room just as Giselle came down from the ceiling. She changed Hailey's dressings for her before leaving for class that morning and she even pulled a stray staple out of her neck. Tomas found another two lodged in her scalp, and Asher was still a no-show.

"Where do you think he is?" she asked Tomas as he twisted her hair into a fancy ponytail. Thank goodness too. Hailey couldn't lift her arms high enough to even touch her hair, let alone brush it.

Tomas shrugged. He didn't care, and as he finished, Fin let himself into her room.

"How's the back?"

Hailey perked up.

"It's just a little raw," she told him optimistically, "and Giselle put some Indispensable Mend-a-Wound on it this morning." Looking down at her backpack, she tried to reach it without bending.

"Stop," Fin said. "I'll carry your books."

"Thank you." She smiled, trying not to look as sore as she felt. Every breath hurt that day, and she sat on the edge of her seat through class, at first because she couldn't rest her back against the chair, but later because Dr. Woodfork lectured on Earth-bound Envoys—she was riveted.

The hour flew, and when Woodfork discovered he'd gone late, he hurriedly gathered his papers and headed for the door, yelling over his shoulder amidst the racket of swinging auditorium seats, "A reminder—instead of Weights and Measures, you'll all go now and meet with your section leads... Oh!"

He spun around with his armful of papers.

"Next time—the White Forest," he told them quickly. "Your assignment: Go into the White Forest *with a partner*, please—we don't need any fatalities this year—and listen to the trees."

He pushed the door open with his back.

"Write fifteen hundred words on what you hear there and how it relates scientifically to paranormal research – due in class next week. Have a good weekend everybody," he added, and the door closed behind him.

As Hailey exited, she had a flashback of her hellish night in Lab 1, and wondered if Asher would bother to show up.

He didn't.

And she knew that meant one of two things: either she was expelled again, or he wanted her dead. She went to the observatory to find out which it was and discovered Asher there staring through his telescope.

"How can you see anything in the daylight?" she asked as the door closed behind her. "What are you looking for anyway?" When he didn't answer, she huffed loudly and turned to leave.

"Forgiveness," he called, and then he turned his gaze to her. "You're injured again."

"It's nothing," she lied. Actually, her back was on fire, but she was too angry to admit it. Not that Asher cared—he went back to his telescope. Fin was right...Asher was bored with her.

"I'll leave you to it," she said softly as she started for the door again.

Asher jumped from his platform, landing loudly in front of Hailey.

"Don't go," he said gently, and Hailey's lip trembled.

Why? Why did she always cry when she was angry?

Asher touched her softly, tilting her chin up, but he didn't heal her. "Why are you sad?" he said.

Hailey looked away. "I'm not," she argued. "I mean, I am. Or angry or scared, I don't know—I tried to find you last night," she told him, her voice going to a croak. She swallowed hard and looked away. "I called for you, and when you didn't answer me, I thought maybe you were waiting to see if I'd die...again. You seem..." She risked a look in his eyes. "Do you want me dead again?"

He brushed her tears away. "Yes," he said. "But only temporarily."

Hailey's blood ran cold. "What?" she managed, stepping away from him.

"Let me heal you," he pleaded, "and we'll talk." He held his hand out for her to take.

Not sure she wanted his help, Hailey stared at the ground stubbornly, and Asher waited.

"Sometimes you scare me," she said without looking up.

"I don't mean to," he coaxed.

Hesitantly, she placed her hand in his. Drawing her into his powerful embrace, he slid his hands around her waist and under her shirt, gently gliding his fingertips across her skin as she silently cried. A torrent of tiny tickles rose up her back, and she cringed slightly under the cold sting of regenerating skin. When he finished his repairs, Asher hugged her tight.

"It upsets me to see you in Pádraig's bed," he told her quietly, and Hailey pushed him away.

"I wasn't *in* his bed, I was on it," she informed him. "And I only ended up there because after you ignored me, I went home, and Fin was there, and he ran out to help me remove a gazillion staples from my back and neck and arms and head, and then I passed out, but you still stayed away, and all I could think was that you were out with Cobon plotting to kill me."

Hailey bit her lips together, squeezed her eyes shut, and slapped her hands over them. "I'm so sorry," she said. She had no right to accuse him of depravity when she'd slept in Fin's bed the night before.

Asher fixed his eyes on her. "Cobon will one day succeed in killing you, but he has agreed to stay away for a short while."

"Wait. You were with him last night?"

Asher dropped his gaze.

"Asher, did you make a deal with him?"

"We discussed a way to save you—an energy swap," he continued, closing the gap between them and reaching for her cheek. "I would have to separate your soul from your body," he said as he stroked her gently. "I would have to kill you temporarily."

Hailey inhaled sharply, but she didn't jump away from him.

"I love you, Hailey, and I don't want to lose you."

"Are you even capable of love, Asher?" Her heart pounding in her throat, she watched him close his eyes, ducking his head slightly.

"Can you not feel my love for you?" he asked, his voice half hurt, half angry.

"Sometimes," Hailey told him cautiously. "Just so you know, it's not romantic at all to talk about killing someone you love— even temporarily. I'm not okay with that. The whole separate-the-soul-from-the-body-thing… I think we should talk about this."

She didn't know if he would even entertain her thoughts on the matter. If he decided to kill her, she was dead, and that was that. She couldn't stop him.

"We will." He brushed a strand of hair over her shoulder. "I brought you something from Pittsburgh," he said with an eagerness Hailey had never seen in him before.

"You were in Pittsburgh?" she asked, smiling a little. Jeez, if she'd known he could flit back and forth so easily, she'd have asked him to bring her some of her things.

Asher nodded and took her hand, leading her into his home and through the doors of his atrium to a wooden bench, built for two, which sat near the two-story stone fountain.

"Sit here," he told her, "and close your eyes."

Hailey obliged, enjoying the feel of her new skin against the back of the bench as the thunder of falling water filled her ears.

"Your uncle sent these for you," came Asher's voice, and Hailey opened her eyes to find her tattered Irish hardshoes sitting on the floor in front of her. She stared at them blankly for several seconds.

"I thought you'd be pleased," said Asher. "Was I mistaken?"

"No," said Hailey softly as she got up. "I just haven't danced since…" Her voice died on her, and she picked up her shoes. "I'm not allowed to use these here anyway," she said holding them wistfully, and Asher touched her hands.

"Dancing makes you happy, and seeing you happy pleases me. You may dance here, in my home, whenever you wish."

"Don't you hate percussion?"

"I do. I find it intolerably annoying, but I enjoy seeing you happy."

As Hailey hugged her shoes to her chest, Asher produced a letter. "From your uncle," he told her. "He kept me waiting while he wrote it, and I confess I listened to his thoughts as I lingered."

"You can hear his thoughts? How?" she asked absently. She already knew. But she needed to hear it from Asher.

"It was Cobon," he said, answering her real question. "Your uncles agreed to watch over your line centuries ago."

Centuries. No wonder Uncle Pix was so grumpy.

"How is he?"

"He insisted I tell you he's well."

"How is he really?"

Asher hesitated. "He worries, and he misses you."

"Maybe he's worried you'll kill me temporarily," she muttered, stealing a glance at him. His face fell momentarily, but she gave him a half-hearted grin, and his mouth twitched in relief.

She opened the note, smiling at the familiar scrawl.

Hailey,

*We all miss you. Looking forward to seeing you dance at
the pub this summer. Remember: love beats like a drum
in the heart of a righteous man. And it can shake even the
most heinous of monsters into oblivion.*

Love Pix

Hailey pulled her chin back, figuring Uncle Pix had been in the whiskey before writing such a cryptic note.

"Do you know what this means?" She held the note out, but Asher shook his head.

"Perhaps he's referring to how you dispatched Adalwolf. But," he added, "he had been drinking with his brothers, and it was difficult to follow his thoughts."

Asher waited patiently as Hailey read the note twice again, and then he stroked her arm. "Hailey, would you join me in the observatory tonight?"

"Sure," she said still staring at her uncle's letter. "What time?"

"After the sun sets. Before it rises again."

"Alright," she chuckled. "I'll see you then."

Hugging her shoes, she left his home smiling. As she exited the ParaScience leaf, Fin caught up to her.

"I'll take that," he said, pulling her backpack off her shoulder.

"Thanks."

"You're welcome…and you know you're not allowed to use those here." He pointed to her hardshoes. Then he slapped her on the back. "Guess you've been to see Asher," he said spitefully, and Hailey gave him a wry smile.

They walked half a block in silence before Fin blurted out, "I'm four hundred and sixty years old."

Hailey stopped slacked-jawed.

"Been meaning to tell you," he added over his shoulder, never breaking stride.

"How?" Hailey asked, running to catch up.

"Curse," he said curtly. "Adalwolf."

Hailey stared at the ground as they walked, not sure what to say or ask or think or feel…

"I stole all your mail," Fin said suddenly.

Hailey pressed her brow down and pulled her chin back. "What?"

"Yeah. Every day," he confessed. "You actually got into to Harvard."

Hailey's jaw fell again, and Fin smiled mischievously.

"I had to get you here," he said shrugging, "and there was no way you were coming to Bear Towne if you knew you could go to Harvard."

"There were an awful lot of scholarships available for Bear Towne…"

"I know!" Fin said excitedly. "I wrote all of those and put them in your mailbox."

"You what?"

"Some of them were pretty good, right?" He smiled proudly.

"Mating habits of the Arctic Ice Worm?"

"I know." He sniffed. "I'm brilliant."

As they walked, Hailey recalled laughing with Holly as they wrote their ridiculous Bear Towne essays, and it made her chuckle.

Fin looked at her expectantly. "What's so funny?"

"I was just thinking about Holly," she told him. "She was hellbent on finding a school we could both go to, and she wasn't afraid to come to Alaska." She raised her eyebrows. "I was, but those ridiculous essays we wrote… 'gave impetus to my spirit of adventure'," Hailey told him, repeating some of the verbiage she'd written for his "scholarships."

"Don't use that word."

"What word?"

Fin shot her a wry grin. "Impetus."

"Why?"

"Because, it makes me want to prove to you that I am not what that word sounds like."

Still smiling, Hailey shook her head. "You're a juvenile. You're a four–hundred-year-old, twelve-year-old, juvenile."

"I'm a four-hundred-and-*sixty*-year-old, twelve-year-old, juvenile," he corrected.

Hailey lowered her head, and her smile widening.

"Impetus," she whispered, and Fin growled.

"I never washed my shirt," he said quickly.

"What shirt?"

"The one you cried all over."

"Which one?" She'd snotted on several of his shirts…and he…never…washed…

"Ew," she said, scrunching her nose.

"Hm," Fin pursed his lips. "Is that creepy?"

"I think so. Or funny. It definitely rises to at least weird."

"I didn't know if I'd ever see you again. Guess I wasn't ready to let go…" He sighed heavily then brightened. "Your turn," he said, bumping into her.

Hailey tucked a strand of hair behind her ear. "I once told a girl at Hullachan's that you used to be a woman," she confessed.

"What?"

"She was really pretty," Hailey said, going red in the face, "but she wasn't very nice, and she wanted me to introduce you to her and get your number and set her up on a date, and I just couldn't stand the thought of you going out with…" *Another girl*, Hailey realized.

"With what?"

Hailey shook her head. "She just wasn't very nice," she said, her heart pounded. "At least I didn't tell her you were the impetus for the—" Fin cut her off by throwing her over his shoulder.

"—oof—condom machines in the ladies' room." She laughed as he threw her in a pile of snow and plopped down beside her. Seeing the last bit of sunlight paint the indigo sky reminded Hailey of Holly's funeral and how Fin stood next to her, hugging her tight when she wept.

"You're the only person I want around me when I'm sad," she said. "And you're the first person I want to find when I'm happy." She sat up and looked at him.

"I didn't want to stay away from you after Holly's funeral," Fin told her, still lying in the snow. "Asher and I had an argument, and he made me go away for a while. Eventually, we agreed you should choose who you wanted to...hang out with..."

He moved his hand across the snow and next to Hailey's, reaching his fingers close to hers, but not touching them.

Watching his hand the whole way, Hailey slid her pinky only a little so it barely brushed his skin.

Then she stood up and crossed her arms.

"Cobon wants me dead, and Asher's the only thing stopping him," she blurted. She just couldn't hold this in any longer. "Now Asher wants to kill me. But, only *temporarily*... Is that possible?"

"Hailey—that's a really bad idea," he told her forcefully.

"Asher said he and Cobon came up with a plan to—"

"This is Cobon's plan?" Fin stood up. "Did it ever occur to you that Cobon is a manipulative, murderous liar?" He shook his head and whirled around at her, putting his hands on her shoulders. "And he's insane! You saw what he did to Holly! He's using Asher, he knows how to manipulate him—this is just a ploy to get Asher to kill you! Can't you see that?"

"What am I supposed to do, Fin? I can't stop them!" She was shaking all over when Fin wrapped his arms around her.

"We'll figure it out," he vowed, and Hailey sniffled into his shirt.

"You better wash this," she chided, trying to laugh.

"I won't," he smiled, rocking her gently in his arms. "I'm sorry I yelled at you."

"You should be." Hailey wiped her face with his shirt and looked up at him. "Save your aggression for the ice."

"You still coming to the game this weekend?"

"That was this weekend?" she asked, feigning surprise as she wiped her last tears away.

"Yeah...you... Did you forget?" he stammered, sounding genuinely disappointed.

Hailey smirked, and he rolled his eyes.

"Are you kidding? I can't wait to see what paranormal hockey looks like."

Fin held her close as they walked into Eureka, saying, "I think you're in for a surprise..."

Chapter Thirty-Two

Paranormal Hockey

"There is no such uncertainty as a sure thing."

— Robert Burns

"This is incredible," Hailey gasped as she took in the extraordinary view—dancing foils of light zinging across the heavens and streamers of glowing warmth in shades of violet and scarlet chasing a glint of yellow through the cosmos, whirling together when they caught it then throwing off sparks of white as they broke apart.

It took her breath away.

She should have guessed Asher's "telescope" used no ordinary optics. But she had no idea she'd be treated to a glimpse into the Aether.

"Now I know why you spend so much time here. It's spellbinding," she marveled. She blinked hard and pulled away from the eyepiece. "You said you were looking for forgiveness. What did you mean?"

Asher placed his hand on the telescope near Hailey's shoulder, so close it warmed her skin.

"When you look through this aperture, you can see into the Aether," he said. "In the Aether, one can find many things. I once betrayed a friend in her most desperate hour. She came to me for protection." Asher's face hardened slightly. "And instead of giving it, I tore her apart."

Hailey froze.

Searching his eyes, she tried to discern whether she saw there more remorse…or annoyance.

"Her name was Kiya. We flung her energy in different directions across the universe, across the Aether. I don't know where she went, but I intend to find her—piece by piece if I must."

"Why didn't you help her when she came to you?"

"I was offended," he answered in a forceful voice, "by her emotions—by the very feelings that you arouse in me."

He stepped toward her, and Hailey took a step back, looking over her shoulder at the edge of the platform. Should she misstep, there was no railing to stop her from plummeting over a hundred feet, and Asher's eyes boiled as he took another step forward.

Instinctively, Hailey put her hands up in defense, which seemed to enrage the Envoy. He lunged at her, and she staggered back a bit too far, teetering on the edge of the mezzanine with wide eyes.

Grabbing her around her waist with one hand, he grasped a tight fistful of hair at the back of her head with the other, holding her over the edge as he glared into her eyes.

"I shouldn't blame you for the perversion of love that has gripped me, but often times, I do," he said, and Hailey let out a whimper.

He was two seconds away from dropping her—she just knew it. She grabbed hold of his shirt and hung on for dear life as he fumed.

"This passion—this *hate* and love—I am maddened by it." He dropped his seething gaze to her mouth. "And just when I think I should rid myself of you, I'm stung by compassion and longing."

"Don't let go of me," she breathed, and Asher jerked her roughly away from the edge, still holding her head painfully tight. She tried to shove him away, but it was like pushing against a block wall.

"Don't fight me, Hailey," he whispered to her ear, and still clutching a fistful of hair, he pressed his lips to hers, unleashing a surge of soothing heat that spread through her mouth, across her face, into her eyes, down her throat, and all the way to the tips of her fingers and toes. As Asher's calm washed over her, Hailey relaxed into his arms and slid a hand onto his shoulder.

When he finished, he released her and gently stroked her cheek. "I've given you a gift, my love," he told her tenderly. "I'll teach you to use it—to tune your eyes and ears to pick up the discord in others before their evil touches you."

"Okay," Hailey whispered, overwhelmed. *Gift?* She'd have to process that later. At the moment, she was still reeling from his biting words. *Rid myself of you.* It played over and over in her head. She pressed her palm to her chest and sneaked a peek over the edge.

"I thought you were going to...let me fall."

"Don't you remember, Hailey?" said Asher tilting his head. "I will never let you fall."

That night, the Aether was different...uncomfortable. The usual pale, soothing light seemed offensively bright and there was a din—a jumble of hideous screeching that grew so loud it hurt. Hailey pressed her hands over her ears and sank to her knees. Then quite suddenly, it stopped, and when she opened her eyes, she was standing inside Fin's room, watching a heated conversation.

Squinting her eyes brought the hazy scene into sharp focus. It was Asher speaking through clenched teeth to Fin, and neither of them seemed to notice her eavesdropping from the shadows. She was only getting bits and pieces of what they were saying.

"I won't do it!" Fin yelled.

Asher's voice faded in and out. "...cannot control...have her... destroy her..."

Fin took a swing at Asher, and Asher caught his fist. Fin let out a yelp, and Asher's voice rang clear: "I've gone mad."

Hailey bolted upright, soaking wet and clutching her chest, her heart beating like a snare drum.

"Was it a good one?" asked Giselle. She was wide awake and sitting on her bed with her legs folded.

"What?" Hailey panted.

"You just had a premonition. Woke me up with your wheezing. Was it a good one? You should try to remember it before it fades away."

Giselle was right. It was slipping through her memory already—just like a dream. She tried to catch her breath and held tight to a few tendrils of images and sound bites...Asher and Fin. Arguing. Fin refused to do something...something Asher wanted him to do...

And then it was too late. The memory was gone.

Fin caught up to her as she walked to breakfast that morning. "Hailey," he called, and she stopped to wait for him.

"Hey," she tried to sing happily, but her despondence rang like a bell. "Ready for your big game today?"

He thrust his chest out and scoffed. "I was born ready."

Flashing a weak smile, Hailey's shoulders drooped.

Wrapping an arm around her, Fin walked hugging her in silent support for several minutes. Then he gave her an encouraging squeeze and said, "So, the student bus leaves from Chinook at noon—you'll be on it, right?"

"I wouldn't miss seeing the Yetis kick some Anchorage Ice Pick butt for anything," she told him, and he beamed.

"Listen, my folks will be there," he said looking less than enthusiastic. "And they want to meet you."

"They do?"

"Yeah," he said apologetically.

Hailey nodded. Then she looked at Fin, confused. "I'm sorry, your parents are alive?"

"Eh…yeah. Look, just pretend that they're normal, I'm normal, you're normal, everyone is normal and nobody's cursed, and Bear Towne is just another university, okay?"

"Okay," she said with a shrug. *Why not?*

"Why do your parents want to meet me?"

"Long story, Hailey. Just—" Fin sighed heavily. "—suffice to say they want to meet the girl I…that I…"

"That you what?"

"That I met in Pittsburgh."

"Oh," she said, sounding more disappointed than she meant to. She recovered with some quick small talk. "What do your parents do?"

"They're both doctors, but now that my dad's retired from his practice again, he's a roof shoveler."

"A *what?*" said Hailey.

"A roof shoveler. He shovels snow off people's roofs in the winter."

Hailey was still confused, and Fin continued, "…so they don't cave in from the weight of the snow…? He enjoys heights."

Hailey shook her head. "Alaskans are just bizarre."

"Said the girl who works for a zombie librarian and lives with a demon."

Hailey bit her lip.

"I'll introduce you to them real quick after the game. Just meet me in the locker room when it's over, okay?"

"In the…like *inside* the locker room?"

"Yes," he said sarcastically. "Hailey, it's real simple. You open the door that says 'Locker Room,' you walk inside and you keep walking until you see me."

Hailey shook her head. "I'll just wait for you outside."

"No, Hailey," said Fin, looking more annoyed. "Everyone will be outside. I won't be able to find you. I'm giving you a backstage pass—use it."

"I don't want—won't you guys want some privacy? I don't want to see…anyone…you know…" Hailey hesitated to say the word "naked," and Fin was at the end of his patience.

"Hailey," he said sharply. "Just come straight down to the locker room after the game, find the gaggle of reporters, and file inside with them."

"Oh. Okay," she answered, more comfortable knowing there would be a whole group going in, and Fin rolled his eyes before jogging away.

At precisely twelve noon, an entirely normal bus, carrying an entirely paranormal group departed from Chinook Hall and bumbled four hours south to Anchorage.

Hailey sat next to the most avoided student at the school... well, second to herself...and the last few students to board the bus actually came to blows over who would sit in the seat across the aisle from Giselle.

In the end, nobody sat there, and the student who lost the fistfight ended up sitting on the floor in the back of the bus.

"I'm not sitting next to that thing," he'd muttered as he sped past her, squeezing himself as far to the other side of the aisle as he could.

At first, Giselle seemed unruffled, but then she turned to Hailey, who stared in open-mouthed astonishment at the jag-off. "I'm never doing this again," she said bitterly.

Hailey rested a hand of solidarity on Giselle's shoulder. "Somewhere," said Hailey, "there's a 'jack' who's lost his 'ass'." She jabbed a thumb at the back of the bus. "Guess what? We found it."

Giselle's scowl softened, and Hailey sighed happily as she stared out the window.

"How is your hair so...pretty?" Giselle asked in a snooty voice. *Wait. Was that a compliment?*

Hailey turned to her roommate, one eyebrow quirked, and she tipped her head to the side. "You know, your hair really is turning blonde," she marveled. "And I will hook you up with my hairstylist when we get back, that's a promise."

Hailey had to bribe Giselle to get her to come to the hockey game, and the banshee had no idea that Hailey's secret hairdresser was actually Tomas the albino poltergeist. She couldn't wait to see how things played out between the two of them.

In the arena, the girls sat near the glass and watched the game—Giselle with a disturbing eagerness to see fists fly, and Hailey with serious zeal, fully expecting a fire-breather or levitating goalie to appear at any moment. But the Yetis and the Ice Picks flew up and down the ice, colliding, fighting, and bleeding within all the laws of physics, and much to her disappointment, Hailey realized it was just a regular game of hockey.

Giselle on the other hand was delighted.

Fin spent a lot of time in play, and he was pretty good. So good, that the most gigantic of the Glacier College players made it his mission to repeatedly chase Fin down, slam him into the glass, and punch him in the face—scuffles that Fin seemed to thoroughly enjoy. He took several blows to the head and more than a few shots to the ribs. At one point, no fewer than three of the Ice Picks had him pinned to the glass right in front of her, and as they beat the snot out of him, he managed to glance up and see Hailey's look of horror.

He gave her a mischievous grin. Then pushed himself away from the glass and landed a nose-breaker on the giant goon. He flew out of the corner in time to get a quick little shovel pass from Sidney, his teammate, and then he fired the puck at the goalie. It ricocheted off the goalie's pad and bounced into the net.

The crowd went wild.

And the pace of the game only picked up. It was constant action. Hailey saw three fights (all of which involved Fin), five goals and at least one tooth get ejected—all before the third period even started.

"It's just...regular hockey," Hailey concluded with a frown during the final intermission.

Giselle, using no more than her disgusted expression said, "No kidding, dumbass," and then she squinted.

"There's something different about you," said Giselle. "Did Asher curse you?"

"What? No," Hailey said quickly then she frowned. "Well, I don't know. He finally kissed me again."

"How was it?"

"Terrifying."

"Told you," said Giselle, and Hailey twisted her lips to the side.

"Anyway, after he kissed me, he told me I'd be able to detect evil." She looked up at her roommate. "I don't feel any different, though."

Giselle stared straight ahead, so Hailey changed the subject.

"Has a guy—or a non-human or whatever—ever kissed you?"

"Do I look like something any guy would ever kiss?" she spat.

"You will once my hairdresser gets through with you." Hailey had an epiphany. She'd been waiting for an opportunity to bring up the Christmas dance. "And if you want, he can do your hair up for Seven Trumpets…"

"Nobody is going to ask me to the ball!" she yelled, and she turned her back on Hailey.

"What about David?"

Giselle didn't respond, which was actually a good sign, and Hailey was encouraged. Now all she had to do was convince David to invite the campus banshee to be his date at the Christmas dance. How hard could it be?

She spent the third period of the game working out her strategy as she watched her favorite bartender bleed, heal, bleed again and then score yet another goal. He actually was phenomenal.

By the end of the game, she couldn't wait to see Fin…neither could the twelve female "reporters" who waited for the all-clear outside the locker room door with her.

When the door swung open, Hailey let the gaggle of giggling girls file in. Then she hesitantly peeked inside and saw a few of the visitors chatting to some of the players. Most of the men were already showered and partially dressed. A few wore only a towel, and one sang loudly in Russian from the shower.

As she glanced around the room, Hailey made a concerted effort to look at the guys from the neck up only. After making unintentional eye contact with far too many bare-chested players, she finally spotted Fin next to a row of lockers. His hair was wet, and he was only partially dressed, but since he was expecting her and since she'd already seen him naked from the waist up, she figured it was alright to proceed inside.

She sped over to him, smiling brightly and still buzzing with the excitement of the game. As he finished giving a sound bite to a scantily-clad "member of the press," Hailey waited patiently with her hands clasped. Fin had shed several pounds and really toned up since the summer. Hailey pointed at his abs, marveling so loud it echoed.

"Wow!" she exclaimed. "You're so small!"

The whole room went silent, and everyone turned to see whose manhood had just been robbed.

"Hailey," said Fin in his best instructor's voice as she pulled her shoulders in, "that's not usually something a man likes to hear."

"I'm so sorry!" She covered her mouth with both hands.

Fin scratched his eyebrow. Then he threw his shirt on and led her outside.

"I meant your belly," she told him in a small voice. "You were getting a little shelf over the summer, but now you have a six-pack," she said desperately.

Fin gave her a cold stare. "A closed mouth gathers no feet, Hailey."

"Are you mad at me?"

"No…" he sighed. "You're just my cross to bear." He hung his arm around her neck and knuckle rubbed her head.

"Ouch!" she laughed in relief.

"Come on, knucklehead," he said, pointing across the parking lot. "There they are."

"Oh, Declan, here they come," Fin's mother cried as the two approached. She raised her hand to her mouth, and his dad straightened up, tugging the hem of his coat.

"Pádraig," he said with a single nod. In a business-like demeanor, he gave his son a firm handshake.

"Declan," said Fin coldly.

Shoving herself between the two, his mother opened her arms wide and squeezed Fin tight.

"So good to see you," she said.

"You too, Meara," he answered curtly.

Hailey stood by, smiling politely until Fin escaped his mother's clutches and stepped back.

"Guys," he said unenthusiastically, "you remember Hailey…"

"All grown up!" Meara gushed. She crushed Hailey in a giant mom-hug.

"Oof—I'm sorry, have we met?"

They both looked sort of familiar.

Meara released her to arm's length, saying "Oh, but it was years ago. You were just little when we were neighbors—"

"—lived right next door," Declan interjected.

"—until the fire," said Meara. "Of course, after Pádraig pulled you girls out of the house—"

"What?" Hailey snapped, casting a flabbergasted look at Fin, who leaned back on his heels with his hands in his pockets and very intentionally but not very convincingly became suddenly captivated by a constellation in the sky.

"You didn't know?" Meara looked with a blank face at her son, who bit the inside of his cheek and continued gazing skyward.

"Sure, even when he's just a lad, he's not afraid of them—so defiant. Well, he saw Adalwolf going for you girls, and he marched right into that house, hell-bent on a rescue, but then, of course Adalwolf exploded, and…well, you know the rest."

Fin tilted his head to the side and set his jaw.

"Nice recap, *Mom*, except you left out the part where you and Declan just stood there and watched."

Hailey just stood there, shifting her weight from one foot to the other, racking her brain to remember the face of the man—or boy or whatever—that pulled her out of the fire as an O'Shea family dysfunction ensued.

"You know very well the control Adalwolf exerted on us," his father said forcefully.

"Funny," said Fin without a hint of amusement, "you looked more scared than hypnotized to me, but…whatever you need to tell yourself so you can sleep at night. Let's go Hailey," he said, grabbing her hand roughly and pulling her along.

"Are you sure it's safe for her there, Pádraig? With…you know…" his mother called out, and Fin stopped.

"She's far safer there with him than she is near either of you."

"Son, we haven't had…an incident in years," she pleaded.

"Well, hooray and good for you," he answered sarcastically, and his mother rushed over to him.

"Take this, son." She pressed a small object into Fin's hand. "It's a gift. From Theon."

"Shacked up with another Envoy, have we?" said Fin, his voice laced with bitterness. "No thank you." He tried to give the object back to his mother, but she stepped back, hands up.

"Just take it, son. Theon is good. He watches over you, and he said to carry it with you—said you'll need that. We love you…" she added as Fin walked off.

"It was nice to see you," Hailey called over her shoulder, and his mother waved sadly.

Rolling his eyes, Fin shoved the object into his pocket. Then he turned to Hailey.

"Come on, you'll ride the bus with the team," he said flatly, and Hailey struggled to keep up with his angry pace.

"Am I allowed?"

"I'm the captain, and I'm inviting you," he said unequivocally. "Besides, you need an opportunity to tell the team how extraordinarily giant I am," he said like a German bodybuilder.

Hailey let out a nervous laugh. "I think I'll steer clear of subtle innuendo for the rest of my life. You're lucky to have witnessed the one moment in history that I actually fit my whole foot into mouth—"

He cut her off by holding his hand up. "Stop talking, Hailey. You're a train wreck."

"What? Why?"

He never answered.

When Fin climbed aboard the bus, the Yetis absolutely erupted. His team obviously adored him. They clobbered him with high-fives as he passed.

Hailey did her best to duck and cover behind him.

"Game puck!" shouted Sidney as he lobbed an object at Fin, who snagged it out of the air.

"Thanks, guys," Fin said. He pointed Hailey to an empty seat.

"Here." He handed her the puck and slid in next to her. "Little souvenir."

"Wow, nobody's ever given me a puck before," she said, hugging it to her chest. That came out sounding sarcastic, but she felt genuinely honored. She couldn't stop smiling.

"You're welcome," he said. He so enjoyed seeing her squirm and laughed out loud as the bus headed north.

"What did you think of the game?" he asked.

Hailey tapped the hockey puck as she formed her answer.

"Hockey looks like an angry ballet on ice."

Fin's smile widened, his eyes sparkling. "...an...angry...ballet..." he repeated with a chuckle.

"...on ice," Hailey said defensively, "except there's more fighting..."

"And more testosterone," Fin pointed out.

"Less estrogen, for sure."

"No estrogen," he corrected.

"Fewer teeth," Hailey chimed.

"No tights…" said Fin.

"…that you know of…"

"Sharper footwear," Fin offered.

"Duller wits," Hailey countered.

"More wood," they both said in unison, and Hailey's eyes went wide. She meant hockey sticks but was pretty sure he meant something else.

"Alexei made some pretty spectacular saves," said Hailey, eager to change the subject.

"He's not bad."

She nodded, staring out the window into the darkness for several seconds before turning to him again.

"Did you really pull us out of the fire?"

"Mmmm… Yep," he said coolly, and then he drummed his hands on the seat in front on them.

"Why…" Hailey shook her head. "…you never mentioned…" her mind raced wildly before she finally took hold of a thought. "What happened that night?"

"Well," he sang, his eyes going far-off for a bit, "Cobon and Adalwolf were going to open the Aether. Cobon had your parents killed and sent Adalwolf to take care of you two. When I got to your room, he had you by the throat…"

Here Fin hesitated, seeming to choose his words.

"…and then he exploded." He shrugged. "The house was on fire; I grabbed you and Holly and dragged you outside."

Hailey shook her head. "Why were you there?"

"A lot of folks were there," he said, " including your buddy Asher—just watching the murders, like it was a TV show…waiting to see what would happen," he said bleakly. "When the other Envoys heard Adalwolf bought it, they hightailed it out of there. I stayed until the fire trucks showed up."

"All this time I thought it was Asher." Hailey dropped her brow.

"Asher can be very manipulative," he said darkly, and Hailey bit her lip.

Asher had never actually said that he'd rescued her from the fire—she just assumed he did. And it bolstered her trust in him. He only said he was there. *Watching...standing by while Adalwolf—*

She shuddered and pushed the unthinkable out of her mind.

"Why did your parents say you were a lad?"

"I was. I was nine years old," he told her. "Well—I was four hundred and thirty-something, living as a nine-year old," he said leaning into her.

Hailey frowned, unable to recall all the details from that night and unable to fathom his curse.

She stared out the window for a long while before she suddenly remembered something...

"Hey, what does your tattoo say?" She'd meant to ask him in the locker room.

"Which one?"

"You have more than one?"

"Yes," he was using his instructor's voice again.

"This one on your arm." She pointed to his bicep.

"You mean this arm?" He flexed in three different ways, which made Hailey laugh again.

"Careful you don't rip your shirt." She feigned her best worried voice.

"That's more like it," he said with satisfaction.

"It says 'Salva nos a maleficio. It means—"

"Save us from evil." Hailey smiled playfully. "Evil hockey pucks?"

"You of all people know what kind of evil is lurking at Bear Towne."

"What do you mean?" She knew exactly what he meant.

"You shouldn't be hanging around with Asher."

"Why not?"

"That guy is serious bad news, Hailey. I heard you're going to Seven Trumpets with him."

"It's not...none of your business who I'm going with." Now he did it. He'd perturbed her into using bad grammar. That made her even angrier.

"It is my business. I promised Pix I'd look after you here."

"You did what?"

"Look, Hailey—" He was using that dang teacher's voice again. "—he's not human. That creature kills people." Hailey rolled her eyes. "Oh, but it's ok if he murders people, because he picked you as the only girl he'll talk to—don't pretend he doesn't scare you." He cocked his head at her and stared. Then he tried a different approach.

"I'm just worried about you." He squeezed her knee. "I want you to hang around a little longer. Who would publically shame me over my tiny manhood if he killed you?"

Now he was just trying to make her laugh.

"I'm really sorry about that," she told him. "Do you want me to tell everyone I was talking about your gut?"

"Don't you dare," he said pointing his finger in her face, and Hailey laughed a genuine laugh.

But as she glanced out the window, her smile vanished. "You know, I've never heard Asher laugh."

"Hey," said Fin, and she turned.

He looked her square in the eyes, his face soft. "You can't have love without laughter, Hailey."

Chapter Thirty-Three

Confessions

There is a smile of love.
And there is a smile of deceit.
And there is a smile of smiles
In which these two smiles meet.

— William Blake

Back at Bear Towne, Hailey walked half a block toward Eureka Hall before she realized she'd forgotten her puck. As she jogged back to retrieve it, she overheard the team chuckling.

Fin was laughing, too.

"Who, Hailey?" she heard him say, and she slowed so she could eavesdrop.

"Pádraig, serious," said one of his teammates. "That chick is *hot*. Tell me you tapped that."

Hailey's jaw dropped.

"You know I did," Fin laughed in a lazy voice, and he slapped his teammate's hand.

A chorus of approval rose from the group.

"Look at you…getting you some freshman tail," one of them sang.

Hailey could hear Fin laughing again, and it made her sick.

"Oh!" yelled another. "You rode the campus pariah!"

"Don't call her that," Fin bellowed through clenched teeth, and Hailey saw him winding up to pummel his teammate, but it was too late.

She was fuming, and she couldn't stop her feet from marching right up to him.

"Hailey?" said Fin. He dropped his fist, his face white.

Hailey pushed two giant hockey players out of the way, stormed over to Fin, and smacked him across the face.

He flinched and immediately began his grovel.

"Hailey," he pleaded. "I'm so sorry—guys, give me a minute." The Yetis dispersed in a hurry.

Hailey walked away as fast as she could, so angry she was shaking, trying to get out of there before Fin saw her cry.

"Hailey, stop!" he yelled, chasing after her. *Nope.* "Hailey, come on. Look, I'm sorry!"

Hailey spun around to yell at him, but she was already crying.

"I can't believe…" she sobbed, "…after you just said you were looking out for me. You don't care about me at all!"

Looking shocked, Fin tried to put his hands on her shoulders, but she slapped them away.

"You don't have enough women traipsing through your room?" she yelled. "You sleep with a different one every night, and you have to lie about me to feed your ego?"

"Hailey, I… I'm sorry," he stuttered, but she was already stomping off. "What was I supposed to tell them?" he yelled after her. "Oh—you want me to say it out loud? That I'm in love with you? There! I said it!"

Hailey stopped.

"Love doesn't act like that," she said over her shoulder, and then she walked away.

"Hailey…" he pleaded. When she didn't respond, he took a few steps after her. "Hailey!" he yelled. "I'm sorry, alright? Hail—"

She never looked back, but she could hear his teammates consoling him in the distance, their voices fading with each step she took, but she still made them out.

"Man..." said one. "You're in the doghouse now, bro."

"Yeah," she heard Fin's strained voice. Then he let out a bellow she would've heard from another block away, and he punched or kicked something that sounded like the side of a bus. Hailey didn't care. She was disgusted and angry and hurt. *Mostly hurt.* How could he ever call himself her friend? And that bit about being "in love"? Hailey scoffed.

...warning me about the evil Asher... She shook her head, disgusted. Asher was the only person—or creature or whatever—the only one who'd never lied to her. Yeah, he was creepy and dangerous, but at least he didn't hide it.

Still boiling the next morning, Hailey woke up a full hour early just so she could seethe.

"You're finally making sense to me," remarked Giselle.

Hailey smacked her books together as she gathered them. "You going to breakfast today?"

"I like morning food," Giselle said, slinging her bag over her shoulder.

"Good." Hailey's anger wanted company.

After breakfast Giselle joined Hailey at the library. While Hailey set to solving the feedback problem in her ghost trap, Giselle worked her way through a pile of beauty magazines, and a gigantic inchworm slithered slowly past, accidentally bumping Hailey's table as he went.

"Matthew!" Hailey barked when he caused her pen to scribble. "I told you to stay out of the lounge. You have to stop drinking tea—just look at you." Hailey threw her hand up. "If you get any bigger, you're going to get stuck in the archway and end up in a dark tunnel. And don't think I'll come running underground to find you."

He slid away, tea sloshing loudly in his stomach.

Hailey turned back to her lab notebook, and she must've just missed seeing Fin rush out of the stacks, because it seemed like he came out of thin air, when he appeared on his knees at her side, wearing a haunted expression.

"Ah!" she yelled, and her pen made another scribble.

"Hailey, I'm sorry—forgive me please," he called out breathless.

"Fin—" Hailey huffed loudly and stared at her messy notebook. "Nothing says, 'I'm sorry' like leaving me the hell alone."

Fin stood up, shoulders hunched. "I'll leave you alone then," he said in a strained voice, "but I will never leave you alone." He placed a folded note on the desk next to her hand and slouched away.

"You were a little hard on him, don't you think?" Giselle asked.

"I thought you hated him?" she whispered sharply.

"*I* do," she said in a loud voice that disturbed Mrs. Spitz.

"SHH!" she warned from the circulation desk.

"But *you* don't," said Giselle in just as loud a voice.

"Trust me. I would rather spend an eternity buried in these library books than spend another second with Pádraig O'Shea."

"Careful what you wish for."

Hailey snapped her head around. "Why?"

"You just shouldn't say things you don't mean."

"Thought you hated libraries," she muttered, recalling the blissful first days of her semester, when her roommate was ignoring her.

"I do. They smell like dead trees. And by the way, I don't understand you at all," Giselle scolded. "Asher very nearly kills you—*wants* to kill you, and you totally blow it off and gush about how—" Giselle put on her best little-girl-Hailey voice. "Oh, I wish he would kiss me again," she mocked. "Pádraig tells one little lie, and you shun him completely."

Before Hailey could close her wide-open mouth, Giselle slapped her magazine shut, got up, and glided out, leaving Hailey alone with her grudge, which quickly turned to guilt when she opened Fin's note.

Inside, she found a magnificent pencil sketch of her praying at Holly's grave with the words "Never Alone" scratched at the bottom.

Her hands numb, Hailey dropped her head to the desk as the squeaky outer door of the library opened.

Fin was waiting at the exit when Giselle walked out, He stopped her by stepping directly in front of her.

"What do *you* want?" she said like a snob.

"Demon," he said, "I need you to tap into your para-empathic, emotion detector thing you do, and tell me if I love that woman or if this is just Cobon's… curse."

"All love's a curse," she said disgustedly, "and you really screwed up."

"Giselle!"

"Pádraig, the very fact that you're here asking me this question should be your answer."

Fin waited for her to explain.

She didn't.

"Giselle, for one minute, pretend you're not a banshee, and stop speaking in riddles. Imagine I'm the biggest idiot you've ever talked to—"

"—that shouldn't be hard."

"Just lay it out for me, okay?"

"Have you ever cared whether you hurt someone who loves you?" she asked him.

Fin straightened up. "She loves me?" he exclaimed, and then he grabbed Giselle by the head and kissed her full on the mouth.

She pushed him away, sputtering and spitting and wiping at her lips as if she'd just been slurped by a dog that had drunk from the toilet.

"Gross!"

"Thank you, Giselle!" he said jubilantly as he jogged away.

"You're still an asshole, Pádraig," Giselle called after him.

Hailey finished up her experimental design, and she left the library that night with her heart in her stomach. The last thing she wanted was a run-in with Fin.

But, as she crested the stairs, she saw him waiting in the hall-way and froze. Staring at the floor, she strode across the landing and made a bee-line for her room.

Fin apparently had another idea and blocked her path. Hailey stopped and looked up at him.

"What?" she demanded half-heartedly.

"Hailey, I need to talk to you." He had her puck in his hand.

"Whatever happened to the whole leaving me alone thing? I liked that plan."

She tried moving past him, but he blocked her way again. Pursing her lips, she stomped down hard on his insole.

Fin yelped and hopped onto his good foot, giving Hailey a way past.

"Hailey, I'm in love with you!" he yelled so loud it echoed off the wall and down the stairwell.

Wide eyed, Hailey turned to look at him, and he hopped closer.

"Hailey," he begged, "you're the most amazing person I've ever met. You're feisty and innocent and unpredictable...I love that you jumped head-first into a vacuum glaze to save a complete stranger then walked around all day stinky and sticky, and somehow you were still the most beautiful girl on campus."

She gave him a cold stare for a good three seconds, but then she dropped her gaze.

"You're beautiful—God, you're beautiful—and you see people. You always see the good in people, you see them for who they are inside. And the way you look at me...I'm in love with you, Hailey. I'm in love with everything about you. I love how you look terrified when you don't know what to say... And then you just blurt out something outrageously honest and totally awkward."

Hailey bit her lip.

"I love that you constantly wrestle with your hair," he went on. "It always starts out so nice but ends up sticking out at some ridiculous angle..."

She tucked a wayward curl behind her ear but resisted the urge to smooth her hands over her entire head.

"Is that it?" Hailey said quietly.

"No," he declared. "I love watching you dance."

Hailey dropped her head, and Fin tilted her chin up in time to see a tear shimmer down her face.

"And I love you, Hailey."

He brushed her cheek, his eyes chasing her shifting gaze until she finally looked at him.

"The whole world went dark when you stopped talking to me," he said gently. "It felt like someone shoved a dull knife into my stomach." He took her hands in his and brought them to his lips. "I always want you next to me, Hailey. I want you to dance with me and drink whiskey and throw things at me when you're angry."

Hailey stood speechless.

"Anyway," he continued, dropping her hands, "I'm sorry I told the team I slept with you. I told them all the truth—that I lied about you. They told me I was an idiot. And I know I am."

He leaned closer, searching her eyes.

"I'm sorry I was an ass. God, I'm so sorry I hurt you.

"You know, if I'd heard another guy say those things about you that I said about you, I would have sent his face home in a box." Fin raised an open palm as he shrugged and shook his head.

Hailey opened her mouth to say something—she didn't know what, but before she could utter a syllable, Fin walked into his room and shut his door. And he took her puck with him.

As Hailey lay in bed that night, she called to her roommate. "Giselle," she said softly. "Are you sleeping?"

"Yes," her roommate droned, but she hadn't yet gone to the ceiling.

Hailey sat up. "Giselle, how do you know if someone loves you?"

"Did he give you the hockey puck?" Giselle was on her bed, talking into her pillow, and Hailey didn't know how Giselle knew about the hockey puck. Her super-banshee senses never ceased to amaze her.

"Um…no. He had it in his hand, but he didn't give it to me."

"He loves you right now," she said in a monotone.

"What? How do you know? What do you mean 'right now'?"

"The hockey puck, dumbass."

"Oh." Hailey said nodding, and then she shook her head. "I don't understand."

Giselle sat straight up and glared across the room at her. "He didn't give you the hockey puck, because he didn't want that idiotic trinket to undermine what he'd just said to you. His words were important to him. If he just wanted to get in your pants, he would've given you the hockey puck and said goodnight."

Hailey's mouth fell open.

"Do you love him?"

"I…I don't know."

"If you love him, go and ask for your hockey puck tomorrow. If you don't, then don't ever talk to him again."

She rolled back into her pillow and added in a muffled voice, "I wouldn't talk to him again if I were you. His love won't last. All men are scum."

That was Giselle's motto.

"I don't really care about the hockey puck," said Hailey.

Giselle shot up again. "Neither does he," she barked. "It's just a token—a metaphor incarnate…"

Hailey shrugged.

"Don't you see? The puck is in his hand. It might as well be his beating heart. You love him? You want him? Go and get the puck," she yelled, and she threw an empty cup at Hailey's head then buried herself in her blankets again.

Hailey dodged the cup, which smacked the wall behind her.

"Thanks, Giselle," she said as she snuggled into her bed. She had a lot of thinking to do.

"You do have a lot to think about," came Giselle's muffled voice. "Start with why you're *really* angry with Pádraig. It's not because you feel humiliated, because you don't. I'm betting it's because he's not strong enough to stop Asher from ripping your soul out."

Hailey pulled her covers to her chin.

Giselle made a fair point. If she wasn't so wrapped up with Asher and his insane jealousy, she'd be head over heels for Fin. Maybe she already was. For sure she wouldn't be mad at him, though.

Because she'd be dead.

Asher would never protect her from Cobon if she chose Fin. In fact, if Asher ever suspected that she was in love with Fin, he might even kill her himself. And she shuddered to think what he would do to Fin.

And Fin couldn't do a thing to stop him. He was no match for an Envoy.

"You know," Hailey called out over her blankets, "if this whole 'banshee' thing doesn't work out for you, you should consider a career in counseling. You have remarkable insight."

Hailey sighed and closed her eyes. "But you should definitely stay away from motivational speaking," she added, and as she drifted to sleep, she thought she heard Giselle giggle.

Chapter Thirty-Four

The White Forest

"It's not what you look at that matters. it's what you see."
— Henry David Thoreau

For her term project, Giselle needed to collect at least five snow embers from the White Forest to brew her latest experimental batch of carnivorous splinter salve—a new balm, which would incinerate a flesh-eating splinter without damaging the surrounding tissue. Very proudly, she'd informed Hailey that Professor Starr was beside himself with excitement over it. It would bear the Indispensable name and no doubt be a big seller.

With their Indispensable Yeti Spray, Tree Repellant, and Magnoggles, the girls headed out fully prepared for any White Forest hazard they might encounter and fully hoping to catch the Northern Lights.

Hailey's nerves were on high alert as the snow-covered trail crunched under her feet. Stepping nervously under the White Forest Gate and reeking of Tree Repellant, she wielded her can of Yeti spray with her finger on the trigger.

"Relax, spaz," Giselle said. "You'll scare away the snow embers."

"I've got our six," Hailey answered, walking backwards.

"Uh-oh," Giselle muttered, and Hailey jumped out of her skin.

"What? Is it a man-eating tree?" She hugged Giselle's arm.

"Worse," she said flatly. "It's Pádraig."

"Ladies…" he said, bowing cordially as they approached him on the trail.

He carried a bulging military-sized backpack.

"What are you doing here?" Hailey said nervously.

"Feeding the animals." He flashed his sardonic smile.

"Jaycen," Giselle said to Hailey with a nudge.

"Oh."

Hailey pushed some snow around with her boot. Not even talk of Jaycen could push the image of that stupid puck from her head. There was no way she could ask for it though. Not without sounding like a total loser, and Fin was leaving anyway.

"See you guys arou—"

"I want my puck."

Hailey bit her lips together. Not the most eloquent way to ask, but at least the words were out.

Fin scrambled to open his bag, and Giselle smirked as she bent to gather the last of her snow embers.

"I've been carrying this with me everywhere," he said as he produced a black object on bended knee.

"You really never gave anyone a puck before?" Hailey brushed her fingertips against it. *Oh, how she wanted that damn puck. But Asher will kill him—and me.*

She pulled her hand back.

"I can't accept this." Her heart plummeted into her stomach. "Asher's…" She frowned and puffed out a cloud of white breath. "I'm with Asher."

Fin studied her right eye then her left, and he wrapped her hand around the puck.

"It's not a ring," he said, standing. "It's just a hockey puck."

As Hailey pressed the puck to her chest, Giselle pointed skyward.

"Hey lovebirds," she called, pulling out her Magnoggles, "Northern Lights."

Lifting her gaze, Hailey gasped.

The sky was…unreal.

"It's like God dunked a great feather into an ink well of pulsing iridescence and dragged it across the sky." Hailey turned to Fin, eyes wide with excitement, and for the first time she noticed how bright his eyes were. Brown and bright and warm and…safe. She blinked a few times before shoving the puck in her coat pocket and pulling on her goggles.

While Fin oooh'ed and Giselle ahhh'ed, Hailey didn't see diddly-squat and huffed loudly.

"They're beautiful, but they don't look any different with these things at all."

Shaking his head, Fin reached over and clicked a switch near her temple.

"It helps if you turn them on."

"Whoa…" she breathed. "This is…it's a slow-motion, glowing electron cloud…and they're making shapes—is that a rose?"

Giselle answered nicely for a change. "They look different to everyone through Magnoggles. Some say you see what's in your heart…" Her voice trailed off.

Both Hailey and Fin turned to stare at the banshee.

"What?" Giselle spat. "I'm sure it's just bullshit."

"What did you see?" Hailey asked her.

Giselle hesitated.

"Something I've never seen before," she said simply.

"You see a rose?" said Fin to Hailey with a knowing grin.

"Yeah," she answered. "But now it's…it kinda looks like…"

Fin—it looked like Fin. Hailey turned away.

"What do you see?" she asked him.

"Heaven," he answered without elaborating, and the three lay in the snow and marveled at the sky for nearly an hour before Hailey shivered.

"It's getting cold out here." She stood when the wind picked up.

"It's not that cold," Fin said.

"You have a layer of man-hair keeping you warm."

"Then your legs should be nice and toasty," he taunted.

"I'll have you know," she said grabbing his arm and turning him to face her, "I actually shave…now that I have a razor…" She gave him a "so there" raise of the eyebrows, stuck her nose in the air, and pushed ahead of him on the trail.

"I'll never know," he said to her back. "You're with Asher, remember?"

"Can you believe she wants to be with that monster?" he said to Giselle, and Hailey glanced over her shoulder.

Giselle shook her head. "Nobody wants to be with a monster," she told him, "especially not a harbinger of death."

"Aw…but you're not a harbinger of death… You're just a big, fat nothing," he said sweetly, patting her gently on the head. "And someday, somebody just as pathetically ordinary is going to see that." Fin used his best mother's voice and squeezed her cheek for good measure.

Giselle shot him a sharp look then her face fell. "Trees," she said grimly, and the forest jittered to life. "Let's get out of here before one of those things eats Hailey!"

"I thought you couldn't sense death coming," said Hailey, who stood frozen on the path just ahead of them.

"You don't have to be a banshee to recognize a slobbering tree." She and Fin raced to her side.

"Well, why did you say *my* name? Why shouldn't we get out of here before one of them eats Fin?"

"Old meat," she said, grabbing Hailey's hand and yanking her out of the path of a small and very spry scrub spruce, which karate-somersaulted in front of them.

"Ankle biter!" Hailey called as another sapling appeared on the trail and took a snap at her foot. Giselle kicked it aside just as a low rumble shook the ground, which sent the man-eating trees scurrying away.

Hailey looked to Fin. "T-Rex?" she asked exasperated, and he threw a somber look at Giselle.

"This is not normal," he said backing away from a menacing snarl that was growing louder, and Giselle bared her teeth.

"Yeti," she growled, and Hailey grabbed up her Yeti spray, holding it out like a shield as the three pressed themselves together.

"Where's it coming from?" Hailey asked.

"There's more than one," Giselle snarled.

The rumble stopped, and the White Forest fell dead silent.

"This isn't good," said Fin with wide eyes. "Giselle, they've got us flanked. Wait for them to show themselves. When you see an out, take it. I'll distract them—you just get her out of here."

Giselle nodded obediently, yanking all three of them out of the way when a giant cottonwood crashed down.

A blinding whirlwind of snow followed, and a gargantuan white blob thundered forth. Hailey blasted it with Yeti spray.

Unfazed, the Yeti made a swipe at them, and Hailey dove out of the way, still clutching her can of utter uselessness. She glared at the container then threw it at the monster's face.

That seemed to enrage the beast.

When it lunged at Hailey's head, Fin pushed her to the ground, taking a slap from the Yeti's giant paw, which batted him across the trail.

"Get her out of here!" he shouted.

Hailey rolled over in time to see the Yeti grab Fin up with both hands and tear him in half, throwing his torso one way and his legs another.

"No!" she shrieked.

Giselle pulled her to her feet. "Let's go!" she yelled, throwing Hailey over her shoulders.

She took off in a dead sprint.

The trees flew past in a snowy blur as Giselle hurdled over the downed cottonwood and galloped down the trail, holding Hailey tight.

"What about Fin?" Hailey cried as they came out of the White Forest.

Giselle dropped her on the ground and glared.

"What about him?"

"Giselle! He's still out there!"

"I doubt it," she said emotionless. "The Yeti would have eaten him by now...and I don't think he'll heal from that," she scoffed. Then she must have seen Hailey's look of horror. "You should be thankful," she said crisply. "Now you don't have to decide who to love."

"We can't just leave him out there!" Hailey yelled, pushing past her.

Giselle grabbed her arm and dragged her toward Eureka Hall.

"Yes," she said sharply. "We can, and we will. If I let you run back out there like the idiot you are, those Yetis will snatch you up in an instant, and then Asher would blame me."

Giselle kept a firm grip on her.

"Giselle, we have to help him!"

"Listen," she said impatiently. "If by some miracle Pádraig survived, I'm sure in a month or two, he'll track down all his parts, wiggle them together, and once again grace us with his presence."

"Really?" Hailey sobbed.

"I hope not. I can't stand him."

Hailey spent all night clutching her hockey puck and blowing her nose.

A little after midnight, Giselle stirred. "Don't even think about it," she grunted from the ceiling when Hailey reached for her shoes.

By morning, Hailey's face was swollen and blotchy. Her throat was raw and her stomach had tied itself shut. Robotically, and with her eyes a slit, she grabbed her shampoo and bathrobe and headed for the shower. For several minutes, she let the water pound over her face before she punched the faucet off and donned her robe.

When she emerged, a familiar Russian voice echoed down the hallway. Alexei, the goalie maybe?

"Yes, eets tonight at Cheenook," he yelled over his shoulder as he headed for the stairs. "See you ullater!" he called as he left.

Hailey tiptoed down the hall, and when she reached the corner, she held her breath

.

Chapter Thirty-Five

Conundrum

"The day breaks not, it is my heart,
Because that you and I must part."

— John Donne, Stay, O Sweet

Hope is manic. The proverbial light at the end of a tunnel. In the same day, it either soothes like a candle in the night, or it blinds then pulverizes like a freight train. As Hailey gripped the corner wall, she clung to the image of her candle in the night and peeked around the corner.

Fin's door was cracked open, and his lights were on.

Very cautiously, she tip-toed closer in her bare feet, hair still dripping wet, her white robe clinging to every goose bump on her body, and she swore she heard a drawer open and close inside his room.

Then a figure crossed in front of the door, and the whole scene felt suddenly familiar. She was in her Pittsburgh townhouse, staring at a door she was sure would open to reveal her lost sister.

And she was scared.

With her heart in her throat, she crept toward Fin's room, and she caught another glimpse of the man, who bore a striking resemblance to her slain friend.

Dropping her shampoo, she quickened her pace and stopped just outside the door.

"Oh, hey Hailey," said the man nonchalantly as he turned to face her.

"Sidney?" Hailey moaned, not even trying to hide her disappointment. "What are you doing in here?"

"Just…catching up…on some team business…?" he said frozen in uncertainty, his eyes bouncing right and left.

Rubbing her head, Hailey slumped her shoulders. "You shouldn't be in here," she told him, her heart dropping like an anchor.

And then the bathroom door swung open.

"I'll see what I can do about getting you more time on the ice," said a voice from inside, and Hailey's lungs quit.

It isn't him, it isn't him, she told herself, tamping down any hope that threatened to lift her spirits.

A foot emerged from the bathroom followed by a body—a whole body.

Fin.

Bolting through the door, Hailey jumped on him. He staggered back, and she clamped her arms and legs around him.

"Fin!"

"Yes?" His normally sarcastic voice was constricted.

"I thought you were dead," she cried as she buried her head in his shoulder.

"I'm not…"

"I'll just catch up with you later," said Sidney with a smirk, and Fin didn't respond as he walked out.

"Hailey," Fin said, "you can let go now." He tried to remove her, but she was attached to him like a barnacle.

"Hailey—" He sounded clearly irked as he again tried to peel her off. Then he dropped his arms and huffed. "Are you naked under this paper thin robe?"

"I saw that Yeti tear you in half!"

She did. She saw it with her own two eyes…blood, guts, and everything.

"No," he said unequivocally. "You didn't."

He made a concerted effort to not touch her.

"Hailey—you're soaking wet!"

"I just got out of the shower," she said, still clutching him. "And, yes I did."

"Hailey—" he grumbled, and she squeezed her eyes shut, begging the universe to make all this real, because it sure felt like a dream.

Pressing her forehead against his, she laced her fingers through his hair and hung on. She couldn't open her eyes, not even to gaze at him. God, she wanted to. But if she did, she might wake up.

Fin lifted his head and brought his lips close to hers, his breath hot against her skin as he kicked his door shut.

"Woman," he said, breathing heavy as he hesitantly touched her thighs, "I am only human."

Hailey slid off him and felt through his shirt for the wound.

"I thought I lost you," she accused, and finally, she found the courage to look up at him. "Am I dreaming?" She searched his eyes for an explanation.

He brushed a tear from her cheek and gazed at her sadly. "No," he said softly, reassuringly. "You're not dreaming."

Wonderful relief washed over her, and she let her hands fall to her sides. Fin wiped another tear from her face then gently tilted her chin up, brushing his lips across her mouth.

"How is this possible?" she whispered as he slowly laid kisses across her cheek and grazed her ear.

"It's—" he inhaled loudly, "—a long story..."

Hailey's own breath sped up, and when she leaned into him, he pulled her even closer and nibbled at her neck, his breath ragged next to her ear. It felt right. It felt like...a sudden jolt. He must've felt it too, because when she wrapped her arms around his waist, something moved against her hip. Startled, Hailey tried to pull away, but Fin's arm tightened and jerked her back.

Sighing heavily, she pressed into him as he moved his lips across hers, kissing her softly even as he seized her by the hips and shoved her into a position more to his liking. Ever so gently, he parted her lips with his tongue, kissing her again and again...

Fire burned in every place he touched—positively raging inside, and she had absolutely no idea what to do. Her arms froze straight from elbow to fingertip even as the rest of her melted into his kisses. Very tentatively, she reached a trembling hand under his shirt, which must've been wrong, because when she brushed his skin, he shuddered, exhaled deeply, and shoved her away. Then he doubled over and pointed emphatically at the door.

"Go and put some clothes on," he ordered in a rough voice.

Hailey stared at him in alarm. "Did I do something wrong?" she breathed, looking from Fin to her hands and back to Fin again.

"No—" he stopped to swallow hard and pant. "You didn't. Look, I'll...I'll take you to dinner, and we can—we can talk." His voice was strained, and he was still breathing heavy. "I'll explain everything," he said, patting the air with his hand.

Hailey backed away slowly, dropping her head. *Why was he so turned off by her?*

"Stop!" he shouted, sounding disgusted and thoroughly displeased. "Hailey, tell me what you're thinking. Right now," he demanded, pointing his finger at the floor.

"No...nothing...I just..." Hailey took another step back, but bumped the wall. "I just wish you wanted me," she said in a small voice, unable to look up at him and trying not to sound like the pathetic little girl that she was. "I just..." she shook her head and pulled her elbows in.

Fin closed his eyes and breathed twice. Then he squared up with her as if he wanted to take a swing at her, set his jaw, and charged. Like an animal, he grabbed her head with both hands and plowed his tongue through her lips, nudging her legs apart with his knee as he pressed and squeezed her against the wall.

When he spoke again, his voice came more like a growl. "Hailey, if you don't leave this room in five seconds, I'm gonna rip your Goddamn robe off."

"Okay," she breathed, and he kissed her again, savagely, his hands sliding roughly down her sides and grasping her hips.

"Dammit, Hailey," he said, breathing heavy, still holding her to the wall. He spoke into the crook of her neck. "I always want you, but you are not just another girl." He kissed her softly, loosening his hold. "And I am trying to be a better man."

"Okay," Hailey breathed again.

"I don't want to screw this up," he told her, taking her hands and backing away. Leading her to the door, he said, "You're the only one I ever want." Very tenderly, he kissed her knuckles and opened his door. "Go get dressed. I'll come get you in ten minutes."

Still on fire, Hailey turned to leave but turned again as soon as she crossed the threshold.

"Is this a date?" she asked eagerly.

"No!" he shouted, and he slammed the door in her face.

True to his word, Fin showed up at Hailey's door exactly ten minutes after he'd slammed his on her face.

He escorted her to the Bruised Moose, where he led her to a booth in the back corner.

"You have to stop showing up naked at my door," he began. Then he leaned back and shook his head. "I can't believe I just said that."

"You have to stop leaving me," she countered. "Promise you will never let me wonder like that again."

"Cross my heart," he said. "And hope to die," he added gravely.

"What happened to you?"

"Your boyfriend's an asshole—that's what happened."

Hailey stifled a laugh.

"What?"

"Giselle says the same thing about you."

"Giselle calls me your boyfriend?" He seemed very interested in that.

"No—she—never mind," she shook her head and licked her lips. "So, you think Asher sent those Yetis after us?" It actually sounded plausible, especially considering the Envoy wanted her dead. Plus he was insanely jealous of Fin.

Fin sighed.

"Honestly, I don't know, but he was there, and he did eventually..." Fin rolled his eyes, "...rescue my legs."

"That makes him an asshole?"

"No. He's an asshole because he watched the entire Yeti attack and only intervened to keep you from spending the next year looking for me."

"So, he healed you," she surmised.

"Yeah," he said reluctantly.

Seemed like a pretty *nice* thing for Asher to do—helping Fin put his parts back together, but... "How did you not die?"

"Actually, I did...die, or whatever." He waved his hand. "I just got slapped back—like a paddle ball."

"That's your curse? What happens to you? What happens if you...say...get hit by a bus?"

"A miraculous recovery."

Hailey's face darkened. "What happens if you burn up in a fire?"

"A more miraculous recovery."

"Does it hurt?" she asked softly.

Fin sighed heavily, his face haunted as he considered his answer. "It feels like a really long exhale," he told her gently. "I've felt it many times."

"How many times?" After her run-in with the poisonous quill, she couldn't imagine feeling the pain of death again and again.

"A lot." He pulled from his pocket a tarnished, antique gold ring and held it up. "This pretty much sums up my existence." He stared at that ring, which seemed more like a plain, men's wedding band than a life story. It was scratched, worn-thin, and bore a deep, crooked score along the side.

"Is that your wedding ring?" Hailey asked.

"Yeah. I mean, it's not mine—I was never married—but it was once a wedding ring. Now it's a reminder," he said. "The man who gave this to me—" Fin paused. "He died in my arms. Right before he died, he pressed this ring into my hand, and he said, 'Love beats like a drum—"

"—in the heart of a righteous man," they both said together. Fin flashed his eyes at her.

"Did you tell Uncle Pix about this?"

"No," he said suspiciously.

"Because he just wrote those exact words in a note to me."

Fin blinked.

"I've never told anyone about that."

"You're the righteous man, aren't you?"

"I… The man who gave me this thought so. He told me I was marred and worn, like his ring, but still worth my weight in gold." He raised his eyebrows and released them, shaking his head. Then he replaced the ring in his pocket, his face darkening.

"I was a slave to the Envoys for a very long time, Hailey." He didn't meet her eyes. "I was made to do a lot of bad things."

Fin reached across the table, taking her hands. "Because of you, the Envoy that tormented me for centuries—the one who marred me—is dead," he told her. "You rescued me from an eternity of Hell. And you keep rescuing me." Fin looked into Hailey's eyes for several seconds, and she gazed back, unsure of what to say to all of this.

"I didn't kill him."

Fin pressed his lips together, smiling.

"Stop saying that. You just don't remember."

But Hailey did remember. She remembered Adalwolf's rotting breath in her face, his skeletal fingers squeezing her throat…

Fin rubbed her hand, and Hailey blinked.

"It's kept you safe from Cobon and the others all these years," he said in a low voice, "so quit saying you didn't kill him, okay?"

Hailey nodded slowly.

"And no matter what happens, no matter what I say to you, no matter what I...do..." He shook his head as he spoke. "...promise me you'll always be the fiery Irish-American girl, who slaps me in the face and tells me to go to Hell whenever I act like an ass."

"I promise," she chuckled, looking at her hands in his. "If you're free now, and they can't control you, what are you afraid of?"

"They still get in my head, Hailey. Especially Cobon. If he makes me break up with you—"

"Break up? Am I one of your women now?" she said smiling.

"What? No." He almost yelled it, but Hailey couldn't stop grinning. "Why are you smiling?"

"I'm just glad you don't think I'm disgusting."

"Nobody thinks you're disgusting, Hailey, half the hockey team asked for my permission to date you."

"What?"

"You have no idea how attractive this cute, disheveled, athletic, nerdy thing is," he told her, gesturing at her with both hands.

"No, I meant, why are they asking for your permission to date me?"

Fin sat back in his seat and chewed his lip for a few seconds.

"Alright, look, I'm not gonna lie to you—I haven't always been the kind and gentlemanly specimen you see before you. I used to date a lot. A LOT. And until I ended things, which was usually very quickly after things started, the guys on the team would respect the relationship for however long it lasted—"

"You mean however short it lasted." *Pig.*

"AND they would wait until I was..." He hesitated before he spit it out. "...done...with whoever I was seeing, before they moved in on her."

"You guys are pigs."

"*Were...* No, they were respectful. I was a... I was fickle."

Hailey curled her lip. *He was a pig.*

"But those days are over," he said quickly. "They were over the day I met you, and in fact, I haven't been with another girl since the day I met you—since my first day as a bartender."

"I've seen you, Fin." Hailey could name ten off the top of her head.

"What you saw was me tying up some loose ends and letting those girls know that I'd met someone."

Fin shifted in his seat and changed the subject. "Listen, Cobon thinks he can make me hurt you...emotionally. The little pervert's been watching my dreams about you."

"You dream about me?" This was news.

"Don't you dream about me?" Fin pulled his cheek back as if he couldn't imagine that she *didn't* spend her nights pining after him, and since he was sharing his innermost thoughts...

"I daydream about you," she admitted.

"Yeah? Tell me more." He leaned forward, looking wolfish.

"In my daydreams, you never kick me out of your room when I show up naked at your door."

"Go on..."

"No." She'd just shared enough embarrassment for at least a decade.

"You don't dream about me at night?"

"No, not you." *Oops.*

Fin pushed back from the table. "Who do you dream of?"

Hailey pressed her lips together.

"It's Asher, isn't it?"

She looked away, hoping he'd just drop it, but Fin fixed a stubborn stare at her.

"That's where I met him," she said, her eyebrows raised.

Fin gave her a look she couldn't quite place, and when she tried to apologize, he cut in.

"Look, there's something I want to ask you," he said rubbing her hand and looking grave. He was going to ask her to stay away from him, she just knew it—to protect her from Cobon, but that was harebrained, and she opened her mouth to tell him so, but Fin held his hand up.

"Hailey," he began, and she made a preemptive frown. "Would you allow me to take you out on a proper date?"

Hailey blinked.

"Yes," she told him, but it came out sounding like, "Finally!" and she couldn't stop her smile from spreading across her whole head. "When?"

"This weekend. There's someplace I want to show you."

"Where is it?"

"You'll find out tomorrow," he said taking a bite of his pizza, and Hailey tried to keep her leg from shaking. Asher would not be happy.

And she didn't care.

Fin wiped his mouth and smiled at her.

"So," he said leaning over the table, "was that your first kiss," he asked, poking his tongue in his cheek and looking very pleased with himself.

Hailey bit her lip.

"No?"

"You left me!" she said pulling her eyebrows together. "You left me all alone, and Asher was there, and I was..." She gnashed her teeth and shook her head, tracing a scratch on the table with her finger and concentrating on not telling him about the second kiss.

"You kissed him?"

"Well, yeah." Asher wasn't exactly gross. Hailey flicked her eyes at Fin's then back to the scratch in the table.

Fin leaned back, crossing his arms over his chest.

"Not like that!" she said waving her hands in front of her. "Not like..." she put her ear on her shoulder, unable to say the word, "tongue."

That seemed to brighten Fin's mood considerably. Leaning forward, he smiled at her, and she could feel her cheeks burning.

"Stop looking at me," she smiled.

"Never."

Fin walked Hailey to her door and kissed her gently. "Pick you up at noon."

"No!" Hailey yelled, and she slammed the door in his face, but she opened it again with a giggle.

"That wasn't funny," he said dead-pan. Making a quick lunge into her room, he tossed her over his shoulder.

"Oof," she grunted. "I thought it was hysterical," she laughed.

"You're gonna pay for that one!"

With her slung over his shoulder, Fin ran down the stairs and out the door. He tossed her kicking and screaming into a six-foot snowbank.

"I'll pick you up at noon tomorrow," he called as he left her struggling to extract herself, giggling and spitting out snow.

Noon on Friday couldn't come quick enough, and Hailey practically skipped to her 9:30 class. She took her usual seat in the first row when something unusual happened.

David, one of the few students at Bear Towne brave enough to even look at Hailey, plopped down next to her.

"Hey, Hailey," he said groggily as he opened his notebook.

"Hi," she answered, confused. Nobody ever sat in the first row with her. She was more than a little suspicious when she saw David had actually combed his hair that morning.

"Are you going to Seven Trumpets?" he said out of the blue.

"Yes—with Asher."

"Do you know if your roommate's going?"

Aha. This was too perfect.

"Yes," she said smiling. "I mean—no, Giselle does not have a date, yet... And I know that," she explained. "But she wants to go..."

"Really?"

Hailey couldn't tell if he was surprised or disgusted. She went with surprised.

"Yeah. I know. It's hard to believe. She's so...um...she has such pretty eyes..."

"Yeah," he raised his eyebrows and nodded. "But—"

"—but she hasn't accepted an invitation, yet."

"You think I should ask her?"

"Well, why wouldn't you? She's very...interesting—and really fun..." That was stretching the truth a little.

"She's a little scary." He came right out and said it.

"She's not scary."

Okay. That was a flat out lie. Giselle could scare the hair off a cat. David drew a doodle on his notebook.

"I guess I could try asking her," he said hesitantly. "Maybe I'll ask her in class—"

"No!" Hailey yelled. "—I mean, you should wait until lunch. She's much more likely to say yes on a full stomach." Especially if Hailey got to her first. She'd have to warn her. And coach her. "...and she's usually all business in class," she added.

That seemed to make sense to David.

"Oh. Alright," he said shrugging.

Hailey hoped he wouldn't lose his nerve before lunch—or try to ask her in class. She'd have to run to catch Giselle in the Pre-Med leaf, and then she'd walk with her to ParaComm while she prepared her for David. And hopefully, she'd have the whole class to convince her to say yes.

As soon as the clock hit 10:30, Hailey bolted. She didn't even wait for the next day's assignment—she'd just get it later.

Hailey caught sight of her roommate just as she passed under the Pre-Med gate.

"Giselle!" She waved and ran to catch up.

"What do you want?"

Hailey needed a second to catch her breath. "You remember…" she panted as the two headed to Trinity, "David from… ParaComm…?"

Giselle didn't respond.

"Well, he just told me he wants to ask you to Seven Trumpets, but he's really nervous…"

Giselle tilted her head away from Hailey, but she detected a slight pull on her cheek—the banshee was smiling!

"Anyway," Hailey said nonchalantly, "thought you should know… just in case he tries to talk to you…"

They walked in silence until they reached Trinity's doors. Giselle hesitated there. "What if he steps on my dress or something?" the banshee said in a weird, almost feigned grouch.

Hailey shrugged as they walked into class.

"Well…uh…wail at him," she said quickly.

"That's funny, Hailey," Giselle told her, once again trying to hide her smile.

The day the banshee appeared in class looking almost happy will go down in history at Bear Towne, because as she continued smiling, Giselle transformed. Most of her wrinkles vanished, and her wiry gray hair took on a golden sheen. David decided he couldn't wait until lunch and just as Professor Mum opened her mouth to begin class, he abruptly stood up and faced Giselle.

Watching David approach her was the whole of their ParaComm class, all shock-faced, frozen in various pre-class poses, and waiting with wide eyes to witness a dumb human try to strike up a conversation with the campus banshee.

David cleared his throat and looked like he was about to lose his nerve when he got close, so Hailey intervened.

"Hi David," she called, smiling kindly, and she jabbed her roommate with her elbow.

"Oh. Hi," said Giselle uncertainly.

"Er...Giselle..." said David with a shaky voice. "...hi." He dropped his head and turned his back on them.

Hailey lunged to grab his arm before he could walk away.

"David, I was just telling Giselle how great it would be if we all sat together at Seven Trumpets," she prodded.

He swallowed loudly. Actually, he looked terrified, and Hailey had to act fast or else he might pass out before he asked Giselle to go.

"...and Giselle really liked the idea..." Hailey gave David her most encouraging smile.

"Giselle," he said going pale, "could...would you..."

Now he was hyperventilating and spoke his next words so fast they ran together.

"Woul-ja-g-go-to Strumpets-with...me...?"

Giselle's face softened. "Yeah sure, I guess," she mumbled.

He smiled widely, but then he passed out at her feet.

Hailey turned to Giselle. "Look," she said pointing at him. "You're a knock-out."

Chapter Thirty-Six

A Proper Date

"It is better to be feared than loved, if you cannot be both."

— Niccolo Machiavelli, The Prince

At exactly noon, Fin knocked on Hailey's door as she scrambled to get her other arm into her jacket.

"Just a second!" she hollered. She didn't know what he had planned, but she did know that it was an overnight date, that Asher would probably go ballistic if he knew, that she didn't care—Asher didn't own her and she was allowed to date whoever she wanted—and that she needed to stop worrying about Asher right now and pack a change of clothes, which her jellied in-between shirt helped her throw together.

"Bring your mittens," he hollered back, and she caught them when her shirt lobbed them from the closet.

"Miss Hartley," Fin said when she emerged. He took her bag and offered his arm. "Ready?"

"Mr. O'Shea. Thank you, and I think so…"

He let out a wistful growl.

"Call me Fin," he said, almost moaned. "I love it when you call me Fin."

"Where are we going, Fin?" Hailey could hardly contain her excitement.

"Up," he said.

"You're taking me flying?" she said, her voice going way higher than she intended.

"As promised."

He led her out the door to his giant red truck, which took them through the White Forest gate.

"Why are we here?" said Hailey, clutching her seat as visions of homicidal Yetis and man-eating trees danced through her head.

"Relax," Fin told her. "The airfield is this way, and I-MET keeps the whole flight area clear of bad things."

Before long, a hangar came into view, and Fin parked his truck next to a tiny red and black two-seater, which stood on skis and bore the Yeti's team logo on its tail.

"Where are the wheels?" Hailey pointed to the airplane's feet.

"In the hangar, I think." He opened the hatch and gave her a boost.

"Why aren't we taking the small one?" she remarked after she bonked her head and bumped her elbows squeezing into her seat.

Fin shook his head as he strapped her in.

"Zip up and put on your mittens. There's no heat back here." With their luggage secured behind Hailey's seat and their headsets donned, Fin fired up the single engine plane, and his voice crackled in Hailey's ear.

"It's a short, thirty-minute flight to the lake and a ten-minute go on the snowmachine."

"The what?"

"The snowmobile," he clarified. "You need to learn some Alaska words—" Fin cut himself off to make a radio call. "Bear Towne traffic, Cub bravo-tango-uniform–tree, taking runway zero-four, departing north, Bear Towne."

He throttled up for takeoff, and Hailey gripped her seat.

"This is incredible," she said, low enough that it didn't activate her mike, and she watched as they rounded a corner and flew over the campus.

Olde Main tilted only slightly to the north, and she could see enough detail to notice two students walk briefly outside the Trinity Center, grab their hoods around their faces, and walk back inside. No doubt they'd decided to take the tunnel. It wasn't below zero, but it was darn close.

Thirty minutes passed in a flash, and Fin pointed out the left window. "There it is," he said, dipping the wings.

Sitting in the middle of a white wonderland was a small log cabin, and the plane descended until it landed without a sound on a white field nearby.

"Where's the lake?" Hailey asked as the engine spun down.

"You're sitting on it." Fin opened the hatch and helped a horror-stricken Hailey outside.

"Holy crap, is this safe?" She stiffened her legs, which in her mind, was the only thing keeping them from falling through the ice.

"I don't know," Fin said as he transferred their gear to a waiting snowmachine. "Better not bend your knees or else the whole lake might cave in," he teased.

He buttoned up the plane then handed her a pair of goggles.

"Relax," he said as he cinched her hood for her. "This ice is at least two feet thick. Now, it might get cold back here, but if you hunker down behind me, I'll block the wind for you." Something serious darkened his expression, but then he smiled.

"Well, hop on."

"How did you get a snowmob—a snowmachine out here?"

Merely winking in response, Fin adjusted his goggles and revved the engine.

Sounding more like a chainsaw than a vehicle, the snowmachine whined and roared as it skimmed across the snow-covered lake and up a gentle hill. They wound around a few trees and parked in front of a beautifully rustic log cabin resting on stilts with a snow-covered roof over its head.

"This is it," he said proudly.

"It's sss-sss-so c-cute." The ride across the lake was a lot colder than she'd expected, and though her parka had kept her chest warm, the wind blew up her sleeves and cut right through her pants.

Fin hurried her inside, where it actually felt colder.

"That's mm-mm-much better," Hailey said with a crooked smile as Fin threw a log into the woodstove.

"Give it a second, and it'll be nice and toasty in here." He lit a fire, and he was right. Less than ten minutes later, she was shedding her parka. By then, Fin had the generator going, lights on, hot chocolate made, and blankets deployed on the couch. Then he clapped his hands together.

"I'll be outside catching dinner," he told her, and he grabbed a fishing pole next to the door.

Hailey knew exactly nothing about ice fishing and had no idea how Fin planned to break through two feet of ice. "The lake's frozen, Fin—how are you gonna catch anything?"

He cocked his head and held up a giant corkscrew.

"It's not frozen solid, my little southerner."

Hailey looked over his shoulder through the window with a skeptical frown.

"Thar be trout in that lake," he said like a pirate, which made Hailey laugh out loud. "And we're gonna eat it—I'll make my special glaze and some rice and beans…" He pointed his finger at her. "And YOU will owe me an apology, ye of little faith. Keep the fire going," he reminded her as he headed out the door.

Through the window, Hailey watched him auger through the ice, bait a hook, and drop it through the hole. Almost immediately, he pulled out a fish. He held it up and pointed at it, nodding his head as if to say, "Told you so."

Smiling, Hailey took a look around the cabin. It was divided by a couch into two small rooms. In the kitchen area was a small propane stove for cooking, a utility sink, a tiny fridge, and a heavy wooden table.

Less than half an hour after he grabbed his fishing pole, Fin was back inside with four trout and a triumphant smile.

"I'll have that apology now," he said as he took off his coat.

"You're amazing," said Hailey, feigning her best swoon. "I never should have doubted your skills on the ice," she continued, and then she bowed her head and batted her lashes at him. "Can you ever forgive me?"

"Alright," he said, matching her sarcasm. "If you ever kiss me, I'll forgive you."

Her playful smile evaporated. "I already kissed you."

"No," he sang. "*I* kissed *you*."

This wasn't fun anymore. She was way too shy to make a first move. Even after last night. So, she tucked her hair behind her ear and changed the subject, like the coward she was.

"How can I help with dinner?" she asked, nervously standing over the day's catch, not that she'd even know where to begin with a fish that still had eyeballs.

"Here," he said as he brought down some plates. "You can set the table and pour the wine—don't tell Pix."

"I won't."

It wasn't that she'd never had alcohol. Uncle Pix had been giving her and Holly beer in a shot glass since they were in grade school, but if he ever found out that Fin fed her wine, he'd probably kill him.

"Do you come here a lot?" If she had a cabin like his, she'd never leave.

"I used to come here…" he said as he lit a lantern on the table, "all the time."

"Alone?"

Fin became very busy at the stove, stirring and studying his secret trout glaze as if he hadn't heard her.

"You bring a lot of girls up here?" she said smiling and pleased to see him squirm for a change.

"Um...no," he answered, still stirring and turning down the flame.

"Just me?" she pressed.

He cut the fire completely. "Time to eat," he said without looking at her.

Hailey watched him shovel a fish onto her plate, and then he pulled her chair out, waiting as Hailey took her seat. Fin sat, too, and picked up his fork but then dropped it loudly.

"Alright, long story short? I brought one girl out here one time—and then she hanged herself, pass the wine?"

Holy shit.

She grabbed the bottle, lifted it to her lips, and downed three giant gulps before passing it to Fin. What else could she do?

He stared at her stark-faced for several seconds until finally, she wiggled the bottle, and he grabbed it.

"*Sláinte.*" He didn't bother with the glass, either.

"I'm sorry I kept prodding you," she said. "It's not your fault."

"What?"

"When someone kills themself, it's never somebody else's fault."

Fin looked up at her with what Hailey thought was a glimmer of hope in his eyes.

"Don't get me wrong, Fin," Hailey said with a chuckle, "you're very handsome and pretty easy to love, but..." her voice trailed off, and Fin searched her eyes from across the table as she continued. "But, you're not all that," she said, chasing her nervousness away, and Fin smiled. "You're not a puppeteer, and you can't know what's going on inside someone's head."

"What's going on inside your head, Hailey Hartley?"

"I'm still glad you don't think I'm disgusting," she laughed. "And I really wish you'd kiss me with your tongue again."

Hailey pressed her lips together and picked up the wine bottle.

"Whoa," she chuckled with wide eyes. "What's in this stuff?"

Fin's shoulders shook. "Sodium Pentothal?" he laughed.

"Well, it's working. Anything else you'd like to know?"

"Yeah," he said, his smile vanishing. "How do I win your heart?"

Hailey gazed at him from across the table, her heart thumping in her ears. His eyes were so bright, so honest. She looked at her plate, and as she did so, a gigantic grin grew across her face.

"You wrote the book on that, didn't you, Fin."

When she looked up, he was still staring at her and looking mighty content.

"Will you tell me about your curse?" she asked, finishing off her first fish. The secret glaze was awesome. Actually, the whole night was awesome.

"It happened when I was seven years old, so I don't remember all the details, though my parents tell me I was very sick—scarlet fever, I think. Anyway, they were desperate. They called on Adalwolf and asked him to save me, which he did. In exchange for saving my life, he demanded an eternity of servitude. My parents pretty much became slaves. And so did I, only…"

"Only what?"

"Only I never killed anyone for him. And it used to piss him off royally," he laughed. "Anyway, I live my life over and over and over. I age until I turn eighty, then I wake up the next morning a seven-year-old. It's a little annoying."

She tried to imagine it… living through grade school—ugh—middle school again… Being thirteen again? Thank-you, no.

"What's your psychotic boyfriend going to say when he finds out you spent the night with me?"

"Nothing good." Hailey pressed her hand to her temple. "Asher gets jealous. I probably won't tell him. Besides, I doubt he'll even notice I'm gone. He hasn't been around much lately, and he only wants me some of the time anyway."

"Well, I want you all the time."

He took her chin with his thumb and forefinger, and she gazed up at him, hoping he'd bring his lips a little closer, but instead, he dropped his stare and finished off the wine.

"I'm going to marry you, Hailey Hartley," he said suddenly, and no doubt fully under the influence of the second bottle of red, so she went with it.

"Where's my ring?"

"In my jacket."

"You're such a clown," she told him shaking her head, but he wasn't laughing—drunk, no doubt.

He put his hand on her shoulder and moved his face close to hers. "No snooping," he said. "I want it to be a surprise when I give it to you."

"Oh, it will be," she said, raising her brow.

While Fin tossed cushions off the couch, Hailey looked around the cabin.

"Where should I sleep?" If he thought she was going to crawl into a sofa bed with him, he was drunk *and* stupid.

"You're sleeping here." He motioned to the bed. "With me."

"I'll just sleep on the floor," she said.

He threw a pillow in her face. "You're sleeping in the bed," he repeated. "*With* your clothes on, my little nudist—no arguments—I'll keep my hands to myself."

That's what he said, but what he did after Hailey donned her pajamas and slithered under the covers was grab her immediately, pull her into a cuddle, throw a leg over her hips, and hold her tight all night long.

And she fought sleep so she could enjoy every second.

"Fin," she whispered long after he'd started snoring, "I think I love you, and I'm scared to death."

Someone else was awake all night, too, and when Fin returned to campus the next day, Asher was waiting for him…with a reminder.

"Good evening, Pádraig," Asher said when he stepped inside the dorm room, and the human had the audacity to roll his eyes.

"What do you want Asher, you wanna talk about Hailey? Fine. Let's talk about how you're planning to kill her, and then I can remind you of our agreement," he said with far too sharp an edge in his voice.

Such disrespect would not go unpunished.

Asher fixed his gaze on Pádraig's eyes.

"Yes," said Asher, boring into the man's mind. "Let's talk about Hailey."

Chapter Thirty-Seven

The Seven Trumpets Ball

"Speak low. if you speak love."

— William Shakespeare.
Much Ado About Nothing

Tacked on doors and message boards all over campus were flyers announcing the upcoming Christmas Ball and Parents' weekend.

Hailey was gawking at one of them when Giselle caught up to her. Each day saw the banshee looking more and more like an angel—long, golden hair, crystal eyes, disappearing wrinkles…

Until she smiled.

It was the razor-sharp demon teeth that gave away her true nature. That and her grumpiness.

"My dress just came," she barked, and Hailey waited to hear why this was a bad thing.

Hailey dipped her chin. "…and?"

"That's all. But I observed that yours hasn't arrived, and the ball is this weekend. Will you be wearing your sweat pants or going naked?"

Dammit. Between completing her term project without Asher's help (he found the experimental vibrations far too annoyingly close to his own death frequency), counting books in the library, reading Professor Woodfork's chronicles, and *not* learning how to use her new "evil-detection" gift, because despite his promise to teach her, Asher rarely even talked to her outside of her dreams anymore—somehow, she had totally forgotten to get a dress.

Now, with only three days left before the ball, she had precious few options. Maybe Fin could drive her into town on Thursday?

She rushed home that Tuesday, hoping to find him before hockey practice. But what she found instead when she opened her door was a gorgeous black and gold gown with iridescent embellishments in hunter green hanging in her closet with shoes to match. Her in-between soldier pants kept it from wrinkling and her jellied shirt nodded its approval.

Asher.

She smiled, running her fingers over the rich fabric. He'd been fairly distant for several weeks after her date with Fin, but in her dreams, he'd promised to be more attentive and hadn't even mentioned ripping her soul out, which greatly improved their relationship—and created for her quite the quandary.

She was intrigued by Asher—by his supernatural strength and new-found emotions—and Fin was right. She was flattered by his attention. Seeing him was mesmerizing, and not just because of his hypnotic gaze. He was simply gorgeous, in a dark, mysterious, brooding sort of way, with his smoldering eyes, thick, dark hair, warm embrace... and he ignited a fire in her that consumed her very reason.

But then there was Fin. Fin talked to her every day, touched her every day—always kissed her hand or her cheek when they parted... Only her hand or her cheek, and she really wanted more. Oh, how she wanted more! And though he hadn't taken her out on another date since their overnight at his cabin, she'd been so busy with school and he with hockey, she'd chalked it up to nothing more serious than a scheduling conflict.

So, when the night of the ball arrived and Fin showed up with a date on his arm, Hailey felt the unmistakable sting of the green-eyed monster as she walked with Giselle to their table. Asher hadn't shown yet, and as Hailey stood and gaped at her thirty-something-looking supermodel banshee roommate flirt with David, a pair of arms surrounded her from behind.

She jumped, and Fin buried his face in her neck, kissing her softly.

"You are a vision of beauty," he murmured. "Save me a dance."

"I will." Hailey smiled broadly.

"And make it early, because I think Asher is going to kill me for good tonight," he called over his shoulder as he returned to his date.

"If he bothers to come," she muttered, but only Giselle heard her.

Dinner came and went, and Asher was still a no-show. While Hailey drummed her fingers on the table, Fin seemed to be having quite a good time laughing and snuggling with Adelaide Martin, the long-legged, blond-haired beauty queen he'd escorted. Then the music started and Hailey's face drained. She grabbed Giselle by the arm, yanking her away from David and into the ladies' room.

"Giselle, you have to help me, I don't know how to dance like a normal person."

"Let me see."

Hailey tried a modified Irish jig, and Giselle raised her lip.

"What am I looking at? You look like a tree on a pogo stick. Try bending your arms or turning or something."

Hailey sighed and pulled her elbows up as she bounced and moved in a circle.

Giselle pointed a finger at her. "Farmer in a tornado."

"Giselle," Hailey huffed.

"Don't bend your arms so much and stop twirling…nope. Now you're a confused windmill. Move your hips or your head."

Hailey tried moving a little bit of everything to the muffled rock-n-roll string quartet, which played through the walls.

"Epileptic Chicken." Giselle settled against the sink and looked at her thoughtfully. "What if you just slid a little across the floor without bouncing so much?"

It felt awkward, and Giselle agreed.

"Moonwalking Frankenstein," she declared. "No, do another one," she commanded when Hailey crossed her arms, and she hopped onto the vanity. "This is fun."

Hailey gave it one last shot, bending her elbows, moving her bum, shaking her shoulders, bobbing her head and swaying side to side.

"Moose stuck in a swing set." Giselle hopped off the vanity. "That's the one. Very Alaskan. Now let's go have some forced fun."

David and Giselle hit the dance floor, but Hailey, still dateless and feeling neglected sat alone, elbow on the table, head on her fist and watched the lights dance across her beautiful shoes. There was no way she was doing the "moose stuck in a swing set," and it was a slow song anyway, so she crossed her arms and sulked.

"C'mere, beautiful."

She looked up to see Fin standing with one arm tucked behind his back, the other extended to her like a perfect gentleman, and she took it, smiling excitedly. He pulled her to her feet, guided her to the center of the room and looked up.

"Mooseltoe," he said, eying a rustic ornament hanging from the ceiling.

"That looks like poop on a spruce branch."

"It is," he conceded with a grin. "Moose poop. But you're supposed to kiss under it. Aren't Alaskans clever?"

With his arm around her waist, he pulled her body to his and held her tight. With his other hand, he grabbed her chin and brushed his thumb across her lips as he swayed with her to the haunting music.

After a few beats, he pressed his forehead against hers. "This will probably do me in," he breathed against her mouth, "but I'm tired of waiting for you to kiss me."

"What do you—"

Fin shoved his lips over her mouth.

She stopped dancing. So did he, and they stood frozen on the dance floor in a heated embrace as he slipped his tongue into her mouth. Her whole body flushed with heat, and she pressed against him. For several seconds, he held her, exploring her mouth with his tongue, then nibbling at her lips, and the music faded—the room faded. He relaxed his hold and danced soft kisses across her cheek until his lips touched her ear.

"Forgive me, Hailey," he whispered fervently, and the room reappeared. Hailey gazed into his pleading eyes, his face ashen.

"For what?"

He sighed heavily, tightened his arms around her and swayed her body to the music. "Everything."

Could he be any more vague? But it didn't matter. Of course she forgave him. For anything. Everything.

"After a kiss like that, I'd forgive you for ripping my heart out," she breathed.

For the briefest instant, his face darkened.

He momentarily loosened his hold on her only to squeeze her tight again. She rested her head against his shoulder, and the music changed, but he didn't loosen his grip. *Another dance, then.* Hailey smiled. She caught a glimpse of his date standing cross-armed in the corner of the room, tapping her foot as she watched them closely.

"She looks angry," Hailey told him, and he glanced over his shoulder at Adelaide.

"Yeah," he agreed with a carefree laugh. "She does. I don't really care. I told her when I asked her to the ball that I'd be dancing with you. Asher's probably got his panties in a bunch by now, though…"

"Asher hasn't shown up." She was going for nonchalant, but couldn't disguise her disappointment at being stood up.

"See? You should've been my date."

He tucked a loose tendril behind her ear.

Blushing, she looked down, pressing her lips together to reign in her giant grin. He so easily lifted her spirits, and she loved him—absolutely and unconditionally.

Fin ran the back of his fingers down her cheek and under her jaw then lifted her chin and smiled sadly. Hailey looked up at him.

"What is it?"

He shook his head, still gazing at her with sad adoration.

"Why did you say Asher would kill you for good tonight?" she asked softly.

Fin sighed and pressed his lips together. His eyes darted away briefly, and he set his jaw, like he was gathering his courage.

Uh-oh, Hailey thought. *This must be pretty bad.*

"He thinks I'll hurt you," he said with no trace of emotion.

"Why would he think that? Because of Cobon?" *Because I'm crazy in love with you, and if you reject me, my heart will implode?*

He answered in a flat voice. "No. Because of the way I am… with women… I guess I get bored easy." The last bit came out sounding strained. "I don't want to hurt you, Hailey," he pleaded.

"Then don't." *Why did it feel like he was saying goodbye?* She opened her mouth to probe further, but now he was looking across the room and his expression hardened.

"Aw, shit."

She turned her head but saw nothing. "What is it?" she asked as he released her.

"Nothing," he said with an icy tone. "I'll be right back." He didn't even look at her as he said it and left her standing on the dance floor looking after him.

After Fin disappeared into the shadows of the hall, Hailey moped back to the table and scanned the room again for Asher. Still nothing.

Giselle appeared, positively glowing.

Hailey looked her up and down. "I think you've turned the corner on the hag issue," she told her. "You look like a movie star."

Giselle smiled, and Hailey pointed at her mouth.

"Except for the pointy demon teeth," she said.

"David just kissed me." She could hardly contain herself.

"Did he survive?"

Hailey was still looking at her roommate's razor-sharp snarl, and Giselle nodded toward the doors where David stood with a dumb grin plastered on his face, surrounded by no fewer than ten of their classmates.

"He's bragging to his friends right now," Giselle said, looking radiant.

As Hailey observed David swoon, something flashed in her periphery, and she snapped her head around in time to see Asher across the room, holding Fin by the throat with one and and pressing his other hand against Fin's forehead. She sprang out of her chair and raced over to them.

"…two months, and my patience wears thin, Padraig. You forget your place, and your soul is still black as pitch with the hundreds of lives you've taken," Asher was saying through clenched teeth as Hailey approached.

Hundreds of lives? Neither man noticed her drawing near.

"Yeah," Fin choked. "You know why?" His face went crimson with rage.

Asher didn't respond.

"Because I actually *have* a soul, Asher. But you wouldn't know anything about that, would you?"

"Asher has a soul," Hailey piped, rather nonchalantly, given the two looked as if they were engaged in mortal combat.

"What?" the men asked in unison, Fin with disgust; Asher in astonishment.

Hailey looked from one to the other.

Asher released his grip on Fin, and Fin took a swing at him. Without shifting his gaze from Hailey, Asher snagged Fin's fist out of the air and squeezed it until it crunched. Fin doubled over, and Hailey's hand flew to her mouth.

"Oh my God, Asher!" She rushed to Fin's side, and Asher seethed. Fin shook his head and held up his good hand.

"Don't touch me."

"Hundreds of lives?" Hailey put her hands on her hips, demanding an explanation.

"It was *one* life," he yelled, standing hastily, and Hailey cringed. Fin's voice went low, hateful. "Over and over and over..."

He put his face close to hers and stared resentfully into her eyes. "And over."

She shrank away, blinking at him, speechless. What was he saying? What life? *His* life? Had he killed himself *hundreds* of times? Maybe after living in hellish torment for hundreds of years...

There were some things I had to straighten out with the Big Guy. That's what he'd told her at the church. It all made sense. Suddenly, instead of yelling back, all she wanted to do was wrap her arms around him. But Asher was watching. Glowering. And Fin was looking at her like she was a cold sore.

"So now you know," he spat at her. He turned his back and walked off. Hailey stared after him and watched open-mouthed as he slung his arm around Adelaide. Then he kissed her so passionately, it turned into a full-body salsa dip. Hailey's heart plummeted into her stomach.

"Hailey," Asher beckoned, holding his hand out. His voice startled her. "Come. We must talk."

She couldn't read his expression or his tone, but it felt like she was in trouble. Tentatively, she put her hand in his, and he led her to the door.

"It's really cold outside," she said, unable to hide the fear in her voice and hoping he hadn't planned on making her leave. For some reason, she felt safer in public, though she didn't really believe a crowd would stop him from killing her.

Asher sighed heavily, whirled around, and cupped her face in his hands.

"You won't be cold with me," he said tenderly, and some of her anxiety abated. He didn't *sound* angry, but if he had seen her kissing Fin...

She swallowed hard. He slid his fingertips from her chin, down the sides of her neck across her shoulders and down the length of her arms. Taking her hands, he gazed into her eyes and walking backwards, led her outside.

Hailey braced for the bite of Alaska's winter, but Asher was right. Somehow, he was shielding her from the icy wind. It was quite comfortable inside his warmth-bubble.

"Look, Asher…" She wanted to tell him that she was in love with Fin, that she wanted nothing to do with Cobon's plan, that she was angry at him for showing up late, though that seemed petty compared to having one's soul ripped out—but her thoughts jumbled and bounced around in her head, and after what she just saw Fin doing with Adelaide… and his hateful tone…

Breathe.

And Fin had dismissed her so coldly, she wasn't even sure he felt the same anymore…or if he ever did feel the same. Plus, Asher might kill her, and she hesitated.

"What is it?" he said very tenderly.

She looked at her hands.

"Thank you for the beautiful dress."

Fear-one, courage-zero.

"The beauty of the dress pales in comparison to the angel wearing it." He sounded exasperated. Then he tilted his head, his eyes igniting into a firestorm, and his mouth twisting into a scowl. Yep, he was angry. "What are you doing, Hailey?" he said bitterly. "I saw you kissing him," he accused, his voice slow. "You promised me there was nothing serious between you and Pádraig." He leaned close to her and whispered, "Do you have any idea what I do to students who lie to me?"

Hailey gasped, her heart quickened. *Was that a threat?*

Jaycen… Unwittingly, her thoughts turned to the southern belle, who was still writhing in agony inside a steel cage in the White Forest with nothing but the sub-zero wind chill to keep her company. Never had Asher spoken to Hailey with such animosity, and for a beat, she wondered if he might tie her soul. Her throat tightened, her eyes went wide, and she instinctively took a retreating step back. She didn't know what to say and stood locked in his intense gaze while her brain floundered and her heart rose in her throat. He stared and squinted, but then his brow knitted together. And she knew in that instant that he—the all-powerful Envoy—was hurting. *She* had hurt *him*, very deeply she'd hurt him, and her heart shriveled.

Asher looked away. He must've seen her remorse and taken pity on her, because when he looked back his eyes were soft.

"He's not the gallant knight you think he is, my dear." He stroked her cheek as he said it. "He will hurt you."

"Well, he never threatened to rip my soul out," she whispered, blinking back tears. "Where have you been anyway? With Cobon?" She wiped her eyes with the back of her hand.

Asher closed his eyes and inhaled loudly. "I only want to rescue you," he told her apologetically. "I know I've been neglecting you—forgive me, please. And no, I haven't spoken to Cobon for quite some time."

What was he doing? His voice was kind. He was staring at her with those gorgeous eyes, full of adoration and heat. Not an hour ago, she'd decided he was a hideous monster, and now…

Hailey trembled and not from the cold. The intensity, the electricity between them sent a shiver down her back, and she raised her shoulders against it.

"Are you cold?" Asher seemed perplexed.

"No," she said, unable to look at him. She could feel her cheeks flush. Asher regarded her curiously for a moment, then without warning, he grabbed her shoulders and shoved her against the wall next to the door. Grasping her chin with one hand and wrapping the other around her waist, he pressed his mouth to hers, hard and hungry. His lips molded to hers, and she kissed him back, running her fingers through his silky hair and melting into him as he pressed the full length of his body against her. This was what she wanted. This was what she craved—love, passion—from the one creature that could rescue her from a fate worse than death.

Oh, it was heaven! He held her there, kissing, caressing for minutes, hours, maybe. She didn't know. She didn't care. She didn't want him to stop.

Fin who?

When he was finished, he held her close. "It upsets me to see another touching you," he breathed against her lips, still caressing the back of her head. He leaned back and flashed his eyes at her. "You belong to me. Do you understand?"

Hailey blinked rapidly, unable to find her voice.

"Answer me," he commanded, grasping her hair and pulling so hard it hurt.

"Yes," Hailey squeaked, her eyes wide, and she was trembling again, this time from sheer terror.

"Yes, what, Hailey? I want you to say it."

Hailey blinked again. What the hell was happening?

"Yes, Asher. I belong to you," she said obediently, and he sighed deeply, releasing her head and rubbing it gently.

"Will you tell me why you think I have a soul?"

She didn't feel like chatting with him anymore. She wondered how fast she could run in her new heels. But wrestling her sudden urge to flee was her paralyzing terror and the realization that— there was nowhere to run, nowhere to hide. Plus, she was still sort of reeling from his kiss and needed a moment to slow her breathing before she could even begin to feel ashamed for wanting him to kiss her again. And right now, she couldn't sort ANY of this out, because he wanted an answer.

"What do you mean?" she asked, searching his violet eyes. "You have a soul... I've seen it in my dreams."

"I don't have a soul, Hailey," he said. "Envoys are pure energy."

"I think you're wrong, Asher. I think you know you're wrong. I think you know you have a soul, but you don't want to admit it. Maybe that's why the Envoys are going mad?" She emphasized the word "mad" maybe a little too much and had to recover. "You wouldn't be able to love me if you didn't have a soul."

She wasn't sure what he was feeling really qualified as love, but she was floundering and suddenly wishing she was safe with Fin again… at the cabin… tucked in his arms…

Asher's eyes calmed down, but he didn't step back. He still had her pinned to the wall.

"I do love you, Hailey," he murmured. "I've tried to be patient with you, but I can no longer tolerate seeing another put his hands on you." His voice was gentle, and Hailey's blood pressure came down. A little. "And I believe I've frightened you. Am I right?"

"Yes," she breathed.

Now she couldn't hold back her tears, and they gushed forth. Asher brought his lips to her cheeks and kissed each teardrop as it escaped her eye.

"Forgive me." He was doing it again. Gazing at her with those hypnotic eyes.

"Asher, I'm sorry," she sobbed.

"For what?" He asked between kisses.

His heat against her face was divine. This was a new side to her monster she'd never experienced before. He was sensual…and loving.

"For disappointing you," she whispered. Suddenly, she felt horribly guilty for kissing Fin when all this time Asher was protecting her, waiting for her.

He kissed her left eyelid then her right and ran his thumb along her jawline. Then he kissed her lips again, unleashing his warmth inside her mouth.

Was he giving her another gift? Invading her mind?

Oh, hell. She didn't care.

She grabbed two fistfuls of his luxurious hair and pulled him into her. He responded by pressing her into the wall, and once again she was putty in his arms.

"Shall we dance?" he asked in his smooth, seductive voice, and Hailey had to get her bearings. She wasn't sure she could stand on her own after that kiss, let alone dance.

"Okay," she breathed.

"I'm going to let go of you now, Hailey," he whispered to her ear. "You're trembling. Can you stand?"

She nodded, but as soon as he let her go, her legs crumpled, and he caught her again.

She clutched his white shirt and willed her legs to stand. "I did that on purpose," she said with a soft giggle, "so you'd hold me tight again."

But the Envoy wasn't amused.

Envoys don't laugh. Fin's voice rang inside her head.

Chapter Thirty-Eight

Torn

"We're fools whether we dance or not. so we might as well dance."

— Japanese Proverb

Asher stepped away and held his hand out to her like a perfect gentleman. "Let's have that dance, my dear."

She took his hand. What choice did she have?

"I wish you could laugh," she said almost to herself, but a slight turn of his head let her know he'd heard.

As he led her across the room, she noticed many turned to look at them. The girls of Bear Towne seemed enchanted by Asher's charm, but their dates sure weren't. The non-humans, of course, avoided him, and the entire hall was a mix of disgust, worry, and adoration.

Asher swooped across the floor, holding her tight, making it easy for her to follow. The dim light, the poignant melody of the strings, the heat from his body, the feel of his hand against her bare back—skin to skin—it was intoxicating. He was so strong, so powerful, and she felt safe with him as she glided across the room.

As the music reached a crescendo, he pulled her tight against his body and kissed her slowly, deliberately, his fingers trailing tickles across her back, and she was lost to the world, lost to him. The music, the lights—they were dizzying. She badly needed a break, needed to catch her breath.

Before she could ask him, Asher was leading her back to the table.

"Giselle." He nodded curtly, and she nervously flicked her eyes at him then back to the floor. "You're looking well."

Giselle lifted her whole head to look at him, her entire face lit up.

"Thank you, Asher," she said, and her mouth twitched in a small grin.

"I think you're the most beautiful woman in the world," David gushed with an almost pleading voice. If he was trying to win a smile from the banshee too, it worked. She even blushed. Then she cleared her throat.

"Hailey," she barked. "I need to speak to you about physical love in the ladies' room."

David spit his drink across the table.

Giselle grabbed Hailey by the arm, shot a begging glance at Asher, who nodded his permission, and she pulled Hailey into the antler-less moose room.

Oh, thank goodness. Hailey's head was swimming; her heart was in a twist. She didn't know which way was up, and she needed some time away from Asher to pull herself together. And Giselle wanted to talk about physical love…? With her…?

"Giselle, I'm not Dr. Ruth," said Hailey as soon as the door closed.

"Don't be stupid. I wouldn't ask you for advice on love." She scowled, looking over her shoulder. "I dragged you in here, because…" She looked over her shoulder again and whispered, "Asher is losing his mind."

"What?"

"He loves you."

"That makes him crazy?"

"Yes!" she hissed, pulling Hailey into a corner. "Envoys don't love. They don't romance, and they certainly don't kiss and caress and cuddle like he was doing on the dance floor." Her expression was grave. "You're in trouble. If he senses that you're rejecting him, he'll rip you apart."

That explained a lot. The Earth swayed under Hailey's feet, and she swallowed hard. Maybe it was wrong, but she liked crazy Asher and his un-Envoy-like romantic tendencies. And she hadn't planned on rejecting him. *Well, not anymore.*

"It doesn't matter if you *plan* on rejecting him."

That was so annoying—Giselle and her banshee-mind-reading thing.

"It's what he thinks is happening," she continued speaking so quietly, Hailey had to strain to hear her. "And as he spirals further into insanity, he'll go totally Cobon batshit crazy."

Cobon. Could she never escape him?

"You need to be careful," she whispered. "And stay the hell away from Pádraig. Asher's jealous of the affection you show him. Plus he's an asshole."

Two giggling girls burst into the bathroom.

"We'd better get back," said Giselle.

"Asher had to go," David informed the girls when they returned, and Hailey blew a sigh of relief.

She instinctively glanced around the room in search of him, catching instead an eyeful of something that turned her stomach.

There in the middle of the dance floor was Fin. With Adelaide. And Hailey stared in disbelief as he stood under the mooseltoe and laid a long, drawn-out kiss on his tall, busty, blonde bombshell date who seemed elated to be stuck to the most handsome man on campus—okay, second-most handsome man. But then, Asher wasn't really a man.

And Hailey really had no right to be jealous, not after her dance with Asher…

But Fin was kissing her again!

Hailey's stomach tightened, even though she "belonged" to Asher. How could Fin kiss that girl after all those things he'd said to her? She wondered if she was even human.

"Giselle, what is that girl?" She pointed to Adelaide. "A suc-cubus?" she guessed. She had to be some kind of demon.

"No. She's just a skank," Giselle said. "Told you his love wouldn't last. Put him out of your head, Hailey," she advised with sad eyes.

It was good to have a friend. But Hailey didn't want Fin out of her head, which was beginning to pound. She shouldn't feel wounded by his behavior. Really—how could she condemn him after the heated moments she'd just shared with Asher?

Hypocrite, she muttered inside her head. Would she even care what Fin was doing if Asher hadn't left her?

Yes.

Fin paraded Adelaide across the floor, laughing and kissing and seemingly unaffected by any lover's quandary, and certainly not one that scattered his thoughts and squeezed his heart.

He was kissing her again...with his tongue? Oh, no! No, he definitely was *not* mired in uncertainty. It seemed he was making Hailey's decision for her.

And if so, there was nothing left to do but say goodbye. She had to. And not just because she was angry...and hurt...and not good enough for him...

It would protect him from Asher's jealousy. She was doing this for the right reason.

All those things he'd said...'I'm going to marry you'—my ass... Hailey sighed and pushed her bitter thoughts aside. As soon as he was alone, she'd just amicably tell him goodnight and goodbye.

There.

Simple.

It shouldn't feel like a confrontation. It wasn't like he was her *boyfriend* or anything, so she wasn't breaking up with him. The thought made her sad. She wanted him to be her boyfriend.

His kisses, his promises... His lies. If she kept this train of thought, she might be angry enough to do this without crying. Or too angry to do it without crying. *Crap.*

There it was. Adelaide excused herself to the no-antlers room, and Hailey bolted upright and strode in his direction. She had her courage and her anger balled up in her stomach, spurring her on. But angry-marching in high heels was a bad idea, and right about the time Fin noticed her approach, right about two paces away from him, her right foot slipped out from under her, and down she went.

Giselle rushed to help her up. Fin just stood there, glaring down at her and looking like he'd just stepped in something squishy.

"Maybe you should stick to flats, little girl," he said in a voice so disparaging, it cut straight to her heart. Hailey rubbed her elbow, which bore the brunt of her fall.

"Why are you being so mean?" she squeaked. That was not what she wanted to say.

"Well, you keep following me around for starters, and you just won't take a hint." His voice was harsh. His eyes were harsh. And she was not following him around. *A hint? What the—? She'd better just get this over with.*

She mustered her friendly voice. "Look, Fin, I—"

"—and my name is Pádraig," he said scornfully.

She waited to see him crack his sarcastic, playful smile.

But he didn't.

"What's the matter with you?" she asked in a voice barely above a whisper.

He cocked his head to the side and stuck his jaw out. "I can't do this anymore, Hailey." His voice was low and honest.

"Can't do what?"

"This big-brother-looking-after-you thing. It's just not me. It was fun almost getting into your pants, but frankly..." He ran his hand through his hair. "I'm bored with you...with this whole situation. And it's irritating when you follow me around."

Bored with me? Oh, no! Is that what he was trying to tell her on the dance floor? And she blew it off. Was that his hint? And now she was following him around? Her heart raced in her chest as fast as the self-deprecating thoughts ran through her head.

He was scowling down at her. And he'd just made this a lot easier.

"Well that's fine, because I was just coming to tell you—"

"Stop following me around, Hailey," he spat in a loud voice. Several heads turned in their direction. "Stop showing up at my door…throwing yourself at me. It's annoying."

Total shock stole her voice, and she could feel her face flush.

"I'll never be your boyfriend, alright?"

Hailey shook her head in surprised confusion. "Why are you saying these things?" *Cobon! Cobon wanted him to hurt her.* She wondered if this was just Envoy shenanigans, but he certainly didn't look hypnotized—in fact, he rolled his eyes at her.

"Look, I had to get close to you after Holly croaked."

Croaked? The air in the room was too heavy to breathe. She blinked rapidly, trying to keep her angry veneer in place for just a few seconds longer.

"I got you here, I gained your trust, I seduced you, and you were eating out of my hand. But now the Envoys have a different plan for you. So, I don't have to keep up this charade any longer."

"That's not funny, Fin," Hailey was holding it together, but just barely.

She had to open her eyes wide to keep the tears in.

He was the one who said they'd figure things out together. *He* had told her he'd help her escape the ripping-out-of-the-soul, temporary death thing. And now he was abandoning her to Cobon's plan.

"You're really freaking me out," she managed between shallow hitching breaths.

"Wait a minute," he said with an arrogant laugh. "You didn't honestly believe I wanted to marry you…"

She blanched.

He gasped. "You did!" He stepped back and clapped his hands together loudly as he laughed at her. Her eyes shot left and right as a gradual hush fell over the hall. "You rise to a whole new level of pathetic," he said loud enough for everyone on the dance floor to hear. "I can't believe you fell for that!" he yelled at her.

She flinched, letting two large drops fall from her eyes, and the whole hall turned to see what was happening. Then he poked her in the forehead.

"Get it through your head, little girl—I'm done with you. You're a weeping cesspool," he muttered. His voice was cold and certain, his eyes frigid, and now Adelaide was coming back. Fin offered his elbow to her.

"Hello my dear," he said, his voice switched back to its smooth, sincere, heart-throb magic.

He didn't even glance back at Hailey as he swaggered away.

She stood gaping after them, shell-shocked, humiliated, and completely hollow.

"Don't feel bad, Hailey," said Sidney, who appeared at her side. "Pádraig does this to every girl he sleeps with."

Hailey continued staring after Fin.

"And that's a lot of girls," Sidney continued. "You get lonely, you can always call me."

"Stop trying to make me feel better, Sidney, I did not sleep with him." Well, actually she did, but not how Sidney meant it. She tore her eyes away from the corner Fin just rounded to stare daggers at Sidney. "And I will *not* be calling you."

Giselle was still at her side.

"Told you," she said softly, gloomily. "He's an asshole." She threw her arm around Hailey and hugged her stiffly. "You okay?"

"Yeah," she whispered.

Hailey shook her head as her eyes welled again. Her whole body trembled.

"At least Asher didn't stand you up."

"Yeah."

Giselle was trying to make her feel better, but she'd heard everything Fin said, and she knew it cut to Hailey's heart.

"Giselle, I'm going to walk home now," she told her in a half whisper. Her feet carried her to the exit, but she couldn't feel the floor under them.

Without getting her coat, she threw open the door and stepped outside. The cold sucked what little breath she had left out of her lungs, and she welcomed the sting of negative ten degree wind on her bare skin. Something to distract her from the ache in her chest.

Giselle ran to catch up, throwing a coat over Hailey's shoulders. She didn't say a word as they made their way to the dorm.

With only a few steps to go, Giselle froze in place, and Hailey followed her stare to entryway, where Asher stood waiting. He opened the door.

"Giselle, would you excuse us?" he asked, indicating her inside.

"Hailey." Asher turned his penetrating gaze to her, and his expression relaxed. There it was again: abject adoration. She bowed her head. He was looking at her like she was the only person on Earth.

She loved it. And hated it. No matter what he said next, she'd want him to kiss her. Actually, he didn't need to say anything else.

"Walk with me to the gazebo." He held his hand out, and she took it.

"Why did you leave?" Her voice was flat.

"Why did you stay?"

He pulled her hand so that she ambled closer to him. Then he wrapped his arm around her.

"I wanted to say goodbye to Fin," she said, her lip trembling, and he stopped mid-stride.

He cupped her face in his hands. When she looked up at him, her eyes pooled, and he brought his lips to hers, nipping her gently, and softly kissing her sobs. She put her hands over his on her cheeks and stroked them lightly.

"I'm so sorry, Asher," she cried. "I feel like such a fool."

"Don't."

His soothing voice was welcome, and he traced his thumb down the side of her cheek to her jaw. "Pádraig was tasked with bringing you here and keeping you here. He did it the only way he knows how—with charm and seduction."

Hailey shivered. It was downright frigid outside, and she wished she had a hat. And pants. And boots.

Smiling kindly, Asher extended his warmth around her. She sighed, all of her muscles relaxed by the sudden reprieve from cold.

"Did you tell him to humiliate me, too?" she asked bleakly, as another round of tears swam in her eyes. "Because that's what he just did."

He drew her into a tight embrace.

"Of course not, Hailey. I told him his job was done and that I no longer expected him to look after you. I had no idea he would hurt you so deeply. Forgive me."

So Asher had put Fin up to it. Fin had played her, and she'd fallen for his deceptive charm—hook, line, and sinker.

She felt sick.

"Hailey, I've neglected you, and I'm sorry. I will be around more often now."

More often? What does that mean?

"Every day," he whispered as if he'd read her mind. "There is no other for me." Her heart found a handhold, and pulled itself partially out of her stomach.

She wasn't sure how to respond.

"What about Cobon's plan?"

Way to kill the mood, she thought, but that was what really worried her...that Asher would even consider—no intend—to hurt her.

He stroked her cheek and lifted her chin.

"Cobon aims to kill you. Soon."

Her heart hit the basement again.

"I know you're afraid," he said gently. "And you should be. If I'm to save you, I have to release your energy to him, and the pain will be excruciating."

Excruciating. She let the word sink in, and her blood ran cold.

"I don't understand it, Asher."

He tilted his head and placed his hand over her heart.

"Your body and soul are bound." He flipped his hand over and stroked her with his knuckles.

"The energy that binds them resonates and was collared in the instant your mother gave you her necklace. Cobon needs that energy—*your* energy—to bring to fruition a centuries-old design. The black rock will open a gateway. Through that gateway, the Envoys will go home."

He stroked her cheek.

"I can hold your soul, release your energy, and rebind your soul and your body with a different energy. The Envoys will leave this place, but I will stay. With you."

Even though she already knew all this, hearing it out loud and in no uncertain terms shocked her brain. It took a few seconds to reestablish the gray matter-to-mouth link. All the while, Asher gazed intensely into her eyes, gauging her reaction. Finally, like a car engine in the winter, her brain revved and sputtered and finally spit out a thought.

"He's already waited centuries. Why can't he wait another fifty years?"

"He's gone mad."

"Oh." *Like you.*

"He wishes to speak with you. Tomorrow."

Asher regarded her carefully. Frankly, she was still shell-shocked from Fin's cruelness and now Asher's cool explanation of why exactly he wanted to rip her soul out. She couldn't register any more shock, so she went with it.

"What time?" That was the normal thing to ask, right? But there was something... Oh, why wouldn't her brain work!

"Evening. He's invited us for dinner."

Hailey pushed him away. The arctic air assaulted her skin.

"I thought you said you hadn't spoken to him!" she yelled. Guess her holy-crap-meter wasn't pegged after all.

"I hadn't." He said it coolly and offered his hand again. As it hung between them, he explained, "He beckoned me from the ball. That's why I left you."

Oh. It was ten below outside his warmth, and she accepted his hand, letting him pull her close and out of the frigid night.

"You eat dinner?" For some reason she found the thought amusing, and she shook her head, stifling what would otherwise be a welcome grin.

"No, I don't eat dinner," he said smiling back at her. "But *you* do. And you need to rest. You're exhausted."

He led her back to the dorm with his arm around her shoulder, his hand gripping her upper arm and her body pulled close.

"You haven't taught me to use my gift," she said, looking up at him. Maybe he regretted giving it to her. "I gotta tell ya, I don't feel any different... Haven't seen any evil coming...or heard any... discord..."

She remembered her premonition dream. "Although..."

Asher's eyes darkened. "What is it?"

Jeez, was he angry again?

"I had a premonition dream. Weeks ago." She looked up at him. He waited to hear more. "You and Fin were...arguing, like usual..."

"Arguing about what?" he asked forcefully, but she couldn't help get the impression he already knew.

She shook her head.

"I couldn't make your voices out."

Asher's expression softened immediately.

"I'll teach you how to use your gift properly. Soon."

"It better be, because I'm not sure I'll survive your assault on my soul."

Asher sighed.

"Don't call it that," he said, sounding irritated.

"What shall I call it, then?" Asher bowed his head. *Yep. Assault.* Hailey thought so. Eureka was close, thankfully.

"Did you enjoy your night?" he asked exasperated.

They stood outside the door, facing each other.

"Not really," she told him apologetically. "Except for the dance. And the kisses—your kisses."

Asher grabbed her right arm and pulled her to him, grasping her hair in a fist with his other hand. He pressed his lips to hers and unleashed a slow, deliciously reassuring warmth, which quickly spread across her face, down her neck and into her shoulders, releasing all of her tension and dazzling her into a groggy stupor.

"Whoa," she breathed when he released her.

She wobbled, dumbfounded.

"Sleep well, Hailey. I'll see you tonight. In the Aether." He ushered her inside and disappeared into the shadows.

Chapter Thirty-Nine

An Invitation to Dinner

"Moral indignation is jealousy with a halo."

— H. G. Wells

Parent's weekend at Bear Towne University was in full swing the next day, and Giselle's mother and sisters had flown all the way from Hell to collect her for the winter break. Hailey only went to the luncheon at Chinook Hall because: she had nothing else to do, was avoiding Fin, she hoped to see her roommate once more before she left, was avoiding Fin, and—oh, yeah—she was avoiding Fin.

Not even close to hungry, she stared blankly at the buffet, completely engrossed in counting the serving spoons when a disinterested voice rang through the hall. "Hey, Prostitute."

Instinctively, and she had no idea why, she turned to look, and when she did, Giselle, who had done the yelling, pointed and laughed.

Hailey rolled her eyes but couldn't suppress a weak smile.

Her roommate stood with three supermodels next to absolutely nobody. It was funny. Even the professors gave them a wide berth. Hailey caught a shiver just looking at them, though with their crystal eyes set into porcelain skin, they were a vision to behold. Like Giselle, the other three banshees were beautiful, tall, and thin, but unlike Giselle, they had long flowing golden-white hair, which was constantly ruffled by an invisible wind that didn't affect Giselle's blondish-gray locks. They almost looked angelic.

Until they smiled.

Hailey wouldn't have thought it possible, but Giselle's family were much paler than she was, and as she drew near she heard them—ringing like crystals. It was beautiful.

Giselle threw her arms around her and lifted her off the ground in a powerful, frigid squeeze.

"Okay," Hailey wheezed. "Put me down!"

Giselle dropped her and smiled.

Her family looked disgusted.

"Where's your uncle?" asked Giselle.

"Ireland," she mumbled. All of her uncles went back to the homeland for Christmas that year, satisfied that Hailey'd be safe under the watchful eye of an Envoy. Her original plan had been to spend the holiday with Fin at his cabin, an idea Uncle Pix abhorred but had finally accepted. But she was pretty sure her invitation had been rescinded sometime between the "don't touch me" and "weeping cesspool" comments the night before. Besides, she'd probably be dead before Christmas anyway.

"Are these your sisters?" Hailey asked, trying to sound upbeat.

"You mean the skanks?"

"…uh…"

"Yeah," Giselle said finally. "My sisters, Marrakech and Amelina." She jabbed her thumb at two of the supermodels.

Hailey extended her hand.

In response, they glared, and Hailey held her hand out for several uncomfortable seconds before finally dropping it.

"My mom, Lorelei." Giselle motioned to the third supermodel.

"Who is this…girl?" Lorelei demanded of Giselle.

Her lip curled as she looked Hailey up and down.

"She's my roommate," Giselle spat in response. "And my friend."

Aw, thought Hailey. *She called me her friend.*

383

Lorelei grabbed her daughter by the shoulders. "Banshees don't have friends."

"I'm not a banshee, mother," said Giselle as she wrenched herself out of her mother's grip. "I'm just a big fat nothing," she said smiling. "And I have a big-fat-nothing friend."

Hailey straightened up and smiled.

"I'm going to stay with her in Pittsburgh this summer."

Whoa. That was news.

Giselle looked at Hailey in a way that let her know she'd better play along.

"Oh, uh...yeah. Giselle is coming to work at our family pub... in the...in the pub."

She looked to Giselle to see if she'd gotten it right, though she had no idea how she would pull this off. Hiding a banshee in plain sight inside the most popular pub on the South Side? Madness. Though contact lenses and hair dye seemed like a logical place to start, and if she never smiled, then maybe... What would her uncles think? She shuddered. Pittsburgh was not ready for an unactivated, mal-tempered banshee.

But, Hailey probably wouldn't survive the school year, so it made no difference to her.

Lorelei, however, radiated thermonuclear disgust.

"If you insist on fraternizing with humans, why don't you just stay here with *them* this winter?"

"Fine!" Giselle yelled. "I didn't want to come home anyway!"

"You're an abomination, Giselle, and a disgrace," said Lorelei dryly. She put her grimace next to her errant daughter's face. "The sooner you lose your soul and die the better for everyone."

Mama Banshee looked at Marrakech and Amelina.

"Girls," she beckoned as she swept toward the door.

The sisters obediently followed their mother without even saying goodbye.

Giselle flipped them off. Hailey shivered and waved dumbfounded as the three disappeared outside.

"Why does your mother want you to lose your soul?" said Hailey.

Giselle turned to her and raised her arms like Frankenstein. Hailey put her hands up defensively, but Giselle threw her arms around her and squeezed.

Another hug.

Embracing a banshee was like standing shirtless in an icy breeze, and it cut right to Hailey's core.

"Because they hate me," Giselle said as she released her. "They always find an excuse to leave me here. I can't remember the last time I spent Christmas with those Gorgons."

She's a Christmas orphan this year too. Hailey smiled and felt her eyes sting again. She was so relieved Giselle was staying. It was her first Christmas without Holly, and she didn't want to be alone.

"You're not alone, you have Asher," Giselle said, and Hailey tsk'ed.

"You mean the omnipotent, bag-of-cats-crazy Envoy? Stop reading my emotions or mind or whatever."

Being with Asher made her feel more lonely sometimes than when she was alone, if that made any sense. Maybe it had something to do with his burning desire to save her by killing her, which still wasn't making sense. She missed Fin.

"Glad you're staying," she muttered, and Giselle smiled, looking rather pleased with herself. She was up to something. "What?"

"So is David," she said proudly.

"Just don't drink the Kool-Aid," was Giselle's advice when Hailey told her about dinner with Cobon. That and wear flats—in case she needed to run.

Asher arrived right on time as usual, looking forty shades of hot as usual, but wearing a rather unusual, troubled, slightly guilty expression when Hailey invited him in. He kissed her cheek and then took her hand in his and slowly brought it to his mouth, gently grazing his lips across her knuckles.

Her breath hitched.

Such a small gesture, and yet it sent a buzzing, tickling comfort down her arm through her heart and all the way into her stomach.

She looked up at him. It felt good, safe in Asher's presence—most of the time—and he was gorgeous. He wanted her to be with him. It was never a secret. He always wanted her next to him.

Except when he wants you dead, her subconscious reminded. *Fin never wanted you dead...* Well, maybe he did now.

She dropped her gaze, pressing her lips together as she caged another wayward synapse.

When she lifted her eyes, she could see that Asher was itching to tell her something.

"What is it, Asher?" she asked after he led her out.

"I've been thinking about what you said to me yesterday. About laughing."

Hailey straightened up. *Really?* She was desperate to hear more, but Fin's stupid voice rang inside her head. *You can't have love without laughter.* She hit her mental mute button.

"In fact, it turns out, it's one of the reasons I search for Kiya." He shook his head, looking baffled. "She embraced her...emotions." He said the word carefully and without disgust, which made Hailey raise her eyebrows. "You see, she wasn't mad, yet she laughed and loved." He looked down at her with confusion and—what was that? Pleading?—etched in his eyes. "I wish to be like that, and I regret destroying her."

"Maybe she avoided insanity, *because* she embraced her emotions."

"I arrived at the same conclusion."

That explained the passionate kissing. Her heart fluttered, and she couldn't stop her smile. When she looked up at Asher, he was smiling too.

It was sweet. For the first time, he actually seemed…young, almost carefree. Without the weight of the Aether on his shoulders, he looked like just another college student.

"So, where are we going?" she asked.

"Pittsburgh."

Pittsburgh? And her uncles were in Ireland, dammit.

"How are we getting there?" It was already after noon. No way they'd make dinner on the East Coast. "You're not gonna throw me, are you?"

Asher flashed a fragile smile. "We'll melt."

Hailey nodded once then looked to Asher. "What does that mean?"

"It means I'm taking a risk. The others might see us." He tilted his head down at her, one eyebrow raised.

"…so, not via Luftzeug?"

"No, Hailey. Not via Luftzeug." He was leading her into the White Forest, and she felt perfectly safe. Not even a carnivorous tree had the wood to challenge Asher.

Hailey tried and failed to stifle a giggle at her private joke. It was her nerves making her goofy, she knew it, but if she didn't laugh, she'd have to cry. She was scared to death of Cobon.

Asher stopped walking and studied her closely. "Have I said something…funny?"

Oh, no. This was too stupid to share.

"No, Asher, I just had a fleeting thought…about the trees…" *And wood—oh, God! Please don't ask me to share.* "So, is melting like being whipped?" Oh, no! Did she really just say that? She could feel her whole head burning up.

Asher's lip twitched. *Was he amused? Fine time to embrace humor.* She shook a lock of hair loose and did her best to hide behind it as she stared at her boots.

"Actually, I don't know what to call it. I'm going to pull you through the energies. I heard it in a song once, and it seemed appropriate. It will feel like the world has stopped, like time has stopped."

He looked down and must've noticed her worried expression.

"It doesn't hurt, so don't be afraid."

Spinning her around so she faced him, Asher wrapped his arms around her waist, pulling her close. "Ready?" he breathed into her ear, which sent a pleasant shiver down her arms.

"Let's get this over with," she whispered, resting her head against his warm chest.

"Melting" felt a lot like being suspended above a movie stuck on fast-forward. The world did stop and drop out from under them. Then it spun in a blur, halted and slammed into their feet.

Cobon's residence sprawled over twenty acres of snow-covered gardens and tailored-to-look-natural forest, with a modern barn situated next to a frozen lake in the distance. His house looked more like a palace and stood on a hill overlooking the Ohio River.

"I know this place," she said, and Asher cocked his head. "Uncle Pix used to take us driving at Christmas time to see the lights on all the big houses. This house… This was always our favorite. We'd save it for last, park on the street, and just sit in the car and gaze at it." She looked up at him. "This was Holly's dream house," she said sadly.

Sliding his arm around her waist, Asher pulled her close as they walked to the porch.

"Remain calm in here, Hailey," he advised. "Do not feed into his madness. Do not enrage him." He paused along the walk, taking her chin in his hand and planting a soft kiss on her lips.

"Ready?" he asked her, and she nodded boldly.

"Yes, Asher. Let's go meet the monster that killed my sister."

Cobon opened the door ceremoniously wide as they approached.

"Ah, Asher." Cobon bowed, looking his creepy, crusty, octogenarian self.

Asher nodded, but almost imperceptibly, and Cobon turned to Hailey.

"At last, Miss Hartley. So glad you accepted my invitation. Please, do come in."

Dinner with two Envoys. What was she thinking?

Cobon had set only one place at his expansive stone table, and he pulled the chair in front of that place out as Asher led Hailey into the dining room. There were four plates, each covered by a silver lid, three forks, three knives, two spoons, four glasses of different shapes and sizes, each filled with a different colored liquid and, finally, there was one napkin.

She focused on the napkin.

At least I know what that's for, she muttered to herself.

In the presence of Cobon, the murderer, she had plenty fuel for anxiety, but in that moment, she fretted over which fork to use for which course. She wondered if Cobon had set the table this way on purpose just to shame her.

"My dear," he beckoned.

Hailey sat stiffly. When she did, Cobon rested his hand on her shoulder for such a quick instant, Hailey didn't have time to shudder away before it quite suddenly disappeared. She whipped her head around to find Asher, eyes blazing and teeth clenched, lifting Cobon in the air by his throat with one hand. With his other hand, Asher clutched Cobon's offending fingers in a tight fist.

"My apologies, brother," Cobon said coolly, his voice unstrained, unworried, and his eyes reflecting genuine remorse. He actually looked and sounded repentant. Asher answered through a barely open mouth.

"I will kill any that endeavor to harm her, Cobon, and you will not touch her."

"Agreed, dear Asher, now put me down, we're being rude in front of Miss Hartley." Asher released Cobon, who straightened his shirt, and smiled kindly at Hailey. "Forgive me, Miss Hartley, but I couldn't resist touching the human that has beguiled and corrupted my oldest friend," he said with an alarming dignity and a gentlemanly bow.

"Please, my dear. You must be famished after so long a journey," he winked. "Eat." He lifted a silver lid from the plate directly in front of her to reveal a small, crisp salad.

"Strangely, I seem to have lost my appetite," she said quietly, curtly.

Eat? In the presence of this monster? Was he out of his mind?

Why, yes, Sherlock, he is, her subconscious piped in.

"Nonsense!" Cobon shouted, taking his seat at the head of the table. He sounded more wounded than angry.

Problem number one: Should she actually eat what he had prepared for her? She looked at Asher, who stood behind the chair to her right. He held her troubled gaze for several seconds before he pulled his chair out and sat next to her. When he did, he placed his left hand on her thigh and squeezed it gently. She supposed that meant she should take a polite bite.

Crap. Problem number two—which fork? She stared uncertainly at her silverware and bit her lip before picking one up, which didn't escape Cobon's attention.

"Dreadful etiquette, I see."

Hailey froze with the fork lifted a few inches from her mouth. She tried her best to do what Asher had advised and remain calm, though she had an irresistible urge to stab Cobon in the eye with the wrong fork.

She lifted the fork again and just before it passed through her lips, Asher seized her hand and shook it loose. It clanged loudly on the marble floor.

Cobon let out a belly laugh followed by a snort and a deep sigh.

"Do you really think I'd poison the girl's dinner?" he said, his eyes gleaming. He laughed again, and Asher stared, impassive.

"Oh, alright," Cobon pouted. "Cyanide," he declared.

With one swoop of his arm, Cobon shoved Hailey's entire, impeccable place setting onto the floor.

Hailey cringed against the racket of shattered china and crystal, the clang of the metal lids.

She furrowed her brow. "Why do you do these things?" she demanded. She chanced a glance at him. "Why do you kill people?"

Cobon blinked a few times.

"I'm bored," he said simply.

He killed Holly because he was bored?

Remain calm, she told herself, echoing Asher's instructions, and he must have detected her rising anxiety, because he squeezed her thigh again.

"Not the reason I killed your sister," said Cobon, guessing her thoughts. "Perhaps I'll enlighten you of the facts—but first you should know—I made two errors in dealing with dear Holly—not typical of me, my dear." Cobon cast an accusatory glare at Hailey. "And it's your fault, you know. I mistook Holly for the end of your family's energy line, but it wasn't her at all. *It was you*," he sneered. "Your mother passed the necklace to you. You broke the rules, Miss Hartley—you took off the necklace. It's you that must die to complete the black rock."

He leaned menacingly forward.

"And then I mistook Holly for Adalwolf's murderer, but once again it was you." Cobon burst out of his chair, knocking it over with a BANG that made Hailey jump. He leaned over the table and continued in a biting voice. "I couldn't put my hands on her to hasten her death—I thought she'd destroy me—I had to wait, and they ravaged her. Had I known, she never would have suffered at the hands of those buffoons—so you see," he told her with a frosty voice, "it's your fault...what she endured. It should have been you."

Hailey felt the blood leave her head, and Asher took her hand in his, brushing his thumb over her knuckles.

"And then there was Mary Lash," Cobon continued, sounding far less affected as he paced around the room. "That was pure rage," he said kindly, but then his tone darkened. "She was supposed to lure your sister into the van, you see—I never told her to take the girl's foot… She did that on her own," Cobon said, frowning. "Well, you can't trust a wretch, can you?"

Something sincere stirred in his eyes—a sadness. He blinked a few times and turned his now penetrating gaze to Hailey.

"But you haven't come to talk about Mrs. Lash, have you? No doubt you're curious about what Asher intends to do to you. I can only imagine your hesitation to oblige him, but there's really no reason to fear this, and I'm on the edge of my seat with anticipation. Do you have any questions?"

When Hailey pressed her mouth into a stern line, Cobon frowned.

"Perhaps you'd like some untainted wine my dear? To loosen your tongue…?"

Hailey shook her head slowly, unable to find her voice, because her brain was still too busy reliving the moment she found Holly's shoe. She shivered in her seat, and Asher leaned to stroke her cheek. Hailey sighed, pushing the memory of her sister's foot from her head as she focused on Asher's touch.

"Something unpleasant was it?" Cobon looked from Hailey to Asher and back to Hailey. "In your mind, I mean—not the image of a foot again, I hope." He pulled his lips back in a wicked smile. Then he whipped his head forward and stared in disapproval at Asher, whose hand still glided across Hailey's cheek.

"Do try to contain your repugnant displays in my house."

Hailey put her hand over Asher's and brought it to her lap. She didn't want to relax too much, and with Asher caressing her face, she was starting to drop her guard.

"Your love for her is but a shadow on the wall of a cave, you know," Cobon said.

Asher said nothing, and Cobon's eyes ignited.

"You compete for her affection with a rogue slave. You've left your challenger unchecked, and when you weren't looking, he touched the one you love in a way she quite enjoyed."

Hailey gasped—unintentionally, which provoked Cobon to smirk.

When Asher continued ignoring him, he slammed his fist on the stone table, sending a fissure down its length. Then he pulled his face into a wretched grimace and let out a cold laugh.

"You like that?" he said turning to Hailey and motioning to the crack in the table. "I learned that from a wretch. He made a similar slice through your sister."

Hailey sat silent and still, though she could feel her brow knit and her throat tightened. If she wasn't careful, she'd blink and a tear could escape. That would give Cobon the satisfaction of knowing he'd made her cry, and *that* wasn't about to happen. She focused on building a wall in her mind and mentally punching Cobon in his rotting mouth.

"Speaking of dear Holly..." he pressed on, still looking directly at Hailey.

She stared straight ahead, squeezing her hand into so tight a fist, her fingernails drew blood.

"She didn't put up much of a fight. Even when I finally pulled her soul, there was only a slight flare."

He shrugged and turned to Asher.

"And how many of our brothers stood by while I destroyed her? All of them, I think. But you were there. You remember...the bystander effect."

Hailey flicked her eyes at Asher, silently pleading for him to deny it.

But he sat straight, saying nothing and giving nothing away.

Heart hammering, Hailey swallowed hard. She couldn't be goaded into mistrust. Not by Cobon-the-raving-psycho-ape-shit-crazy-Envoy.

"Did the mortician piece her together like a puzzle and stitch her up like Frankenstein, I wonder?" Cobon's eyes studied Hailey. "Fodder for your dreams, Hailey-Khu..."

Hailey furrowed her brow. That was a Tomas word—one he'd used *before* DOPPLER got him. And it wasn't German. It was obscure. He must've picked it up from somewhere, and now Hailey knew where. *But why would Tomas be hanging around—*

"—Still, I never wanted to hurt her," Cobon continued, and a perfect tear rolled out of his eye.

Cobon let his tear drop to the table, where it glowed beautifully under the chandelier.

"I had a plan, brother," he said to Asher. Then he turned to Hailey.

"And these are the facts, my dear, so pay attention. I needed only grasp her soul at the very moment of her death to release her energy, and then I would've rebound her—she was going to live," he sniffled. "But those wretched humans...they were supposed to kill her quick. I couldn't stop them once they had her, and when she cried out for help, what could I do with the others watching?"

He pressed a hand to his chest as another tear escaped his eye.

"They might have destroyed her soul if I had intervened... maybe shredded me as well—I had to let her die slowly, in agony to save us both."

If this admission surprised Asher, he never showed it.

"But I took her mind into the Aether, and I stayed with her there until the end, and that was my greatest show, don't you think?"

Cobon looked hopefully at Asher, who looked stoically back.

"You believed it, that I shredded her soul, didn't you?" He wiped another tear from his cheek. "But I did no such thing. And I chose the perfect image to sell that lie. Who would believe I conjured that wretched memory of dancing myself?"

Cobon swallowed, and when he spoke again it was in a whisper.

"I held on to her soul. I would have restored her, had the black stone sent the others home. I would have restored her..." He turned his gaze to Asher. "Holly was mine, you know. And I loved her."

Asher dropped his eyes then looked lovingly at Hailey.

"She's a lot like my Holly," Cobon said. "Oh, I do see the draw. If I still had a muse like this, perhaps I might like to linger here a bit longer." He looked Hailey over as one might inspect a horse. Then he strode behind her and leaned in close, sniffing her hair.

"She smells like her sister—nowhere near as fair, but, yes, I do see the draw. May I borrow her, brother?"

Hailey couldn't stand it anymore.

"If you cared about her, how could you hurt her? Why did you do it?" she demanded, her eyes swimming with angry tears. Asher squeezed her shoulder, but she shrugged him off, staring defiantly into Cobon's swirling eyes.

"Why, to rid the Earth of the others, of course." Shrugging, he smiled at Asher as if this should have been obvious. "I could not show my affection for her with them skulking around. Envoys can be so cavalier, casting about their judgments and executions. That's why Asher brought you to me, my dear. He wishes to rid the Earth of them for the same reason, surely he's told you?"

Hailey looked away but couldn't keep her lip from curling in disgust. Cobon was far worse than crazy if he thought Holly would ever love him. That was just gross.

"You would judge me unworthy, Miss Hartley?" Cobon spoke slowly, briskly articulating each incredulous word. He paused, squinting a glare at her. "Enlighten me, won't you, young Hailey, how would you judge one—say Asher, for instance—if he had lied to you to gain your favor...your affection?"

"I would forgive him, Cobon. I know that Asher is inherently good."

"God forgives, Miss Hartley. Humans forget," said Cobon. He turned his eyes to Asher. "And we do neither.

"And what can you give to her, Asher?" Cobon said as he wandered behind Hailey, pausing to feel the back of her chair.

Hailey cringed away, and Asher stood, knocking his chair over, his chin lowered, his brow dropped in warning.

Releasing Hailey's chair, Cobon held his hands up. "Love?" he scoffed. "We don't love, we covet." He brought his finger to his chin, tapping it thoughtfully. "Perhaps you'll give her…oh, what do you humans call it? A pickle tickle?"

"Cobon, that's gross," Hailey snapped. It was like hearing her uncle talk about the birds and the bees, only Cobon sounded like a dirty old man. She didn't grunt her disgust, but she couldn't stop her nose from wrinkling.

Asher slowly turned his probing gaze to Hailey, his head tilted ever so slightly.

She looked up at him. *Oh, no. He thinks I'm talking about him…* As the realization dawned on her, her face fell.

"Not… It's not gross to… That…" Hailey stammered, and Asher watched her closely. "I didn't mean it would be gross to… with you…" She shook her head, but she might as well have just blurted the word "penis."

This was a disaster. *Did Asher even have a penis?*

She bit her lip before she blurted that too.

"That expression on your face," Cobon said, leaning uncomfortably close to her. "Tell me what it means—what are you thinking?"

Abject, vomitus horror at the mental image of you naked.

"It's the look of verbal restraint, Cobon—you're…" Hailey looked to Asher, who seemed interested to hear what she had to say, but not near as attentive as Cobon. "You're rotting and disgusting."

Cobon stepped back, looking genuinely offended.

He glided to the grandfather clock and studied his reflection in the glass.

"Humans are superficial," he said as if it were some sort of cosmic revelation.

"If I may, Asher…" Cobon turned away from his reflection and waved his hand at Hailey. "At the risk of sounding…pharisaic, let's say." He grinned as if amused by a private joke. "This little affair with your human is dangerous in so many ways—forget the wrath of the others—tell me, what *won't* you do to her when she rejects you?"

Both Asher and Cobon suddenly shifted their gaze into the distance, momentarily distracted. Hailey looked around the room, listening intently, but she perceived nothing out of the ordinary.

"You hear it too," Cobon whispered. "Hideous sound, is it not?"

Asher narrowed his eyes at Cobon.

"What darkness are you hiding, brother?" he asked, turning his head ever so slightly, and Cobon sneered.

"Time for you to leave, I think," he said coldly, his eyes bulging. His next words were measured, commanding. "Tomorrow, Asher. No more stalling."

Hailey's heart jumped into her throat. *Tomorrow? Did he want to kill her tomorrow?*

Chapter Forty

The Tipping Point

"Go confidently in the direction of your dreams."

— Henry David Thoreau

"Come along, Hailey," Asher said gently and without explanation as he slid her chair out, and when they returned to campus, Hailey unloaded six months of confusion.

"What was the point of that?" She stood on shaky legs after the floor of Asher's atrium slammed against her feet. She didn't know if she was more wobbly from melting or from the prospect of Cobon ripping her soul out. Honestly, if he were hell-bent on doing it the next day, she would rather Asher just did it right then and there and got it over with. She didn't want Cobon's creepy, scaly, corpse hands on her.

She shuddered.

"We accomplished nothing, Asher, Cobon is...is..." She shook her head, bewildered.

"Cobon has clearly gone mad."

"Clearly. He sounds like a psychotic maniac—Asher, why did he kick us out? What was the hideous sound you two heard?"

Asher creased his brow. "It was a very sudden, very brief, and very faint percussion—barely audible, even to me, but just as suddenly as I heard it, Cobon concealed it from me."

"He can do that?" Hailey's eyes darted left then met Asher's fierce gaze. "Why would he do that?"

"He hides something..." His voice trailed off, and Hailey watched his eyes erupt. "Cobon is a skilled deceiver. He can project images and sounds—as well as obscure them from the minds of humans and Envoys alike."

"But why would he do that? What...?"

She dropped her shoulders and huffed, exasperated. Cobon made absolutely no sense. But in his ramblings, he'd mentioned so much. "Asher, were you there when he killed Holly?"

The mood in the atrium shifted. He stood unmoving for several seconds, gazing impassively, no doubt weighing his answer though his hesitation spoke for him and punched her in the stomach.

"Why didn't you stop him?" she breathed.

At least he had the decency to look contrite.

"I wanted to, Hailey, but I couldn't stop him. We spoke of this—the others would have surely intervened, and then you would have been in danger."

"You didn't tell me you were right there, watching as she—"

Just like he had when Adalwolf came to kill them.

Hailey turned her back on him, pressing one hand to her forehead and clutching her shirt next to her belly with the other.

Asher moved so he stood directly behind her. Very gently, he grazed his fingers down her arm from her shoulder to her elbow.

"There was no way to rescue her."

"You told me she didn't suffer." Her voice barely rose above a whisper, and Asher sighed.

"Forgive me, please. Cobon shielded her mind. Holly experienced no pain."

"You lied to me."

"I sought only to protect you."

"Did you?" she asked absently. Then she shook her head. None of this mattered right now. "Does Cobon want you to kill me tomorrow?"

Asher stroked her hair. "Yes," he breathed.

"Are you going to?" she demanded, her heart racing.

Asher nodded. "If I don't do this, Cobon will, Hailey," he implored.

"How do you know this will work, Asher? What if the same thing happens? What if it fails and the others are there? How do you know you won't kill me permanently?"

Asher knit his brow together and drew a great breath.

"Because I would die before I hurt you," he said slowly, and as the words left his mouth, his expression darkened, as if he'd just awakened to an undesirable realization.

"But it *will* hurt me." Her voice rose barely above a whisper as she imagined having her soul pulled. An image of Jaycen, bloodied and writing in agony on the floor of her dorm room forced a gasp, and when she spoke again, her voice wavered. "Will you…shield my mind from it? Like Cobon did for Holly?"

Misty-eyed, Asher shook his head, and Hailey pressed her arms to her belly, clutching her shirt in tight fists as she hugged herself tight. "Cobon has much experience in manipulating human minds. I'm afraid it's a skill I've never honed."

"And what if I hurt you?" She shook her head, swallowing hard. "Cobon thought Holly killed Adalwolf. Now he thinks I did. You guys have no idea what happened that night, do you?"

"You killed Adalwolf, Hailey. There was nobody else in the room. You and Holly and—" He cut himself off and turned away.

"You just don't know, do you?"

He said nothing.

"Well, what if you touch my soul, and it kills you?"

Asher spun to face her, pressing his forehead against hers, closing his eyes.

"Then you'll be safe," he declared. "From all of us."

There was no place Hailey could hide. No one but Asher could protect her from Cobon, and even though he planned to kill her the next day, she wanted nothing more than to curl up in his arms and feel safe. Even if it only lasted a couple hours. That night, she dozed only once, only briefly and woke with a start, relieved to find herself still lying in Asher's bed, tucked in his powerful arms. He squeezed her tight, his chest pressed against her back.

"You were in a nightmare," he murmured. "I was just coming to rescue you."

"Oh," she breathed, trying to bring her heart rate down.

She snuggled in his embrace.

"That's sweet," she said, "but you would've been rescuing me from yourself."

He didn't respond.

"I'm really scared, Asher. I don't want you to kill me, even if it is only temporary." Her heart pounded just thinking about it, and she squeezed his arms so they pressed tight against her hollow chest.

"I won't do it until you're ready, but know that Cobon won't wait, and if he comes to claim you, I don't know if I can stop him," he warned.

Her insides went cold at the thought of Cobon's crusty, gnarled hands. She shook away a shiver.

"I don't want him touching me."

Asher let out a scoff, or was it a laugh? "I don't want him touching you, either."

"Where does that leave us?"

Asher shifted, propping himself up on his elbow. Turning so she faced him, she gazed up at him expectantly, hopefully. Surely he had a solution.

"There's no escaping this," he told her, impassive. "Your fate was sealed the night your mother gave you that necklace. Cobon's desperation grows, and his patience wanes." His eyes darkened as he paused, and Hailey waited, anxious to hear his genius plan to liberate her from her dark fate.

"I must go," he said.

"You can't leave me!" Holy buckets of ice water. He was getting up.

"I will speak with Cobon." He grazed his fingers next to her ear. "Perhaps I can persuade him to wait."

Hailey hopped to her feet, her brow pulled together.

"Don't go… please…" She reached out, grasping his arm as she stared despondently into his eyes. "I need you, Asher. I'm so afraid. Please don't go."

He pressed a slow kiss onto her lips.

"You're safe here," he murmured. "I won't be gone long, and I'll be watching you. I can be at your side in an instant."

He kissed her again, and she closed her eyes. "Don't be afraid," he whispered, and when she opened them again, he was gone.

Don't be afraid.

Okay. Hailey nodded bravely.

Don't be afraid.

Her eyes darted around his bedroom, desperately searching for a distraction from the fear, which hovered menacingly over her head.

When pacing frantically through his obnoxiously opulent house didn't shake it, she dropped her shoulders and sighed. She couldn't just sit there and wait for cruel fate to find her. She threw on her coat and ran out the door, resolved to take matters into her own hands or at least find some answers, form a plan maybe…

In the end, she knew she had to face death by Envoy. Hopefully it would only be temporary. And there was no way she'd let Asher touch her soul if it would kill him. If she had indeed killed Adalwolf, she needed to know exactly how it happened and exactly how to stop it from happening again. She didn't know how much time she had.

As she jogged to her dorm, she closed her eyes briefly, envisioning herself wrapped securely in Asher's embrace, breathing in his after-rainstorm scent and letting her heart swell with love for him.

Hurriedly, she gathered her books from her room, grabbed her backpack, scribbled Giselle a note and taped it to the mirror.

G—
Meet me in the library--asap. Asher's going to rip my soul out.
—H

That should get her attention. Giselle had experience in the soul-touching arena, and Hailey desperately needed her expertise to sort things out. She bolted through the hallway, down the stairs, and exploded out the door just in time to run face-first into Fin.

"Whoa!" he yelled.

She ricocheted back and fell on her bum, flinging her armful of books up in a spectacular flourish, which left her notes scattered across the ground in all directions. She should've taken the extra thirty seconds to pack them into her backpack before she'd left the room. She shook her head in self-admonishment.

"Sorry!" she shouted automatically as she hastily gathered her papers.

Wait. Why am I apologizing to him?

"Watch where you're going," he muttered irritably, and he stood over her, arms crossed, watching as she struggled to gather her papers before they blew away.

"*You* ran into me!" she yelled up at him, and then she threw her leg over a page that lifted into the air. Darn the wind. *And thanks for your help, Fin.*

"Please…" he scoffed. Turning away, he seized a page out of the air. "Hope's greatest fool, Hailey, you're pathetic."

Like she ran into him on purpose! Is that what he thought? What a jerk.

Rushing to her feet, Hailey snatched the paper from his hand. He held it tight, so she had to pull again.

Ask me nicely, he should've said, but he only scowled.

Hailey blinked, and for one hopeful moment, she imagined his thumb grazing her hand. Finally, he released the page, and she staggered back.

"I said I was sorry, Fin," she said, as a traitorous lump grew in her throat.

Dammit. She meant to call him Pádraig. And she didn't have time for this now. Didn't he know this was her last day on Earth? Maybe he did, and he didn't care. The thought pricked her eyes, which welled with tears. She had to get out of there.

Shoving the whole messy pile of notes into her bag, she ran off with her head bowed, eyes fixed on the ground.

You're a weeping cesspool... Well, yes, she was weeping, but she didn't think she was infectious waste. His cruel words reverberated in her head, bouncing around, turning over and over. *Hope's greatest fool...*

Oh, stop it! Why did she keep torturing herself? *Because those words are familiar*, her subconscious reminded her. A memory...it was a memory—she'd seen those words before, but where...?

Hailey glanced back, keenly aware that it might be the last time she laid eyes on him. His head was bowed as he trotted off.

"Goodbye," she whispered.

Fin burst into Asher's house without knocking, hell-bent on a confrontation that would hopefully end with his death—once and for all, sparing him another second of living with the agonizing heartache that sucked the air from his chest. He'd hurt the only woman he ever loved, and he'd probably lost her forever. Not that he deserved her anyway. He didn't deserve to even look at her.

"Asher!" he barked, storming from room to room. When the Envoy didn't answer, Fin bellowed as loud as he could, gritting his teeth, his face crimson with rage, "Asher!"

"Where is she?" Asher answered urgently, appearing suddenly in the doorway behind him.

Fin pivoted and lunged at the Envoy.

"You listen—"

Asher grabbed his neck and squeezed. "Cobon obscures my vision, Pádraig. He may already have her, where is she?" Asher repeated, his eyes a volcanic fury. He eased his grip enough for Fin to speak.

"I just saw her leaving Eureka—five minutes ago," he croaked, his voice partially strangled. "She had her books, library?"

Asher tossed Fin to the floor and spun around.

"I'm going to tell her the truth, Asher!" Fin shouted as soon as he caught his breath, and Asher turned back scowling hatefully.

"You will tell her nothing, slave," he said slowly.

"Suck it, Asher. I won't miss another second of her life." He said it with conviction, because he *wanted* it to be true. He *wanted* to stay with her forever. But Asher would never allow it. He'd destroy her, and Fin's heart would turn inside out. He'd die a thousand deaths if he ever did something to hurt her again. No, this was the end for him. He couldn't bear to face another dawn without her. He knew what he wanted. An end. And Asher was the only one that could provide it.

"You delay me with your misplaced defiance when her very life is at risk. And you will tell her nothing!"

It was working. He was angry. Maybe even furious. Fin shook his head.

"I'm going to tell her the truth," he repeated, his voice weary, defeated.

"Wrong answer, *Fin*." Asher grabbed him up by his neck again.

"What are you going to do, Asher? Kill me?"

He tried to hide the hope in his voice as he egged the Envoy on.

"Oh, I can do far worse than kill you..."

Matthew the book worm did his best to fetch Hailey some helpful references from the stacks, but honestly, he was so gorged with tea, he moved more like Jabba the Hutt than a zinging inchworm, and it took him ten minutes to return with *The Banshee's Guide to Handling a Soul*, which read like cell phone instructions.

Hailey slammed it shut. While she waited for Giselle, she returned to straightening and smoothing her crinkled notes. As she made her way through the pile, something strange caught her eye. There among the mound of windblown pages, she found a handwritten note. She recognized the print immediately...the phrases...the metaphor... *Oh my God!*

> *This lonely soul by solitude stalked,*
> *whose Sandman's sand makes said what's not*
> *what God knows. And now it's got*
> *your Rose, a fool, in deception locked.*
> *Who else but me would make this hell?*
> *Who else but you could break this spell?*

Hailey clutched her stomach. *The rose...the lonely soul...the weeping cesspool...* She gasped. *Hopes greatest fool!* Fin wasn't insulting her—he was trying to talk to her—to tell her in a code that only she would know—a code he'd used before—it wasn't Asher who'd carried her home from Holly's grave. It was Fin! He was begging for help!

Realization hit her like a freight train. *The rose... The sketch of her at Holly's grave...* All this time he was trying to tell her, and all this time, she was too stupid to get it.

She had to find him.

She pushed back from the table, but when she stood, her legs buckled, and she fell back into her chair. The room went black. Her breath caught in her throat; her ears filled with muffled silence. And she was falling, through the chair, through the floor, flailing her arms at the nothingness in desperation, anticipating—no dreading—the impact.

Then with a whole-body quake, she woke, and she was watching Asher and Fin from the shadows of Fin's room again—just like she had in her premonition dream, only there was no haze, no mistaking the words they exchanged.

"Did it ever occur to you in all your cerebral-ness that Cobon lied to get you to do exactly what you're doing? To kill Hailey?" said Fin.

"Hailey belongs to me. I will do what I please to her."

Hailey's heart stopped. He sounded so cold.

"We had an agreement, Asher, don't you remember? Hailey will choose who she wants to be with, and we will respect her choice," he said firmly, but Asher was unmoved.

"I love her," he told the Envoy. "And she loves me."

Hailey's breath caught.

"You think you love her, but you do not. Cobon uses you, Pádraig. You will drive her into despair, and you will destroy her."

"No," Fin said firmly. "Nobody is controlling me, Asher, I'm free."

Asher stepped toward him, a furious storm swirling in his eyes as they traced a path through the distance. "You will always be our slave," he concluded. "Forever was the deal your parents made with Adalwolf, and forever you will obey."

"I'm not a slave to the Envoys anymore, Asher," Fin said irritably.

"Are you so sure?"

Fin took a swing at him, but Asher caught his fist and held it.

"Perhaps you'd like to live this life with one hand," he said, and he squeezed Fin's fist until it collapsed with a sickening crunch.

Fin howled and fell to his knees.

"That's more like it," said Asher coolly, and Fin's mutilated hand turned to dust in his grip. Asher brushed his hands together, and Fin gnashed his teeth.

"I won't do it!" Fin cried out.

"Perhaps I'll take your arm, then. You won't heal from this, you know." Asher's voice was menacing, hateful, even.

He snatched him up by his arm and cremated that as well.

"Go to hell!" Fin yelled, as he pushed himself to his feet. Squaring up with Asher, he spit in the Envoy's face.

Asher's eyes exploded. Grabbing Fin by the neck with one hand, he seized him by his manhood with the other.

"Shall I take something more valuable?" he threatened, and Fin squeezed his eyes shut.

"Tear me limb from limb, Asher. I love her, and I won't hurt her."

Asher released him and tilted his head as Fin surveyed his shoulder stump.

"I've gone mad," said Asher suddenly.

"I know," Fin panted.

"If I cannot have her, I will destroy her," Asher said with pain in his voice. "I cannot control my rage." His admission sounded more like a plea. His eyes darkened, and quite suddenly, he grabbed Fin up by his neck again.

"I once saved you from an eternity in Hell, Pádraig O'Shea. It's time for you to repay your debt to me."

Asher raised Fin higher and plunged his hand through his chest.

Fin struggled to breathe.

"Is this the fate you want for her? You would drive me to rip her apart, to shred her soul, to slash and tear until there is nothing left of the woman we both love?"

"She'd—destroy—you," Fin grunted.

Asher squeezed Fin's neck until it cracked and tossed him to the floor.

"No, Pádraig," Asher said while he waited for Fin to heal. "We both know what destroyed Adalwolf. It was a confluence of impossibilities, *a cosmic accident when he exploded. And you can't make it happen again, or I'd already be dead, Righteous Man."*

Fin's neck cracked back together, and he rolled onto his side.

"We can do this all night," Asher said grinding his teeth, and he grabbed Fin up by his neck again. "I would do worse to her!"

"Alright I'll do it!" Fin shouted. "I'll do it," he moaned, resigned.

Asher released him and stepped away.

"She'll know you did this," Fin panted nodding to his missing limb, and Asher surveyed his one-armed slave.

"On your knees, Pádraig," said Asher gently, and Fin obliged, his face etched with shame.

Asher placed his hand on Fin's back and watched as an arm grew perfectly out of his shoulder.

"Make it public, Fin, and make it hurt," Asher said, turning to leave. "I'll be watching."

"Wait," Fin said.

Asher stopped and looked back.

"If you cared about her, you wouldn't force me to hurt her."

His eyes searched Asher's for a flicker of compassion.

"I will comfort her. I will protect her from Cobon," the Envoy reasoned.

"Can you protect her from yourself?"

"And what would you do?" he spat. "How would you save her light, human?"

"With my dying breath, Asher. I would die or spend an eternity in agony before I hurt her."

"Then you're a better man than I, Pádraig the Defiant."

Chapter Forty-One

To Die, but Only Temporarily

"It requires more courage to suffer than to die."

— Napoleon

Hailey blinked hard as Giselle's voice faded in to her ears.

"...but you're not going to find anything helpful in a library, and I already read these magazines the last time you dragged me in here, so how much longer do you want to stay in this pulverized-tree crypt?"

Hailey finally focused on Giselle. She was holding *The Banshee's Guide to Handling a Soul* in one hand and pointing to the magazine rack with the other.

"What's the matter with you? Did you just have a vision?"

"I did!" She shot out of her chair. "Oh my God, Giselle, I have to find Fin!"

Hailey swayed shakily, leaned against the table to steady herself, and straightened to leave, but an explosion in the reference section threw her back into her chair.

Matthew, who had been snoring peacefully next to Hailey's desk, was thrown toward Mysteries, and Hailey scrambled to her feet only to find herself face-to-face with Cobon's rotten sneer.

Staggering back, she bumped into Giselle, who grabbed her arm and shoved her aside, wedging herself protectively between her and Cobon.

"What's this?" Cobon laughed. "Do you mean to protect the human? You? A demon abomination?" Cobon tossed his head back and cackled. Then without warning, he backhanded Giselle across the face, sending her careening across the room until her body slammed limp against the stone wall and crumpled to the floor.

"No!" Hailey screamed, and she lunged toward her roommate.

Cobon grasped her by the hair and jerked her back, flinging her against a bookcase, which he then toppled over on top of her. All six hundred and eighty-seven books, which Hailey had meticulously counted, thundered down, thumping her head and neck and back. She scrambled as fast as she could against the onslaught, but when the heavy oaken shelf crashed down, it smashed her legs above the knee into the cold marble floor.

She couldn't force air to scream.

Cobon grabbed Giselle up by the neck and held her high.

"My work here could be done," he said over his shoulder to Hailey. "But I'd much rather stay until you expire completely, my dear, you're losing blood at a fatal rate, did you know? If you can speak, please tell me why you care about this one—I'm curious—she's an abomination, which I should happily rid from this wretched planet."

"No," Hailey gasped. "Don't—" Pain stole her breath.

Cobon poised his hand over Giselle's chest, and then he turned, smiled, and winked.

"Ah, Hailey…" He shook his head, clicking his tongue in disapproval. "Quite a spirit you have. Imagine my disappointment when Asher told me you were reconsidering our little arrangement.

No matter, we don't need Asher, do we? He's had second thoughts as well and is no doubt right behind me, so I'll be quick. Embrace your fate, my dear. Your death is only temporary. And I'll spare this demon. What do you say?" He plunged his hand through Giselle's chest, and she let out a guttural, agonizing screech.

Hailey's mind fogged with pain and desperation. *Six hundred and eighty-seven.* She frantically focused on her consciousness. If she passed out, she'd die—or he'd kill her—he'd kill Giselle for sure—no, she had to stay awake—keep him talking, figure something out. She knew she'd never killed an Envoy, but Cobon didn't. Maybe she could scare him. But how?

Six hundred and eighty-seven. It kept intruding—rattling in her head—she'd shelved these books, which now buried her—all six hundred and eighty-seven of them. That number. And Tomas was wringing his hands in the polished marbled floor next to her, worrying over her.

Tomas—the ghost trap—the frequency Asher abhorred—690 Hertz—it was too annoyingly close to—

Mrs. Spitz is clairvoyant!

In all her frenzied anguish, it made her giggle.

"Six hundred and eighty-seven," she sputtered, and Giselle nodded, her eyes determined.

The banshee opened her mouth and let out a howl that made Hailey's ears bleed. The library windows shattered. Hailey squinted against the noise.

Cobon dropped Giselle and slammed his hands against his ears. He kicked the wailing banshee against another bookcase with such force, it fell over on her, and then he bolted.

Finally the commotion stopped and Hailey scanned the area, finding the overturned shelf where Giselle had been.

"Giselle?" she cried frantically. "Are you alright? Giselle..."

A low moan rose from the rubble, and Hailey held her breath. "Giselle?" she breathed hesitantly.

A hand emerged in a loose fist, which stretched toward the ceiling. Very slowly, she raised her middle finger.

"You're alive," Hailey breathed. She was never so happy to be flipped off. "I'm stuck under this shelf," she added and laughed painfully.

"I really hate libraries," Giselle muttered flatly as she struggled out of the pile. "How did you know Cobon's death frequency?"

"What? I didn't." Hailey blinked back the darkness. Was she making sense?

Giselle froze. "You didn't? You told me to wail his death frequency. It made him think he was going to die. How did you know his death frequency?"

"That was..." she breathed. "...the number of books on each of these shelves."

Thank you, Mrs. Spitz!

Hailey wanted to laugh, but realizing the gravity of her injuries, thought better of it.

"Giselle," she moaned urgently, pushing away the darkness that eclipsed her periphery. "Can you call an ambulance? I think I'm hurt."

"You're under a bookcase, bozo," Giselle noted as she scrambled across the books toward Hailey. "You're probably crushed."

"It's on my legs," Hailey breathed, feeling nauseous.

Giselle pulled several books off of Hailey, tossing them this way and that until she'd uncovered her enough to assess the situation. She grabbed the bookcase and heaved, but she might as well have been trying to lift the pavement off a road. The bookcase didn't budge.

"Hailey!" Giselle barked. "Wake up!"

"Still here," Hailey responded.

"Shit," she grunted. "It's too heavy for me." Then she rested her hand gingerly on Hailey's back. "Do you want me to wail for you?"

"No!" *Was she kidding?*

"Fine. I've got to go and get some help, then." Giselle's voice dripped with worry.

"Okay," Hailey bleated, trying not to think of dying alone.

"Before I go, guess what?"

"What Giselle?!"

"I still have my soul," she smiled. "Cobon grabbed it—you know, if I leave you, you might die alone." She was stalling. She actually was worried, and that worried Hailey.

"Giselle!" she huffed. "Go!"

"Alright," she said. "Just don't die, okay?" *Wow. She really cared.*

"Okay," Hailey breathed, and Giselle sprinted away.

Shortly after she left, Mrs. Spritz strolled over, paused in front of Hailey with her hands on her hips, and shook her head in disgust before she continued on her way, calling over her shoulder as she strode off, "The three of you will clean this up, Hail…" Her muffled voice faded, and darkness pushed Hailey's eyes shut.

"You're badly wounded, my dear. Do you want me to heal you?" Asher's voice pierced her mind.

Was he really there? Did he really have to ask? That was exactly what she wanted.

"Yes…heal…" she moaned painfully, her voice barely a whisper.

Her eyes half-open, she watched Asher touch the bookcase, which instantly turned to ash and crumbled with a puff into nothing. She didn't feel any weight lift. She didn't feel anything except the muffled darkness poised over her head, ready to drop like a guillotine.

Kneeling beside her, he placed his hands on her back.

"You're close to death," he told her in his velvety soft voice.

With one swift tug, he pulled her out from the pile of—she couldn't remember how many books anymore—and into his lap, cradling her gently against his chest.

"It's time, Hailey."

Time for what? Was he going to pull her soul out? Or... Her breath came in labored hitches. *Oh, no...he's letting me die...no, no, no, not yet. I have to see him...*

"Fin...?" That's all she could manage. His was the only face she wanted to see. Where was he?

Asher stroked Hailey's cheek and pressed his thumb against her lips.

"Shhh. Hush Hailey," he murmured. "Don't be afraid. You know what's happening. You'll live again. I cannot stop this." As he gazed lovingly at her, a single, iridescent tear ran down his face. He drew a breath, and his expression hardened into one of focused determination.

He's letting me die.

Comprehension hit her like a toppled bookcase. This man— no, this monster—his was the last face she'd ever see. The last voice she'd ever hear. She didn't want him touching her. He'd taken from her the one person she always wanted when she was scared—forced him away—forced him to hurt her. Asher was a monster. And she hated him—for taking Fin, for watching her die when he had the power to save her...

Darkness crumbled around her. *Count to eight,* she recalled Fin's soothing voice, and she held her breath. Then she looked up at the Envoy. Despite her anger, she was glad she wasn't alone. As monstrous as he was, he comforted her, and she let him. She convulsed once and fought the permanent night that pushed through her mind. She was so tired. So cold.

Still holding her breath, she turned her thoughts to Holly. Would she be waiting for her on the other side? Had she been this cold when she died? She fixed an image of her smiling sister into her mind's eyes and waited.

She shivered once more and stilled.

Asher rested his hand on her cheek, and kissed her gently.

"I'll see you soon," he whispered to her ear, his words echoing into a lifeless hush. And then, the light left her, the air left her—it was the long exhale.

Asher pushed his hand through her chest, poising it expectantly over her soul. Patiently he waited to catch it as she expired in his arms. *She*—his beautiful girl, lying motionless, helpless in his lap as his love for her mixed with rage.

She'd cried out for him—that wretched, defiant human. Even so, he would still rescue her, still heal her beautiful, broken body. And now that he'd removed his defiant challenger, he would court his love without Pádraig's constant interference. And Hailey would finally be his—only his.

And Cobon…Cobon had *harmed* his girl, but he'd deal with him later. Right now, his focus was singular—protect Hailey. He would shield her from death, rebind her soul.

She was looking up at him with the primal fear of impending death. He knew that look. It wouldn't be long. Cobon's attack had left her at death's door. It might've been a blessing, really, sparing her the searing pain of a pulled soul. Now, he need only wait a few moments longer, and her soul would free itself—shed its Earthly body, and when it did, Asher need only grasp it and rebind it.

She shuddered once. She was holding her last breath, clinging to life, and he could see the desperate fear in her eyes fade into death's infinite stare.

Her soul loosened itself, and he clutched its gorgeous luminescence, gently pulling it away from her lovely, limp body, which lay like a rag doll in his lap. With his free hand, he pulled the stone from his pocket and watched as it glowed and pulsated an ever more intense and bright purple. He launched it a safe distance through the broken window and quickly returned her soul to its home, gathering the binding energies from the universe to fix it in place. At the same time, he rebuilt her broken body, readied it for life, which lit her eyes in an Aethereal lilac. As life returned and colored her cheeks, she drew a hitching breath, her eyes finding their focus on his.

"Welcome back," he murmured, and she blinked—his girl.

His girl. Finally, he could have her, touch her, love her. The others would leave, and she would be *his*.

From outside grew a rumble. Asher's face hardened. The stone exploded, quaking the Earth and throwing bright rays of violet ripping through the window.

The vortex arrived next, and feeling its pull, Asher scrambled to escape its reach. This wasn't right—it was too close—too powerful.

How?

He had whipped the black rock a hundred miles across campus—more than a sufficient distance, yet it opened just outside the library.

Someone brought it back...

Someone betrayed him.

"Cobon!" he screeched, but his brother ignored him, and there was no time for revenge anyway. He was caught in the slow, unyielding pull—an iron filing to an electromagnet, powerless to escape the grasp of the Aether.

In desperation, he grabbed Hailey tight.

The Aether would incinerate her body, but he could keep her soul...hold her there with him forever. He couldn't fathom letting her go—not now—not when he was so close to winning her heart.

This will hurt her. He pushed the thought away, and she cried out.

"Asher...?"

Her slight, barely conscious voice pleaded for reassurance as fear once again etched in her eyes...those big, bright, uncertain eyes. He gazed into those innocent eyes with a plea of his own—a regretful, aching want for forgiveness for what he was about to do.

"No!" he shouted against his selfishness. His eyes ignited into a firestorm as the Aether drew him in—he couldn't bear to let her go. But to save her delicate, human body, he had to.

"I love you, Hailey," he breathed.

As the vortex pulled them both outside, he grabbed her roughly by the head and pressed a deep, mournful kiss onto her exquisite mouth, pouring all of his hate, all of his love, all of his heartache and regret into her. Scrambling against the increasingly powerful haul, he drew a great breath and with it, as much energy as he could muster. And he shoved her away...far away...miles away...away to safety, out of the Aether's reach, and out of his arms—forever.

Chapter Forty-Two

Something Borrowed

"Every new beginning comes from some other
beginning's end."

— Seneca

The sound of her breath was her only company when she woke.
Had she survived another night of captivity, or had she only dozed
for a couple minutes? She couldn't tell. There were no windows in
her basement prison…no indication whether it was day or night.
Just the monotonous beat of her heart and the occasional rattle of
her chains when she felt the urge to move.

The box he'd given her still sat on the floor, just out of reach.
Was it Christmas?

The thought was depressing. Her hope for a rescue diminished.
She didn't know if anyone was even looking for her. And Tomas
hadn't been by for a visit in months, it seemed. She wondered how
much longer she could endure.

She tested her bonds again, happy to find she could slip her
left hand out of the cuff. If only she could free her ankle, then she
could escape this hell hole. But her foot was stuck; it wouldn't slip
out, so she'd been working the hook, which anchored her to the
cinderblock wall.

It had taken many, many days—she didn't know how long—months, maybe—but it finally wiggled. She just prayed he didn't notice. How would she survive if he noticed?

Interrupting her despair was the click of the lock at the door to her "room."

He was back.

Pulling her knees to her chest, she fixed an impassive stare at her favorite crack in the floor. She hadn't looked at him since he chained her to the wall, and it made him angry, but it was the only bargaining chip she had—the only distraction she could use in case he tested her chains.

"Would you like to open your gift now?" His voice sounded different, younger, relaxed even as he stood over her.

She stared at the crack in silence.

Crouching down, he opened the brown box.

"I think you'll like it," he coaxed. "Call it a motivational decoration for your room," he said brightly, and then he produced for her a second box, wrapped in green silk—lime green, her favorite color. He placed it at her feet, and when he moved to check her bonds, she reached for his gift.

Gasping his delight, he forgot the bonds.

With dispassionate hands, she opened the box and stared blankly at its contents.

"I know they're not yours, but your sister won't be needing them. Not where she is…

"If you would only show me a little affection, my dear," said the Envoy Cobon as he squatted in front of her.

Though he now appeared to her as a kind-faced Scandinavian in his twenties, she still recoiled when he stroked her cheek, dropping the box, pushing herself against the wall, and hugging her knees to her chest.

Cobon pressed his lips together and picked up one of the tattered Irish dance shoes, which had tumbled from the box.

"I may be inclined to restore your foot and allow you to wear these." His thumb rubbed the soft black leather of her beloved sister's shoe. Then he flicked his finger against the bedazzled buckle so it made a shrill TING!

"Now that the others are gone, you can make as much noise as you want." He inched his face close to hers. "And if you're especially agreeable, my dear Holly," he added in a kind but dark voice, "perhaps I'll bring your darling sister here to join you."

Book Two

Sneak Peek

Darkness and dust in the air, so thick it made him cough kept Fin from getting a clear view of his surroundings. He was horizontal—that much he knew. And the earthy, musty smell told him he was probably underground. Possibly in a coffin.

He clawed at the lid above his face until his fingernails came off—all ten of them. When they regrew, he clawed at it again. It felt like wood. If it was and if he kept scraping, it might give way… after a few years…

He gnashed his teeth and let out a loud, primal screech, as he scratched and punched and flailed at the lid. But it was no use. It didn't give. He dropped his arms and sobbed.

"Hailey," he moaned. *Hailey…* His love, his life.

She'd be saying, "Your first poem was much better." And he'd answer, "Well, I had more time to write it." He actually smiled at the memory of her melodic voice, her feistiness. And that memory gave impetus to his escape. He recalled her sly expression at taunting him with that word, and he let out a giggle—then stopped. His breath was shallow, his thoughts jumbled. The air was getting thin.

Hypoxia.

He squeezed his eyes shut, panting still. Soon the real torture would begin—suffocation. Then he'd wake, cough, gag, choke and suffocate again.

Over and over and over…

Think!

He had to tell Hailey…had to tell her the truth before she… before the Envoy…

She never killed an Envoy.

She couldn't defend herself. And if Asher swapped her energy, there was no telling how she'd come back.

"Asher…" he gasped.

The Envoy didn't answer.

The Envoy…the Envoy…the Env—

He had to hurry…had to hurry while he still had breath.

Frantic, Fin wiggled his arm down and reached into his pocket, where his bloody fingertips found it—the gift from Theon the Envoy.

But in that moment, it seemed more like a gift from God.

Acknowledgments

It never fails. As soon as I step naked into the not-yet-warm shower, there's a knock at the door followed by my spastic, stumbling, shivering sprint for a robe before our toddler invites a stranger inside. But what has this got to do with Eerie, you ask?

Nothing.

And everything. You see, the shower is also where all of my strange ideas sprout and therefore the need to immediately fact check every dismemberment, magnetic swirling vortex, Irish dance reference, and police procedure said strangeness demands in a book such as this. Here is where I thank every person who answered my strange calls and still called me "friend" after hanging up. Since I suck, I know I'll forget to mention somebody here, and I hope they forgive me.

First and foremost, thank you Elizabeth Riley for believing in me, for taking a chance on a new writer, and for making my publication dreams come true.

The first person to read all the eeriness that came out of my head was my mother, Debra Shipman: Thank you, Mom, for loving my story, and I'm sorry the dismemberment disturbed you, but also happy it did so in a very Poe way. To all my beta readers—especially Adria Goetz, my sister, Sherry Anderson, my loving husband, Billy O, my Irish and dancing friends: Sarah Adair, Sara Barker, Jenna Richey, Laureen Laffey, and Myra Watters, who also corrected some of my grumpy-old-Irish-man-isms; Annette Thompson—thank you for wanting to call off work to finish the book; MATCOM dispatchers: Carol Hayes, Brittney Miller, and the awesome Amie Jo Nash, who read the extended version in 3 days, while working 12-hour shifts on the North Slope—thank you for falling in love with Hailey's adventure; Ruth Canfield: thank you for breaking away from the ICU to tell me everything you know about rigor mortis. Where would I be without my law enforcement friends: Alaska State Troopers Peter Steen and David Eastwood-Kolezar (thank you for putting up with my clumsiness during my ride-along), and Wasilla Police Sgt Bill Rapson and Lt Ruth Josten as well as Center Township Police Officer Andy Hill for never flinching when I inquired about procedure, lying to the police, how to stage a crime scene, and how to hide a body. Fin would not be Fin without Joshua Jackson, who provided infinite inspiration.

My critique partners, especially: Sarah Adair—thank you for helping me with my Irish and my character arcs; Laura Irrgang—thank you for playing the snarky teen reader; Rachel Geffrey—who beta-read like a line editor and fixed all things from story arc and logic gaps to comma splices; and Giovanna Adams—who helped me better visualize my fantasy world.

For believing in me when my confidence in all things writerly faltered: Michelle Johnson, Jessica Schmeidler, Michelle Hauck, and Genevieve Gagne-Hawes. And for holding my hand through the contract negotiations, the cornucopia of publaw knowledge and wisdom: Susan Spann.

Editing is like the vegetables of writing—not really anybody's favorite part, but essential none the less. Thank you Lisa O'Hara for shaping up my novel-baby, for e-slapping me when I needed it, and for letting me keep my favorite lines.

Last but never least, I could not have begun this journey nor seen it through without my husband's patient support and my son's willingness to share me with my very strange imaginary friends.

About the Author

C.M. McCoy is an Irish dancer and former military officer living in the Great White North. Though B.S.'d in chemical engineering and German from Penn State University, she's far happier writing stories involving Alaska and a body bag (with an awkward kiss in the mix.) While working 911 dispatch for Alaska State Troopers, she learned to speak in 10-codes, which she still does...but only to annoy her family. C.M. is represented by literary agent Michelle Johnson.

CPSIA information can be obtained
at www.ICGtesting.com
Printed in the USA
LVOW08s1436130617
537962LV00001B/133/P